Playin

Grant Campbell

2

For Papa Jack

PROLOGUE

Khost Province, Afghanistan

The subtle pink hues that bathed the eastern horizon gave the first hints of daybreak. It also brought the distant sounds of rotor blades coming from the west. Just a little while longer to hang on...

It seemed to take a monumental effort to look at the two guys lying beside him. Specialist Manuel "Manny" Torres was very quiet and very still. His respirations were shallow and slow, his body armor vest was opened from the left shoulder, and his ACU top and undershirt were cut vertically from neck to waist. His usually tapered and well-defined abdomen was terribly distended. Two field dressings were pressure-wrapped around two wounds that were soaked through despite frequent changing. A large-bore IV line was in each arm, but the last remaining fluid bags were now empty and there was blood backing up in the line to the closed white plastic clamp. He was eerily pale and had not spoken in almost two hours.

Staff Sergeant David "Booger" Tripp was slightly better. His breathing was substantially less labored after the placement of a chest tube on his right side. The small linear slit of an entry wound was around five inches below his armpit, and there was no exit wound; the bullet probably entered through the small space between his armor plates. It had been hard to get his armor vest off and get access to his chest without causing further pain to his badly burned hands. His vitals were stable enough to give him intramuscular narcotics to ease his pain which gradually drifted him into sleep. Booger was going to make it; Manny could be a different story.

Major Michael Reece didn't really need his four years of training in medical school, four years of residency, along with countless hours of Army training in combat medical care for him to know what was going on in his own body. The shivering and worsening feeling of cold along with the more ominous drowsiness told him he was dying. The tourniquet he had applied on his left leg had slowed the bleeding some from its initially frightening rate. The pain was beyond

5

excruciating, but the analgesia that narcotics offered was not an option for the only one remaining that could defend them against the same people that had blown their vehicle apart seven hours ago. The welfare of the two men beside him on the ground was keeping him from giving in to the overwhelming desire to go to sleep.

The mission had been a straightforward one, but it had taken days to get the go-ahead from command. A small village less than ten kilometers from the perimeter of their Forward Operating Base (FOB) had been very helpful to the mission. A courageous collection of people there was tired of the constant bloodshed and harassment from Taliban fighters and decided that the soldiers of the 82nd Airborne offered the best hope of bringing some degree of normalcy to their lives by ending the conflict. This decision had brought a wealth of intelligence to American forces stationed there, which resulted in devastating losses for the Taliban.

This, however, had come at a price for the village. The wrath of the Taliban would often be expressed by executions of villagers suspected of aiding the infidels. Sometimes they had killed people who had given valuable assistance to American forces; other times the victims had been wrongly accused. Children had been killed or abducted, women raped and executed, and supplies had been taken. In the midst of all of this misery, a cholera outbreak had occurred.

The treatment for cholera is not only simple but very inexpensive. The medicine could be taken to the village in one vehicle with personnel in another to teach the villagers how to administer it. Security vehicles in the front and rear would bring the total to four, and it would take less than an afternoon to accomplish. The mission would not only be a statement of gratitude for those that would help the mission to push out the Taliban, it would be an example of the goodwill that can come from American forces when locals decide to help.

Less than forty-eight hours ago, word had been given to a select few villagers to expect the supplies the following day. That select few apparently had not been select enough.

In the beginning, the mission had been as smooth as anyone could have hoped. The ride to the village was uneventful. It had taken less than an hour to unload the needed supplies to treat the infirmed given the small number of people who lived there. Within five hours of

6

leaving FOB Salerno, as the sun was setting in the west, everyone was loading up and preparing to return. The ambush that followed was a textbook example of surprise and precision.

Heavy mortar fire rained down on the FOB from multiple directions within two minutes of the destruction of the rear security vehicle by a particularly deadly form of IED known as an "explosively formed penetrator" (EFP). All three of the personnel were shredded instantly. Heavy small arms and RPG fire destroyed the supply vehicle and wounded enough of the lead security vehicle to render them ineffective. Reece's vehicle was third in the line and received an RPG just behind the front driver-side wheel, completely disabling the vehicle. The resulting fire forced Reece, Torres and Tripp to exit the vehicle, but not before Tripp had burned his hands getting out. The small arms fire outside was overwhelming, and Torres took two rounds in the abdomen just below the lower edge of his armored Improved Outer Tactical Vest (IOTV) within seconds of exiting the vehicle.

As they pulled Manny to meager cover—a few large rocks approximately fifty feet from the now burning Humvee—Reece began working on his wounds while Booger returned fire as best he could. The wounds were ominous. As he pulled Manny's armor vest open, the bleeding was already significant. Reece applied pressure dressings to the wounds and started large-bore intravenous lines in both of Manny's arms. He didn't use the QuickClot hemostatic sponges on the entry wounds, because the source of the majority of the bleeding was inside the abdomen and not on the surface. He did, however, apply it to the one exit wound in the left side of Manny's back just under the rib cage, underneath which Reece was pretty sure the spleen had been shredded, with disastrous consequences.

"I can't feel my fucking legs Doc," Manny whispered rapidly, leaving Reece little doubt where the second bullet had lodged.

"It's just because of your pain. Your legs are fine." Reece knew that his reassurances were likely untrue, but he had to give Manny (and himself) hope while the sounds of AK-47s from the distant line of trees exceeded the sounds of Tripp's efforts to keep them from advancing on their position.

The pounding percussions of fifty-caliber fire erupted on the Taliban positions from the severely disabled lead security vehicle. Two final shots reached out to the convoy before the Taliban fighting position was silenced. The first was a final RPG striking the top turret of the lead security vehicle, killing the remaining soldier that had so bravely raked over the insurgents who would have surely overrun Reece and his companions. The second was an AK-47 round that ricocheted off the rock Tripp was using for cover, piercing his vest perfectly between his armor plates and entering his chest.

Reece noticed the enemy fire had stopped right before Tripp fell backward onto his feet.

"Goddammit...I'm hit!" Tripp screamed. The pain from his hands had been masked by adrenaline during the firefight, but this wasn't enough to overcome the chest wound he had sustained. He fell backward onto Reece's heels.

Reece pulled out his feet and turned around, ripping the Velcro side flaps of Tripp's IOTV and pulling it off. He was so wired from the surrounding events that he forgot to take off Booger's helmet first, resulting in a delay and a good whack to Tripp's nose. He was, however, able to avoid hitting his burned hands. The small amount of red froth in Tripp's mouth and the location of the entry wound were telltale signs that there was bleeding in the chest cavity. He knew that this was much more of a threat to the foul-mouthed but beloved Staff Sergeant from Mississippi than his hand burns at the moment.

"Booger, I'm going to have to put a tube in the side of your chest so your lungs won't collapse. I'm not going to lie to you; it's going to hurt like a motherfucker."

"Just don't fuck it up then sir," was Tripp's short reply, as he mentally started to prepare for the pain, his breath getting more and more difficult.

Reece pulled a pre-loaded 2 percent Lidocaine syringe from his aid bag and injected 10 cc's of it into the proper site for the chest tube. He made a small incision with a disposable scalpel and then pushed the tips of a Kelly clamp through the intercostal muscles and inner chest wall lining.

"Son of a bitch!" Tripp said through clenched teeth as Reece put his index finger through the defect and swept the chest wall. Quickly he inserted the tube, securing it in place with one silk suture, then sealed the surrounding area with tape. Blood streamed out at an alarming rate for a few seconds before abating, and Tripp's breathing began to immediately improve. Silvadene cream and gauze were placed on both of his hands (a proper cleaning would have to wait), followed by 5 cc's of morphine in his thigh muscle.

The crack that Reece heard shortly after that was immediately followed by the most intense searing pain that he had ever imagined. He had been shot in the leg. Two more rounds bounced off the rocks above his head. The expanding crimson stains on his multicam trousers shook him out of his daze from the pain. Using the bandage scissors from his aid bag, he cut the trousers away from his left calf. A bright red fountain of blood announced that he had a severed artery in his leg. Fighting off the urge to vomit, he placed a tourniquet above his left knee to slow the blood loss. There was no time to dwell on the injury.

Bullets impacted on the rocks that provided their somewhat meager cover. For the first time in his career, Reece pulled his M9 out of the holster attached to the front of his armored vest and returned fire. His hands shook and he had no illusions that he had killed whomever had fired at them, but it did have the intended effect of sending the bad guys further away for better cover.

"Lay the fuck down!" was the short instruction Reece gave Tripp as the latter tried to sit up and shoulder his weapon to help. "Your hands are bandaged and you're drunk from the morphine. You're just as likely to hit me as anyone." He was surprised that he had adopted Tripp's salty language to give him an order, but he was beyond wired from excitement, pain...and fear. Looking over his right shoulder, he noticed Manny wasn't making any effort to move and was moaning quietly.

The next shots fired toward them seemed to be from further away. Reece returned fire this time with Manny's M4 rifle, both because he was running low on 9 mm ammunition and because he hoped it would give the bad guys the impression that there was more than one soldier fighting back at the moment. Stomach acid burned the roof of his mouth and his heart

9

raced. He could hear the mortars from the direction of the FOB and he said a silent prayer that someone would be coming soon to help.

The darkness and the belief that there was more than one American capable of returning fire seemed to keep the Taliban fighters at bay for most of the night. This allowed Reece to keep watch on his two patients, the steady deterioration of Manny periodically interrupted by somewhat wild and unaimed exchanges of fire between Reece and whomever the hell was out there...all the while his own blood volume continued to leave him through the gaping wound in his left leg.

Along with early hints of daybreak came the sounds of Blackhawk rotors. Reece was fighting unconsciousness more and more. He wrote "two abdominal entry, one exit" on Manny's cheek with a Sharpie pen and "right chest wall entry with tube, 5 cc morphine, hand burns" on Tripp's right upper trouser leg in case he lost his own battle before the helicopter arrived.

Almost instantly after that, there was someone crouched in front of him. Reece dropped his Sharpie and went for his M9, but the gloved hand grabbed his arm.

"It's Airborne sir. We got ya," said a baritone voice in the closing tunnel vision in front of Reece.

"Manny's bad..." was all his slurred speech could give to the figure in front of him as the tunnel walls continued to close in.

"We've got 'im, sir. Let's lay you back and take a look at you."

Darkness...

CHAPTER 1

In OR 7, the circulating nurse and medical student watched the robotic instruments move in the pelvis on one of the three monitors that were mounted from the ceiling. The assistant surgeon sat at the right side of the patient, passing sutures through the assisting port and occasionally irrigating and suctioning the operative field. The OR scrub technician, stood at the patient's left side by a table of sterile instruments and interchangeable small robotic arms, each with a different tool at the end. Dr. Michael Reece sat at the operative console of the DaVinci robotic system looking through eye ports that showed him a three-dimensional image supplied by the laparoscopic camera inserted in a small incision just above the patient's navel. His fingers were placed in sensors that allowed the robotic surgical instruments inserted through small incisions to mirror the motions that he performed at his console. Two pedals near his right foot controlled unipolar and bipolar cautery currents that could be attached to instruments to seal bleeding vessels. Two pedals on the left side controlled movement of the camera and centering of his instruments, respectively. The forward of the left-side pedals had a folded surgical towel taped on top of it to allow Reece to distinguish between the two without taking his eyes from his console viewers—a modification accommodating for his left prosthetic foot. The whole setup was designed to do major surgical procedures inside the abdomen and pelvis with four small incisions, each less than one inch in length.

He had already dissected the eleven-centimeter tumor from the wall of the uterus, and his assistant had removed it bit by bit with an instrument called a morcellator, which essentially cut the tumor into strips small enough to remove through the twelve-millimeter surgical port one at a time. He was now using the robotic "hands" to suture the defect in the left side of the uterus to stop any bleeding. He used a suture called V-Lock, which has multiple tiny barbs throughout the length of it that grab and hold the tissue to keep the edges together. This was easier and faster than tying knots with the robotic hands, which, as Carl liked to say, could resemble two blind pelicans trying to have sex. The muscular wall of the uterus had a rich blood supply, and consequently a quicker closure meant less blood loss which Reece had an almost maniacal obsession with minimizing. Once the defect was closed, he placed a small sheet of collagen—which would help prevent the formation of scar tissue—between the uterus and the side of the pelvis.

A hysterectomy, or removal of the entire uterus, was a much more common procedure for such a large tumor. Rashonda, however, was twenty-eight years old and had not had children—despite two successful conceptions, both of which resulted in miscarriage, possibly due to the significant distortion of the cavity of her womb by the large mass. She was desperate for a family of her own and had avoided surgery of any type as long as she could. However, the continued growth of the tumor—called a *leiomyoma*—had given her relentless pain and now was compressing the left ureter, which carried urine produced by the kidney to the bladder, and there were now signs that the kidney was starting to show diminished function.

Several weeks ago, Reece had sat with the patient and her husband and talked about their options. They had all decided on removing the tumor with the hopes of repairing and preserving the uterus and, consequently, her ability to have children. Attempting to do this procedure with the robotic approach could be technically difficult but would allow for a quicker recovery and less post-operative pain. Both saving the uterus and avoiding a large open incision, Reece had explained to them, was not always possible, and it might become necessary during the procedure to either remove the womb or convert the surgery to an "open" procedure, requiring a ten- to fifteen-centimeter incision in the abdominal wall. He assured them that he would do everything in his power to avoid this.

They were an incredibly likable couple whom Michael had gotten to know very well over the past several years, including walking them through the devastating news of two miscarriages as well as trying to treat the terrible pain from the tumor. With two children of his own, he knew firsthand the joys of parenthood, and he wanted Rashonda and Craig to be able to experience it as well. He had cried right along with them as he explained their second pregnancy would miscarry just like the first. They had even joked that they would time their attempts at conception around his ninety-day deployments, to which he was occasionally subject as a member of the United States Army Medical Corps (Reserve).

Once he was satisfied that the incision on the womb was closed properly, the assistant irrigated and suctioned the surgical field once more. He was happy to see the left ureter had lost its dilated appearance and had returned to its normal caliber now that the mass was no longer compressing it. The uterus now had a normal size—approximately the dimensions of a closed fist (in a non-pregnant patient)—and had a linear sutured incision along the left side covered by a collagen sheet. Both ovaries and fallopian tubes were normal. *That's more like it.*

"OK, I think we can undock," Reece told Carl as he watched the two robotic instruments being removed through the ports that were positioned on each side of the belly button.

"Nice job, Doc," Carl said.

"You could have probably done it faster."

Michael wasn't really kidding. The staff in the robotic room was so proficient that it was more of a well-rehearsed team than one surgeon along with several assistants.

"The towel works like a charm," Reece said to Brian Renner, the company sales representative for the robotic system who occasionally came by to check in on everyone or just watch Reece operate.

"I think you should call me MacGyver," Renner joked.

Renner enjoyed being in the operating room with Reece. He didn't have the superior air about him that many surgeons carried with them, and he was not afraid to ask questions of anyone, because he didn't care if he admitted not knowing something. This is a characteristic that is often absent in doctors, especially surgeons. He was a very enjoyable person to talk with, over medically-related topics or more everyday subjects like movies, his family, or his beloved University of North Carolina Tar Heels. The only rule he had was no chit chat while the surgery was occurring. You usually would get a second or third chance on this rule before you would see the rare appearance of his surliness. Nothing was to distract him from giving his best effort to his patients in the operating room, and that was a rule that was easy to respect as far as Renner was concerned. It also didn't hurt that Reece was a genuine war hero, especially in the eyes of Renner, who was a veteran himself.

Reece had only the slightest limp as he walked over to the sink to re-scrub his arms and hands. He had a fresh sterile gown and gloves placed on by Carl and began closing the small robotic port incisions while the circulating nurse rolled the massive system of robotic arms away to the side of the operating room. "Windows Are Rolled Down" by Amos Lee, Reece's preferred "closing music," came from the ceiling speakers.

Once satisfied that the incisions were closed properly, Reece turned and gave the scrub technician their traditional fist bump, signaling the end of another successful procedure. He walked toward the Biohazard bag and pulled off his disposable surgical gown, gloves, and shoe covers. He grabbed the patient's medical chart and told everyone he would see them in about two hours when the next surgery was scheduled to start.

He dropped the chart on the physician's work counter in the Recovery Room and headed to the waiting room. The chart wouldn't be going anywhere, and he had been taught by one of his mentors that nothing should happen after the surgery is complete before you talk to the family and let them know that all is well.

The talk with Rashonda's husband Craig started with an embrace. Anyone who had spent any amount of time with Reece knew he was a hugger. You usually got a handshake the first time you met him, and he would "bring it in for the real thing" after that.

"Everything came out without a problem and the uterus looks fine."

Craig's eyes started to reflect light a little stronger. "Is she awake yet?"

"Kinda sorta. She's waking up but she's still high as a kite which is good because she is not in any pain. Her main issue this evening will be bloating and soreness. We gave her some nausea medicine before she woke up to prevent her stomach from being upset from the anesthesia, and I don't want her to hesitate to ask for pain medicine. I don't give medals for being in pain and I don't want her trying to impress us with how tough she is. I know patients will often go home the same evening, but I want to keep her overnight to monitor how her kidney is doing now that it's not so backed up. We should get her home in the morning if she does well and can pee on her own."

Reece purposefully avoided using a lot of medical terms when talking with patients and their families. It wasn't because he didn't think they could understand it; he just thought it sounded detached and, at times, arrogant, and he wanted no barriers to patients and families being comfortable asking him questions. For the same reason, he insisted on his patients calling him Mike instead of Dr. Reece.

"I don't foresee any problems with you guys getting pregnant, and we're going to have a better ending next time."

"I can't thank you enough Mike."

"You guys have a bunch of kids and spoil them and that will be more than thanks enough."

They embraced again and Reece headed back to the recovery room to do his paperwork. He wrote for her bladder catheter to come out in eight hours and prescribed a "Patient Controlled Analgesia" protocol, which allows the patient to control the amount of narcotic pain medicine (in this case morphine) that she receives (the system has an automatic lockout that can be set to avoid any overdose risks). He also wrote for three doses of an intravenous anti-inflammatory called Toradol every eight hours, which allows the patient to get good pain control without large doses of narcotics, which can upset the stomach. Only clear liquids and Jell-o would be allowed today and she could have a normal diet in the morning if she didn't have any nausea. She would get 125 cc's of Lactated Ringer solution with Dextrose every hour through her IV line, since she wouldn't be drinking very much. She could get out of bed only with assistance tonight since the morphine could make her a little unsteady on her feet. Zofran was written for "prn" (as needed) for nausea, as well as Tylenol, Pepcid, and Chloraseptic spray for headache, heartburn, and sore throat, respectively. He both wrote and dictated operative reports, making sure to have a copy of her dictated report sent to her primary care doctor.

All the paperwork complete, he took the chart to the recovery room nurse and checked in once more on Rashonda. She was snoring—always a good sign of adequate pain control. All her vital signs looked good, and there were no signs of bleeding on the small dressings on each of her four small incisions. He thanked the nurse anesthetist (CRNA) who had monitored her throughout the procedure and headed to the surgeon's lounge at North Charlotte Regional Hospital.

"What's up Ahab?" was the greeting Reece received from Dr. Gabriel Drake.

"Nothing much, 90210."

Drake was a plastic surgeon on staff at North Charlotte Regional. He had finished his case for the morning and had already changed into an impeccable shirt, tie, and slacks from Brooks Brothers, along with a perfectly starched white lab coat that announced "H. Gabriel Drake, M.D., F.A.C.S." above the left chest pocket. His dark wavy hair with a hint of gray at the temples was held back with gel and ended just above the shoulders. His brown leather shoes probably cost more than a monthly payment on an economy car. He catered to wealthy clients who wanted to reclaim youth by way of a scalpel, and he dressed the part—hence the nickname "90210." He was an unabashed womanizer with two ex-wives in his rearview mirror and was known to be cocky and brash both in the operating room and life in general. He was an outstanding surgeon and knew it, and he rubbed many the wrong way, especially the countless women who had been intense, but often brief, objects of his desire.

But Reece seemed to be completely immune to his often boorish presence, and they got along very well, earning them the moniker "The Odd Couple" among the hospital staff. Reece's unassuming and happy manner was often the polar opposite of Drake's, and their friendship seemed to have every reason not to work, but it did.

"Ahab" was one of Drake's nicknames for Reece alluding to his artificial left lower leg. "Gimpy" and "Peg Leg" were some of the others. Drake didn't mean any malice with his nicknames; it was just the way he was, and it never seemed to bother Reece at all.

"Are we doing lunch today?" Drake asked.

"Sure."

"Is it possible that we could go somewhere different than that goddamn sushi place you always go to? You're like fucking Rain Man sometimes."

16

"You pick. Just nothing heavy. I'm back in the OR this afternoon."

"Let's go somewhere with a lot of people. It helps my image to be seen dining with Charlotte's favorite son."

"Kiss my ass Drake."

Drake's jokes aside, the description was fairly accurate.

CHAPTER 2

Reece had become a celebrity since returning from Afghanistan. Already a well-respected physician by his peers and patients, his service to his country and subsequent injury in combat had not been missed by the media across the country, but especially in North Carolina where he lived and had grown up. This attention had highlighted a life story that the news media couldn't resist.

He had been born in the rural foothills of the North Carolina mountains into extreme poverty. His father had left when he was less than a year old, and his mother had died of cervical cancer when he was eight. He was placed in foster care in the same county until he had staggered into his second-grade class one morning with a broken arm, split left eyebrow, and a fractured skull, compliments of a horrifically abusive, drug-addicted foster father who had unleashed on him for using the last of the milk for his cereal that morning. The bruises and cuts he had previously worn to school could no longer be ignored, and the state stepped in once again.

It was at this point that Reece received what media figures would later call the "lottery ticket of his life." He was placed in a home for orphaned boys named Sycamore Place in Asheville. The home housed eleven boys ages five to fourteen in a suburban setting, offered meals, clothing, counseling, and school transportation, and was able to boast that their largest benefactor was the Honorable James A. Haxton—the wealthiest real estate developer in Western North Carolina and the current Congressman from the Eleventh District. Haxton was said to have wealth and influence that the Asheville area had not seen since George Vanderbilt. He had won his congressional election overwhelmingly on his first attempt over an incumbent mired in a tax-evasion scandal. After that, his status and well-publicized charitable endeavors made him wildly popular among the people of his district, and he hadn't had a serious re-election challenge for twenty years.

Then, in 1992, he made the jump to United States Senator by similar landslide-like numbers. There he still served and counted numerous politicians, heads of industry, celebrities, and even the President as people who sought his counsel from time to time. He was involved in countless charities dedicated to the welfare of children, but always sited Sycamore Place as his proudest effort, visiting there regularly even as he rose through the ranks of power and influence in Washington.

Sycamore Place's mission was to take in young boys who had nowhere else to go and who had been dealt a very unfair hand in life. They offered a healthy environment, allowing kids to heal their physical and emotional injuries and receive an education as well as a chance at the American Dream that, as Haxton had proclaimed, "every child in America should have as a birthright."

Reece's physical injuries healed quickly, but his emotional scars proved harder to overcome. His first two years at Sycamore Place had been a time of fear and withdrawal. He feared being alone and also being in the dark. He feared adults he did not know, mainly, his counselor concluded, because "he had never had an adult close to him that didn't leave him or hurt him." He was exceptionally kind to other children and showed hints of being very intelligent, but he lived in a world dominated by his fears. Everyone at Sycamore Place had prayed for a turning point in his life for the better...which came shortly after his tenth birthday.

In 1986, the cook for Sycamore Place retired after his medical problems became too much for full-time work. As with all employees at Sycamore Place, Haxton ensured that he had a generous retirement income, as a thank you for working to help those who needed it the most. Charlie Potts was hired as the new cook shortly thereafter. Potts was a kind and gentle soul that stood in contrast to his massive frame and towering height. A Vietnam veteran who had received two Purple Hearts in combat with the United States Army, he had returned home to the foothills like many vets at the time: ignored and unappreciated. After several menial-labor jobs, he had been hired in the kitchen at Highland Country Club as a cook. Highland was where the wealthy and important of Asheville congregated to socialize, play golf, and congratulate themselves on being the masters of their own small worlds. The legion of well-to-do members at Highland included James Haxton.

Haxton got along well with all the staff and took time to ask them about their lives and families, often in contrast to other members, who either viewed them more as personal servants or didn't view them at all. Potts would engage in conversation with anyone there and became known as a gentle giant who had a kind word for anyone who needed it. He seemed to appreciate the greetings and statements of gratitude that came from "Mr. James," and when the vacancy at Sycamore Place presented itself, Haxton asked Potts to take the position—which included a substantial raise from his current earnings.

Shortly after his arrival at Sycamore Place, Charlie Potts seemed to make a connection with little Michael Reece. He would talk with Potts and even laugh at his jokes. At times, when he was fearful, Michael would look for Charlie and often stand beside and slightly behind him, holding the side of his pant leg. The sense of security that he felt having Potts at the home allowed him to open up and interact with others, and he began to play with the other kids; counselors heard his laughter out loud for the first time. He began to do well at school, often doing his homework while sitting on the floor of the kitchen while Charlie cooked the evening meal for the kids and staff.

Charlie would do more than kid around with Michael, though. He taught him the importance of manners and saying "yes, sir" or "yes, ma'am" when speaking with adults. He made him open the door for women and told him to sit straight at the table at meals. He would sneak him extra desserts after dinner when he heard about good things Reece did at school, taught him to ride a bike, and let him help in the kitchen if he finished his homework.

Staff at the home recognized the special relationship the two of them had and the remarkable change in Michael's progress since Charlie's arrival. No Christmas or birthday Michael had celebrated since his arrival came close to rivaling his eleventh birthday, when he was given new privileges: riding with Charlie to buy food supplies on Mondays and Thursdays and attending church with him on Sunday mornings. Reece became somewhat of a mascot for Red Creek A.M.E. Zion Church. The congregation accepted this shy little white kid with open arms that Charlie Potts brought to church every Sunday, with unconcealed pride, as if he was his own son.

One of the results of Michael's turnaround was that his teachers at school noticed that he was an exceptionally intelligent child. As he lost his fear and shyness and began to engage in class, he performed academically at levels far beyond his other classmates. By the second semester of his fifth-grade year, he was performing high-school-level math, with reading-comprehension and vocabulary-aptitude testing in the ninety-ninth percentile for children his age. He had read every book on the shelves at Sycamore House and had become proficient enough in Spanish to speak with workers at the produce supply store he and Charlie visited on Mondays and Thursdays, just by reading the "Spanish, Level One" text and an English/Spanish dictionary that had been collecting dust on the bookshelf at the home. The staff at the public elementary school that "Sycamore Kids" went to expressed to administration that they could no longer challenge him academically and recommended exploring other educational options for him.

The two preeminent private schools in the Asheville area both seemed enthusiastic about the prospect of having Michael at their institutions. Without a doubt, they were inspired by his story, but they also saw an opportunity to have the attention and gratitude of Congressman James A. Haxton, who called both school superintendents personally to ask for consideration in taking Michael on as a student. Both Vanderbilt Academy and Highlands Preparatory School said they would welcome young Master Reece into their student body.

The Sycamore staff sat down with Michael one spring afternoon and talked to him about the amazing opportunities he had to choose from for the next school year. Vanderbilt Academy was less than four miles away and boasted the highest college-placement results in the city. Highlands Prep was a prestigious boarding school that attracted kids from all over the country and boasted alumni that included two Asheville mayors, countless doctors and lawyers, and one Honorable James A. Haxton, who had also taken a special interest in Michael's remarkable progress as a young man. Cost was not an issue, since the Senator would be paying the tuition out of his own pocket with pride.

Many of his counselors recommended Highlands Prep, due to its well-regarded program designed for academically gifted kids. Senator Haxton even tried to persuade him to go to "H.P." like he himself had as a young man, by taking Michael on a trip to his beach estate on

Figure Eight Island to meet colleagues of his, including many Highland Prep alumni. None of this had one grain of swaying power, however, because Highlands Prep was a boarding school, which would mean moving away from Sycamore House and, more importantly, Charlie Potts. So Michael enrolled the following year at Vanderbilt Academy—with the stipulation that Charlie would be the one to pick him up at the end of the day when his work allowed him to do so.

His first two years at Vanderbilt's "Middle School" were notable for astonishing academic and social progress. Michael devoured course material of all disciplines, consistently outperforming his classmates by significant margins. For the first time in his life, he also began to develop a small circle of friends, although that happened slowly, because it took time for him to open himself up to others. Up to this point, he had focused his interactions with other children to Chris and Darnell Tyler who were twins at the home that Michael had begun to regard as younger brothers given that they had arrived to Sycamore under similar horrible circumstances; spending time with them and teaching them to read. He excelled in sports and developed an interest in and talent for football, which he and Charlie to watched on Sunday afternoons after services at Red Creek. Highlands Prep made a brief and futile attempt to convince him to switch over for his high school career the summer after completing his eighth-grade year. Even the monthly trips with the Congressman to Figure Eight Island yielded absolutely no success in convincing him to change.

His years at Vanderbilt Academy's "Upper School" continued to show his promise as an incredibly gifted student—with a new twist. A new characteristic began to emerge that no one who had observed him as a timid, fearful, and withdrawn child would have ever predicted: Michael was showing skills as a leader. He continued to play football and was selected to be team captain in both his junior and senior seasons along with cultivating the Tyler twins' interest in playing sports themselves. Although he never possessed the size or skills to attract any serious college athletic interest, he played inspired ball as an inside linebacker, directing the defense on the field. He developed friendships with several team members as well as many other students and was elected Student Body President his final year. His academic appetite continued to be unquenchable, posting very high SAT scores and ranking at the top of his class every year at "Vandy." His high school record was unblemished...with the exception of one incident.

During his junior year, when a student pushed him against a locker during an argument, Michael responded with an onslaught of savage punches that only stopped when fellow students pulled him off. His teammates thought it was a sign that he was tough and wouldn't back down. But the Headmaster sat down with him and explained that he would have to show more control during disagreements, and any further incidents would be more formally documented. There was a call made to the Sycamore House, informing them of the incident and explaining that he wasn't being punished but would be held accountable if it happened again. Michael apologized to the counselors, promised it would be his only show of violence, and was utterly devastated when he had to tell Charlie about it. Charlie gave him a paper towel to wipe away his tears of shame and, told him he was disappointed in his actions, but also that he forgave him and believed everyone deserved a second chance. The fact that Charlie had given him his forgiveness gave Michael a palpable sense of relief, and he vowed to never do anything again to disappoint him.

College brochures and letters of interest began to flood the Sycamore House mailbox from all over the country. During the fall of his senior year, he was awarded the prestigious Morehead Scholarship at the University of North Carolina at Chapel Hill, which cemented his decision to go there. He knew the school was one of the best in the nation, and he would still be close enough to Asheville to visit Charlie and his other friends at Sycamore House. Life seemed to be falling into place. And then devastation hit Michael's life again.

Patty Wilson had pulled out of the lot only five minutes before driving Bus No. 244 on her way to her morning pick-up route for Pine Valley Middle School. Being in a school bus, she was elevated above the road, so she was just able to just catch the brake light illuminated down a steep embankment to the side of rural Joel Maynard Road. She pulled off on the shoulder, activated her hazard lights, peered down the slope, and could tell that the car was still running. It was still dark and the slope was far too steep to walk down to investigate further. She used her CB radio in the school bus to have the school district bus offices contact the authorities.

Trooper Walt Hough of the North Carolina Highway Patrol arrived about fifteen minutes later, followed shortly thereafter by the fire department. A ladder was placed down the embankment to allow one of the firemen to go down and check on the older-model pickup truck. Hough used his flashlight to get the tag number so he could call in registration information, noting the Vietnam Veteran sticker in the back window.

Michael was inconsolable when Theresa, the lead counselor at Sycamore House, informed him that Charlie had been found that morning by the highway patrol. It appeared that he had likely fallen asleep driving home and went off the road, unfortunately where the embankment was quite steep. He was already gone when he was found, and it appeared to have been an instant death from a broken neck along with trauma to the head. Hoping to comfort Michael, Theresa told him that Charlie hadn't felt any pain. It was a Wednesday morning.

He was kept home that day from school, and several classmates and staff at Vandy who were close enough to Michael to know how much Charlie meant to him called to offer sympathies while the Tyler twins kept a vigil by his side. His grief had not improved at all the following day, and the now Senator Haxton stopped in Asheville on the way to his Figure Eight Island retreat to pick up Michael to stay there until Sunday's funeral. He hoped to lift his spirits and walk him through what was a devastating time in his life.

Upon their return to Asheville on Sunday morning, Michael was no longer sobbing, but he was a very different person than everyone had gotten used to at Sycamore House. Haxton told Theresa that he had told Michael that Charlie would want him to face this with a stiff back and his chin up. Even though he was no longer here with him, Charlie would still be proud to see that he weathered this storm and continued to succeed as a tribute to everything Charlie had done for him.

Michael carried himself with a silent focus throughout the day, including the funeral, at which Haxton had arranged for full military honors to be rendered. Michael followed the sharply dressed Army pallbearers at the rear of the casket. He stared forward and showed no emotion throughout the ceremony, including the remarks by Reverend Webber from Red Creek and an eloquent eulogy by the Senator. The one exception was when he embraced Charlie's

24

elderly mother Betty; he silently sobbed while she held him tight and told him how much he meant to Charlie all these years. After the service, he asked to remain behind and drive back in the old car that the home allowed him to use on occasion after he had gotten his driver's license the year before. He remained at the gravesite while the funeral home crew covered the grave, and then he left without saying a word.

He finished his senior year withdrawn from others but continuing to excel in academics. He had chosen to enroll in summer classes in Chapel Hill starting only two weeks after his graduation from Vandy, where he led the procession of seniors as the Valedictorian. He deferred his opportunity to give the traditional student speech, an honor awarded to the year's top student, instead allowing the salutatorian to give it.

Two weeks later, in May, 1993, he hugged Theresa and the other counselors goodbye and thanked them for giving him a chance at a good life. He promised Theresa that he was going to be all right and that it would get better when he got away from Asheville for a while. He said goodbye to the other boys at the home and spent some time with the Tyler twins, who were four years younger than him, telling them to be strong and work hard to get independence and success. He climbed into his 1988 Honda Accord—a gift from the congregation of Red Creek church, where he had continued to go every Sunday after Charlie's death—and headed east on I-40 headed to Chapel Hill. He would never return to Sycamore House.

*****

Three years at the University of North Carolina marked the transformation of Michael to a man. He relished the numerous academic pathways one could choose and basked in the anonymity of being at a larger university where you didn't have to wear your past as a birthmark. His scholarship freed him from worrying about tuition and expenses, and he discovered a love of history.

But his interest in medicine was aroused after volunteering at the North Carolina Children's Hospital. He continued to work on a bachelor's degree in history but took the required courses for a pre-medical track as well, which qualified him to receive a minor in

25

chemistry. He achieved Dean's List every semester and scored very high marks on the Medical College Admissions Test (MCAT), all the while developing a passionate love for Tar Heel basketball and everything Carolina. Because of summer courses and the credits he'd attained through AP courses he had taken and excelled in at Vandy, he was on track to graduate in three years. He had found a home he loved in Chapel Hill, so he applied "early decision" to medical school there and received his acceptance. This, however, was not remotely his greatest achievement in college, according to him.

During his sophomore year in Chapel Hill, he happened to meet Anna West, who was working on a degree in accounting. They had first met when he was volunteering at Children's Hospital and she was doing a summer internship with UNC Hospitals' administration department. It took several months of spending time together for Anna to decide this hard-working young man, who was friendly to everyone but maintained a very subtle distance from those he didn't know very well, was someone worth dating. Michael, on the other hand, fell in love with her the first day he met her. He had been on a smattering of blind dates and set-ups from friends during high school and early college, but Anna was his first real girlfriend in the truest sense of the word. He planned for her to be the only one he ever had as well.

Their relationship became very serious during his third and final year of undergraduate studies, and they would occasionally talk about what the future would hold. Anna came from a loving and successful family in Charlotte; her father Walt worked as an executive with Wachovia Bank, and her mother Tina was an English professor at Wingate University. His troubled and non-traditional childhood was never a concern of Anna's, but Michael often felt that her family would have misgivings about this mountain-country orphan who had had a rough road to Chapel Hill. He couldn't have been more wrong.

Michael's introduction to the West family was a relief beyond measure. They had obviously raised a brilliant and confident young woman and, therefore, trusted her judgment in the person to whom she gave her affection. Because of this, they accepted him without reservations. His comfort with them grew quickly, and he found in the Wests a family unit that he felt a part of from the start. He began to believe that he could let his guard down and enjoy his new life.

He entered medical school in the fall of 1996 while Anna finished her masters in accounting. He took her to Asheville for the first time that year and showed her where he went to school, and then he introduced her to Betty Potts. They all went together to Red Creek the next day, a Sunday, followed by a visit to Charlie's grave. Betty told him that Charlie would be very proud of him, and she absolutely loved Anna. Betty's approval and Anna's complete lack of concern over his background gave him a clarity about what he had in her. That night back in Chapel Hill he dropped her off at her apartment on Rosemary Street and told her he had to take a trip the following day to a rural clinic for students to observe primary care medicine. This was the first lie he had ever told her.

Waking at five thirty the following morning, he drove his trusty old Honda to Charlotte and asked to meet Walt for lunch. They met at Dickadee's on East Boulevard, where he didn't touch his sandwich and stammered through the words he had practiced the entire way down I-85 South that morning. He told her that he loved Anna in a way he had never known and that he couldn't imagine a life without her. He promised to try hard every day to make her happy and to never disrespect her. He wanted to ask her to marry him, but wanted Walt's approval first. He felt it would be what Charlie would expect him to do as a gentleman. Walt said he would be thrilled to have him in his family and seemed somewhat surprised at how relieved Michael seemed to be; Michael, in turn, was surprised that Walt's blessing came so easily. They called Tina at work and Walt told her about their conversation. Michael thanked her for raising such a wonderful woman and said he treasured the love they had given him and would let them know ahead of time the day he was going to propose.

He and Walt embraced outside the deli, and Walt got in his Audi and headed back uptown to work. Michael got in his car, elated, and then began wondering how he would buy a ring and whether Anna would say yes. He quickly opened his car door and threw up in the parking lot. He wasn't nervous about getting engaged, but he was terrified that he might not be good enough for someone as perfect as Anna. She was the all-American girl from a nice family who had no limits on what she could do or who she could be with. He was an abused orphan who happened to be smart enough to get a scholarship and who still had nightmares about his childhood. Would she be as happy as he about the prospect of spending the rest of their lives together?

He took what money he had saved over the years and traded his Honda for a small motorcycle, telling himself he lived only four blocks from Berryhill Hall and the hospital anyway. After spending three days shopping for a ring, he finally found the one he thought reflected her—not to mention one he could hope of paying off one day.

He asked her on a beautiful spring day by the Old Well on campus, after having lunch at Spanky's on Franklin Street. His shaking hands and profuse sweating on the way to the Chapel Hill landmark pretty much gave away his intentions even before he stuttered his way nervously through his proposal. The fact that she said yes gave him such a sense of relief that he forgot to put the ring on her finger after showing it to her, until, after walking to her apartment, she asked if he thought she might be able to wear the thing since she had said yes. They called her parents and Mrs. Potts to share the news, then they made love. He watched her sleep as the curtains in the window made the dim moonlight flicker on her face, and he silently thanked God for sending her to him.

They were engaged for a year and then married at Myers Park Presbyterian Church in Charlotte in the spring of 1998. The service was led by Rev. Foster of Anna's church, along with Rev. Webber from Red Creek. She took a job with UNC Hospitals with the group she had done her internship with earlier, while he finished medical school. He had decided on Obstetrics & Gynecology as a specialty after doing a rotation with their oncology team and learning about treating cervical cancer, which had taken his mother away from him at such an early age. His academic performance was as outstanding in medical school as it had been in college, and he matched with his first choice for residency training, at Emory University.

Residency was the time during which Michael earned a reputation as an extremely hard worker and a gifted surgeon. He was a favorite with the nursing staff because he always took the time to share compassion with his patients. It was also the time that Michael and Anna welcomed their first child into the family, a daughter named Elizabeth. As graduation neared, Michael and Anna both looked to Charlotte as their home, and he accepted a position with North Charlotte Women's Group in 2004. The following year blessed them with a son, Charlie, and in 2007 Michael was commissioned in the United States Army Medical Corps Reserve, as a way of giving back to a country where even he had a chance to find success.

Winter of 2008 brought a call to active duty with the 82nd Airborne in Afghanistan as a Field Surgeon, which gave him experiences and friendships that would stay with him for life. But it also took part of his left leg, with a Silver Star (with a V-device for Valor) and a Purple Heart awarded as marks of his sacrifice. The odyssey that began that fateful night in Khost Province took a path to waking up in Landstuhl, Germany, and realizing he had survived, followed by three surgeries at Walter Reed Hospital and intense physical therapy to learn to function again with his prosthetic device. The medical team had talked with Anna about his nightmares, but she knew he had battled them long before Afghanistan.

The Reece family returned home in May 2009 to a hero's welcome. His life was a whirlwind of work, speaking engagements, physical therapy, and catching back up with his family, who was happy to have Dad back home and not always keen to have to share him with so many others who asked for his time. He had been interviewed by all the local media outlets and even occasionally some national organizations. He was North Carolina's returning beloved son.

CHAPTER 3

"You know, you are allowed to go to more than one place to each lunch on occasion Doctor," Drake complained as they walked into Ishi and selected a corner booth. As usual, outside the surgery department, Drake was dressed like an editor from *GQ* while Reece wore his scrubs.

"If it ain't broke…"

"Don't fix it I know. God, what a fucking hillbilly you can be sometimes."

Reece was known by many close to him as very much a creature of habit. If he found something that he liked or was comfortable with, be it food or the company of others, he stuck to it with dogmatic consistency. It wasn't that he feared trying new things; he just appreciated finding places where you could be at ease.

Ishi was a place where he had lunch easily three times a week. He didn't waiver very much with his menu choices, and he had developed friendships with the staff. He knew all of their names and asked about how things were going in their lives. The restaurant was owned by a Vietnamese family who were very friendly and appreciative of Michael's company (and business).

Reece drank his sweet tea without lemon, which was brought without him having to ask, while Drake began ranking the attractiveness of the waitresses. After ordering their lunch, they chatted a little about work, and then Drake just leaned back and stared at him.

"What?"

"How are you doing?"

"Fine, Dr. Drake. Thanks for asking."

"I mean it, no bullshit. You haven't had a lot of downtime and you're always being pulled in multiple directions. I mean, I'm happy you have pulled back your hours a bit at work, but I think that was more out of necessity than choice. You OBs are masochistic when it comes to work schedule. It's no wonder you guys die early." This last remark gained him a little bit of a harsh look from Reece. "I guess what I'm trying to say is that I see you working less at the hospital, but I also see you substituting that work time with some other demand rather than smelling the roses on occasion."

"I'm trying to find my way to some degree...looking for a better balance."

Drake thought that there was more than a little bit of bullshit mixed in with that response. He had noticed changes in Reece since he recovered from his injuries, but he couldn't find the right words in his mind to describe them. Reece carried himself lately with a thinly hidden exhaustion or anxiety or something else. Drake was a skirt chaser and an egomaniac, but he also cared about his friend across the table very much. Reece seemed to personify that which Drake wished that he could be more often. Drake would ask him more direct questions about things than others would—mainly because he didn't really think too much about whether his questions would offend or irritate, but also because Reece didn't seem to mind.

"I tell you what I think. I think you don't like the attention you're getting about this. I personally think you should enjoy the perks of being a hero a little bit more if you ask me..."

"Don't call me that."

"Call you what?"

"A hero. Don't call me that. I'm not comfortable with it and I don't think I deserve that kind of label."

"Dude, save the awww shucks act for—"

"It's not a fucking act. Don't call me that and I'm not going to ask you again."

There was real anger in Reece's eyes. Drake realized there was a line here and that he had stepped over and it was time to pull his foot back. He didn't have to understand why it bothered him to notice that it did.

"Fair enough. Just promise me you will sit down for a while in the near future and just hang out with your family with no commitments that you were too nice or too fucking soft to say no to. You know I am nothing like you even when I should be, but you also know I would run out into traffic for you."

"I know. Just give me a while to sort out how to arrange this new life."

Their food arrived and the conversation took a back seat to eating. Reece picked at his Hurricane Roll while Drake had shrimp tempura. Drake decided the conversation needed to take a turn to the less serious.

"Did you notice how friendly the waitress was being to me?"

"Well, I guess that means you haven't dated her in the past, then."

"Fuck you, St. Michael the Faithful. I'm just a man who appreciates beauty from all over the globe."

They finished their lunch and it was Drake's turn in the rotation to pick up the tab. Michael climbed into his Toyota 4Runner and headed back to the hospital. He saw Drake going the other direction in his Mercedes S550, toward his office, which had its own operating suite where he could charge the surgeon's fees as well as the facility fee. Reece smiled as he thought about how different they were but also how well they got along. The irony was that he was much wealthier than Drake, due to a combination of two incomes, speaking engagement fees since returning, as well as some very good investments. It also helped that he didn't pay alimony to two ex-wives with sizable lifestyle expectations. He had reached a high level of financial independence, which also aided his substantial devotion to supporting two charitable organizations: The Wounded Warrior Project and Big Brothers/Big Sisters of Greater Charlotte. He had lost count of how much money he and Anna had either donated personally or helped raise through volunteering, mainly because the actual figure didn't matter to him. He also had directed his financial advisor to set up fully funded college accounts for the two children of the late Manny Torres.

He knew Drake's questions and advice were not meant to intrude on his personal life. Drake really was a good friend and cared about the Reece family very much. Despite the fact that his demeanor (and often his personal behavior) upset others fairly frequently, he also had an ironclad devotion to them. He knew that Drake had done many things for his family while he was away and during his recovery and could be counted on to do things for your friend that you wouldn't receive praise or credit for. Anna often didn't know whether to hug his neck or strangle it sometimes, but she also appreciated that he was a reliable friend in good times and, especially, in bad.

He pulled into the physician's parking lot at the hospital, checked on his patient in the preoperative area, and made sure she had everything she needed. While the anesthesia team went through her pre-surgical checklist, he went upstairs to the surgical floor to make sure his patient from this morning was doing well. Rashonda was sleeping comfortably, and he was happy to see her urine output was excellent—a sign of two happy kidneys.

The second surgery went smoothly and, after speaking to the family and writing the necessary orders, he noticed there was a message to call the office as soon as he was done.

"North Charlotte Women's Group, this is Julia, how can I help you today?"

"Hey Julia, it's Mike. I had a message to call after surgery."

"Hang on dear; Tricia needed to talk to you."

Tricia was a nurse at the office who had been there longer than he had. She was very proficient at her job and the patients adored her. She ran a tight ship in the clinical area, and Michael jokingly referred to her as his immediate boss.

"Dr. Reece, there is someone here to see you. He's been waiting for about an hour."

"I didn't think I was in the office this afternoon."

"You're not. It's not a medically related issue. I think you should just come on over."

Tricia's voice didn't seem alarmed, but she did sound serious. He had learned long ago that if she gave you advice on what you should do, it was almost always right. Besides, his office was actually attached to the hospital in the Medical Arts Complex.

"No problem. Be there in ten minutes."

He checked in on his second surgery patient of the day one more time and headed over to his office. He walked in the staff entrance, turned the first corner, and stopped dead in his tracks, as he was facing an impeccably fit man dressed to perfection in an Army Dress Blue ASU, including a ribbon collection five rows high.

"Booger?" It was the first thing that came to his mouth, because this was utterly unexpected.

"Great to see you, sir. Sorry for the surprise, but I've got something I need to talk to you about," Staff Sergeant David Tripp said.

They embraced and asked each other about their families. Reece introduced him to the staff and showed him around the office. Tripp then asked if they could talk in private.

They stepped into Reece's office and, after about fifteen minutes, they emerged. Tripp said goodbye to the staff he had met and told Reece he would catch up with him tomorrow and they could talk more. Reece offered for Tripp to stay at his family's home tonight, but he had already checked in at a local hotel and unpacked. "Besides," he said "you and Anna will need some time tonight to talk about this." They embraced and Tripp took his leave.

"Is everything OK?" Tricia asked after Tripp left.

"Yeah, umm, everything's fine." Reece looked like he was in a fog that he couldn't shake out of his head. "It looks like I've been awarded the Medal of Honor."

CHAPTER 4

The Medal of Honor was first authorized in 1861 for the Navy and 1862 for the Army. It was to be presented by the President "in the name of Congress, to such non-commissioned officers and privates as shall most distinguish themselves by their gallantry in action, and other soldier-like qualities..." It was created to recognize soldiers in the Civil War but was changed to a permanent decoration by Congress in 1863. (Because of this, it is often thought erroneously to be named the Congressional Medal of Honor.) It is the highest decoration that can be awarded to a member of the United States military. The current criteria to be a recipient is to demonstrate "conspicuous gallantry and intrepidity at the risk of life, above and beyond the call of duty, in action involving actual conflict with an opposing armed force." Although initially created for recognition of enlisted soldiers and non-commissioned officers, it was later expanded to include commissioned officers as well. Over two-thirds of recipients since World War II were killed in the actions that earned them recognition. Although not a requirement by military regulations, it is customary for other soldiers to render salute to recipients regardless of their rank.

These were a few of the thoughts that made Michael feel more and more that he was undeserving of such recognition. He had gone back into his office and sat down and stared vacantly at the wall for over thirty minutes. *I don't belong among them.*

He walked down the stairs and headed to the physician's parking lot in a daze. He had random thoughts about the recipients he had learned about during the Officers Basic Leadership Course at Fort Sam Houston a few years ago. He viewed their accomplishments as far beyond anything he would ever be capable of. He had visions of the paintings of them he had seen in books or documentaries. Instead of elated that he would be joining one of the most elite groups in the history of the world, he felt unworthy.

Traffic was agreeably light heading west on Harris Boulevard toward Mountain Island Lake. Lake Norman was certainly considered by most as the trendy destination for waterfront living in the Charlotte area, but Reece felt like Mountain Island Lake suited him and his family. Although the Reece family was more than comfortable financially, Michael and Anna both had an aversion to the prevailing need to "keep up with the Jones" that was so popular among many of the well-heeled residents of Mecklenburg County. They aspired to remain casual and approachable and gravitated toward neighbors who were the same.

The Reece family home was on a larger-than-average lot backing up to one of the many coves of Mountain Island Lake. The backyard was wooded, with a wrought-iron fence that contained a large play set built by Michael himself that had become the official rally point for all the kids younger than ten in the neighborhood, which was just fine with the Reeces. They both enjoyed the presence of the neighborhood kids and had become accustomed to a mild degree of chaos existing in the house and yard until all would disperse for dinner or bed in the evening. Tiny, their three-year-old Great Dane who topped out at 185 pounds, was the kids' favorite attraction. He was the consummate gentle giant who both played with the kids and, much to Mike and Anna's delight, by his appearance alone discouraged strangers who may have ill intent. He also would never be more than twenty feet from little Charlie, even when it was time for bed. Elizabeth wasn't jealous, because Tiny "snored like a train," and she enjoyed a quieter atmosphere at bedtime.

"Hey Dr. Mike," Charlie's friend Will said as Michael climbed out of his truck in the driveway. Will Katz lived next door and was Charlie's partner in mischief. The two families were so close that each viewed the others' children as much as their own as the ones they had conceived themselves.

"Hey buddy. Where's Charlie?"

"Getting his stuff. He's staying at my house tonight."

He high-fived Will and headed to the door through the garage where Charlie intercepted him with a leaping hug. "Hey Dad, I'm spending the night with Will." He grabbed his football and ran with Will next door to his house.

Michael found Anna standing in the kitchen. "David called ahead." She preferred David to "Booger," since she didn't know the story behind the nickname and thought it was juvenile. "Elizabeth is staying with Madison."

He wrapped Anna in his arms and just held her there, not saying a word.

"I'm so proud of you honey."

He didn't know what to say. He was baffled by his reaction, to be honest. He couldn't put his finger on why he wasn't beaming with pride, but he felt like someone had made a mistake. "I'm not sure how I feel about this, Anna."

"David said you seemed completely shocked, and he said that was normal."

Anna absolutely adored David. In her eyes, he was a man who appreciated Michael for the unassuming and dedicated man he was. She also remembered that he called one of them every day during Michael's recovery, even when he was still in the hospital himself. He had told her, and she believed him, that he would do anything for her husband, that he was honored to be his friend...and that he would be dead without him. She looked forward to the times that he would visit—as did all of her girlfriends in the neighborhood, who weren't blind at all to the fact that he was well over six feet tall, with a chiseled physique and a face that reminded everyone of Ryan Reynolds. He was hard not to be liked by anyone.

It was a Thursday, and he was glad he was out of the office tomorrow with no commitments. David, a Silver Star recipient himself, would come over and walk them through what would happen from here. Right now he sat on the couch with Anna and stared forward. Anna held his hand in her lap and let him sit in silence. She had known him long enough, probably better than anyone alive, and wasn't surprised when the tears began to roll down his face.

"What moron thought I deserved this? If they wanted to give an award for what happened, I would be happy to tell them to give it to Manny, who I couldn't even keep from dying."

37

"Don't you say that." She turned his face to hers with her hand. "You did everything you could. If you couldn't save him, then he couldn't be saved by anyone. There is a guy coming over tomorrow who would have died that night if not for you."

Anna knew that he harbored terrible survivor's guilt about Manny. He had set up college funds for his kids and talked with his widow Giselle about once a month. He had a framed picture of himself with Manny, taken by Tripp about one week before his death, hanging in his office. They were both smiling and were obviously joking around about something. Many a tear had been shed from Michael while he held that picture since he came home. It was a gift from Giselle, who had received it in the mail a week after Manny was killed along with the last letter he ever wrote her. Every doctor and medic would agree without hesitation that Michael had done everything he could to save him, but his injuries were just too severe.

She also knew that he often referred to himself as "not a real soldier," because he didn't have the most dangerous job and had shorter deployments than his non-physician friends in the Army. She had tried to argue with him; Tripp had simply told him "that's the biggest bunch of bullshit I've ever heard." But it was just his way. He seemed to have trouble seeing himself as worthy of any admiration. She thought of this as she held his hand and let him cry, her eyes falling on his prosthetic leg. *You have nothing to prove to anyone.*

They ordered take-out, which he picked up, and they sat in the living room in front of the fireplace eating sesame chicken and drinking a Far Niente Cabernet Sauvignon. Tomorrow would hopefully bring some clarity as to what came next, then they would talk to the kids. Tripp had said that it would be released to the press on the following Monday, and the circus would begin.

*****

He finally gave up around four thirty a.m. after a fitful struggle to sleep. Swinging his legs over the side of the bed, he fixed his stump below the knee into his prosthesis and walked to the bathroom in the UNC gym shorts that had served as his pajamas for as long as Anna had known him. He brushed his teeth, threw on a Carolina Panthers t-shirt, and walked quietly out of the bedroom into the living room. Tiny met him in the kitchen, somewhat out of sorts due to the pre-dawn activity in the house and the fact that Charlie was not in his bedroom, where Tiny slept between him and the door faithfully every night. Michael let Tiny out the back door to handle his particulars while he found a Gatorade in the fridge. He grabbed the leash hanging at the door to the garage and took Tiny with him on a run as the first hints of sunrise began to peak over the horizon. He had kept out of the habit of running with his iPod, since it's forbidden on any Army post for safety reasons, and he used Tiny's long strides and breathing as his cadence.

He finished a three-mile route he used many times, which ended at the clubhouse of the neighborhood. He used his magnetic membership card to gain access to the workout facility after giving Tiny a drink from the outside spigot. He did his weightlifting and jump-rope routine while watching CNN as Tiny napped in the corner. The warmth of the morning sun was chasing away the condensation on the grass when he emerged from the gym and walked with Tiny at a leisurely pace to the house.

The smell of the brewing coffee machine greeted him as he came inside the house. He kissed Anna on the cheek as she waited for her morning caffeine fix to finish. He smiled as he heard Tiny drink from his bowl, which at his size sounded like a child stomping through a puddle. After calling the post-operative floor at the hospital and checking on his two surgical patients from the day before, he called his partner on call and asked if she could round on them this morning since Michael was off that day. He gave no one a hint of the news he had received yesterday and had asked Tricia to not share it with anyone yet. With that taken care of, he ate a toasted bagel while reading his favorite news sites on the laptop on the kitchen bar counter.

It was summer recess, so Elizabeth was spending the day at her friend's house and Charlie was going to Great Wolf Lodge Water Park with Will and his parents; both of them wouldn't be home until late afternoon. He had about two hours before Tripp would be at the house, so he gave Tiny a bath in the driveway with dog shampoo and the hose, then jumped in the shower, shaved, and got dressed. He kept his morning busy so as to avoid thinking about what the next several weeks had in store for him. He wasn't thrilled about the attention this would cause, but what he dreaded most was the required trip to Washington, DC.

*****

Staff Sgt. David "Booger" Tripp opened the front door and called out for Michael or Anna. Friends that share the kind of experiences they had don't have to knock or use the doorbell; they are much more like family than friends. Reece saw the imposing figure coming over the front threshold of the house and came up to meet him. They embraced along with back slaps.

"Oh my Lord. Look who they let in the neighborhood," Anna joked as she kissed him on the cheek and hugged him like a brother whom she hadn't seen in a long time.

"I'm going to guess that wonderboy here didn't sleep much last night and has been busy but quiet all morning."

"How'd you guess?" Anna said as Tripp grabbed her coffee mug on the way to the machine to get both of them a fresh cup. He knew Michael never got the taste for it, even during the endless and unpredictable hours of overseas combat deployment. They all settled into chairs in the living room.

"I thought I would give you both the broad strokes of what will happen over the next couple of weeks, and then Mike promised me he would take me out on the boat today," Tripp winked at Anna as he said the second part, as a code for *I'll feel him out when I get him alone and let you know how he's doing.* He learned a while back that Major Michael Reece was "Mike" when they were alone together or out of uniform, and that was non-negotiable, he had been informed that if he called him "sir" out of uniform, he would be kicked in the nuts.

"Sounds good," said Anna, "but if you leave before the kids get to see you, they will lose their minds."

"Not a problem," he said to Anna. "I'm not leaving until tomorrow."

"Then you're staying with us tonight, and that is not up for discussion."

David offered no resistance. Truth be told, he wanted to spend some time with them before he left. He and Mike had a bond that would never change, and he had grown to love the Reece family as if they were his own. The unpredictable life of an active duty non-commissioned officer in the 82nd Airborne had not been conducive to him having a family of

40

his own other than nieces and nephews and the occasional girlfriend, none of which had been able to stand the strain of being in a relationship with a warrior during times of combat. He knew he owed his health—his life, actually—to Michael; his wounds had completely healed, including the burns on his hands, with minimal scarring and no loss of function.

Michael's leg was working as close to a normal one as any Tripp had seen. He went on runs and had only a barely perceptible limp. He had even had an attachment made for a fin so he could continue his favorite hobby of scuba diving. But his inner wounds, Tripp feared, were still far from healed.

"OK, so the Pentagon will issue a press release on Monday that will include your official citation, your most recent promotion photo, and a brief bio of you. I've got the bio for you to look at and make any changes you need, and I will send it to them tomorrow. You will be flown up to Washington on Tuesday to meet with the Secretary of the Army, the Joint Chiefs, and the Secretary of Defense. That's when everyone will set a date for you to be formally presented with the medal by the President." Tripp saw the color of Michael's face slowly fading. "Listen, I will be there with you through all this. The Army has assigned me to be your aide for the next three weeks."

Michael almost blurted out that he had things scheduled for work but felt immediate shame for that being his first reaction. More often than not, recipients of this honor had given their lives for something greater than themselves. He may have been struggling with whether he was worthy of this honor, but he had almost God-like admiration for the men and women in uniform. "I'm going to have to make a few calls today to move some things around."

They spent about two hours talking about how their lives would be very different for a while. Tripp assured them that the Army would help them navigate the process and the demands for his time. He said that the fact that he was a reservist would be another factor that would attract a lot of attention, since this was a fairly rare occurrence. It was becoming very clear that the Reece family would have a big portion of their lives dictated by others for the near future.

Michael and David decided to take the boat out for a bit then all three would go out for lunch. After making a few calls to his practice, they were heading through the backyard to the boat dock.

After firing up the engine on the Stingray 235LR, they cast off the dock lines and cruised out of the cove area at idle speed. They rode around the lake mainly talking about their time overseas and catching each other up on updates of some of their common friends. They made some preliminary plans for a diving trip in the next several weeks—a hobby Tripp had gotten into because of Michael. They planned to go to Dominica and spend several days diving, drinking beer, and eating at local dives. Drake was going to meet them there in his sixty-nine-foot Sunseeker yacht, aptly named *The Sculpted Lady*, which he was going to spend about four weeks cruising around the Caribbean. Drake was not someone Tripp would have struck up a friendship with independently, but he liked him and enjoyed his company mainly because he knew Reece did. After about a half-hour cruise around, they dropped anchor in one of the many coves and sat down to talk.

Tripp opened a Diet Coke and dropped into one of the seats, his arms seeming to stretch the sleeves of his t-shirt to a ripping point. "Before you say anything, I know that this is a shock to you and you really don't know what to make of things right now. I also know your life schedule is going to be turned upside down, but this is a big honor, sir." He raised his hands defensively when Reece cut him the evil eye; Tripp had called him "sir" out of uniform.

"I know it's a big honor, it's just an honor I don't think I should be given."

"Well, that's bullshit, and you're going to have to come to grips with that fact ricky-fucking-tick. I was there and I saw what you did." Tripp thought he needed a little shake into reality right now. "Look man, you know I would do anything for you, and I would pray every day if I had a son that he would grow up to be like you. I also know your humbleness is not an act, but you have to accept that this is happening and that you represent something far greater than yourself now. It's time to come to grips and move forward. Or do you want me to go all barking NCO on your ass?"

"I need you to tell me something and you have to be straight with me," Reece said, leaning toward him from the seat directly across from him. "This is not the result of a goddamn politician nominating me and pushing it up the chain, and you know who I'm talking about."

"Well, the easy answer is that it doesn't make a difference, but the truth is that it was originated in the Army and not any office in Washington."

"You know this for a fact? I'm trusting you right now not to tell me what I want to hear."

"I know that's a fact, without any reservation."

"How?"

"Because I'm the one that asked Colonel Tyson to put you up for it."

Reece was at a loss for words. Colonel Greg Tyson was the Commanding Officer (CO) of the unit he was assigned to during that fateful deployment. He had come to respect him tremendously as a CO as well as someone who looked after his people. He knew that Tripp and Tyson went way back and had served together in many different locations and capacities.

He also knew that Tyson had already sent a letter to the promotions board strongly recommending if not demanding that Tripp be bumped to Sergeant First Class as soon as possible. Tripp had been somewhat undercut for promotion by an Executive Officer in his last deployment, out of jealousy for Tripp's beloved status with the men, which was not an opinion they had of the ribbon-collecting desk jockey the XO had been. Tripp had known what happened but was too much of an honorable man to say it. Reece felt Tripp was ten times the soldier that he would ever hope to be, and that made it hard to believe that he could be seen as a hero to him.

"I don't feel remotely worthy of this medal Booger."

"That's exactly why you should get it Mike."

Tripp realized that it was beginning to sink in. There was a look of resolution—and a small hint of pride—in Michael's face.

"You're going to be there with me, right?"

"You know the answer to that brother."

At Tripp's direction, the conversation steered away from the daunting events that were coming in the next few days, and they talked about the boat and the upcoming diving trip, as well as the idea of putting a reunion together for their circle of friends from "Rocket City" (their nickname for FOB Salerno, due to all of the incoming fire that was directed there from Taliban forces). The anchor was pulled after about an hour, and they headed back to the dock. Over their shoulders, there were a few hints of storm clouds building in the distance, making them secure the boat cover after tying up.

CHAPTER 5

Senator James A. Haxton sat in his spacious office in the Russell Senate Office Building, which afforded one of the choicest views of the Capitol Building, from the intersection of Constitution and Delaware Avenues. Office square footage and location can be a reflection of status and seniority, and he had both. As always, he was sharply dressed in a custom-tailored suit complete with the ever-present North Carolina flag lapel pin. He carried a lean frame that stood slightly over six feet in height. The cherry table that stood behind him was littered with pictures of the Senator with countless dignitaries, including the President of the United States. The centerpiece of this picture arrangement was one of Linda Haxton, who had passed away in 1988. Haxton remained a widower, and he and Linda had never had any children of their own— which may have had a lot to do with his devotion to Sycamore House. Currently he had an old friend sitting in front of him who, like the Senator, swirled Johnnie Walker around ice cubes in a crystal glass.

"Well, is it true?" Harold Sutton sat in the soft leather chair looking at his friend who was framed in the window by the Capitol Building as the Washington shadows grew long in the late afternoon. Sutton had known the Senator since their college days at Duke University, after which he had entered Wake Forest School of Law while Haxton left for Harvard to pursue the same degree. His career had ended with retirement after four years in the Governor's mansion. Many people could claim to be in important circles in North Carolina politics, but these two were the ones around which those circles rotated.

"It certainly is. My guys have some friends in the Pentagon, and it's confirmed. The Secretary of the Army gave the green light two weeks ago, and the President signed off on it on Tuesday. Michael was notified yesterday and will be coming to Washington on Monday to be briefed on the process leading up to the ceremony."

"You going to get together with him next week?"

Sutton was already thinking about the almost endless PR possibilities that this would present. An abused child abandoned by society and taken in by the benevolent James A. Haxton, who helped him rise from the proverbial ashes to become a successful physician and now the epitome of an American hero. The current President was in his second term, and there had already been rumblings that Senator Haxton could be a strong candidate for the next election. This kind of attention could go a long way toward getting him to 1600 Pennsylvania Avenue...and a pretty prime cabinet position for his best friend.

"I know what you're thinking Harry, and don't get started," he admonished him with a waving finger. "Michael is his own man and not an election prop. He wouldn't take kindly to being placed in that position, and I won't ask him to do it. Besides, the reporters will do the storytelling for us. If we push it ourselves, it will look forced."

"I defer to your brilliance, Mr. President." Sutton raised his glass as he earned himself a reproaching glare from across the desk.

Harold Palmer Sutton was a man that could be as in his element speaking to campaign donors in the towering bank buildings of Charlotte as he could at a Biscuitville in eastern North Carolina talking with local farmers. He hailed from Lillington, in the heart of tobacco country, which for so long had been a prerequisite to gaining high political office in state politics. He had worked for years in private practice as a plaintiff attorney in Raleigh before winning a seat on the city council and, shortly thereafter, the title of Wake County District Attorney. His aspirations for a prominent judgeship changed course after several high-profile murder prosecutions made him a legitimate star in the state. A cakewalk of an election to Lt. Governor put him in a position to advocate for billions of federal dollars for tobacco farmers hit hard by an industry on the ropes. He and his congressman college buddy were able to steer huge subsidies to help farmers transition to corn and soybeans in a very profitable way. The resulting gratitude swept him into the Governor's mansion, where he spent four years serving the state. After a long career of public service, he decided to retire instead of running for re-election, to "spend time with his family." Sutton's "retirement" had been spent being a power broker from Raleigh to Washington, DC, as well as a highly paid "consultant" for various think tanks, lobbyists, and news networks. Being the ultimate insider was much less stressful (and much more profitable) that holding high public office.

They had dinner reservations at Citronelle that evening, so he decided not to push the PR angle any further for now. Jim was probably right anyway. The bulk of the coverage that would elevate him from advocate for the youth of America to political saint would occur without any prompting from them. It was just too perfect of a story.

*****

Michael and Anna knew there was absolutely zero chance of having the attention of their two children after they came home to find "Uncle Dave" at the house. Tripp was the prototypical favorite uncle. Elizabeth and Charlie always had a willing participant in him for anything from backyard football to Justin Beiber karaoke. His good nature and gentleness contradicted his bodyguard appearance. From the time he was released from recovery for his chest and hand injuries, he had spent countless hours with the Reece family, as Michael faced a much longer road to health. He had formed a special bond with little Charlie; the young man had struggled with seeing his father humbled by injury, when up until that time he was nothing short of Superman in the child's eyes. Uncle David had talked to him in a way that calmed him down and made him believe that his father's injuries were actually another reason that he was indeed Superman...and he would get better. In his eyes, they were as close to his own children as he would ever have, and his love for them was unconditional. It also didn't hurt that he had probably never uttered the word "no" to either one of them, sometimes to the consternation of Mom and Dad.

The parents both smiled as they watched Uncle Dave get his ass kicked for the umpteenth time in Mario Kart by a six-year-old boy, all the while having his driving skills mocked by his surrogate niece. They were both wearing new 82nd Airborne t-shirts that he had bought for them at Ft. Bragg, with Charlie also wearing Tripp's Red Sox hat that was constantly falling over his face while he operated the Wii remote. Mom and Dad were great parents whom the kids dearly loved, but Uncle Dave was quite simply Captain Awesome.

There had been many trips with Uncle Dave to amusement parks, concerts, and UNC games while Daddy had been going through difficult surgical recovery or intense physical therapy. To the kids Tripp's face shined with pure unconditional love, while to the public he resembled a Doberman guarding his puppies. It was fair to say that Mom and Dad felt the same way about Uncle Dave that the kids did.

Dinner tonight would be burgers and hot dogs from the grill on the back deck, and then Mom, Dad, and Uncle Dave would talk with the kids about what would be happening in the next few weeks. Anna's parents would be coming over tomorrow, along with a few very close friends, so they wouldn't be blindsided by the news on Monday. Negotiations had already begun between the kids and Mom about being able to stay up later than usual tonight since Uncle Dave was here. She knew resistance was futile, since he had already said that they could rent a movie, watch it on the floor with blankets and pillows and stuffed animals, make popcorn, etc. She secretly wished that he would one day settle down and have kids himself, if for no other reason than it would give her and Michael a chance to spoil them rotten as revenge.

After dinner, they all gathered in the living room, with the kids sitting on each side of Uncle Dave (the only way to avoid violent jealousy and conflict).

"Guys, do you remember us telling you about the night that Daddy and Uncle Dave got hurt?" Michael said to the kids.

"Yes sir," said little Charlie, earning him a rub on the head by Uncle Dave.

"Some bad guys tried to hurt you and Uncle Dave, and Mr. Manny died," Elizabeth added.

"That's right. Well, Daddy is going to get an award pretty soon for that."

"I got an award this year in school for winning the potato-sack race at Field Day," Charlie announced, letting everyone know he knew what an award was. Elizabeth rolled her eyes.

"You're darn right, my man," Tripp said as he high-fived little Charlie. "Your Daddy is getting an award from the Army that is the most special award they can give to someone. You see, your Daddy was very brave that night and helped protect Uncle Dave after he got hurt." Both kids nodded as he spoke.

Michael leaned forward toward the kids. "We wanted to tell you before anybody else, because you guys are the most important people in the world to us." He leaned back in the chair and held Anna's hand. "After everybody finds out about this award, there will be a lot of people that want to talk to Daddy about it, so we may have to travel to different places from time to time. A lot of times you guys will go with us, but sometimes it may just be me and your Mommy, or sometimes just me. Is that OK with you guys?"

"Way to go, Daddy," Charlie said. "Can we go to Blockbuster with Uncle Dave now?" Charlie knew that "Blockbuster" with Uncle Dave also meant a stop for ice cream. Tripp was doing a poor job of containing his amusement.

It was one of the many reasons that Michael and Anna loved their kids more than life itself. They didn't get caught up with all the confusion and superficialities of life. They loved their Daddy, and they weren't surprised that evidently other people loved him, too. The accompanying ballyhoo and celebration didn't affect them, because they just didn't care about it.

"I guess so," said Anna, with a bit of a snigger herself as well.

Elizabeth slipped off the couch and hugged the neck of her father. "I'm proud of you, Daddy." Michael bit his lower lip and kissed her on the forehead. That statement meant more than anything he could ever receive, the Medal of Honor included. He couldn't help thinking about the Torres children, and felt an inner anger that they couldn't have a moment like this with their father.

"I'm proud of you too sweetheart."

As the kids raced each other to get shoes for the movie and dessert run, Tripp looked at Michael and Anna. "Don't you wish it were that easy with everyone?"

*****

The evening temperatures had not reached the stifling levels that late summer could bring to the Charlotte area, especially since there was a mild breeze that gently swayed the pine and willow trees in the backyard near the water. As they walked to the door leading to the back deck, the Reece parents grinned at the scene on the floor: little Charlie perched on the back of Tripp's massive frame, the soldier sprawled on his stomach beside Elizabeth, watching *How To Train Your Dragon*.

Anna reclined on Michael in a cushioned lounge chair as they watched the slow-moving motor and pontoon boats gliding over the lake, the setting sun now requiring them to use their operating lights. Two lit citronella candles kept the mosquitoes away, and the only sounds were the gentle lapping of the water on the shore and the early chorus of frogs in the distance. They soaked in the tranquility, since it was going to get very hectic in the near future, and shared a glass of Cabernet as she rested the back of her head on Michael's chest. It was probably the millionth time he silently thanked God for sending Anna.

"You're going to have to come to grips with the fact that you're the only person who thinks you shouldn't get this honey."

"I know. I will. I promise I will try to keep this from overrunning our lives."

"We'll just take it one day at a time. But I want you to know that I'm proud of you, too."

"I love you. Tripp and I fly out early Monday morning to Washington."

Anna looked up to his face as he kissed her forehead. "Behold, I send you out as sheep amongst the wolves." They both laughed, his a little more forced than hers.

*****

Walt West sat in the Reece living room with his wife Tina, looking thunderstruck. "Jesus."

"My thoughts exactly Dad," Michael told his father-in-law.

Walt had never served in the military, but he was the son of a United States Marine who had fought in the Pacific. After World War II, Hiram West had opened an insurance agency in

Charlotte, where he had built a good living and earned enough to send Walt and his sister Mary to college. He was a fiercely patriotic man who was well respected in the community as an honest and hard-working neighbor. Walt could remember his father telling him stories about one of the greatest Marines in history—John Basilone, who had received the Medal of Honor for actions in Guadalcanal. He remembered the look of reverence and awe on his father's face when he told stories about him—including his one encounter with Basilone, on Iwo Jima, which turned out to be a few hours before he was killed in action, earning a Navy Cross that was given to his widow, Lena.

"Well, I think they couldn't have picked a better man to give it to if you ask me," Tina said as she kissed Michael on the cheek.

"When will the presentation take place?" Walt asked.

"I'm not sure. I fly to Washington on Monday for several meetings at the Pentagon and the announcement will be given as a press release that day. David said that the presentation at the White House will probably be within a couple of weeks of that."

Uncle David was currently at Carowinds with the Reece kids, continuing his mission to make them the most rotten kids in Mecklenburg County. A few close friends and co-workers were coming over that evening, but Michael and Anna wanted to tell her parents first in a more personal setting. Second only to Charlie Potts, they were the closest thing to parents Michael had ever had. Michael and Anna stressed the importance of not telling anyone until it was released on Tuesday. They all embraced and he promised to call them when he got back from Washington.

*****

Around the same time, Colonel Greg Tyson grinned as he read his official notice that a soldier under his command would be receiving the Medal of Honor on his AKO email account. The aged government-issue desk chair creaked as he leaned back placing his large hands behind his chocolate-colored shaved scalp.

51

He held fond memories of the doctor who worked tirelessly to save the wounded soldiers under his command in Afghanistan. His initial decision to nominate Reece for the Distinguished Service Cross was amended to the next higher award mainly because of the insistence of Tripp. Tyson was always a commander who gave great weight to the desires of the men who were at the tip of the sword rather than the Command Post and had no reservations about his nomination after Tripp's description of the events that occurred that fateful night.

He remembered Reece's popularity with the unit soldiers, particularly the medics whom Reece always said were the reason that most wounded soldiers survived their battlefield injuries and had no hesitation in asking young enlisted men over ten years his junior to teach the officer combat medical skills. On the night that Reece was cut off during the attack, the medics on the FOB had to be physically restrained from going outside the wire on foot during a firefight to try and rescue him.

The thin and gray-accented mustache spread as Tyson's smile broadened. "Hooah Doc...Hooah."

*****

As per the usual custom, the late afternoon had started off with small talk and catching up. Catering platters from Chik-Fil-A had satisfied the children in attendance, after which they had all been settled into the upstairs home theater room to watch *The Lion King*, with the two teenage kids acting as chaperones/gophers. Anna had ordered a taco bar catered for the adults, and everyone helped themselves and sat at the large dining room table enjoying the meal with glasses of wine or bottles of beer.

The attendees to this casual gathering represented what would be a fairly small inner circle of Michael and Anna's closest friends and colleagues. They all knew this had been put together on fairly short notice and that there was going to be some kind of announcement. Because everyone here was at ease with each other and there were no strangers that were trying to impress others, no one tried to pry any information and knew it would come when it came.

In addition to Tripp, Drake, and the Katz family there were two of Michael's partners at the practice: Richard Phillips and Susan Banks. Rich and Susan were his closest friends in a practice where all the doctors got along very well. In addition Jon and Monica Tate, who had driven in from Wilmington after getting the phone call about there being something important that they needed to be a part of tonight. Jon and Monica were college friends of Michael and Anna, respectively, and had been set up on their first date by them. The fact that their only child was named Anna was a testament to how close their friendship with the Reece family was.

After dinner was over and plates and cups had been put away, they all gathered on the back deck and Tripp made the announcement to the assembled friends. There were gasps followed by applause followed by hugs and back slaps. The Reeces thanked everyone for being there and told them they wanted them to know tonight rather than as a surprise on Tuesday when the press would begin reporting the news. Questions were asked about what came next, and Michael and Anna shared what answers they had. Everyone understood that this was not information to be shared, and there was no one in this tight circle of friends that couldn't be taken at their word.

Rich and Susan spent some time with Michael and made a suggestion that seemed like a very good idea. All senior partners at North Charlotte Women's Care could take a four-month sabbatical during which they wouldn't share in the office revenue but also they wouldn't be responsible for any of the overhead expenses either. This had been enacted several years ago to help prevent burnout in a specialty that was especially demanding on one's time and effort. Michael resisted at first, due to the practice having to cover for him and do extra call coverage when he was deployed overseas, but both Rich and Susan would have none of that; compared to his sacrifice, this was nothing, they said. Besides, Rich had joked that going somewhere and getting part of your leg blown off shouldn't really be considered a sabbatical. Michael couldn't argue with the logic of the idea and, in all honesty, it was a relief to know that it would be one less thing to juggle in the craziness that was to come. He felt that he could take care of all the currently scheduled surgical procedures and other commitments in three weeks, and then his sabbatical would begin.

After being the recipient of praise and congratulations and general good fellowship that only close friendships can bring, the evening ended with Michael raising a toast to three people that he kept as close to his heart as anyone: Anna Reece, Manny Torres, and Charlie Potts. In a brilliant tactical move, Tripp had given the catering staff an extra bonus to stay and clean up, and after the kids had been put to bed the hosts all collapsed in the living room.

Tripp had planned to visit the following day with an old Airborne friend who now lived in nearby Salisbury, and Michael and Anna decided that their best use of Sunday would be to spend it as a family, with no scheduled events whatsoever. All three of them went to bed fairly early, and Anna made sure that Michael's evening was topped of in fine fashion indeed. The combination of wine, good food, and making love to his wife had allowed him a good five hours of sleep before the nightmares began.

CHAPTER 6

Michael and David crept out of the house for an early-morning run on Monday, accompanied by Tiny. There was very little activity on the neighborhood roads, as the early morning haze promised a warm and humid day to come. Their conversation was limited due to Reece's disdain for chatting during a run; he always joked that he was working hard enough just to breathe. David smiled to himself thinking of how far Reece had come. He had actually gone on Michael's first jog with him after the injury once he had been cleared for that kind of physical activity. After barely over one mile his friend was terribly out of breath and had a bleeding stump inside its prosthetic insert. Reece was more than a little discouraged but also determined to overcome this obstacle. Over the past several months, Tripp's pace setting had become faster as Michael had slowly healed and gotten back into shape. They both knew that David could run at twice the pace and twice the distance without breaking a sweat, but running beside his friend was far more important than running ahead.

The house was coming to life when they returned, Michael panting and David pretending to be more winded than he really was. The kids were having cinnamon bagels and blueberries for breakfast, while Anna was sipping her coffee mug. All three would take the men to the airport this morning, then the kids would go to their half-day summer camp activities. After initial bickering, it was decided that Charlie would sit beside Uncle David on the way to the airport but Elizabeth would get to do the same when they were picked up on Tuesday.

Those details settled, Michael headed to the bathroom to shower up and dress for the flight. As the steam was evaporating from the mirror, he looked at the man scraping the morning's stubble from his face. He didn't see a celebrity or a super soldier...and certainly not a hero...but he pledged to himself to try to live up to the honor that was being bestowed upon him. The temples were gray in his close-cropped hair, and although he worked hard to be fit, he was not remotely the match for the chiseled physique of his battle buddy. He leaned into the front of the sink to compensate for his mauled left leg, which lacked its prosthesis at the moment. He slipped on his dog tags and dressed in his ACU uniform; he had a special insert in his left boot to make up for the small post above his artificial foot. He pinned on his Combat Action Badge on his left breast and made sure all the Velcro tags were in their proper position. He wanted to be squared away since he would be meeting with many soldiers today who were far above his O-4 pay grade. He had been assured that Tripp would be by his side for the entire agenda today.

The departing-passenger drop-off area at Charlotte Douglas International Airport was typically congested for a Monday morning. Hugs were exchanged and both men listened to the requested souvenirs from the kids. Tripp threw his overnight pack over his shoulder while Michael extended the handle on his Pullman. They both had small hang-up bags carrying their Class A uniforms in case a change was required. As is often the case while in uniform, they were waved toward the first class check-in counter instead of the much longer line for coach tickets. They checked their bags and headed toward security, where they removed their laptops and placed their backpacks on the conveyer belt. Dog tags, keys, and watches were placed in the hard plastic bowls at the entrance to the scanner, and Michael waved to the TSA agent to try to tell him he would need to be scanned.

"Come through the detector please, sir," the agent instructed him.

"I'm going to need—"

"Just come through the detector, sir."

Michael sighed but walked through, eliciting a beep.

"Please back up, check your pockets and come through again."

"I'm going to need to be hand-scanned."

"Just follow my instructions please, sir."

Michael waved off David, who was about to insert himself into the conversation. He looked at the crew-cut, pot-bellied man and knew the futility of trying to reason with him at the

56

moment. He walked through again, earning yet another reproaching beep, and opened his mouth to speak.

"Did you check your pockets, sir?" The agent belted out while scanning the line.

Reece had had enough. He backed through the detector once more, unlaced his boot, and pulled off his prosthesis. He dropped into on the conveyer belt with a loud thunk and hopped through the detector.

Silence.

"Better?"

The agent's neck was flushed red and he avoided eye contact. "Thank you, sir."

The two agents behind the scanner were speechless, but their faces offered an apology while he thanked them and grabbed his things. He hopped to the nearby bench and began squaring himself away.

"Fucking asshole," filled the agent's ears; he could smell the coffee on Tripp's breath as his face was about two inches from his. The agent looked down while he checked off the boarding pass, which was fiercely snatched from his hands by the hulk of a man in uniform before him.

The USO lounge at Charlotte Douglas is a point of pride for the city. After checking in, they walked down the hall adorned on each side with countless coins of excellence and unit patches donated by hundreds of soldiers and veterans grateful for this special place on the second floor above the bustle of thousands of travelers. The hall opens to a large room on the right, with a dozen leather recliners facing a large flat-screen television and a kid's play room on the left. Around the corner past the television lie multiple Internet terminals and plug-in outlets, followed by a private movie room and a video game room. The lounge is stocked with coffee, beverages, snacks, and even hot food, all donated by local airport vendors. Its staff are all volunteers whose purpose is to do anything they can to make the travel process a little easier for one of the country's most precious resources. Michael grabbed a complimentary *USA Today* while Tripp looked over the food selection.

"There's always one fucking guy who desperately needs a good beating," Tripp said softly through clenched teeth. He imagined his blood pressure reading would be off the charts right now. He knew this was the perfect time for Reece to utter one of his most often used lines.

"There are far worse tragedies going on in the world right now my friend."

It was one of the reasons he was a good officer and leader. He could be angry when he needed to be, but he didn't dwell on things or hold grudges. He seemed to be gifted with a tremendous amount of perspective and patience. Tripp knew he himself had an abundance of the former and very little of the latter, but let it go while he watched his friend lift the handle to a footrest on a recliner and attack the crossword puzzle.

It wasn't long before there was the sound of two pairs of feet walking down the hall with purpose. The two friends looked up to see the aforementioned TSA agent trailing behind another who was older and appeared to be a supervisor of some sort. The older gentleman did not look happy, and his companion looked as though he had just seen his own ghost. The supervisor had a small Kuwait Liberation Campaign ribbon replica pin on his collar.

"Sir, my name is Cecil Gardner, and I'm the shift supervisor here today for security check-in personnel," the older gentleman said as Michael shook his hand.

"Nice to meet you, sir. I'm Michael Reece."

"Sir, I have been made aware of what occurred during your security walk-through earlier, and I wanted to personally apologize for the improper behavior that you had to witness. There are no words that can excuse what happened to you today. I believe Agent Daniels has something he would like to say to you if that's OK."

The overweight agent shuffled forward and made only occasional eye contact. "Sir, my actions were improper and disrespectful, and I apologize."

Agent Gardner stepped forward again. "Sir, I will be happy to present a complaint on your behalf to our department head supervisor if you so wish. I assure you that this matter would be dealt with swiftly and convincingly," his eyes cut to the withering younger agent.

58

"That won't be necessary Mr. Gardner. I'm pretty sure that your colleague learned a valuable lesson today and he will certainly approach it in a different manner should this situation arise again in the future." His remark was met with a vigorous nod by Agent Daniels. "I think we're all good here, and I appreciate you coming to talk with us. We are all entitled to a bad day now and then."

They all shook hands and Agent Daniels gave one more apology before leaving the lounge, undoubtedly heading to another location where Mr. Gardner was planning on chewing the rest of the young man's ass off.

Tripp shook his head as he watched them leave. "I don't know how you do it, sir."

"I find forgiveness can be liberating. It helps you cast off things that weigh you down. Don't get me wrong, it pissed me off. But if I had insisted that he be fired, it probably would have happened. It wouldn't change what had happened earlier, and some guy who probably has a wife and kids would be out of a job. Now he feels like he has a second chance and I'll bet you the next soldier that comes through his line will be treated like a king. In the end, everybody wins."

"All due respect sir, but this is the same guy that still blames himself for Manny."

While David was prohibited from addressing Reece as "sir" when not in uniform, the sergeant insisted on doing so in these situations. He hoped this comment didn't cross a line, but he had known him long enough to recognize the excessive amount of criticism he would lay upon himself.

"Don't you think forgiving yourself would be just as liberating, especially when you didn't do anything wrong?"

"'Forgive many things in others, nothing in yourself.' Ausonius."

"You can be an enigma sometimes, sir."

Reece grinned and returned to his crossword. Tripp spotted two soldiers in the lounge with Airborne patches, and he went to chat with some fellow paratroopers. They had about an hour to kill before boarding their direct flight to Reagan National.

*****

Chip Johnson stirred two Splenda packets into his Starbucks café mocha with an extra shot of espresso. After purchasing a copy of the *Washington Post*, he headed toward Washington in his Volkswagen Jetta on the congested George Washington Memorial Parkway from his home of Alexandria. The stop-and-go traffic allowed him to check his numerous messages on his Blackberry while sipping his first caffeine infusion of the day. The young chief political advisor to Senator James A. Haxton was known as the next wonder kid in political circles and sat at the grown-up table on the staff of his boss. He had been noticed by many for his savvy political analysis, but more so for his superb skill at using the media to advance the agenda of whomever was lucky enough to hire him. At the young age of twenty-nine he had a Rolodex full of everyone that mattered in the media in Washington and, to a slightly lesser extent, in America.

He had a bachelor's degree in political science from George Mason University that he completed at the age of nineteen, and a JD from The University of Virginia. He had never set foot in a courtroom and had never worked in a law firm. Instead, he took an entry-level position in Feldman, Creasy, and Jones, which was a high-powered political consulting firm in the nation's capital. He was very opinionated about assignments he had, which mainly dealt with media relations for political figures—especially political figures that had been caught with their pants down, literally or metaphorically. His co-workers, for the most part, despised him and thought of him as an obnoxious pain in the ass, and he somewhat floundered in his position until after two years he was part of the consulting group for one Congressman Paul Butler. The distinguished gentleman from South Carolina had been caught carrying on a three-year affair with his Chief of Staff, part of which time overlapped with his wife's pregnancy with their third child. Chip's firm had been hired to salvage not so much the Congressman but his party's hold on the office that he would obviously step down from. They assigned him to the team handling the media management of the affair, mainly because he hadn't really impressed anyone and this seemed like a loser—which wouldn't stop them from billing countless hours generating a proposal that would essentially say "lay low and don't run for re-election."

Five days after the story had broken, the Congressman met with the team to hear their proposal of how to land as softly as possible from this disaster. They were all in agreement that he would do three interviews: CNN, CBS, and the local Columbia news station at home. He would wax poetically on his sorrow and pray for forgiveness from God, his family, and his constituents. He would announce that he would not run for re-election, in order to focus his time on healing his family. He would take a four-week leave of absence to spend time with his children and his pastor and try to win his wife's trust back, and would beg the people of South Carolina's Second Congressional District to not let his personal failures make them give up on the issues that his party would continue to fight for without faltering. Advocating for the poor and victimized was far more important than one man who had surrendered to weakness and strayed from his family and his God. They all agreed this was the way to go...all but one.

Chip thought that this was his chance. He had not uttered a single word about his wariness of their plan, but had spent every night after their long days working on what his proposal would be. He was fully aware that he had not had an impressive tenure thus far at the firm, and there were rumors of him being let go for more promising young talent. This was his opportunity to make a big splash by going all in on a contrary recommendation—a recommendation that he had not shared with anyone beforehand to avoid it being deep-sixed before he had the chance to test the waters.

He smiled as the Congressman buried his face in his hands and muttered, "Jesus...this can't be the only way."

"With all due respect, Congressman, I don't think it is the only way. I don't even think it is the best way," Chip announced with a firm purpose in his voice. In tandem, every face from his team turned to him in shock followed by silent rage. He knew he had better jump in to his idea immediately before someone shot him right then and there. "Sir, you have worked too hard for your constituents to just quit without a fight. You made a mistake, but it doesn't have to overshadow everything you are and everything you have done for YOUR people!" The look on the Congressman's face told him immediately that catering to his vanity was exactly the right move.

He launched into an aggressive media campaign proposal that would fight the charges head on with the goal of not only salvaging his reputation but also sealing a successful bid for re-election. He had prepared a Power Point presentation that was detailed and clear and laid out a two-week timeline of carefully choreographed press releases and interviews that would cast doubt on the authenticity of the accusations and would, as a bonus, possibly crush some of his opponents, despite the fact that they had nothing to do with the story breaking. It had suggested networks and reporters for each release and interview and why. It had a list of political allies who either owed him a favor or needed him for a vote and, therefore, who could be approached to aid in his media resurrection. He suggested possible bad guys that could be cast as suspects for falsely suggesting this tawdry tale in order to ruin this honest family man who fought for the little guy. He had a detailed plan of how to walk his wife through this and convince her of playing along for the good of the people and what rewards there would be if she did. He walked Butler through how to ask his party to give him four weeks of this before they turned their collective backs on him in order to try to keep his seat on their side of the aisle, and he offered three case reports on political figures that had been caught in similar circumstances, two of whom kept their seats in the next election.

He was passionate and relentless in his presentation, and by the end the Congressman may have even doubted he had an affair in the first place. He had faced personal and political ruin less than an hour ago, and this young man was giving him the proverbial "get out of jail free" card. His narcissism made him easy to convince that the people of his district would be lost without him, and he was too good of a representative of the regular guy to give up this easily. He also was independently wealthy and had plenty of money to spend on the efforts that this Johnson kid was proposing. He turned to the other end of the long mahogany table at Felton Creasy and announced he was going with Mr. Johnson's plan. Butler left the office building like a man who had just found out that his brain tumor was inexplicably gone.

"You little fucking weasel!" One of the more senior team members seemed to voice the consensus of the group after the Congressman had left. "You've got less than an hour to pack up your goddamn desk and get the fuck out of here." Blood vessels were clearly visible in the man's neck and temples.

"Hang on everyone. Let's all just settle down," Creasy said to the team. "I'm not happy with what you did at all young man. Getting a reputation as an undercutting backstabber is not going to get you very far here. However, Butler wants to go with his plan. Therefore, if we kick the kid out the front door, we have lost our client." Creasy placed his tanned hand on his chin as he looked down at the floor for a moment. "OK. The team will go with Chip's plan, and he will take the lead. No bitterness or petty bullshit from anyone will be tolerated. If it works, you will be the next boy genius in town. If it doesn't, I will fire you and then I will fucking crush you. You'll be lucky to get on as assistant campaign manager for someone's city council run in Slingshit, Utah. Does everyone understand?"

There were nods all around, and Creasy walked away to his plush office hiding the smile on his face. The kid had a lot of balls, and he was an original thinker. He didn't care for his ambush in the conference room, but there was something to be said for someone who was willing to stick their neck out in this town.

What followed was a media campaign that is still talked about in public relations circles to this day. Butler held a press conference back home, where he defiantly stated that he was being slandered and he wouldn't go quietly into that good night. He said that even though this baseless nonsense was threatening to tear apart his family (his wife was not by his side, by Chip's design), he would fight for the ideals that he believed in and the ideals that caused the good people of his district to elect him in the first place.

Chip used what meager contacts he had with the media to create a domino effect that made it up to the top echelons of the big networks. Very quickly everyone in the media knew that Chip was calling the shots, and anyone who wanted in the game would have to go through him. It was the big story at the time, with all the ingredients of a media circus: a possibly philandering member of Congress, a wronged family, possible favoritism on his staff in exchange for sexual favors…Everyone wanted more, and Chip was the one who decided who could break something new. To get a new detail or access to Butler, interviewers had to agree to avoid certain questions and were skillfully manipulated to steer how the interview would play in public. Networks and newspapers were for-profit entities, and their viewers/readers wanted the freshest information, so many reporters and news executives made decisions to alter their coverage in exchange for access. It was quite simply a feeding frenzy, and Chip Johnson was the only one with a snack to offer.

By the end of three weeks, Butler had been so skillfully presented that public opinion had changed from the initial disgust and outrage to sympathy for someone they believed to have been set up. Network anchors who had reported the affair and seen emails giving damning details about it were now stating that consideration must be given to the possibility that the rumors of infidelity were untrue. Stories were planted and set up by Chip that offered possible conspirators, from anti-union business leaders who wanted to silence a defender of workers to the South Carolina Republican Party Chairman. A portion of the substantial fees charged by the firm were quietly distributed through multiple shell corporations to the mistress, who held a press conference announcing her resignation and vehemently denying anything improper took place. She said she was profoundly saddened that such a good man and a fresh wind of change in Washington had been attacked, and she hoped with all her heart that the perpetrators of these lies would be found and exposed.

The coup de grace was the ex-husband of the mistress coming forward and stating that he had made it up and released the information to the press, including the falsified emails, to get back at the woman who had left him. He came forward because he was "overcome with guilt for soiling the reputation of a good man and husband." He prayed he would someday receive forgiveness from the Congressman, and he had decided to move away from the ones he had caused such harm.

Butler's final interview on the matter came the next day, with his wife now by his side, holding his hand. He stated that he had spoken with his family and his pastor and said that he had decided to forgive the man who had caused so much damage to him. "We are all imperfect creatures in God's eyes, and we should forgive others as a tribute to the teachings of Jesus Christ." The Butler family was whole again and had survived an attempted character assassination, and it was now time to move forward and do the work that he had been elected to do. Several weeks after the final interview, Chip gave the hometown newspaper exclusive access to do a piece on the healing family, complete with photographs of Butler and his wife walking on their property hand in hand and one of the Congressman on his front porch swing with all three children, looking off into the distance and knowing nothing on the horizon could threaten their love for each other ever again.

The jilted ex-husband had almost completely dropped off the face of the earth, leaving a statement that he wanted to get away and try to earn his honor back. Rumors of his location placed him all over the country and even abroad, but only Chip knew that he had moved to rural Oregon, with a significantly elevated net worth.

Election Day came around, Butler won by a staggering margin, and the new boy genius had his coming out party. The behind-the-scenes movers and shakers in Washington knew the value of someone who could pilot a media campaign against the odds to the desired outcome, and he was the hottest free agent in town. It was even more impressive that the entire PR campaign was based on utter bullshit. One of those admirers was freelance consultant and lobbyist Harold Sutton, who knew there were introductions to be made.

Chip's entry to the staff of Sen. Haxton as Chief Political Advisor and Director of Communications ruffled some feathers on the staff, but they were told that this matter was decided and everyone should get used to it. He had received countless offers after the Butler affair, but he recognized the best wagon to hitch himself to. Haxton was considered by many to be one of the two or three frontrunners for the party nomination for President. If that were to happen, Chip would be an integral part of senior campaign staff and, if successful, a shoe-in for White House Director of Communications, with his other benefactor, Governor Sutton, as Chief of Staff.

He saw that the lead email on his phone said he had a new meeting scheduled this morning with the Senator, Gov. Sutton (he insisted on being called *Governor* Sutton), and no one else. It certainly tickled his curiosity, but he would find out soon enough what it was about. He laid his Blackberry on the passenger seat and listened to CNN on satellite radio as he crept up the congested highway.

CHAPTER 7

The short US Airways flight was uneventful and landed at Reagan National Airport a few minutes ahead of schedule. Michael and David were met at baggage claim by Staff Sgt. Elaine Woods, who would take them to their hotel and act as their driver today. They claimed their baggage and walked with her to her vehicle, which was a standard American-made sedan with Department of Defense labels at the top middle area of the windshield.

"Sir, I will take you to your hotel where you can freshen up if you need to do so and change. The uniform for today's meetings will be Class A," SSG Woods informed them. "Here is your agenda for today."

Michael looked over it and noted it was shorter than he expected. They would meet at the Office of the Secretary of the Army at 1330, followed by a meeting with the Army Office of Public Affairs. To Michael's relief, "SSG David Tripp" was included on the agenda. He wasn't afraid of the meetings or the people he would see there; he was just intimidated sometimes with the Army process. Being a reservist, he didn't have daily exposure to the "Army Way" and was constantly worried that he would do something outside of protocol or just plain stupid. That worry was amplified by the fact he would be meeting with some pretty senior people today. Tripp's presence set him more at ease in these situations, since he had far more experience at being a soldier. Tomorrow was breakfast with Secretary of Defense Frank Dietz and General Andy Shaver, Army Chief of Staff, at 0700, followed by a meeting with Major General Tommy Butts, Commanding Officer of the 82nd Airborne Division, and Major General Catherine Kniesl, Commanding Officer of the US Army Medical Corps at 0915, after which they would be taken to the airport for their flight home.

They arrived at the Hilton Garden Inn in Arlington. It seemed clear that SSG Woods was not aware of the purpose of their being here today, but she had been instructed that they were distinguished guests for some reason. She offered to take their bags, which they both politely declined, at which point she hurried into the lobby to take care of their check-in. They stood

66

near the lobby bar and watched SportsCenter on the television for the few short minutes it took Woods to get their keys.

"Your rooms are both on the fourth floor and here are your keys. I will wait here in the lobby and we will need to leave here by 1230. I've arranged for some food items to be in your room if you would like to eat something before we go. This card has my cell phone number on it and you can call it anytime today or tomorrow if you need anything or have any questions, sir."

"Sergeant Woods, I was under the impression that Sergeant Tripp and I would have the Honeymoon Suite here tonight," Reece said with as straight a face as he could muster.

Woods blinked hard and struggled to find something to say.

"Look Sergeant, we are both pretty easygoing guys. I would like for you to try to relax a little bit. The last time I checked, I'm not the Pope."

"No problem, sir," Woods said with a grin. She turned toward the lobby sitting area and they headed to the elevators.

Michael made a trip to his bathroom and then nibbled on the sandwich plate that was in his room. He didn't have much of an appetite and was a bit nervous, so he kept the intake to a minimum. Afterward, he washed his face and changed into his Class A uniform, making sure that his shoes were not scuffed and his tie was straight. He had taken his trousers to an alterations shop back home that had put in a silk inner lining. Although Tripp joked it was the "metrosexual-issue Class A trousers," it was done because Reece still had some contact sensitivity to the never fully healed areas of his left leg. He still had what was often referred to as "phantom pain," which felt as though his foot was still there and was hurting. The low-dose Elavil tablets were the only residual medications he still took from his recovery, and they were quite helpful for this type of nerve communication confusion that his brain couldn't quite process.

He knocked on Tripp's door and said "Room service" in his pitiful-woman impression. Staff Sergeant David Tripp opened the door and Reece felt his testosterone levels fall just by looking at him. Tripp could have been taken off an Army recruiting poster with his broad shoulders and barrel chest, tapered like an inverted pyramid to a thirty-three-inch waist. His left chest was emblazoned with ribbons just under a jaw line that would make Superman jealous.

"Jesus, you make me look old and soft."

"Would you like me to carry anything for you, sir?" Tripp said in his overly loud official voice.

"Kiss my ass."

They met Woods in the lobby and Michael asked her if she had gotten a chance to eat.

"I'm squared away, sir," was her reply. He noticed she didn't say that she *had* eaten, which made him suspicious that she had sat there and waited the entire time. He decided against pressing her for an answer, because he didn't want her to feel uncomfortable. She seemed to have read his mind anyway. "I'm having chow during your first meeting, sir."

The drive up I-395 to the Pentagon was fairly short. They were directed to the Distinguished Visitors parking area. The number of service men and women walking in the outer area made for a continuous routine of saluting and returning salutes. Woods brought them to an area just outside the entrance where a sharp-looking Captain executed a sharp salute to Reece who quickly returned it.

"Major Reece, I'm Captain Phil Sullivan and I will be escorting you and Staff Sergeant Tripp to your meetings today. It is beyond an honor to meet you today, sir."

"Thank you Captain," Reece said. *Looks like someone has briefed the Captain on what is going on today.* Sullivan already had badges and passes for them, and they went through the entrance heading toward the Office of the Secretary of the Army.

The sheer size of the Pentagon is awe-inspiring when it's viewed from the outside, boasting over 6.5 million square feet. Reece was surprised, however, how regular it looked on the inside. One quickly forgot how large the building was once you were walking through the countless corridors. They remained in the outermost, or "E," ring of the complex, which usually was the real estate of the most senior of officials here. The walk was fairly long, and he had to work a little to keep up with the brisk pace set by CPT Sullivan. He couldn't help but notice the amount of men and women who had stars on their shoulder boards, reminding him that he was in the physical heart of the American military. He also noticed that Tripp had taken a more formal appearance as they walked, positioning himself slightly ahead and to the left of Reece. This was the customary position for a soldier to be in when walking with a superior officer, which dated back to centuries ago where it was believed that this allowed the junior soldier to draw his sword with his dominant hand and place it between his superior and whomever may wish him harm.

After about five minutes of navigating the hallway with their escort officer, they reached the door which read:

Office of the Secretary of the Army

Malcolm J. Winters

It opened to an anteroom with several staff members. One walked directly to meet them and told them the meeting would begin in about five minutes. Coffee was offered and declined, and they both sat in fairly plush leather chairs with Reece clasping his hands in his lap to keep them from shaking. His mouth was as dry as cotton and he felt the humidity of perspiration under his arms.

"Don't worry, sir. Remember, you're here to get *your* ass kissed today," Tripp said with a grin, sensing his anxiety. "They are probably just as nervous about looking stupid in front of you."

"I really doubt that Booger. Do you think they would notice if we made a break for it?"

"I think that would be generally frowned upon, Major, in my humble opinion. Just relax sir; I've got your six. I already checked to see that your fly is zipped and you don't have any shit in your teeth. Just try not to crack a nervous fart during the meeting."

Reece noticed an older soldier walking toward them with more ribbons than he thought could possibly fit on a uniform. As it registered to him who it was, he noticed Tripp pop out of his seat and turn to face him.

"Good afternoon, sir," the man said to Michael. "My name is Command Sergeant Major Leslie Morris. I will be taking you into the conference room for your briefing with the Secretary." Morris was not just a Command Sergeant Major, but he was Command Sergeant Major of the Army, which is the highest rank possible for an enlisted soldier in the Army. "It is an honor to have you here today, sir."

"It's my honor to meet you, Command Sergeant Major. This is—"

"Staff Sergeant David Tripp. It's a pleasure to meet you Sergeant." The perfect white teeth of his smile contrasted his milk chocolate skin. He was a friendly man, but you could tell there was absolutely no bullshit tolerance in him at all. Tripp looked as though he had just met Michael Jordan. "I'm glad you were able to come with Major Reece."

"It was my honor, Command Sergeant Major. Thank you for having me."

They walked the short distance across the anteroom to a door labeled Main Conference Room. The conversations on the inside were muted by the door. Morris opened the door and belted out, "Group attention!"

Every soldier in uniform bolted straight upright at attention as they walked in. It took a moment for Reece to register that they were standing at attention for him. "As you were," he stammered. Telling a group of men that included Major Generals that it was OK to have a seat made him feel like he just walked through the door to the Twilight Zone. The men around the conference table smiled and began a thunderous applause, along with several shouts of "Hooah!"

Everyone in attendance came and shook his hand and then settled into their seats. He saw on the projection screen there was an image of the five-pointed star below a perched eagle standing on the word VALOR hanging below a light-blue octagon adorned with thirteen stars flanked on each side by blue ribbon. An image of a helmeted Minerva was in the middle of the five-pointed star, and a laurel wreath was behind it. It was the symbol of the highest honor that can be bestowed upon a soldier, and it was a very small fraternity.

Secretary Winters welcomed everyone to the meeting and echoed the sentiments of all present that he was honored to be sitting in front of a hero today. He made a few statements about the history of the medal and the gallantry that is required to be considered for it and introduced everyone at the table. Reece nodded at the kind remarks and also as each person in attendance was introduced. He found himself turning his gaze often to the image on the screen. The gravity of this was finally starting to sink in, and he found himself breathing a little more rapidly and perspiring even more. He noticed that the Secretary was smiling.

"Major Reece, I believe you are trying your very hardest not to completely freak out right now aren't you?"

"That would be correct, sir." There was a smattering of chuckling around the table.

The Secretary continued, "Major Reece, this is the third time I have sat down with a Medal of Honor recipient like this, and every time their reaction has been just like yours. If there are any take-home points from this meeting, it is that everyone in this room is convinced beyond a shadow of a doubt that you are well-deserving of this honor, and you can't run out of this room right now because we'll catch you." His remarks had the intended effect of decreasing the tension in the room and allowing Reece to relax a bit.

The meeting actually didn't reveal a lot of new information. The Secretary explained that there would be a Public Affairs Officer (PAO) assigned to him between now and the medal presentation, which would take place at the White House. The PAO would help him navigate the requests from the media as well as other invitations that would range from speaking engagements to throwing out the first pitch at a baseball game. The advice was not to get overwhelmed by those things and to let the PAO handle them; the PAO had been trained to do just that, and Reece didn't have to say yes to every request. There would be some that he would be strongly encouraged to do, but he would have a fair degree of autonomy when it came to his time. Evidently this award allowed you to call a lot of your own shots, and he would be afforded deference on a number of things, even if he was *highly* outranked. He was now part of a very exclusive club.

The presentation at the White House would occur sixteen days from today, and he was allowed to request the presence of those who he thought should be there and was encouraged to hand over those names as soon as possible. They would do everything in their power to get them there, but he understood that sometimes it would not be possible. He would not be permitted to wear the medal until the President had done the presentation. He was also given a packet that would explain the additional benefits that he would be entitled to after receiving this honor, including access to a person in the Veterans Affairs office whose sole job was to handle any concerns or questions of MOH recipients. The meeting was followed by a briefing by the Public Affairs Division, and he was introduced to Lt. Colonel Dwayne Collins, who would be attached at Michael's hip for the next couple of weeks and would help make any arrangements for media engagements or other events. Collins had been the PAO for the most recent MOH recipient and tried to set him at ease that it would be much smoother than Reece might think it would be.

During both meetings he found himself glancing at the image of the medal on the wall, and his mind would occasional drift to making a mental list of whom he would want to come to the presentation. He began to realize that some of the people he would desperately want to be there were no longer with him.

At the end of the briefing, Secretary Winters asked if there was anything he needed at the moment or any further questions. He surprised himself by answering yes to that inquiry. "Sir, it's my understanding that during this time of the year that Arlington National Cemetery closes at 1900..."

*****

"Good morning Sandy," Chip said as he walked into the offices of the Honorable James A. Haxton, Senior Senator from North Carolina and Chairman of the Senate Appropriations Committee.

"Good morning, Mr. Johnson. Did you get my email about the morning meeting?"

"I did. Any idea what it's about?"

"No sir. I was just asked to put it together early today." Sandy Patterson didn't care for the haughty little shit that stood before her, but he enjoyed pretty much carte blanche with Haxton and therefore was untouchable. "It's set for about eight forty-five; he requested you and the Governor only."

Johnson went to his own office and looked at his upcoming week. He had three television appearance set up so far. Any legislative initiative that required funding, i.e., all of them, had to go through Appropriations, and Haxton sat on the throne of the powerful committee that controlled the purse strings of the federal government. As a result, the opinion of Haxton's office was often sought after when items were working their way through the Senate. Handling the numerous requests from the media was one of Chip's chief responsibilities, and he decided who would get the Senator and who would not. Haxton would only personally do a small number of requested interviews, and Chip was often the one to stand in for him and be the voice of the Appropriations Chairman. The usual setup was the anchor along with two staff members or party representatives on each side of the issue, discussing the pros and cons of whatever the political flavor of the day was. It was almost always a moderately civil exchange of prepared talking points that, occasionally, were actually related to the question the anchor would ask. No new information or revelations came from these, but it was how the game was played.

Chip knew which anchors and moderators were sympathetic to their way of thinking, and he would reward their requests first. Being able to land the Appropriations Chairman for their show was a big deal for political journalists, and they would often cross the line of objectivity to get such a coup. Many times they would do this without even knowing it, which was one of the things that Chip Johnson was a master at choreographing. He was very talented at making reporters believe that they were "keeping them honest," when in actuality they would only call politicians out who didn't march to the drum of the reporter's personal political beliefs. It was easy. You held out the carrot of landing the Senator while playing on their vanity by telling them that they were "the last true advocate of the people" and that they showed pure courage by standing up to power and being the "voice of the masses." The reason this

73

recipe of reward and flattery was time-honored was because it worked. He sent an email to the week's interviewers, highlighting the points that needed to be made in order for the viewers to have an accurate reflection of the issues, and headed to the Senator's office.

"Good morning, Senator. Good morning, Governor."

The two titans of politics sat in the office. The room itself was adorned with the usual trappings of power and influence. The solid-cherry-paneled walls were covered in numerous awards and honors along with photographs of the Senator with various supporters, admirers, and colleagues. A framed photograph of one of Duke University's Atlantic Coast Conference Championship teams supported a cut basketball net on one corner that had been given to one of their many distinguished and successful alumni. The front right area of the office had a low table surrounded by plush leather chairs, and the left had a scale model of the Capitol Building on a waist-level table, which also sported an antique globe. The smell of Café Ruiz coffee permeated the room from an antique serving set to the right of the massive wooden desk. The silver-haired gentlemen sat by the low table, porcelain coffee cups in hand.

The Senator smiled at his young media phenom. "Morning Chip. Grab some coffee and join us."

Chip poured himself a cup of the coffee that would cost more than two weeks' supply of his Starbucks beverage of the morning. "So what's the big mystery that has brought us together this fine morning gentlemen?"

"Sycamore House," said Gov. Sutton, "and it's most successful alumnus."

Chip sat down and looked at the table for a moment while pulling up information from his memory. He had learned the life of Haxton along with his likes, dislikes, accomplishments, special hobbies and interests, and acquaintances. "Michael Reece."

Haxton shifted in his chair to face Johnson. "Tell us what you know about him."

"Modern day Oliver Twist. Abused kid rescued from horror and placed in an environment that allowed his brilliance to emerge. Brilliant student and now successful doctor and family man who stepped up to serve his country after 9/11. Gave his time and part of his leg for the Global War on Terrorism. It's like someone made him in a lab for me to run a campaign for one day."

"Well, he is going to be on a lot of newspapers this week."

Sutton put his coffee cup in its saucer on the table. "It will be announced tomorrow that he is getting the Medal of Honor."

"Holy shit!" Chip sat wide-eyed in his chair, then he looked at Haxton. "How did you manage to make that happen?"

Haxton wagged his finger at Chip. "I didn't have anything to do with it Chip. He performed some heroic acts in a terrible situation and the Army decided that he was worthy of this honor. There's no horse trading going on with this."

"The inevitable connections are going to be made between his time at Sycamore House and the patronage of the Senator. We do *not* want you to start pushing this on the press to play it up. We want it to happen on its own, but you need to be aware of it and prepare how we should handle it," Sutton explained.

"Wow. It's awfully early for it to be Christmas but it certainly feels like it."

Johnson's mind was already in overdrive thinking of the endless opportunities for favorable coverage for his boss, not to mention the perfect timing, as talk was already beginning about potential candidates for the party nomination for President.

"Give me the day to get all of the information together. We can have prepared information for the press when they request it that will go over the history of the Senator's charitable interests and efforts, including Sycamore House. The packet can have contact information for selected people to interview along with a bio of Reece's life and accomplishments. The culminating event should probably be a story followed by a joint interview. I would lean toward a venue like Dateline or maybe Oprah."

"No joint interviews or appearances. He is his own man and has never used his connections to me to his benefit. He has never been politically active and would see it as political opportunism." Haxton adopted somewhat of a protective tone in his voice.

Chip looked as if his favorite toy had been taken away without warning. "Look, I understand you care a lot about his guy and don't want him to feel pressured. It's all about how he's approached about it...I've already got some ideas on how to do that."

"No joint appearances period. He won't like it and we risk the chance of being seen as using someone's genuine acts for valor for our political gain. I don't give you many hard lines Chip, but this is one you can't cross."

Johnson raised his hands in surrender. He certainly wasn't giving up on this, but he would fight that battle another time. The Senator had a soft spot in his heart for kids in need (especially ones who had come through Sycamore House), and Chip would have to figure out a way to get him to see the light. It was all about the process. He saw manipulating others to make them see things his way as a kind of seduction and he was one of the best around at doing this, but now wasn't the time to press the issue.

"If it's being announced tomorrow, we will need to be ready. Someone will make the connection within days, probably a local reporter. Give me about six hours and I'll have the broad strokes for you to approve and I'll work on the final package tonight and it'll be ready for you in the morning."

"That sounds good. Not a word of this to anyone, including your contacts until the official announcement has been made tomorrow."

Johnson left the office and began running the plan through his mind. *Thank you God.* This was the kind of story that PR people dream of at night. It had the potential to take on a life of its own...and to take them to the White House. He stopped at Sandy's desk on the way back to his office.

"I'm going to need everything we have on Sycamore House, as well as Michael Reece, who used to be a kid there. Drop anything else you're doing currently—this comes from the boss." He raised his hand in appreciation as he walked away.

Sandy bit her tongue as he crossed the threshold of his office, which was far bigger than her area. *You're welcome.* She had been working for the Senator since before he was even a Congressman. She had become his secretary at his land development company and had followed him everywhere since then. She had cut many of the Senator's checks to the Sycamore House over the years, as well as the ones to Vanderbilt Academy for the young Michael Reece. She had even met him once, when Haxton had brought him to the office before taking him to his beach house on Figure Eight Island. He was very polite but exceedingly shy. He seemed to be a little afraid whenever she looked at him. *I probably would be too if I had been abused that badly.* She had followed his success through conversations with the Senator as well as with Ms. Theresa, the head counselor at Sycamore. At any rate, if this would highlight the good things the Senator had done, she could tolerate being a gopher for that sanctimonious little prick that strutted around the office like a peacock.

*****

The shadows from the trees were getting long as SSG Woods drove the government sedan up Memorial Drive toward hallowed ground. Arlington National Cemetery had officially closed to the public thirty minutes ago. The vehicle came to a stop, and Reece and Tripp emerged. They had asked to return to the hotel first so they could change back into their Army Combat Uniforms.

A man in a blue suit was waiting for them. They both noticed the small United States Marine Corps pin on his lapel. "Major Reece, Sergeant Tripp, my name is Steve MacGregor, and I am the Superintendent here at Arlington. It's an honor to meet you both."

Michael shook his hand right after Tripp. "It's nice to meet you as well. I apologize if this is keeping you later than usual…" Reece saw MacGregor raise his hand to that remark.

"Sir, Secretary Winters called personally and, under threat of dismemberment if I blabbed it, he explained why you're in Washington today. I'm proud to help you today and appreciate your sacrifice to our nation. If you gentlemen could follow me, I will get you to the site before it gets too dark."

Tripp turned toward the vehicle. "Sergeant Woods, you are welcome to join us if you would like." She nodded and joined the three men as they walked toward the visitor center.

"Sir, we have a golf cart for your use if you would like," MacGregor said to Reece.

"I would rather walk if I could."

The Superintendent nodded, and they walked east along Eisenhower Drive towards Section 60. The orchestra of birds and insects were beginning their evening performances, but otherwise there was not a sound. Reece and Tripp walked side by side in step behind MacGregor, with Woods a few steps behind them.

MacGregor came to a stop and turned to them. "Sir, his stone is the sixth one down this row." He pointed a few yards back. "I will be waiting here for you. Take as much time as you want."

"Mr. MacGregor, I saw your lapel pin. I would be honored if you would join us."

"The honor would be mine, sir."

Reece walked with the remaining three behind him to the sixth marker of the row, which read:

MANUEL JESUS

TORRES

SPC

US ARMY

PURPLE HEART

BRONZE STAR

OPERATION ENDURING FREEDOM

They stood in silence for several minutes, and then Reece pulled a folded piece of paper from his pocket, cleared his throat, and quoted Spike Milligan.

"Young are our dead
Like babies they lie
The wombs they blest once
Not healed dry
And yet - too soon
Into each space
A cold earth falls
On colder face.
Quite still they lie
These fresh-cut reeds
Clutched in earth
Like winter seeds
But they will not bloom
When called by spring
To burst with leaf
And blossoming
They sleep on
In silent dust
As crosses rot
And helmets rust."

Reece stared at the stone marker for a while longer, then turned to SSG Woods and MacGregor. "I present to you Specialist Manny Torres. He was a fine father, husband, and soldier. He gave his life for his county and for the two men that stand with you today."

He stood himself ramrod straight, swiveled back toward the gravestone, and all present offered a crisp salute, until Tripp whispered, "Order arms."

Tripp placed his hand on Reece's shoulder and took two steps back, turning toward Woods and MacGregor. "Why don't we wait over there for a minute?" He motioned several yards away.

Reece did not make one sound as they waited behind him, but all could see the rhythmic bobbing of his shoulders as he quietly sobbed over his fallen friend. He reached once again into his pocket and pulled out the ribbon from his Class A uniform that designated him a recipient of the Silver Star and placed it on the stone marker. He gathered himself and walked toward the rest of them, and all walked in silence back to the vehicle. Mr. MacGregor seemed visibly touched by what had just occurred.

As they reached the visitor's center, MacGregor turned to them. "Can I offer you all some coffee?"

Reece smiled warmly at him. "That sounds great Mr. MacGregor."

"I only share my coffee with people who call me Steve sir."

"Well, I will only drink coffee with those who call me Mike." His usual aversion to coffee would be ignored out of respect for the man offering.

They walked into the empty building, and Steve quickly returned with steaming cups of coffee along with various sweeteners and creamers. They all sat and chatted about their lives and other small things. Tripp asked him how long he had been at Arlington.

"Eighteen years, the last six as Superintendent."

This was Reece and Tripp's first trip here. They were both medically unable to attend the burial service for Manny, and they had spent other visits with Manny's wife at her home in Texas.

"I know you never get used to the tragedy here, but you seemed a little broken up on the walk back today," Reece asked. "If I'm intruding, please don't hesitate to tell me to stuff it."

"You saw that?"

Tripp pulled his coffee cup away from his mouth. "He doesn't miss much Steve. Don't ever play poker with him."

"About twenty paces from Specialist Torres is the grave of Lance Corporal Christopher MacGregor. He is my son, and he was killed near Camp Leatherneck in Afghanistan two years ago. My job allows me to spend time with my son every day, but not how I would wish it."

"My God," Reece said as he sat his cup down.

"Afraid so. His vehicle was hit by an IED. He made it back to base, but he died there. His bleeding was just too heavy. You see, sir, I know you're a doctor and I'm pretty sure that Specialist Torres died despite your best efforts. I can tell it tears you apart, and that means you're a good man. But here's the thing, sir: this is a war, and in a war soldiers die. Sometimes you can do everything you can and they won't make it. I have no doubt that they did everything they could for my son, but it was his time. God was ready for him to come home. I miss him as much today as I did the minute I found out he was killed, but his injuries were just too severe. It's OK to grieve the loss of your friend Major, but he didn't die because of you. He died because a bad guy killed him. A lot of people thought that me working here near my son's grave would send me over the edge, but it hasn't. I think about him every day, but I'm at peace that it was meant to happen. That allows me to spend time with him or with his memory without letting the grief consume me. You don't have to let go of their memory to let go of the pain sir."

Tripp gave MacGregor a grateful smile. He had often worried about his friend when it came to Manny's death. Survivor's guilt is a very real issue for soldiers who have witnessed death...especially when the deceased is a friend. It seemed, however, that there was more to it than that. It's hard to understand that moving forward from tragedy isn't the same as abandoning the memories of the fallen.

As they walked to the car, MacGregor and Reece paced behind them, talking, with the Superintendent's arm around the other man. At the car door, he handed him a card after scribbling on the back side of it. "If you ever need to talk Mike, just give me a call."

"Thanks Steve," Reece said as they embraced. They shared the scars that war can give...both seen and hidden.

CHAPTER 8

Secretary of Defense Frank Dietz only stood about five feet six inches tall but had a force of personality that leveled him with others. The former amateur Golden Glove winner and Naval Academy boxing champion from Brooklyn had spent eight years in the US Navy before going on to earn a doctorate in business and management from the University of Maryland. He had rapidly climbed the corporate ladder at Triton Technologies, which specialized in military ordinance delivery for naval vessels. After a successful tenure as Chief Operating Officer, he had been asked to serve as Secretary of the Navy for the prior administration and was promoted to his present position by the current President.

He had added a bigger emphasis on special operations and pushed the military brass to find ways to make mobilization of troops more rapid, including doubling the number of locations around the world where there were turnkey inventories of military equipment, ammunition, and logistical supplies that troops could use immediately upon landing. He had purchased large numbers of aircraft that could move soldiers and equipment to remote locations requiring much shorter runways and had also begun to make plans to reduce some of the bureaucratic redundancies that plagued the armed forces, which would make his initiatives cost-neutral. He was a no-nonsense guy who didn't mince words, but his history of proven results allowed him to avoid bitterness in his colleagues.

He stood along with General Shaver as Reece and Tripp were escorted into a small private area of the Pentagon Dining Room. The facility was not open to staff and visitors until lunch, which afforded them a further degree of privacy. They shook hands and made plates from a mini buffet set up by staff beside the dining table. Stewards poured coffee, and there were assorted juices at the end of the serving table. Reece made a light breakfast, mainly because he was worried about spilling food on his uniform in front of these titans of the American military. Tripp even showed a small degree of nerves this morning.

Dietz, in his usual style, wanted to set everyone at ease. "Gentlemen, this will not be a formal affair this morning. I wanted to get together to show my gratitude for your service and congratulate you on this honor. The White House Office of Protocol will be getting in touch with you about the presentation coming up, and the General and I will be available to you any time if you have any concerns or questions. Now, if you see my wife, you are to tell her that I had fruit and wheat toast this morning and you will deny all knowledge of the omelet sitting in front of me right now." Everyone chuckled and the tension seemed to evaporate from the room.

"Have you gotten over the shock of it all yet?" Shaver asked as they unfurled their silverware from the cloth napkins. Shaver was a recipient of the Distinguished Service Cross himself, which is second only to the award Reece would be receiving in two weeks' time. In Vietnam, as a young Second Lieutenant fresh out of West Point, he had charged two machine gun positions by himself in order to secure a landing zone to evacuate his wounded men. His position before being appointed to the Joint Chiefs was Commander, US Special Operations Command (USSOCOM), and he shared Dietz's vision of the future of the American military.

"Not really, sir. I think I have come to grips with the fact that I'm getting this medal, but I'm still struggling with—"

"With the question of if you should get it right?" Shaver responded.

"Yes, sir. I have seen countless soldiers do braver things than me over there, including the one sitting beside me here."

"Well Major, I have read what you did and have spoken with Colonel Tyson. I'm not struggling one bit with whether you should get this. The fact that you question it means that you have a heart as big as your balls."

The remark had the intended effect, and Dietz had a good belly laugh at it as well. Reece looked to his friend and then the General. "Are you and Staff Sergeant Tripp related by any chance, sir?"

"I don't know a Staff Sergeant Tripp, Major," Shaver said as he waved to a staff member at the door who brought a manila envelope to him. He stood and said, "I met a Sergeant First Class Tripp this morning. Sergeant Tripp, could you please post before me?"

Tripp's jaw was hanging from his face momentarily, then he shook it off and stood up and faced the General with the Secretary and Reece flanking him.

"By the order of the President of the United States and the Secretary of the Army, you are hereby promoted to the rank of Sergeant First Class. Your accomplishments reflect the best traditions of the United States Army, and this rank is a token of gratitude from a grateful nation."

Shaver handed the pins to a for-once speechless SFC David Tripp, along with the General's coin. Salutes were exchanged and hands were shaken. It wasn't every day that you got your promotion presented by the Army Chief of Staff.

"According to Major Reece, this promotion was somewhat overdue. In order to ensure that doesn't happen again, I have entered a personal letter of commendation to your personnel file."

They engaged in light conversation for the remainder of the meal. Reece was quite happy not to be the center of attention for at least an hour after their impromptu promotion ceremony.

Breakfast was followed by a meeting with the Commander of both the Eighty-Second Airborne and the Medical Corps. It was mainly a congratulatory meeting, with both expressing hopes that at some point Major Reece would be willing to speak with their respective units. Michael said he would be honored to do so, and both stated they would contact his assigned PAO and work out dates and details. They handed him a packet that the PAO had left for him to review over the next few days, and Reece walked out of the Pentagon probably for the last time as someone no one there would recognize.

After stopping at the hotel and changing back to ACUs, they were taken to Reagan National by SSG Woods. Security went much smoother this time, and they sat in the USO lounge reading the paper and waiting for their flight to begin boarding. The Pentagon press conference was scheduled at 1400, at which time both of them would be about thirty thousand feet above Virginia.

*****

"I don't understand. Why will I be getting a lot of requests for interviews? Has something happened?" Theresa Williams was saying to her unexpected caller.

"Everything is perfectly fine Mrs. Williams. In fact, there will be an announcement later today on the news which will help explain everything. It will be very good news and will bring very positive attention to the great things you're doing there." Chip Johnson was starting to work his magic.

She had confirmation from Sandy that this man worked for Senator Haxton, but she had never met him before and thought he sounded like someone who would call you during dinner to sell you a timeshare. "I hope you understand that any information about our residents here and any issues they may have would be confidential, and I wouldn't discuss that with anyone."

"It won't be anything like that, Mrs. Williams. This announcement will no doubt show that Sycamore House has been nothing short of a salvation for many kids who had not been given a fair shake in life. I ask you to trust me that it will all be clear this afternoon after the announcement on the news. The Senator wanted me to call you personally to make you aware so you wouldn't be surprised by anything. I assure you that the pride he feels right now will be a pride you will be sharing this afternoon. I'll be sending you an email with my contact information, including my private number. I would like very much for you to call me after the announcement this afternoon."

"Well, which news will it be on?"

"All of them. It will all make sense this afternoon and I look forward to speaking to you later today if that would be all right."

Theresa had no doubts about the Senator's commitment to the Sycamore House and felt certain that he wouldn't put her in a difficult situation. Over 50 percent of their operating

85

budget was now covered by him personally, and the number of residents had now grown to eighteen boys. "Well, sure, I guess. Should I call you after this announcement then?"

"Why don't you let me call you? That way I can contact you at a time that I can devote my full attention to your needs." *It's just too easy sometimes.* He said goodbye and went to step two of what could be his masterpiece.

*****

The Pentagon Press Room is a rectangular area that has an elevated floor at one end of its long axis. The wall behind it is draped with blue curtains with an oval emblem of the Pentagon to show viewers where the announcement is taking place. A single wooden podium faces multiple rows of barely padded chairs, with a circular Department of Defense seal attached to the front. A single American flag hangs from a post over the right shoulder of the podium speaker.

There had been a notice this morning that there would be a press conference at two p.m., with the subject being the "announcement of a major decoration to be awarded." There weren't many decorations that would be announced at a Pentagon press conference called the same day, so it was well attended. Given its early-afternoon time frame, most of the major cable news networks decided to carry it live.

When the Secretary of the Defense and the Secretary of the Army walked onto the podium, the reporters knew this was not an announcement about a new flavor of salad dressing in the Pentagon cafeteria. Most of the cable network cameras showed a glowing red "live" light on the upper front frame. The camera shutters clicked randomly like a bug zapper on a back deck in the summer. Anchors sitting at desks at CNN, Fox News, MSNBC, and the like informed their viewers that they were taking them now to the Pentagon, where a major announcement was about to be made.

Secretary Dietz motioned for those assembled to have a seat. "Thank you all for coming. It is my honor to announce that two weeks from today Major Michael Scott Reece will be presented with the Medal of Honor by the President for actions in Afghanistan in December, 2010. He was stationed at the time at Forward Operating Base Salerno in the Khost Province of

Afghanistan, where he was assigned as a Field Surgeon with the Eighty-Second Airborne Division. I will read his formal citation and then will take a limited number of questions.

"The President of the United States of America, authorized by Act of Congress, March 3, 1863, has awarded, in the name of Congress, the Medal of Honor to Major Michael Scott Reece, United States Army, for conspicuous gallantry and intrepidity at the risk of his live above and beyond the call of duty.

"Major Reece so distinguished himself in action with an armed enemy in the Khost Province, Afghanistan, on December 10, 2010. While participating in a humanitarian mission with Second Battalion (Airborne), 325th Infantry Regiment, Major Reece and his team were in a convoy of vehicles when they were ambushed by enemy insurgents. With his vehicle disabled and cut off from other team members, Major Reece pulled a severely wounded team member to meager cover and administered medical aid while under withering enemy fire. The other occupant of his vehicle was also wounded in the firefight, and Major Reece alternated between offering lifesaving medical aid to his team members and engaging the enemy, exposing himself to enemy gunfire and grenade attacks with no regard for his own safety. Major Reece continued these activities for several hours until reinforcements could arrive, sustaining a gunshot wound to his left leg that led to the loss of his foot. Badly wounded and near death himself, Major Reece refused medical care until his wounded team members were removed from danger. One of his wounded team members would not have survived were it not for his quick thinking and bravery. Major Reece's extraordinary bravery and heroism above and beyond the call of duty are in keeping with the highest traditions of the military and the United States Army.

"Staff members are passing out packets with the official citation along with a biography of Major Reece. As I said earlier, the official presentation of the award will occur two weeks from today at the White House. I will take a few questions."

"Mr. Secretary," said Cynthia Stone of CNN, "is Major Reece still attached to the same unit that he was with at the time of the attack?"

"No, ma'am. Major Reece was activated from his reserve unit and deployed to Afghanistan for a ninety-day rotation with the aforementioned unit."

"Follow up, Mr. Secretary," Stone stood with her hand up. "Does that mean that Major Reece is a member of the US Army reserves?"

"That's correct. Major Reece is a member of the US Army Medical Corps Reserve. He currently is not on active duty and practices medicine in Charlotte, North Carolina."

"Secretary Dietz, Miles Dent of CBS News. Is this a rare occurrence, for a reservist to win the Medal of Honor?"

"First off, I want to clarify that one does not win the Medal of Honor. They receive it. Now, to answer your question, it is rare for any soldier to be awarded the Medal of Honor. It would also be fair to say it is even rarer that a reservist and also a doctor receives it. As anyone who has been in the military or spent time with members of the military will tell you, bravery and heroism can come from any soldier at any time. No one can predict when one would find himself in circumstances that would require such actions as the ones of Major Reece, but it is without debate that his actions were well above and beyond the call of duty."

"Ted Mitchell, *Washington Times*, Mr. Secretary. How accessible will Major Reece be to the media during the next few weeks?"

"I am going to let Secretary Winters answer that question."

Secretary Winters traded positions at the podium with Dietz. "Well, as Secretary Dietz had mentioned, Major Reece is currently back at his civilian job as a physician in Charlotte, and he is currently not on active duty with the Army. Therefore, he will generally not be on an Army post during this time and will essentially be as available as any civilian would. He is a very busy physician at home, and I would ask the members of the press to consider that when trying to contact him. There will be no official appearances until after he is presented the award by the President."

Dietz stepped to the podium again. "Thank you, everyone. That will be all."

Short and sweet. The members of the Pentagon press had become accustomed to Dietz's brief style. He was not rude or evasive; he just got to the point without wasting time or unnecessary words.

They recognized that this wasn't your usual Medal of Honor award. This was a doctor and a reservist. The packet contained the citation and a skeleton biography, with emphasis on skeleton. It listed his place of birth, city of current residence, education beginning with college, and the fact that he had a wife and two children. They had work to do and, as it was with just about any story, each one of them wanted to do it first.

*****

Dr. Gabriel Drake stood in the Surgeon's Lounge of North Charlotte Regional Medical Center in silence, with several other physicians on staff there. The Pentagon press conference had just wrapped up, and commentary was being made by someone at the news desk who didn't seem to have much more information than was in the packets just given to the onsite reporters, who were going through it on a split screen with their respective networks. Several of the doctors looked at Drake, with one voicing everyone's question: "Did you know about this Gabe?"

"I just found out about it this weekend and he swore me to secrecy. Rich and Susan knew too, but they made the same promise. He didn't find out himself but a few days before and, needless to say, he's adjusting to it. I'm sure it won't surprise anyone that he doesn't think he deserves it."

"Good for him. It's nice to see one of the good guys get praise once in a while," said Eric Daniels, one of the anesthesiologists on staff who had watched Reece deliver all three of his children, including an emergency Cesarean section on the last one due to a dangerous complication known as *placental abruption*. His wife and Anna were very close friends, and he and Michael took their equally horrible golf games to the course together once or twice a month, where they fought for the spoils of the exorbitant bet of twenty-five cents per hole, with the one who lost the least amount of balls during the round buying the beers at the clubhouse.

89

Drake saw a picture of Michael come up on the screen. He recognized it as the official photograph of him on the hospital website. *Damn those guys are quick.*

All present collectively raised their coffee cups in the air toward the television in salute to their friend's accomplishment.

*****

Anna Reece sat in her living room with kids, her parents, and a few close neighbors. Tears were streaming down her face. Her arm was across little Charlie's chest as he sat in her lap. She held her father's hand while Elizabeth sat on the love seat with "Mimi."

She had known that Michael had done something special by the conversation she had had with David. But Michael would not talk about it all, and Anna had never pressed, because she believed that it brought back painful memories of Manny dying. The magnitude of the honor, as well as hearing the description of the actual events read aloud, made her very proud of him but also startled at how very close she came to losing him forever. He was three days out from his injuries before she was allowed to travel to Germany to see him. He had already lost his foot, but she never knew how close to death he had actually been. She knew he had saved David, because he had told her so, but hearing it made her appreciate why he had such an unconditional devotion to her husband. She rested her head on her father's shoulder. "I think I married pretty well Dad."

Walt squeezed her hand and kissed the top of her head. "I think we all knew that long before today, didn't we?"

"We certainly did." She dried her eyes and gathered everyone for the trip to the airport to pick up "her men," as she called David and Michael when they were together.

*****

Theresa Williams watched the television with the other staff and the current young residents of Sycamore House. Her hand was placed over her heart as she listened to the narrative. She was very proud.

She never complained about the lack of contact Michael had with them since leaving for Chapel Hill. She understood that he had about as complicated a childhood as any kid in America. Still, she continued to hope that time would allow him to return and see them. The time hadn't come yet, and there was a small hint of disappointment about that.

They all applauded after the broadcast came to a close. This certainly explained the phone call from the man who had given her a small degree of wariness when they had spoken. She didn't know what time he would be calling again, and there was no reason to speculate on what their conversation would be before he did.

*****

There was wild applause and hugs in the waiting room of North Charlotte Women's Care by patients and staff alike. With Michael's permission, Rich and Susan had gathered the partners in the practice at lunch and told them what would be announced this afternoon. Michael had called Tricia the night before from his hotel in Arlington, because he felt she should know before the staff, since they had worked together for so long. The only other recipient of a call that night was the Reverend Earl Webber of Red Creek AME Zion Church, who, as a former Army Chaplain, praised the good Lord with tears in his eyes after hanging up the phone.

*****

Chip Johnson sat in his office with his feet propped on the desk as he watched MSNBC providing the same coverage of the press conference as every other network. He had a squash game with a colleague in an hour at the Potomac Squash Club, and he fully believed that the connection with the Senator would be made by someone in the national press before nightfall. He smiled like a man who already knew his horse would be a winner of a race yet to be run. He would call the lady at the boy's home when he got back from his match. The Senator would not have any chance of being approached by reporters until tomorrow, given that he had already gone home for the day and Chip had told him to not answer the phone unless he knew the caller wasn't from the press.

*****

It was simply an after-effect of the twenty-four-hour news cycle and society's almost limitless access to information at their fingertips. An accounting software salesman on a layover at Charlotte Douglas International Airport sat at the bar at Phillip's Seafood in Concourse C. He had tired of working on his laptop and sat back and watched the news while drinking a cold beer. He found it ironic that the soldier who would be getting the highest award the military had was from Charlotte, which was where he was stuck at the moment. The news networks were in the second half-hour cycle, and the information now included a picture of the recipient. *He's from Charlotte, I'm in Charlotte.* One had to try anything to occupy their mind when stuck at yet another airport on yet another layover. He ordered a second large mug of beer, since he would be going straight to a hotel in Phoenix when he got there, and the second drink would help him sleep on the plane while just starting to lower his inhibitions.

Michael and David emerged from the Jetway at gate C17 after a short and smooth flight from Reagan National. Reece was sure his travel companion was walking a little straighter with the new Sergeant First Class insignia square attached to the front of his ACU top. Michael had just finished a story about little Charlie streaking through the living room when they had the newest partner at the practice over for dinner, and Tripp's laughter matched his stature,— booming and hard to ignore. The laughter caused the salesman to look up over the rim of his beer mug as he had lifted it to his mouth. He saw the military uniforms of two men walking toward him and turning onto the long middle walkway heading to baggage claim. He had made it a habit to pick up the check of soldiers eating at restaurants he was in at airports. He always imagined that they were either heading away from loved ones to somewhere less pleasant or, hopefully, on their way home to the arms of their families. He never asked the waitress to tell them who had picked up their bill; it was one small way he could say thanks to the nation's finest and bravest.

That's when something clicked. He was missing something that was screaming in the back of his mind. Looking closer, his eyes went up to the faces of the men now turning into the walkway, and that's when it connected: *Holy shit...that's the guy.* He looked up to the television, which just happened to have the hospital photograph displayed at that moment, and was positive it was the same person.

He threw a twenty-dollar bill on the bar, told the bartender to keep the change, grabbed his Pullman, and walked quickly out of the eatery. "Wait...Sir!"

Probably two dozen men turned their heads at the sound, including Reece, who could tell that the man was walking straight to him with a purpose. He was disconcerted for a moment to see this unfamiliar man speed-walking up to him, seemingly oblivious to the crowds he was almost bowling through.

"Sir! I'm sorry to bother you, but are you the guy on the news right now?"

At first he didn't have any idea what this guy was talking about, and then his brain started to catch up with the surprising encounter unfolding in front of him. *The announcement happened while we were on the plane.* He could tell that it was connecting for David also, since he was relaxing from his initial reaction of positioning himself between the harried man and his friend. There was a small audience, forming not only out of curiosity but also because the three men now stopped in the middle of the thoroughfare had caused a mini bottleneck of the constant foot traffic.

Michael searched for the right words and stammered, "Um...yes, I guess I am."

"Holy shit...I mean, excuse me, sir. I just wanted to shake your hand, and I'm sorry for startling you." Michael grasped the outstretched hand and got a vigorous shaking. "This is a huge honor, sir."

Michael smiled and was gracious to the excited man in front of him. "It's a pleasure to meet you, and thanks for your kind words."

There was confused mumbling from the surrounding crowd. The salesman looked around to the people in the walkway and the seating area for gate C15. "Hey everybody, this man just won the Congressional Medal of Honor!" There were several people who had been waiting for the boarding call at the gate while watching the CNN Airport Network, and the clouds started to lift for many of them. A chorus of handshakes, back slaps, and hugs began to grow around them as people began to realize the man in front of them and the picture on the news were the same person. Michael looked as if he had just landed on Mars to find that there was a keg party going on.

As they slowly walked down the concourse and waiting passengers went from confusion to realization, the two men were flanked on each side by thunderous applause. The people whose flights were not about to immediately board began to form a mob around Reece and Tripp. The love and gratitude was overwhelming, and about a third of the mob were holding their cell phones above their heads trying to catch a snapshot. The people behind them would dissipate like the spreading condensation trail behind a high-flying jet plane as they went back to their gates talking excitedly to each other or trying to upload their snapshots to Facebook to share their brush with fame on the web. There were many, however, that stayed right with them, and the mass encircling them continued to grow and their walking pace continued to slow.

Tripp leaned his face toward Michael's ear as they approached the common area where all the concourses converged, which contained eateries, coffee shops, newsstands, rocking chairs for waiting passengers...and the USO lounge. "We're going up to the USO instead of baggage claim. This is about to get out of hand." Tripp took lead as if they were walking outside the wire on patrol, letting his massive frame cut into the mob like the sharp keel of a ship.

They reached the stairs, which tapered up to the open area of the second floor. They climbed up and headed into the hallway on the right which led to the USO. "USA! USA! USA!" was being chanted by the excited passengers below as they entered the lounge only open to current military, veterans, or retired service men and women. They checked in with a front desk volunteer who hadn't figured out what was going on. As they walked the short hallway toward the television area, several soldiers recognized Reece, and a large Navy Master Chief in uniform who was waiting on a connecting flight to go home for two weeks' R&R from overseas rose from his seat. "Attention on deck!"

It was an automatic response from training; all of the soldiers in the uniform sitting in the lounge sprang to their feet and braced themselves straight. Recognition could be seen in the widening of eyes starting from the front of the room and working its way back toward the large flat-screen television on the wall that had his face emblazoned on it.

"They're not going to move until you tell 'em it's OK, sir," came the whisper from Tripp in his ear.

Reece snapped back to reality. "As you were, gentlemen."

The room erupted with shouts of "Hooah!" and applause. Michael was humbled to be praised so vocally by those here that he saw as infinitely more brave than he ever would be and who tackled tougher jobs than he had every day they were downrange. He shook many hands and actually had several autograph requests. He finally raised his hands to the men and women and thanked them and wished them all the best in their travels. "If you want to honor me for this, you can do it by staying safe and getting home to your families."

Word had spread to employees about who was at the airport, and TSA Supervisor Cecil Gardner happened to be back on duty today and came up to the USO lounge. He shook hands with Reece and Tripp and he arranged for their luggage to be brought up from baggage claim. Michael called Anna and told her to come to the shuttle gate at the Arrivals section of the airport. An agent met her there and opened the gate to let her through, where they instructed her to park in one of the airport security vehicle spaces. A uniformed Charlotte-Mecklenburg police officer introduced himself to Anna and asked would they be going home from here. She told him that was the plan, and he waited outside her car.

"OK, sir," Mr. Gardner said, "we will escort you outside the baggage claim area where your wife is waiting. Congratulations sir, and thank you for your service."

Michael shook his hand again and pointed to the small veteran's pin on the agent's shirt collar. "Thank you Mr. Gardner, and thank you for your service as well. Could I just slip in here before we go?" He pointed to the restroom. With all that had unfolded around him in the past half hour, he suddenly felt the need to take a leak.

When he came out of the bathroom, he noticed there was hardly anyone in the lounge anymore. When he exited the USO and started down the stairs, he realized why. A human corridor had been made, of TSA personnel and the soldiers who had been in the USO. He turned right after descending the stairs and walked past the applauding TSA agents and airport passengers. The soldiers offered crisp salutes as he passed, which he returned with pride. It was not protocol to salute indoors, but if they didn't care he wouldn't care either.

Anna's mouth was agape in shock as she saw "her men" with their escorts come out of the building amid applause. The kids ran up and hugged Dad and Uncle David. After the luggage was put in the back of Michael's 4Runner, they headed out of the Arrivals area. When they emerged from under the covered area onto the road leading off the airport grounds, they saw two Charlotte-Mecklenburg Police vehicles take position in front of and behind their car, with lights flashing. The police escort that followed them all the way to their house was something that little Charlie wouldn't stop talking about for weeks.

"Welcome to your new life," Tripp said as they pulled into the driveway.

CHAPTER 9

The phone call from Chip Johnson came that same evening. Theresa closed the door to her office so she could speak without distraction. She had always kept her office attached to the main common area at Sycamore House and made a point to keep her door open as much as possible, both to make the boys feel like they could talk to her whenever they needed but also to provide herself the ability to watch them interact with each other and the staff, which often would give her the first clue that there was something wrong. Abrupt changes in one of the boys' personalities would often prompt her to chat with him a little extra when the time presented itself.

"Hello Ms. Williams, I trust you saw the press conference today."

"I certainly did Mr. Johnson. What a pleasant surprise that was." She didn't know this man well enough yet to adopt a more informal note to her conversation.

"I agree. I have become familiar with Dr. Reece's story by working here with the Senator, and what I heard today made me quite proud of him."

"There are many things about Michael that made me proud of him long before today, Mr. Johnson." The wariness she had felt during their first conversation was still there. Maybe she wasn't being fair. It seemed that he had the confidence of Senator Haxton which carried a lot of weight with her.

"Right you are, Ms. Williams. Right you are. Well, the reason for my getting in touch with you is that my specialty with the Senator, among other things, is interacting with the press. I don't think it will take very long for members of the press, especially ones in your local area, to connect the dots between Dr. Reece and Sycamore House. That will, in my opinion, be a fascinating and inspiring angle to his story, and the press will certainly want to explore that. When I say 'the press' I mean newspaper reporters and television news people."

"I'm familiar with the term." *I have a master's degree in social work, young man. I'm not an idiot.*

"Excellent. Well, I also think that when they make the connection between Dr. Reece and Sycamore House, it won't take long for them to make the further connection with Senator Haxton. Now, as inspiring as this story is, Senator Haxton was emphatic that I not set up any interviews with anyone to talk about Dr. Reece or Sycamore House. He is immensely proud of the miraculous work done there, but he didn't want to make this about himself. He thinks any credit for things that happen there is deserved by the kids and dedicated staff like you. But he did want me to make myself available to you if you had any questions about how to handle inquiries from the media...of which I think there will be a lot."

"That's very kind of you Mr. Johnson. I appreciate that." Maybe she was being too hard on him. She knew the Senator wouldn't want the credit for this, and maybe this young man (he sounded young anyway) just wanted to help.

"It's my pleasure, Ms. Williams. Between you and me, the Senator has been talking a lot about Sycamore House lately, with all the news about Dr. Reece. I'm not supposed to know this, but he is planning to make a donation outside of his usual ones to celebrate this event. I'm probably going to do the same. It's obvious that you all are making a huge difference for a lot of great kids there. It's an honor to be able to work with someone like you."

"Wow. That is great news about the Senator, and that's very generous of you as well, Mr. Johnson. We try our best and, with God's help, I think we do make positive changes sometimes." She was beginning to feel guilty about her first impressions of him.

"Not at all Ms. Williams. We all need reminders of the goodness of humanity...especially here in Washington...and you are just that." *Like shooting fish in a barrel...*

They ended their phone conversation by agreeing that she would contact him on his personal cell phone when she started getting requests from the media for information or interviews. He would "walk her through the process" and told her he would be willing to come to Asheville personally if she decided it would help.

*****

Wednesday would be a fairly easy day for the Reece family. LTCOL Dwayne Collins, the PAO assigned to him, came to their house and spent about an hour talking about what to expect before the presentation ceremony. Reece would have no official appearances as a Medal of Honor recipient until after then, but there would be numerous requests to speak with him before that occurred. Collins had taken the liberty of arranging a short interview with the *Charlotte Observer*, who would then share that information with the Associated Press, with the stipulation that the AP run the story only after it appeared in the *Observer*. It would entail simple questions about how he felt about the award, along with some questions about his family and his work here in Charlotte. There were to be no questions about details surrounding the night the award citation described. A photographer would be present to take a few pictures. If that went well, they could do a short piece with one of the television networks with similar guidelines.

Beyond that, there would likely be no further media obligations until the ceremony. This was welcome news to Michael, since he would be working a good bit of that time in order to square things away before beginning his sabbatical. Anna's work had been very supportive and was willing to give her any flexibility she needed with her schedule for the next several weeks; she worked for Wells Fargo, which was building a strong record in Charlotte for community support, especially among the military members and spouses who worked for them. It didn't hurt that she was well liked and did superb work there, along with the fact that her father had been with the company for decades, starting back when it was still Wachovia Bank.

Collins was the perfect match for the Reece family in this situation. He was not a career desk jockey in the Army. He had three combat deployments to his credit, with the last ending with a severe injury that cost him his right hand and made him non-deployable for combat. He had a degree in psychology from San Diego State and had spent a year overseeing the development of Warrior Recovery Units around the world, where injured soldiers could go to recover and adjust after injuries. After that he transferred to Army Public Affairs, where he had developed a solid reputation as a hard worker and someone who was easy to work with. He had a unique perspective on how the media works, since his wife was a reporter for the *Wall*

99

Street Journal. His two sons were both in college, one at West Point and one at Columbia, and he planned to retire in two years after a distinguished career serving his country.

He quickly developed a rapport with Michael and, more importantly, a trust with Anna. She was very protective of her husband, who could be a little too trusting of others and could be taken advantage of at times. She liked the fact that Collins saw his job as helping Michael as well as protecting him. He didn't push anything and merely said things that he thought might be a good idea, and he always wanted to know what the both of them thought. He would be staying in Charlotte for the time leading up to the White House ceremony, but he understood that Michael had a life outside of the Army, including a family he loved dearly and patients that he had to take care of as well.

Michael agreed to the interview with the newspaper later that day and said he would call Collins after it was over. He decided to go to the office to see everyone and start working on the details of getting all his surgeries and other clinical commitments arranged before going on leave.

He went in the back entrance of the office and found Tricia. Besides Anna, he probably spent more time with her than anyone else, and he wanted to talk with her first. They hugged and talked about the trip to Washington and the craziness at the airport. He would be back at the office in two days, and they had already arranged to block out any appointments that were still open before he went on leave. They were also moving the dates of some surgeries that were currently scheduled after his last day to next week, and everything looked good to go. He also spent some time with his office manager and talked individually with each partner, and they assured him they would take care of any of his patients' needs while he was gone. He thanked them for their support, not only with this but also his previous deployments. Each one of these had meant more work and call for each of the doctors, but they accepted it willingly, as a gesture of support for the sacrifices he was making. He left the office once again reminded of how lucky he was to work where he did.

He had time before going back home for the interview, so he stopped at the florist and bought a dozen long-stem roses for Anna, who continued to be his constant as the rest of his life was ever-changing. He wrote on the card, "For too many reasons to ever be able to put on paper. I love you always, Michael."

*****

In the employee break room at Lowe's Home Improvement in the coastal town of Shallotte, North Carolina, one man sat sipping a Sprite from the nearby vending machine. He had just come inside from having a smoke and had about ten minutes before his break was over. The television was currently on Fox News, and he had seen the most recent updates on the big story about an honored soldier. His head was shaved bald and his black skin was weathered and dry from working in the outdoor garden section of the store, along with several years of multiple, mainly menial jobs.

He had been a drifter for several years, never settling down in one place for more than a year or two. He had initially come to the coast following construction jobs, as it was one of the few places that still had them after the housing market had tanked. Unfortunately, within a year the real estate crisis had even reached the recession-resistant coastal market, and he found himself out of work. He had worked on a shrimp boat for a while, followed by brief stint working with a crew who repaired the numerous canal docks in the neighboring beach communities like Holden Beach, Ocean Isle, and Oak Island. When that operation had shut down due to lack of business, he had gotten his current job at Lowe's.

Chris Tyler had come from the western part of the state, where he had gotten away from the bad crowd after finishing high school. He had found problems back home after being busted for selling weed on one occasion and being involved in a night club fight in another, and came to the realization that if he didn't get away, he was going to end up in prison or even killed. He had tried to convince his twin brother to do the same, but the latter had taken his troubles one step further and had found addiction with heroin. After two months of trying without success, Chris decided to go, but he said a prayer every day that his brother would find God and sobriety before anything worse happened. So far, those prayers had been unanswered.

He shook his head as he threw away his plastic soda bottle and turned to leave the break room. He took one last look at the television and the face of the man who had told him and his brother to be strong many years ago, right before walking away, never to speak with them again.

*****

"Hello, Dr. Reece, my name is Jason Ecklund," the reporter said as he shook hands at the Reece family home front door. "I appreciate your time today, and congratulations on your award."

"Thank you Mr. Ecklund. It's a pleasure to meet you. Please come inside."

They entered the house and Reece was introduced to Karen Riggs, the photographer. The journalists suggested that they do the photographs first, since Riggs felt the lighting outside was the best it would be for the rest of the day. They took several shots of Michael alone and also with his family, inside the house and outside as well. The kids then left for McDonald's with Uncle Dave, who would be leaving in the morning to return to Ft. Bragg until it was time to travel back to Washington. Michael sat down with Ecklund, with Riggs occasionally snapping a photograph during the interview.

"Dr. Reece, what would you prefer to be called during the interview?" Ecklund asked.

"Michael or Mike is fine."

"Let's start by asking how you felt when you found out that you had won the award."

"Well, it's important to understand that no one wins this award. You receive it. Most circumstances that result in such an honor include injury or even tragedy," Michael said without trying to sound condescending. "I was absolutely floored when I found out. I think I still am. It has been somewhat of a fog the past few days. It's like I'm in a chronic state of disbelief."

"You almost sound as if you're not sure you should get this award..."

"To be perfectly honest, I'm not. Please don't misunderstand; I'm very honored to have been selected, but I feel like I just did what I had to do given the circumstances. I just feel like I

102

was surrounded by countless soldiers who faced harder situations and showed more courage than me on a daily basis. I have always seen myself as someone in the Army whose job it was to support others who were injured or needed medical assistance. I was rarely put in situations where direct contact with the enemy was much of a possibility. It was just a very unusual situation and I did the best I could until help could get there."

Ecklund had a recorder going for the interview, but he also took occasional notes to reference comments he wanted to emphasize or revisit. "Tell me why a man who has a family, a successful career, and not a lot of spare time enters the Army reserves."

"I wish I had a long eloquent commentary on why I did it, but the simple reason is because I felt there was a need for more doctors and I could help. I had seen reports of how the military was very short of doctors, especially surgeons, and it was putting a strain on meeting the needs of our troops. I knew it would be a challenge, but we are a nation at war, and I think we forget that. We see reports on the war and see it as an abstract event and forget that the men and women over there fighting and dying are our citizens. I understand injury and death is a part of war, but I couldn't accept injury or death occurring because we didn't have enough doctors to help our soldiers."

"Do you ever regret your decision?"

"I never have once. Don't get me wrong, it's a challenge. Being deployed requires sacrifices by my wife, my children, and my co-workers. Despite all of that, I feel the Army has given me way more than I have given them. My time over there was tough sometimes...even frightening, but I have had the privilege and honor to work with the greatest men and women our country has to offer."

Ecklund smiled. "You sound like a recruiter."

"I'm not. Look, this is not for everyone, and there have been many times that I wasn't sure I measured up as a soldier. All that being said, I can only say it has been an experience that I wouldn't trade for anything."

"You mentioned the sacrifices those around you have made, but you didn't talk about the sacrifices you have made. I can't help but notice that you lost part of your leg that night."

Reece looked down at the prosthesis entering his New Balance running shoe. He seemed to stay in that moment for a while before speaking, in an almost detached tone. "I feel lucky. It was a tough recovery at times, but there were several men who didn't survive that mission, and my sacrifice pales in comparison to theirs. Despite the celebration of what I did that night, there was a man that started that mission with me alive and didn't survive. Any recognition I get, I accept in his honor. I'm sure his family would rather he be home with them than any medals being handed out for that night."

"Do you think you failed him Michael?"

"I don't think I failed him; I know I did. I was the doctor there and he was injured. When that happens, the men look to me to fix what's broken. No one asks me over there to charge an enemy position or call in an air strike. They ask me to treat injured soldiers and make sure they get home to their families healthy."

"Sometimes injuries are too severe no matter what you do..." Ecklund said less as a question and more as an effort to comfort the man who was quite melancholy at the moment.

"Maybe so...maybe so..." Michael had what many combat veterans refer to as "the million-mile stare."

Ecklund decided to change the direction that the interview was going. "Why don't we take a little break and then we'll pick back up in a few minutes."

Michael seemed to pull himself back in the present and smiled at the reporter. "Thank you. That would be great."

Ecklund said he had some phone calls he needed to make while they took a break, and Michael offered the use of his office to do so. He asked if either of them needed anything to drink or anything else and showed them the bathroom location in case they needed it. Then he stepped out to get some fresh air. Anna poured Riggs some coffee while she looked through the digital images of the shots she had taken so far.

"Would you mind if I take a few shots of the house while everyone takes a break?" Riggs asked Anna as she leaned on the granite counter separating the den and the kitchen area.

"No problem. Help yourself."

Riggs took a few shots of the den, including some framed photographs of Michael's time in the Army. "He doesn't like this kind of attention does he?"

Anna thought for a moment before answering. "It's not that he's shy...You'll learn, if you get to know him, he can talk to anyone. I think he is a little overwhelmed by everything."

Riggs sipped from her coffee mug while she looked around. She liked this family. Working in the news, it's not uncommon to have to do interviews with people who are famous. She has seen more than a few people with public attention see themselves as more special than others, better than others even. The Reece family seemed the very opposite of that. They were easy to talk to and opened their home to them. They both seemed to feel a bit embarrassed about the attention, and Michael even seemed to feel unworthy.

"He is really special to you isn't he?"

"He is indeed. He and our children are the most precious things in my life. He has overcome so much and still remains as humble as anyone I have ever known. He has a genuine care and love for others that you don't see very often anymore."

Riggs put her coffee mug down on the counter. She could still hear a muffled phone conversation from behind the glass office doors near the front of the house, so she knew Jason was still occupied. "Thanks for the coffee. Would you mind if I went outside for some fresh air before we start back?"

"Don't mind at all. The back door there goes to the deck and you can take the stairs down from there to the yard if you like."

She grabbed her camera and bag and went out on the deck. It was a warm Carolina mid-afternoon with thick humidity in the air but not oppressively hot. The twirling notes of cicadas could be heard in the distance, along with the rhythmic lapping of water against the shore about forty yards away. Beyond the backyard fence was the boat deck, which is where she saw him, sitting on the edge of the deck, a somewhat distant gaze on his face, with both his real and his prosthetic foot hanging over the side. His right arm was slung over the shoulders of a massive Great Dane. She put the 300-zoom lens on her Nikon D80 and took several shots from the deck, where her presence had not been detected. Looking at the images on the back of the camera, she knew she had her shot for the story.

The interview resumed and continued for about half an hour. They covered generalities, like how the Reeces felt about meeting the President, Michael's work here in Charlotte, the kids, and his recovery from his injury. It was overall a pleasant encounter for all involved, and the newspaper employees took their leave after shaking hands with Michael and Anna.

He called LTC Collins afterward and let him know that everything went well. They went over the questions, and he assured him that the reporters didn't pry into areas that were uncomfortable or which had been declared off limits. Reece said he would be OK with doing a local television interview tomorrow.

The kids would be home soon, and they planned to go out to dinner as a family with David, since he would be leaving in the morning.

*****

"If my boss even new I have stood near you talking about this, he would not only fire me he would probably kill me," Chip said to Matthew Weinrib as they sat in a booth at the Warehouse Bar and Grill in Old Town Alexandria. Chip had gone all out with the conspiratorial undertones. He had called Matt on his personal cell phone and told him, in hushed tones, that he wanted to meet with him. He said he had something he wanted his opinion on, but it had to be on the down low. He insisted on meeting away from his office, suggesting their current location after regular working hours. He wanted not only to dangle the prospect of information that would not be out in view but also to make Matt feel like he was special.

Weinrib had been at *The Washington Post* for about six years. He had received his BS in journalism at Ohio State University after growing up in economically depressed Youngstown. After graduating, he knew he wanted two things: to work in political journalism and to get out of Ohio. He had used persistence and tenacity to land an entry-level job in the *Post*'s political section. Over the years, he had endured countless bullshit writing assignments that often never made print or were dissected by his superiors so they could use the better parts and claim them as their own. He wasn't ignorant of the condescension and, at times, utter contempt that his Ivy League-educated contemporaries felt for this working-class kid from a—gasp!—public college. He desperately wanted to get the contacts in his Rolodex that the big boys had. He wanted politicians to fear him and his pen, and he wanted to be invited to trendy Georgetown cocktail parties. In short, he wanted to be a player, and he wanted it badly.

This was exactly why Chip had chosen him for this meeting. In Weinrib's eyes, Johnson was a big fish. He was "the guy" on a staff for a powerful Senator who had realistic aspirations of making it to the White House. In Johnson's eyes, Matt was a guy who wanted to get in the game so bad that he could be manipulated. Chip would play the conflicted staff member who was reaching out to a reporter from the biggest political newspaper in the land for advice. He needed the guidance of someone who was in the political media game and, before the evening was over, he would have Matt believing that the story he suggested would actually be his own idea. Chip couldn't help thinking of himself as the modern-day Gordon Gekko of the Washington political game.

"Listen Chip, we're off the record tonight. I appreciate you calling and I'm happy to be a bouncing board for you," Weinrib said, trying his best to act in a way that would hide the feeling that he was on the first date with a girl he had had a crush on for years. He leaned back in the booth and adopted as casual a pose as his excitement would allow. Warehouse Bar and Grill was one of the trendy places where young movers and shakers would meet, and he wanted to be one.

"Thanks man. I have been rolling this thing around in my head for a couple of days and I'm really conflicted." He sighed heavily and tapped on the table a couple of times, then he ordered a second drink, playing the nervous confidential source. "I'm sitting on something big. Something that needs to be told, but my boss doesn't want it out. It's the kind of information that would have the whole country talking and could even send him to the White House."

Matt felt a hot flush go into his neck, and he prayed it wasn't visible to his friend. He was glad he hadn't eaten already, because he probably would have shit in his pants out of anticipation. "Well, why don't you walk me through it and I'll tell you what I think," he said, praying that he wasn't looking too eager.

But he was. Chip had seen the flush of the face and the shifting in the booth. He had hoped to get the fish to nibble on the bait, but he was already trying to swallow it. Better not to rush it and risk the play becoming obvious. He decided to put the brakes on the seduction just slightly. "I don't know Matt. You have to promise me you won't talk to anyone about this. I need someone in this town I can talk to sometimes. I want to do the right thing, and it's hard to decide that on my own sometimes. This may sound bad, but I can't really talk with all the Ivy League douchebags that roam the halls where I'm at. Does that make sense? I know that sounded like a shitty thing to say." *Just going to try the buttons of the blouse first...*

"Believe me, buddy: I know exactly what you mean. Sometimes I feel like the folks at the *Post* don't think you can be trusted to wipe your own ass if you didn't write for *The Harvard Crimson* in college." Matt ordered another beer to calm his nerves. He didn't know that he was the only one who was actually nervous.

"Look, I have been in this town for a while now and I have seen many big players try to silence people who have unflattering information about them, but I find myself in the opposite situation. My boss has done some amazing things for others that didn't have a fair shake in life. It wasn't part of an image-building campaign, because he did it long before he was even running for his first public office. He has never asked for any credit or praise for it because that's just who he is. Now I know of a story about someone he helped that could qualify him for sainthood, and he doesn't want any credit for it—and believe me, it's a person who is famous. He's a good man, Matt, and people should know about this. But I have been sworn to secrecy. There aren't many truly good people left in this town." He threw his hands up in the air theatrically. "This is a story that doesn't come around but once in a generation and no one is going to hear it."

"I'm not really following you Chip. What is so big about this?"

"Look, this isn't some puff piece of inspiration about somebody doing a good thing where everyone can smile and feel warm and fuzzy inside. We are talking about someone's life literally being saved and redirected, and now he's a fucking icon." Chip glared a bit at his companion. "If you think I'm just trying to get you to do a touchy-feely article about my boss, I can get dozens of people to do that by picking up my phone. This is different...way different. If this is not something that's worth your time, I understand." *Playing a little hard to get never hurt...*

"No, that's not what I'm saying at all. I guess I need more details before I can really understand your quandary." Weinrib felt a hint of panic as he thought he could be losing his possible meal ticket.

The first step of his play with the young reporter went easier than he thought. Now that he had him on the line, it was time to pull back and let him worry a bit about it. "I don't know. I need to think about this a little. I will call you in a day or two and we can talk more." He pulled out two twenty-dollar bills and put them on the table. "Drinks on me buddy. Thanks for listening." He shook Weinrib's hand and left the bar.

Matt sat there in the booth for a while, initially confused about what just happened and then worried that he had blown it. He was so close to getting a seat at the grown-up table he could taste it, but he resisted the urge to chase after Johnson and push him for more. It was time to be patient and see how this unfolded.

Chip smiled to himself as he drove home from the restaurant. He had done this long enough to know that he already had him, and it was now just a matter of timing. He would let him fret about possibly missing out on a big story for a couple of days, which would make him even more willing to try to please him when he called again. Haxton wanted this to break on its own, but it wouldn't hurt if it got a little directional nudging. He thought of the wooden furniture and warm colors of the White House Director of Communications Office that would be his after going down in history as the youngest campaign manager in a successful bid for the Presidency...

CHAPTER 10

He awoke with the vague knowledge that his screaming in the dream had been some sort of sound in the real world. He could hear his rapid pulse in his ear against the pillow that was damp with perspiration and noticed that the corner of the fitted sheet had been pulled away from the mattress, since part of it was clenched in his fist. He waited in silence, worried that he had woken Anna and glad that they had spent the extra money on a motion-isolation mattress a few years ago; he was still shaking. He gently pulled the comforter away from him and sat up, reaching for his prosthesis as he swung his legs over the side of the bed. His back felt cold as the gentle breeze from the ceiling fan hit his back, which was damp with sweat. He went to the bathroom and grabbed a t-shirt from the closet. His mouth was dry and he could feel the stinging sensation in the back of his throat from stomach acid.

Trying to be as quiet as possible, he walked to the kitchen, where he filled a cup from the drying rack with cold water and drank it all without pausing. He chewed two antacid tablets while he stared out the back window toward the water. It was still dark outside, and the clock on the microwave read 5:40 a.m. He jumped slightly as he felt the wet nose of Tiny push against his hand. He had become a pro at not waking the family with his bad dreams or just simply getting up early for work, but he could never get past this massive dog that always came to check on him. He scratched the top of his early morning companion's head, which came up to his chest, while he drank another half of a cup of water. Going back to sleep wasn't going to be possible. He let Tiny outside while he changed into his running clothes, and they went out to the neighborhood streets for what Michael often called really cheap therapy.

Upon returning he grabbed the newspaper from the driveway. There were no lights on in the house, so he went to the back deck, filled Tiny's water bowl, and dropped into one of the chairs. The dawn symphony of birds and insects had begun as he opened the paper and was greeted by the same thing he'd see by looking up at the shore behind his house. There was the picture of himself with Tiny, sitting on the dock, just under a headline titled "Major Michael

Reece: Charlotte's Reluctant Hero." The article was essentially a recap of their interview, along with commentary of his mannerisms, his family, and his home. He turned the paper toward Tiny and said, "They even mention you in here." Tiny seemed unimpressed as his massive frame took up the entire deck couch beside him. Michael was surprised to see that they had gotten comments from the hospital administrator, two of his partners, and even one of his patients. He initially bristled at this intrusion into the doctor-patient confidentiality, until he realized that the patient was also an employee of the newspaper. It included his most recent Department of Defense promotion photograph, along with a picture of him with David in Afghanistan, a digital copy of which he remembered giving to Ecklund at his request. There was a separate section that described the history of the Medal of Honor, along with his official citation and an illustration of the medal itself.

A small tapping on the door turned his attention to little Charlie pressing his face against the glass, trying to look goofy. He came outside, wearing his prized Sponge Bob Square Pants pajama pants and his Airborne t-shirt from Uncle David, and climbed into Michael's lap. "Look, Daddy, Tiny's in the newspaper."

Michael cherished the grounded reality that a kid can bring to your world. "That's right buddy...He doesn't seem to care that he's famous now." He put the paper down and sat watching the lake with his arms around his son. The peace was as short-lived as the attention span of his son, who dropped out of his lap to go inside to the Cartoon Network. Tiny followed little Charlie, and Michael picked the paper back up and found the Sports section. Training camp for the Panthers had begun, and he saw that their second-round draft pick wide receiver had pulled a hamstring in practice yesterday. Football practice was ongoing for the Tar Heels as well, and prospects for a bowl game were better than fifty-fifty.

He came inside and started the coffee maker for Anna and headed for the shower. Reece knew that she often pretended not to wake from his nightmares. He had never really wanted to talk about it when it happened, and she didn't want him to feel compelled to try if he didn't want to. Many times, she would simply lean over and kiss him on the cheek as he came back to bed. She knew him so well, and it was one of the many reasons she was the perfect match for him.

When he returned to the den, he could hear the bickering over which cartoon to watch and knew that another Reece family summer day had begun. Little Charlie was lying on the floor reclining against Tiny while he explained that he had gotten up first and, therefore, deserved dominion over the remote control. Elizabeth rolled her eyes and hugged her Dad on the way to their bedroom to watch her show of choice in there. Anna was sitting at the counter reading the paper. She lifted her chin for Michael's good-morning kiss. "The article is really good honey. How was your run?"

"It was good. I'm not getting irritated at all anymore since they refitted the cup to the prosthesis. Probably going to go to the office for about an hour this morning."

"Okay. The interview isn't until late afternoon, so you have time for a nap if you need it," Anna said, tipping her hand that she had indeed known that he had had another nightmare last night.

"I'm good." He walked over to start toasting waffles for the kids as well as to take his medication for his phantom leg pains. He had never been one to require much sleep, which was probably a good thing, since part of his job was delivering babies who didn't give a damn what time it was when they decided to come.

*****

"If he finds out, he will cut your balls off," Gov. Sutton said to Chip. They had met for breakfast at the Grand Hyatt Washington, where Sutton often stayed on trips to the nation's capital he took for business with one of the many consulting jobs he had. When he wasn't on official business, he more often than not stayed at the Senator's home, but he certainly enjoyed the perks of a suite in one of the more posh DC hotels, courtesy of an expense account, when he was "on the clock."

Chip smiled as he stirred his coffee. "Well, I'm not going to tell him, and I'm pretty sure Weinrib won't since he is ready to drink poison at my command to get the story. That leaves you, Governor."

"I want no part of that firestorm, young man. He won't find out from me. What did you say to Weinrib?"

"Nothing yet. Really overplayed the torn-conscience-of-a-senior-staffer routine and reeled him in slowly. I told him I needed a few days to think about it. By then, he'll eat his own shit if I ask him to."

Sutton wouldn't admit it, but Chip knew that he was on his side with this. He agreed that it would look better if the link between Reece and the Senator broke on its own, but he thought it *appearing* to break on its own was just as good if not better, since they could mold the message a bit. He shared senior White House staff aspirations with Johnson, but he knew more than he that this would have to be played very carefully...and delicately.

*****

Matt Weinrib sat at his cubicle desk at the *Washington Post* headquarters on Fifteenth Street NW, rolling over the conversation from the night before. He had picked up his iPhone several times to dial Chip but then thought better of it. Feeling like a teenager after a first date wondering whether he should risk being seen as too eager, he checked his email for the umpteenth time since arriving: nothing. He didn't know what this story was, but he was sure it was big, and he was sure he was on the precipice of being the one to break it wide open. His eyes drifted over his disheveled desk surface and stopped at his Rolodex. It was anemic in appearance and content, but he hoped that was about to change.

He tried to focus on the little bit he did know. He knew it involved Senator Haxton and, by the tone of the conversation, it seemed to be something that would reflect upon him in a positive way. It involved "saving" a life. Did he literally save someone's life, or did he save one metaphorically?

He knew that Haxton was a widower and had no children. His wife had died of cancer many years ago, and he had not remarried. Maybe he had gotten involved with cancer charity work, and that was the meaning of saving someone's life. It seemed a stretch, since countless politicians had their pet projects and charities, and healthcare was a common pursuit. The suspense was killing him, and he had a mental picture of Chip sitting in his office beginning to

113

reconsider sharing this news, or even worse, beginning to reconsider himself as the recipient of the scoop.

He had just finished some crap write-up on a farm subsidy debate that he knew had about as much chance of making the paper as a monkey climbing out of his ass right now, so he opened his laptop and decided to start translating his random thoughts into Internet searches. Maybe he would get lucky...

He started with "Haxton saves life" on a Google search. Thousands of hits came up, with nothing that seemed to be a likely jackpot. Most articles were about legislative initiatives that had a talking point in the text about "life-saving" resources or bringing medicines to poor communities that could "save lives." It all seemed the usual political claptrap collection of stories, with nothing that seemed to garner much attention to the reporter.

Healthcare charity seemed a much more likely angle, especially considering the loss of his wife. He entered "Haxton healthcare charity" into the search engine, again resulting in countless results, many of which were the same as the previous search. He had been a supporter of the Susan Komen Foundation for research into breast cancer, which was what had taken his wife from him. Articles related to this mentioned the charitable funds contributing to "saving countless lives" or providing for "life-saving treatments or care." There were mentions of contributions to the local hospitals, mainly for cancer treatments, for those who couldn't afford it, and pictures of him running in the annual Race for the Cure. There were certainly laudable efforts all over the articles, but nothing that seemed to be related to saving a particular individual's life. He bookmarked a few articles that had a glimmer of promise but felt like he wasn't even getting warm yet.

He checked his messages again: nothing.

He dropped the "healthcare" from the previous search, and the results broadened somewhat. It appeared that Haxton was quite a philanthropist, especially in his native North Carolina foothills. There were features about hospital fundraising, the Ronald McDonald House, children's charities, restoring historical buildings in the Asheville area, donations to Duke University (his alma mater), as well as many other worthy efforts. The collection of articles gave

114

an overall impression of Senator Haxton as a charitable guy and someone who wanted the best for his community, but there were no lights flickering in the back of Weinrib's mind yet. Searching "Haxton benefactor" revealed a list of recipients that included Duke University, Asheville Memorial Hospital, Highlands Preparatory School, Buncombe County Battered Women's Shelter, an orphanage called Sycamore House, and the Greater Asheville Food Bank among others. All worthy causes, no doubt, but nothing that seemed to garner the type of cloak-and-dagger behavior from Chip.

Matt felt like he was randomly throwing things at the wall to see if anything would stick—probably because he was. His iPhone and email both still showed no check-in from Chip, and he was hungry. He threw on his leather Bosconi messenger bag—a graduation gift from his parents—and headed out. He walked into Panera Bread Company, ordered a sandwich, and grabbed a table outside, hoping to get an epiphany about what do next.

*****

The cramping had been off and on since about four a.m. They were not labor contractions, because she had experienced those before. Renee Carson was still about two weeks away from her due date and had her repeat cesarean section scheduled in eight days. This would be her third such procedure, thanks to her first child, a daughter, tolerating contractions very poorly since the umbilical cord had been around her neck. She had chosen to have a repeat "C-section" for her son who came two years later. Her current baby, another daughter, would be her final child. Like her first two children, this one was scheduled next week to be brought into the world by Dr. Michael Reece.

Renee was a nurse in the pre-operative area of North Charlotte Regional Hospital. She had known Michael since he had come to practice and was one of the first patient's he had delivered at the hospital. They had become good friends, and their families spent a lot of time together outside of work. She remembered his calming presence when he explained to her that she needed surgery to deliver her first child, who was not doing very well on the fetal monitor. He talked to Renee and her husband while holding her hand, telling her that he wouldn't allow anything bad to happen to her or her daughter. The surgery went well, and they celebrated the arrival of a beautiful baby that night. They had been close friends ever since.

115

She had increased her fluids and had lain down to see if the cramping would go away. She had Michael's personal cell phone and had been assured that he would be there for her third delivery, scheduled or unscheduled. The passing time brought increasing intensity of the pain, and she was beginning to think that these might be closer to contractions than cramping. She texted her next-door neighbor, who was on standby to watch the kids in case anything happened, and called her husband at work to give him a heads-up that she might need to go to the hospital. He told her he was on his way to the house just in case. Being a pre-operative nurse, she decided to stop eating or drinking anything just in case surgery was in her near future.

Her neighbor came in the front door and started gathering pajamas and other things for the kids in case they would be having a sleepover at her house, while Renee got her packed hospital bag from the bedroom. She now had to pause when the contractions came. She heard the garage door opening while her husband pulled in. She gave a look to her neighbor, a mother herself, which told her without words to tell the kids to come on over to her house and grab their overnight items. Her water broke about thirty minutes later, and she picked up her cell phone to call her good friend.

"How's my favorite one-legged doctor today?" she asked when Michael answered the phone.

Michael could hear the discomfort in her voice. "Something's telling me that we are not going to be keeping our date for next week, are we?"

She told him what was going on, and they agreed to meet up at the Maternity Center. He had other things going on today, but they were all secondary to promises made to his patients...especially ones that were also dear friends. He kissed Anna goodbye and got in his truck to head to the hospital. He had the number for the interviewer at the television station and would call him on the way.

*****

Chase Ranson hit the button to kill the intercom on the phone and high-fived his cameraman. The six o'clock anchorman for WCHR Channel 7 News had just got off the phone with Michael Reece. The doctor was apologetic and explained that he had a long-time patient going into labor and who would require a cesarean section. He probably wouldn't be done until about thirty minutes after their interview was scheduled to start taping at his home. He was happy to still do the interview and felt bad that it would inconvenience everyone on the interview team.

Ranson reassured him that it wouldn't be a problem, and then a brilliant idea hit him. "Why don't we do the interview at the hospital?" he had asked him on the phone. The team could come to the visitor's lobby and wait there until he was finished. Ranson had wanted to find an additional element to the interview that wasn't in the newspaper article this morning, and this could be it: a popular hometown physician who had received such a prestigious award for heroism, interviewed at the local hospital where he worked. He was certain that the administrator of the hospital wouldn't mind, which was quickly confirmed by his assistant; this kind of good publicity was hard to come by, and the hospital was all for it.

Reece was agreeable to the idea and was apologetic for the change in plans. That accommodating veneer was only broken when Ranson suggested that they include footage of the surgery and speaking with his patient. That was an absolute no-go for Dr. Reece, who said that his patient's privacy and right to enjoy their new baby in peace trumped any media request. The tone of his reply made it clear that it was not up for negotiation. It would have been nice, but there were so many angles to go with this story that it wasn't essential, so Ranson let that one go. They would plan to do the interview outside; the administrator had asked that the hospital signage be somewhere in the shot at some point. This wasn't a problem at all, since a good amount of advertising revenue for the channel came from the hospital system.

They still had about two hours before they needed to leave, and his assistant was still working on background information to feature along with the interview footage. This would be the first television interview of their hometown hero and probably the only one until after the White House presentation ceremony. He knew that he couldn't ask about details of the mission and thought that asking about Reece's political views would be seen as in poor taste. This would be a feel-good piece through and through, with some solid questions but also some

117

softball tosses as well. He had chosen the shirt and sport coat with no tie to portray "Chase Ranson: Regular Guy"—not to mention it had a tendency to convey, subconsciously, that the interviewer and the interviewee had a personal friendship, even though they had never met.

*****

Reece pulled into the Physician's Parking section of North Charlotte Regional Hospital and went into the back entrance of the building. He swiped his ID badge at the entrance to the surgeon's lounge, which was currently empty, and headed into the locker room to change into surgical scrubs. He texted Renee to tell her he was at the hospital and would be up to see her in a couple of minutes.

He took the stairs up to the third floor, as he had stubbornly done since his return home, refusing to acknowledge that his injury would be any kind of limitation to him. He had to use his badge again to gain access to the maternity floor, since security was a little tighter there, mainly due to patient privacy, but also because of the occasional stories about nutcases showing up at hospitals with the intent of stealing someone's newborn to keep as their own.

Dr. Eric Daniels was coming out of a patient room after placing an epidural for a laboring patient. "Hey buddy. I thought Susan was on call today."

"She is. Renee Carson broke her water and I promised I would do the C-section for her."

"That's right. You're going for the hat trick with her." Daniels knew Renee also from the pre-operative area, and she was well-liked and respected by everyone there. He had also been on call for her second baby. "Well, if it's a go for today, just give me a call."

"Thanks buddy. I'll let you know."

It was his first time on the maternity floor since the announcement, and there were many hugs and congratulations by the staff, including a tearful embrace from Gail Wade, whose son had been killed in Fallujah in 2004 while serving with the Third Battalion, First Regiment of the United States Marine Corps. He whispered to her that her son was more of a hero than he ever would be, and she responded by kissing his cheek and heading to the break room to have a moment to herself.

118

He found Dara Walker, the nurse in charge of the OB Triage area, which evaluated patients to see if they would be admitted or sent home. As usual, she had everything already in order, which reminded him for the thousandth time that maternity care was 99 percent nurse and 1 percent doctor. Renee was in Triage 3. She had a positive nitrazene test, which confirmed that her water had indeed broken. The baby's heart rate was in the 140s, with good variability and no decelerations, indicating that everything was fine with her unborn child. Contractions were irregular, ranging from every five to twelve minutes. Her cervix was two centimeters dilated out of ten, and her vital signs looked good. She wanted to have a tubal ligation at the time of the C-section, which she had already discussed earlier in the pregnancy, since she wanted no more children after this one.

Michael walked into Triage 3 with Dara and hugged Renee and Keith Carson. "Well, I guess we can cancel next week's surgery." He pulled the paper printout of the fetal heart monitoring tracing and concluded that everything looked good. "How's your pain?"

"Not too bad. I was actually surprised that this happened today. Things were a little more painful a few hours ago. Before I forget, Charlie had left his baseball glove in my car last week and we brought it for you."

Michael smiled at that. Renee was as casual about this as she would be going to the grocery store to pick up bread and milk. She had been in this situation two times already, not to mention she had worked in the medical field for many years now. She also had a close relationship with her doctor and complete trust in him. He was honored to have her trust and still enjoyed the welcoming of a new child into the world as much as he had when he was a third-year medical student in Chapel Hill.

"Oh, and I won't say anything else about it after this because I know you hate to be praised, but we are very proud of you." Renee held Michael's hand as she said this, and Keith patted him on the back.

"Thanks guys, but today's about you. I'm going to give Dr. Daniels a call and we'll get you guys ready to go if that's OK."

He took her clipboard over to the physician's work area and filled out the "History and Physical" that was required for any patient being admitted to the hospital. It was a narrative of what brought them to the hospital, along with their medical/surgical history and current assessment and plan. He filled out the admission orders and paged Daniels. Discharge prescriptions for pain medications were called into Renee's pharmacy for when she went home. He had just finished texting Anna to let her know the change in plans when the unit secretary said Dr. Daniels was on line 2.

"Hey buddy. It's for real. Baby looks fine on the monitor."

"No problem. I'll be up in a couple of minutes and we will start getting her ready."

The unit secretary came over to Reece and told him that the television crew had arrived and was in the visitor's waiting area. He stuck his head in the door and let them know he would find them as soon as everything was done, and they told him that they would be right there. He waved to Renee's parents, who were waiting there as well, and promised to take good care of their daughter and their granddaughter. He ran into Susan as she was coming up to assist him with the surgery, and he walked with her as she got a cup of coffee—the required fuel for most on-call obstetricians.

"So much for your day off," Susan said as she stirred a creamer into her coffee.

"I'm not knocking it. It's nice to be doing a normal routine lately." He nodded to Keith, who was popping into the waiting room to update the family once more before they went back to the operating room.

Michael and Susan walked to operative suite and got shoe covers and hats. Renee was walking with Dara back to the operating room, where she would receive her spinal anesthesia—an injection in the fluid around the spinal cord that would make her numb from the chest down and allow her to have the procedure painlessly and awake. She had changed into the standard hospital gown often the subject of ridicule for not quite giving one's backside adequate coverage. Dara was pushing her rolling metal intravenous fluid tree holding the lactated ringer solution she would receive prior to the "spinal" to prevent her blood pressure from dropping from the anesthetic.

Dr. Daniels came in and gave Renee a quick hug and helped her get into position, which was sitting on the side of the operating table with her legs hanging over, with her back hunched over like an angry cat. The anesthesiologist cleaned her lower back with an iodine solution and felt her lower spine with sterile gloved hands, finding the space between her lumbar vertebrae where he would inject the numbing medication. The spinal injection went without problems, and Renee was laid back on the operating table and covered on her chest and shoulders with warm blankets. The surgical technician began cleaning her abdomen with iodine solution while the "circulating" nurse called to the front desk to let the doctors know they could come back and "scrub."

Michael told Keith that as soon as they got in the room and made sure Renee's level of numbness was good for the procedure, they would get him in the room and get started. He enjoyed small talk with Susan as they scrubbed their hands with sterilizing soap at the sink outside the operatory. He asked Renee if she was doing OK as the surgical technician helped the two surgeons get into their surgical gowns and sterile gloves. Sterile drapes were placed over their patient, and he pinched her belly with a sterile surgical pick-up instrument and asked her if she could feel any pain. When she informed them that she couldn't feel anything, they brought in Keith to sit by her head behind the sterile drape. Michael asked for the scalpel.

He made a side-to-side incision over her previous scar, which was barely perceptible. He divided the thin fatty layer under the skin with an electrical instrument called a "Bovie," which cauterized bleeding vessels as it separated the tissue. The dense layer under that was called the fascia, which he divided in the same direction as the skin incision, and then he separated the rectus, or "six-pack," muscles vertically. The final layer before being inside the actual abdominal cavity was called the peritoneum and was cut with scissors and then extended vertically with the Bovie.

Now the uterus was exposed, and Michael carefully made a shallow incision across the bottom front, going deeper by very small increments so not to cut the baby immediately behind the wall of the womb. Once the inside was reached, he carefully delivered the head and suctioned out the nose and mouth. After making sure there were no loops of umbilical cord around the neck, he delivered the shoulders and the rest of the body while Susan pressed the top of the abdomen. The welcome cries of a newborn echoed in the room as Michael clamped and cut the umbilical cord and carried their newest daughter around the curtain so Renee and Keith could see her before the nurses cleaned her off under the warmer and wrapped her in a blanket. Keith fought back tears as their little girl was given to him while Renee looked on.

After tying the fallopian tubes per Renee's request, Michael closed the open areas carefully layer by layer, finishing by running a thin continuous suture just under the skin to bring the edges together, making the scar as thin as possible. Small adhesive strips were placed across the now-closed incision, and a dressing applied. He thanked all the staff and pulled off his surgical gown, walking around again to let Renee and Keith know everything went well.

Crouching down to hold Renee's hand, he congratulated both of them. "Everything went great. We'll get you to recovery room soon so you can take a turn at holding this little angel."

"I know you were off today, and it means a lot that you came in for this." Renee was filled with the emotions of being a new mother again along with the slight melancholy of this being the last time she would experience this moment.

"It means a lot that you would want me to come in." He shook Keith's free hand and left the operating room to dictate the surgical report and fill out the post-operative orders. Once that was complete, he went to the lobby.

He held up his hand as the television crew stood and started to speak and walked over to Renee's parents, congratulating them and letting them know that Mom, Dad, and baby were all doing well. He then turned to the anchorman.

"Sorry, but patients and families come first."

"Not a problem Dr. Reece. Thank you for still agreeing to speak with us today."

"Happy to do it Mr. Ranson. I apologize that we had a last-minute change of plans, and I hope I haven't inconvenienced everyone too much."

"Please call me Chase, Dr. Reece. It's an honor to meet you, and we will make this go pretty quickly."

"I much prefer Michael or Mike to Dr. Reece. What do you have in mind?"

The female producer talked him through the process. They would get footage of him and Chase walking in the hospital hallway, and then they would have the interview in a separated area of the main lobby, since there were some of the classic Carolina summer thunderclouds on the horizon outside. Not knowing that it was his usual working attire, she loved the fact that he was still wearing his surgical scrubs. They fitted him with a small microphone to the V-neck portion of his scrub shirt, running the wire under it to a pack clipped to his waist at his lower back. She asked if he wore a white coat, and he said he hadn't since he was a resident several years ago.

After walking down the hallway and talking about nothing in particular while the anchorman did his best attentive nodding, they sat down for the formal part of the interview. A lot of the questions were virtually identical to the ones asked from the newspaper, and his corresponding answers were not much different either. The questions then turned more toward Michael Reece the person.

Legs crossed, with a slight backward lean into the chair, Chase Ranson had perfected the relaxed but in-charge posture that he used during one-on-one interviews. "Dr. Reece, you are often described as a dedicated family man. Would you say that is your main driving force in life?"

"Absolutely. I have been blessed with the greatest wife in the world, and we have had two wonderful children together. I see my main purpose in life as being a good husband and father and giving my children a good example to follow. Being the spouse of a doctor with pretty strange working hours, as well as a soldier who has to leave home periodically, is a very tough job. Anna inspires me every day with how she handles it with grace and devotion. I am very lucky to have my family."

Ranson smiled as he nodded slowly during the answer. "You are a man of humble beginnings. Did you imagine yourself having the life you have now when you were younger?"

"Probably not, but I think everyone has challenges to overcome in life. I was able to come in contact with people that helped me realize that I could shape my future and find success."

"Do you feel sometimes like you hit the lottery in life?"

"No. Seeing myself as winning the lottery would imply that I stumbled upon the things that I have done. I have worked extremely hard to get where I am and have had to overcome some pretty tough obstacles. Nothing good comes easy, at least not for most people. I believe luck helps many along the way, but usually success comes from hard work." Reece didn't want to show his irritation at that particular question, since it was probably asked without any bad intent, but his initial reaction was to say *I wouldn't consider getting my leg blown off being part of winning the lottery.* "I wouldn't say I'm a self-made man because that would do a disservice to people that have been a big help to me along the way. But you have to set a goal and be willing to put in the work required to get there."

"How has your injury affected your life since coming home?"

"Well, the recovery was very hard. Luckily the surgeons and physical therapists that took care of me brought me back. I owe a huge debt to them for working with me and helping me learn to adapt to life after my injury. I really try to not let it affect me at all now. Just ask my wife—I have a good stubborn streak in me. I felt like I had an obligation to the men that didn't survive that night to carry on and live my life to the fullest.

"I have a great friend named Sergeant David Tripp who was with me that night. He told me that we were living testimonies to those who fell and we had to make them proud. It really put my injuries into perspective, and I thought of them when I felt like quitting during my recovery. I insist on doing the things I used to do. I run four times a week, play golf, and I can even still go scuba diving, thanks to my diving instructor, who helped custom build an apparatus to have a prosthetic fin for my leg."

Ranson smiled. "Are you still a good golfer?"

That question brought a chuckle from Reece. "Unfortunately, I was never a good golfer. I guess I can say that I'm not any worse than I used to be. I try to get my golfing buddies to give me a few more strokes, but they aren't being very charitable." Both men laughed.

"What do you see the future holding for you now?"

"Hopefully it will be more of the present. I am a happy guy and feel blessed with what I have. I enjoy my work and taking care of my patients, and I plan to continue serving in the Army Reserves as well. I know life is going to be a little different for a while with the attention that comes with this honor, but I hope that it doesn't change me and sometime in the near future I can return to my regular life."

"How would you feel about being called for active duty again?"

"That's my job, Chase. You don't serve in the reserves to play soldier on the weekend and wear a cool uniform. You are there to serve when the Army needs you, and you have to be willing to set aside your civilian life from time to time to do that. If I complained about going back again, I feel like it would be a slap in the face to the men and women who have died doing their jobs over there or ones who have sustained much worse injuries than mine."

"What about your disability?"

"Please don't call it that. There are many injured soldiers who have gone back to active service with worse than what I have. If the Army finds something that they need me to do to help the mission, I would go without hesitation."

"Dr. Reece, it has been an honor to speak with you today, and we wish you the very best in the future."

"Thank you Chase. I appreciate the opportunity to speak with you."

The lights indicating active recording went out on the two cameras facing them. Michael felt like the interview had lasted only a few seconds, but was relieved that is was over. "I hope I did OK."

Chase shook his hand again. "You did great." He gave Reece his card and said he would be happy to speak with him again if he ever wanted, and they broke down their equipment and headed to the van outside. He had about two hours to get everything put together for it to be the leading story on tonight's evening broadcast. NBC, their national network, had already requested it for their broadcast, and he knew there would be many more to follow. He also knew that they would allow anyone to use it after tonight's initial broadcast as long as the upper left hand corner of the screen showed "Courtesy of WCHR, NBC News 7 Charlotte." The other networks would have the story for their respective audience as long as they advertised that they were beat to the punch by their competitors.

Reece headed back upstairs to check on the Carson family one more time. He felt a sense of relief that his media obligations prior to the presentation ceremony had been completed, and he hoped for at least a few routine days before leaving for Washington.

CHAPTER 11

Behind the music in his iPod ear buds, Matt Weinrib could hear the rhythmic swishing of the elliptical machine he was operating at the Gold's Gym in Herndon, Virginia. He wanted to be closer to Washington proper or the more trendy Old Towne Alexandria area, but his current pittance of a salary at *The Washington Post* did not make that very likely at the moment. It was early morning, and last night had not been overly restful. He had tried several more approaches with the almighty Google with the hopes of getting a hit that would explain what was going on at the office of the Honorable Gentleman from North Carolina. None of his attempts had borne fruit, and he had tossed around in the bed during a night of fitful sleep trying new angles in his mind. The early morning showed no new emails or messages from Chip, so he grabbed his bag and headed to the gym with plans to shower and change there and take the train to work. Being a junior political reporter certainly didn't merit one of the most prized commodities in the DC area—a parking space.

The CNN station on his satellite radio on the way to the gym gave pretty much the same rotation of stories that were going last night when he had given up on the computer and went to bed. No earth-shattering events had happened in the past several hours. He was also relieved that there were no breaking stories involving Haxton signaling that someone else had gotten the golden ticket.

He wiped the sweat from his brow as he picked up the pace on the exercise machine. His eyes darted between the two televisions in front of him, one showing Headline News and the other SportsCenter. He was keeping one eye on the sports channel in case any story was done about the Buckeyes' upcoming season. *I may not have written for The Harvard fucking Crimson, but at least I had a real football team to go see on Saturdays.* He noted Headline News was doing a story on the guy who had won the Congressional Medal of Honor. They seemed to be showing footage of an interview of him done by a local station. Funny that he was in scrubs; Weinrib must have missed that he was a doctor or nurse or something. Matt did remember someone mentioning that he was a reservist and that was rare, which would explain him not being in uniform. The interview footage was followed by images of the press conference at the Pentagon, a picture of the guy in uniform which looked like it was taken overseas somewhere, a likely high school yearbook photograph, and a brief interview of a woman from a local affiliate in Asheville outside of what looked like a large brick house with a big play area in the back; the name banner said Theresa something. He looked down at the display and saw that he had about six minutes to go, and then something started to gnaw at him in the back of his mind.

He began to have the feeling that he had missed something of consequence. Was it something flashing from the his memory of his Internet searches yesterday, something from the conversation with Chip, something he heard on the radio this morning…or something he had just seen? He snapped his face back up to the televisions. The news station was doing a story on rising gas prices now, and the other set was showing a report from the training camp of one of the likely NFL contenders this year. The nagging feeling was becoming more pronounced but not any clearer. He began to feel almost sure that it was something that he had just seen on television. There was urgency in his thoughts, and it took him over two minutes to realize he wasn't moving on the elliptical machine anymore. It was right there, just over the horizon of his conscious thought, but it wouldn't reveal itself.

Whatever it was, he was convinced that not only was it important but it was related to what had kept him up the night before. He went to the locker room, grabbed his bag, and headed to the train station, not bothering to shower and change. He checked his email on his phone: nothing. He had decided he would play it cool until mid-afternoon, and then he would send Chip a text. Nothing pushy, but he would tell him that he was around if he wanted to talk.

It seemed like an eternity for the train to reach his stop near work. He passed the elevator and headed up to his floor, hopping two stairs at a time since he had only a few minutes before the top-of-the-hour news stories recycled.

He received a few odd looks as he came to his cubicle in gym clothes with sweat marks still visible. He threw his bag in his chair, grabbed a notepad, pen, and his phone, and headed for the nearest conference room. It was empty, and he turned on the television inside, which, much to his delight, had a DVR with which he could pause and rewind live programs. He saw that the conference room wasn't reserved for two more hours, so he shifted the sign on the door to Occupied and locked the door. He dropped into the chair with two minutes before the top of the hour. He realized that he should have taken a piss first, but there wasn't enough time now.

Sure enough, six minutes into the top-of-the-hour broadcast, the story began and he grabbed the remote, turned up the volume, and rested his right thumb on the pause button so he could strike it quickly if anything caught his eye. He paused it at the end of the story and started to rewind it. It was in here somewhere...he was sure of it. He watched it again, pausing frequently as well as scribbling notes about the comments being said. He didn't think it was something anyone said, because he hadn't heard the broadcast in the gym. It had to be something he had seen.

Pausing on the image of the press conference, he looked at everything on the podium and studied the two men in front of the cameras: nothing. He paused the picture of Major Reece (he had picked up the guy's name by hearing the story) and looked at him, his uniform, the men around him, and there was nothing causing alarms to go off. He started to feel some anticipation as the yearbook photo came up and looked at the young man wearing what looked like a prep school uniform with a slight smile. There was nothing in the background of the picture, and he felt like he was grasping at straws now. Next came the interview of the lady outside the brick house. Her name was Theresa Williams, and she was talking about Reece and how he was a special young man and how proud she was of him. *Fuck!* It was maddening. He paused it again right before it switched from the Williams interview back to the morning host. He paced around the table and thought about his Google searches, his conversations with Chip, and what he had learned about Haxton. He kicked his empty water bottle in frustration, and it ricocheted off the wall beside the television...and that's when he saw it. Just over the left shoulder of the Williams lady were dark brown letters in an archway over the front entrance to the brick house: Sycamore House.

His mind seemed to go into overdrive once he saw those words. He began pacing again and, after about two minutes, he stopped and grabbed his things and went running back to his cubicle. He threw his notepad and pen on the desk and shook his mouse to awaken his computer from the sleep mode.

He typed "Sycamore House" and several matches came up, including the home page for the house itself. He learned that Theresa Williams was the head counselor there and that their mission was to help young boys who either didn't have parents or they had been taken from them. He went through the different headers of the website that showed the staff, the mission statement, and a link to make a donation. The next eureka moment came when he clicked on the "Board of Directors" tab. The new page came up with several professional photographs of distinguished-appearing men and women with short biographies next to them. He didn't go beyond the first picture, however, which showed the Chairman of the Board of Trustees: The Honorable James A. Haxton, Senior Senator from North Carolina and longtime philanthropist in the Asheville area.

By now his need to piss had become an overwhelming urgency. He walked briskly to the bathroom and stood over the urinal as he thought over what he had seen. He knew he had the link. A Medal of Honor winner who grew up in an orphanage whose biggest benefactor happened to be Chip's boss. Great story, no doubt, but there was something missing.

Upon returning to his cubicle he decided to search some more. He looked over the Sycamore House website once more and was satisfied that there was nothing more of substance to him there. Then he searched "Haxton Sycamore House," and got a lot of puff pieces in local newspapers but not much more. He then typed in "Haxton Michael Reece." Some of the same matches came up, but the number was much lower. He clicked on Google Images, and the first one listed was what made the final connection.

It was from an article written by the local newspaper in Wilmington and was on the Senator's home at nearby Figure Eight Island. The article itself was pure fluff and seemed to be an afterthought filler piece put in the Sunday Lifestyle section, but when he enlarged one of the photos from the article he knew he had hit the jackpot. It was a great shot of an older man in khaki shorts, a golf shirt, and topsiders—clearly Haxton—holding the hand of a young boy. They were walking toward the end of a dock beyond which was the Intracoastal Waterway. The sun was setting off to the left. The caption read "Congressman James Haxton walking with Michael Reece, one of the many young children who have benefited from his philanthropy."

He bookmarked the article on his browser and leaned back in his chair feeling quite self-congratulatory. Chip had given him just enough information in his cryptic remarks over drinks that allowed him to crack the code. He smiled as he looked at his mobile phone. Waiting until mid-afternoon no longer seemed necessary, and now he wanted this before anyone else figured it out. He hit the text function on the phone and selected Chip Johnson from his stored numbers: "Sycamore House. We should talk soon."

*****

Theresa Williams sat at her desk and stared at an old photograph of a young Michael Reece hanging upside down from the play set. She remembered the day like it was yesterday. She had taken the picture mainly because it was when he had started to come out of his shell, which had been around the same time that Charlie Potts had arrived at Sycamore. She was convinced that it was not a coincidence. He had one of the most infectious smiles that a child could have, and she was so thankful when it finally began to emerge that she took the picture so she could remember the day. It also brought back less-than-pleasant memories of Michael's reaction upon learning about Charlie's death.

A melancholy descended upon her as she sat in her desk behind a closed door (which was a rare occurrence in itself) and thought about the years since Michael had left for college. She rejoiced at the opportunity he had to escape painful memories and strike out his own claim in the world and had encouraged him to take in the college experience and enjoy a life outside of what he had come to know as home. She had been disappointed, however, by the complete lack of contact since that time. She didn't feel betrayed, because although she was one of the best youth counselors around, she couldn't comprehend what kind of psychological toll growing up as he had before Sycamore could take on a young mind. But it was just that surely he would want to keep some contact with the people he had grown up with and who had been so dedicated to helping him overcome such terrible circumstances, not to mention some of the childhood friends he had gained at the house. She thought in particular of the Tyler twins, who seemed to struggle with his absence from their lives after he left.

The twins' lives didn't follow the inspirational tale that Michael had experienced. They had also come from abusive homes; both parents were incarcerated for drug use and trafficking. They had certainly benefited from their new home and the guidance that staff had given them, but it seemed that they couldn't break free from their past as easily. Both had experienced behavioral issues at school that seemed to worsen after Michael left, and they struggled academically, with Darnell dropping out of school the day he turned eighteen and Chris barely graduating. Both had descended into lives of substance abuse and petty crime after that, with only Chris finding some degree of escape by leaving Asheville and essentially becoming a drifter; he did seem to have embraced sobriety, though. He would come back occasionally with the hopes of getting his brother away from crime and drugs, but always left disappointed.

Darnell had been incarcerated on three separate occasions since entering adulthood, twice for drug possession and once for breaking and entering. Theresa had only sporadic contact with him. She pleaded with him to get clean and offered of any help she could give. His rebuke was not only immediate but also laced with contempt. The day he quit school had told the staff at Sycamore that he would never have anything to do with them. He had gathered his things and threatened to fight his brother if he tried to make him stay. Chris let him go and, unfortunately, had followed the same path a few months later.

Both the brothers had enjoyed a good relationship with Michael and even looked up to him, as he was succeeding in school and was a few years older than them. No words were ever said on the subject, but it appeared that Michael's lack of contact had confused them at first. Eventually it led to resentment.

Theresa couldn't find the reason for one doing so well and the other two taking a vastly different path. All three were very bright boys, and they had all enjoyed the same resources and dedication from the Sycamore House staff. They had all received words of wisdom from the members of the Board of Trustees and had been taken on trips by them to see a world outside of what they had known. Senator Haxton had put aside funds for the twins' further education, just like Michael, but those funds were never put to use. The twins had reacted to the prospects of help after high school with contempt and, in Theresa's opinion, ingratitude.

It wasn't Michael's fault that they did poorly as young adults. But she couldn't help but wonder if there would have been a different outcome had he chosen to keep in touch. They missed him after he left. She missed him after he left. Did everything that they had gone through together and all the help that he had been given not matter? She couldn't help but feel a little cast aside, and she was sure that the twins had felt that even more strongly than her. No, she wasn't angry at Michael. But she was disappointed in him. She believed every positive thing she had said about him to the reporter and loved him like he was her own son, but he could have done more after he left, and you have to be honest with the ones you love.

She pulled out a piece of stationary and began writing him a letter from her heart. It would not be an angry letter, but it would be honest. If he chose to continue to keep the distance between them the same, that was his choice. But he would know that she still loved him and that she had expected a little more from him over the years.

*****

Standing on the elevated balcony area of the Capitol rotunda, Johnson looked at the camera that was set up in front of him while he listened to the discussion through his earpiece. He was currently part of a roundtable discussion via satellite feed with MSNBC discussing the proposed tax code changes that were filtering through various congressional subcommittees. He had already put forth his talking points and had made his counterpart representing the opposing view stumble in his rebuttals. He had chosen one of his better Brooks Brothers pin-striped dark blue suits with a starched white shirt and light blue silk power tie. His lapel sported an American flag just lateral to the small clipped microphone, whose cord snaked around his side and down his back under his coat. The conversation had now shifted to the upcoming presidential election and potential candidates for the party nominations.

Chip smiled at the inevitable casting of the line hoping for information. "Well, Jason, I can tell you that right now the Senator has plenty on his plate serving the needs of his constituents back home. He's certainly flattered by all the talk about him being a strong candidate on our party's ticket, but he has no current plans to enter that race." It was a line he had said dozens of times in the past several months, which contained about three dozen words but actually said nothing.

"That didn't sound like a firm 'no' to me Chip," he heard through his earpiece.

"I haven't met a single person yet who can predict the future Jason, so who knows what that holds. I can only say right now that Senator Haxton is very happy serving the many needs of the good people of North Carolina." He heard the surrender in his ear.

"It's always a pleasure to speak with you too, Jason."

When the red camera indicator went out, he pulled his earpiece free while the producer helped him untangle from the microphone wire. He flashed his smile at the camera crew, thanked them for helping him out, and headed back toward his office, thumbing his phone for new messages as he walked. Weinrib's was the third one down the list of texts he had gotten in the past hour. It looked like the kid was a little more resourceful than he originally thought. Chip had hoped for another day, but the connection was going to be made sooner or later. It didn't change the fact that he could control how it was presented by framing the information he gave the reporter, along with the dangling carrot of possible exclusive access to the Senator himself at some point for an interview.

He typed a reply: "How about we meet at 7:00 at Fontaine Café and we can talk?"

The texted reply of "C u there" took less than thirty seconds to come, which let Chip know the he was still very much in control. He dialed Sutton's number.

"It's Chip. Weinrib has made the connection with Sycamore House. I'm meeting with him tonight." He nodded as he listened to the other end. "I understand. Don't worry, he will write what we want him to, and he will firmly believe it was his idea all along." The Governor could be a patronizing old shit but there wasn't a bigger player in politics in Haxton's home state, and his list of connections and favors owed inside the beltway was staggering.

The elevation of the Honorable James A. Haxton from distinguished statesman to saint would begin tonight at a coffee shop in Alexandria.

*****

It was ironic that his last surgery before going on leave was not a scheduled one. He had been called to the Emergency Department to consult on a fourteen-year-old girl who had developed fairly sudden severe pain in her right lower abdomen. It was followed shortly thereafter by nausea and vomiting and a call by her mother to the pediatrician, who advised them to go to the hospital to be evaluated. The emergency medicine physician initially assumed appendicitis, but that changed when she saw there was no fever and no elevation in her white blood cell count. Her pain was impressive, and she reacted to any pressure in that area on exam.

Dr. Carol Tilghman wasn't sure what was going on but believed the patient's parents when they said their daughter was not one to complain and was in terrible pain. Tilghman ordered a computed tomography (CT scan) of the abdomen and pelvis to look for structural explanations for her pain. She started an IV drip and gave her a dose of Demerol for the pain. Shortly after, she received a call from the radiologist, who said she had about a nine-centimeter mass in her right pelvis that looked to be part of her ovary. He recommended an ultrasound to evaluate it further, which Dr. Tilghman agreed.

Pelvic ultrasound confirmed that the mass was part of the right ovary and also showed the more ominous sign of no blood flow to the area on Doppler studies, confirming the diagnosis of a right ovarian torsion, which was essentially a twisting of the ovary on itself, cutting off the blood flow necessary to keep the organ alive. There would be little time to correct the problem before the ovary was lost in a teenager that still had childbearing ahead in the faraway future.

Although Reece wasn't on call that day, Carol knew he was around since she had seen him about an hour ago in the doctor's lounge. She had a teenage daughter, and if she needed surgery on her ovary she would want Michael to do it. He was a good surgeon and also happened to be her personal doctor as well, so she picked up the phone and dialed his pager number.

Michael heard the Emergency Department unit secretary answer on the other end of the line. "Hey Becky, it's Mike. Somebody paged."

"Hang on just a moment Dr. Reece. I'll find out who needs you." It didn't matter how many times he had asked Becky to call him Mike, she would always call him by his formal title. After a while, he gave up and respected her decision.

"Hey loser," Carol said as she picked up the phone.

"Hey butthead." It was a playful picking at each other that dated back to their time as residents at Emory University.

"Listen, I know you're not on call, but because you love me so much I know you will want to help me out with a patient I have here."

"Whatcha got?"

"Fourteen-year-old with acute onset right-lower-quadrant pain. Afebrile with normal white blood cell count, and urine pregnancy test is negative."

The last part made Michael shudder, since it wouldn't be that many years before Elizabeth would be that age and the boys would start chasing...especially since she was every bit as beautiful as her mother.

"CT scan showed an adnexal mass. Ultrasound confirmed it's an ovarian mass, and Doppler studies show no blood flow to the ovary. Negative surgical history and she has no medical problems. It's an ugly-looking mass, but I hope the ovary can be saved. She already has an IV in and her parents are here with her. Since it's your last day before sabbatical and since I am your favorite ER doctor ever, don't you want to take care of her?"

"OK, give me about five minutes and I'll be there."

"Thanks sweetheart." She went to the patient's room and was happy to see that the Demerol had helped with the pain. She sat down with the parents.

"Mr. and Mrs. Thompson, your daughter has a large cyst on her ovary that has caused it to twist on itself. This cuts the blood flow that goes to the ovary to keep it alive. Fortunately, you came here pretty quickly and there is a good chance we can fix this and save the ovary. Unfortunately that means she will have to have surgery to correct the problem. This is not a

136

life-threatening situation, but we will have to do the procedure pretty soon. I took the liberty of calling one of our GYN surgeons and telling him about the case to see if he would be willing to do this. He was happy to do it and is on his way to meet you. He is an outstanding surgeon and he also happens to be my own doctor."

No parent wants to hear that their child needs surgery, but Carol's outstanding bedside manner helped them be at ease with the decision, and she answered their questions completely and patiently. They thanked her for her excellent care, and the father had an unrelated question for her as she was about to leave the room.

"Doctor Tilghman, isn't this the hospital that has the doctor that just won the Medal of Honor?"

"That's right Mr. Thompson. He is here. In fact, he is about to operate on your daughter." She smiled as she saw his mouth fall open. "And he is just as good with ovaries as he is with gunshot wounds."

*****

Darnell Tyler stumbled out of the bedroom in the dilapidated single-wide trailer that he shared with three other men. Several of the windows had taped cardboard over them, and the inside reeked of cigarettes and spilled beer. More often than not, at least one of the four roommates was away in county lockup for drug-related offenses. They all ran in the same crowd of people who occasionally worked at odd menial jobs to help pay bills and support their drug habits and robbed homes or people when they needed more than the low-paying jobs supplied.

Darnell had a terrible headache, compliments of last night's heavy drinking. He would still be asleep in these early-afternoon hours if his craving for drugs had not awoken him and pulled him out of bed. He was angry but not surprised to find that his stash had been lightened by someone in the trailer. The guys tapping into each other's drug supply for their own withdrawals had been the source of countless arguments and fights and even one stab wound. There was enough still there to carry him over until he could get in touch with his dealer.

After initially just using beer and weed, he had graduated to more potent forms of recreational pharmaceutics and by now had developed a serious addiction to methamphetamine, more commonly referred to as "crystal meth" or "ice," as well as heroin. He used about six times a day, and the withdrawal symptoms would come swift and severe if he ever went more than about ten hours without it. He wanted to stop but had failed many times to do it on his own. He regretted every day not listening to his brother, who desperately wanted him to come with him and get away from the degenerates who stole his drugs and took his cash if he wasn't looking but who still thought they were his "homies."

He harbored tremendous guilt for reaching this point. He had initially used drugs and alcohol as an escape from a painful past, but he had fallen quickly down the slippery slope. He was a shell of the young and handsome man he had once been. His previous muscle tone was nearly absent, thanks to poor nutrition and chronic poisoning of his body, while any look in the mirror reflected a face with multiple sores and several missing teeth. He was what many people called him: a meth head.

The withdrawal symptoms were starting to become more pronounced, and he doubled over as his stomach cramped and brought on a sense of urgency. He grabbed his stash and raced to the bathroom. The absolute filth of the toilet and shower areas would have shocked anyone who hadn't lived here, and the counter was covered with syringes, charred spoons, and empty plastic packets.

He barely made it to the toilet before the explosive diarrhea began. All the while his stomach continued to cramp and he felt his saliva increase as the urge to vomit threatened also. He smoked the last of his ice while sitting on the toilet, smelling the alternating odor of drug fumes and shit. As he looked down at the dirty floor and the unwashed underwear that clung around his ankles, he began to cry. He cursed the life that had been dealt to him and at the same time felt the shame of wasting the chance he had been offered but did not take. The effects of the drug began to rise in his system, which pushed away the urgency that withdrawal could bring.

He stood up and wiped the tears and snot off of his pock-marked face. Addicts often describe their "rock bottom" moment, and he was pretty sure that this was his. He walked in the living room where one of his "homies" was passed out on the couch. He fished a cell phone from the guy's back jeans pocket. He sniffed and tried to collect himself as he dialed his brother's phone.

"This is Chris," his brother said as he answered the phone.

"Hey bro, it's D." Darnell deepened his voice with the hopes of hiding the fact that he had been crying. "How's it goin'?"

"I'm good. What's up with you?" There was a hint of suspicion in his voice. Darnell was not one just to call up and chat out of the blue. Most of these calls involved either needing to be bailed out of jail or simply needing cash to feed his habit. "You in trouble?"

"I guess you could say that." The tears were coming again and his voice was cracking as he spoke. "I think I need some help bro. I can't do this anymore. If I don't get out of here, I think I'm goin' to die. I don't know where you are right now, and I know I shoulda come with you before. I'm sorry bro. I'm really, really sorry. I just gotta get out of here."

No matter how frustrated Chris had been with his brother, he loved him and wanted him to get better. Darnell wasn't one to cry, and Chris was alarmed. He didn't know whether to be happy that he finally was ready to get help or suspicious that it was all bullshit. But it didn't matter. If his brother needed help, he would be there for him. Drugs, alcohol, arguments, and fights were no match for a brother's love.

"All right, bro. I'm at the coast right now. Let me talk to my boss and I will be there as soon as I can. It might be a few days, but I'm coming. Can you hang on until then?"

"Yeah, man, I can hang." Darnell was afraid, but knowing his brother would come would help him get through the next few days. "I'm sorry bro."

"Don't be sorry D. I love you man, and we're going to get you better. I'll have this number with me all the time until I get there."

They hung up and Darnell dried his face and blew his nose with a crinkled fast food napkin that was on the floor. He kept the phone he had taken from his sleeping housemate. He knew the phone was probably stolen and his friend would simply steal another one. He called his dealer to set a meet. There was no way he could stop cold turkey right now, and he needed to score more drugs to keep from "getting sick." He programmed Chris's phone number into the cell phone and headed out the door.

*****

Michael studied the monitor that hung from the operating room ceiling in front of him. It conveyed the image from the camera he had inserted through a trocar, or port, that went through a small incision in the young patient's navel. Two other smaller trocars were inserted on each side of the camera with laparoscopic instruments that he held from the outside. The patient was lying on her back with the head of the bed slightly lower than the foot to allow the intestines to fall away from the pelvis.

He was looking at a large ovarian mass that almost completely filled the pelvis. It was made up of a fluid-filled cyst, and the attachment between the right side of the pelvis and the ovary showed several corkscrew-like twists confirming that it was indeed a torsion of the ovary. The tissue was a darker blue than usually seen, showing that it was starving for essential oxygen-containing blood flow.

He used a "spatula," a small instrument that used electrical current to function as a knife, to make a shallow half-circle incision at the base of the cystic mass. He alternated using the electrocautery and graspers to separate the large cyst from the remaining ovary and "buzzed" several small bleeding vessels on the surface of the ovary. Now for the part where he mentally crossed his fingers...

He reversed the twisting of the infundibulopelvic ligament, which contained the right ovarian artery, and held his breath. After several agonizing seconds, the ovary began to lose its dark blue appearance and reflected its normal pink-tinged pearly hue. This told him and everyone else in the operating room that they had done the surgery in time and the ovary wasn't dead—great news for a fourteen-year-old.

He changed to a smaller camera and put it through one of the smaller trocars, allowing him to insert an instrument through the larger navel port called an "Endopouch." Once he saw the end of the pouch was in the abdomen, he pushed a plunger released a clear plastic pouch, like a small Ziploc sandwich bag, tethered to the instrument by a sterile string. He used a surgical grasper from the other port to place the large cyst into the pouch, but he didn't close the drawstring mechanism yet. He then removed the grasper and inserted a tube with a short needle on the end that had a 100 cc syringe attached to the other side. He punctured the cyst with the needle and began drawing the clear-yellow fluid into the syringe while watching the cyst collapse in the bag. Once the syringe was full, he would remove it from the tube and empty the fluid into a sterile collection basin and start again. Three minutes and nearly a liter of fluid later, the cyst wall was all that remained in the bag. He pulled the drawstring closed and it easily came through the less-than-two-centimeter incision in the navel.

After irrigating the pelvis with an instrument that would also suction the fluid out, he checked to make sure the now-healthy ovary was not bleeding. He placed two small sutures to "plicate" the ovary to the side of the pelvis to prevent it from twisting again in the future. He then looked at the other structures in the abdomen and pelvis to make sure there were no other abnormalities, removed the instruments and trocars from her abdomen, and sutured closed the small incisions with a Vicryl suture that would dissolve on its own.

He took care of all the necessary charting and paperwork and shared the good news with her parents that her ovary was fine and she could actually go home in about an hour. He stopped by the Emergency Department to let Carol know how everything went, and she rewarded his favor with a big hug and kiss on the cheek. All that done, he walked out to the physicians' parking area behind the hospital and pulled away in his truck, now officially on sabbatical and free from work duties with his practice for the next four months.

*****

The Fontaine Cafe and Creperie was a consummate Old Town Alexandria establishment. It was a popular hangout for the young and trendy in the area and had excellent coffee and sweets along with occasional beer and wine tastings. The inside was fairly small, with pastel-colored walls and wooden tables and chairs and just the right type of music piped overhead to make you feel like you were on the cutting edge of intellectual hipsterness. The aroma was of coffee beans with hints of pastries and old wood.

Chip was pleased to see that Weinrib was already there and had a table. *Still the eager young reporter on the cusp of his breakout story.* He put his briefcase in a chair, draped his suit coat on the back, and looked at the reporter. "I'm going to get a drink. You need anything?"

"I'm good thanks."

He ordered a local microbrew that was currently featured and passed on any food. He mentally prepared to portray the Washington player who had been bested by the young upstart newsman. If people didn't possess vanity, his job would be orders of magnitude harder. He returned to the table and made a show of collapsing into the chair and sighing heavily.

"I tip my hat to you sir. You have put me up against the proverbial wall, and I guess I need to know if you're going to force my hand with this."

Matt had rehearsed how to answer this question, since he was sure that it would come. "Look Chip, I know you are torn about what to do with this, but I'm not blind to the fact that there is more than altruism making you want to turn this story loose. I know Haxton is one of the rising stars with the upcoming primaries should he choose to run, and you would play a big role in the campaign as well as on Pennsylvania Avenue if he wins. I appreciate your compliment, but it really didn't take a ton of work to arrive at this information, which means that someone else will make the connection pretty soon as well. In other words, it's coming out. You just have to decide if it comes out by someone who can work with you."

Matt thought the carrot he was dangling was a good one. *Let me be the one who breaks it and I'll give you a role in shaping the story.* He leaned back in his chair and sipped his Sierra Nevada Pale Ale and waited for a response.

"Fair point." *Let him think he's holding all the cards and that I'm eternally grateful for his benevolence.* He gave the reporter the impression that he had just been given an easier way out of his dilemma. "You would do that for me? I mean, you would be willing to work with me on this?"

"Of course I will Chip. You trusted me in the beginning to talk to about it. I owe you that much. I just might need some help on my end too." *Nothing's free in this town buddy.* "We can work on this tonight and tomorrow, but I want to put the story out in two days. Like I said, somebody else is going to make this connection before long, and it's better for you and me if it occurs on our own terms."

It took more than a little bit of effort not to smirk at this kid. He really thought he was the cock of the walk right now and that he was doing Chip the favor. He was sure that Weinrib believed his dick had grown at least two inches since this conversation began.

"You're probably right. How about this? We can go through the details tonight and you can sleep on it. I can't change my schedule tomorrow without raising suspicion, but we can get together for about an hour and a half late tomorrow morning. That gives you several hours to follow up anything and verify the facts, and I can help you as to how to do that fairly easily. Then you can call the Senator's office asking for a comment about the story that will come out the next day. That will go to me, since it's part of my job there. I'll go to Haxton to let him know that it's out and will give you a comment an hour or so after that. That way, you will be in way before the printing deadline."

"I'm OK with that—plus one more thing. I want an interview with Haxton before the medal presentation ceremony for a follow-up story, and he can't talk to anyone before my second story comes out. I don't want to see a sit-down spot with a cable TV reporter between my interview and the following morning. The printed press gets their asses kicked on scoops these days, and I don't want it to happen this time. You and I can sit down together after the interview to go over the broad strokes of the story after it's done. I think that's more than fair." Matt thought he was giving Chip the equivalent of a media blowjob with this offer.

"You've got yourself a deal," Chip said as he shook hands with the reporter across the table. It really did feel like his birthday and Christmas all together. He was going to offer Weinrib way more than that, but he was happy with the exclusive interview, and Chip was going to be able to damn near co-author the two stories. No reason to give him more, since any extras could be used to garner further favors either from him or another member of the press.

They spent about two hours talking about the ascent of the heroic Major Doctor Michael Reece courtesy of the Honorable James A. Haxton. Chip had worked on this earlier

143

today and walked Weinrib though the details and the timeline. He suggested that a good confirming source could be Theresa Williams at the Sycamore House, as well as another person he had spoken with already at Vanderbilt Academy. Weinrib was happy to hear that the photograph of Haxton and Reece he had found on his internet search was actually the property of the Senator and not the newspaper that had published the story, since Chip gave him a CD containing a digital copy of it along with some other supporting documents.

Once Weinrib felt he had enough information to shape the basic tenets of the story, they shook hands and parted ways, with the plan to meet up at ten the next morning at the Capitol Building Restaurant to tie up any loose ends. He didn't know, nor did Johnson for that matter, that the information didn't come close to giving a complete picture of the story.

As he watched Johnson head for the adjacent parking garage to go home, he went to a nearby sandwich shop to grab some takeout for the train ride to Herndon. It would be a long night of writing and he would need some food, not to mention a shitload of caffeine.

CHAPTER 12

The trembling had begun deep inside but was now working its way to the surface, and he could feel his own hands shaking as he sensed the weight of another's on his shoulder. He reached for the white-trimmed door frame. The air smelled of salt, but the back of his nose was burning from the stomach acid that was in his throat. There was nothing beyond the door for him, and the familiar sense of hopeless resignation began to return. The other hand squeezed gently and pulled him slightly back from the door.

The dark circular blur of the ceiling fan blades came into focus as his eyes jerked open. His frame of vision was blocked on the left side and it took him a moment to completely emerge from the drowsy haze of sudden awakening. It was a foot. Little Charlie's right foot rested on his shoulder and left cheek. Just above the ankle was the hem line of Star Wars pajama pants. He remembered sometime in the night his son coming in and asking to crawl in bed with them after a bad dream. He now lay sideways with his head resting on Anna's right side and Michael could hear the faint snore that only a small child's nose could make.

The dusty yellow glow of a nearly full moon was the only light making its way between the blinds of the bedroom, and the clock showed that sunrise was still about two hours away. He could feel the goose bumps on his shoulders as the breeze from the fan passed over his perspiration…sleep would not be coming back for him tonight.

He saw the large head of Tiny peer over the foot of the bed while he moved Charlie's leg and sat up. The massive family dog had taken up his nighttime watch there after his charge had come down to sleep with his parents. Michael slipped on his prosthesis and stepped over him on the way to the bathroom to relieve his bladder and splash some water on his face. Tiny formed up beside him as he came back through the bedroom and headed to the kitchen for a long pull on a cold bottled water.

After throwing on a hooded sweatshirt he headed out the back door onto the deck and onward into the backyard. By the time he had reached the water's edge, Tiny had taken care of his morning necessities and rejoined him. He sat down on the dock very close to where his picture had been taken just a few days ago, the moon giving enough light to see quite a distance. The gentle slapping of the water against the edge of the structure was the only sound in the predawn air. He slipped off his prosthesis and gazed at his leg while absently rubbing Tiny's back who was lounging at his right side.

The leg came to a blunted end about six inches below his knee. The reddish-purple scar went from the side of his knee down the stump and back up to the other, where the two flaps of muscle and skin had been brought together almost like the closing jaws of a Venus flytrap.

He remembered how it looked shortly before he blacked out in southern Afghanistan. A large chunk of tissue had been blasted away where the tumbling bullet had exited the inside of his calf, and the exposed end of his shattered tibia jutted out. The surrounding skin had a sickly pale bluish hue from the tourniquet that he had applied to himself above the knee. He had tried to periodically release the tension to give some oxygenated blood flow to his mangled lower leg, but the frightening velocity of the blood loss each time he did it made him stop trying. The initial white-hot pain after impact was gone after a while as the tissue began to die and shock set in.

The realization that he would probably lose his leg came around the same time that he started to believe that Manny was probably dying right in front of him. He remembered deciding that he would gladly give his leg up in order to keep the tourniquet tight and, therefore, himself conscious, giving the best change to continue to give aid to his wounded buddies.

Did he think clearly that last hour before the chopper came? Had his blood loss clouded his faculties impairing his ability to give the best care he could to Manny? If he had abandoned the chance of saving his own leg earlier, would he have thought of something else to keep him alive? The mangled leg that hung over the edge of the dock this morning represented his heroism to many around him, but to him it represented his failure. He had two men under his care during those hours, and one of them came home in a flag-draped box.

He began thinking about "The Soldier's Creed," which he was made to memorize during OBLC at Ft. Sam Houston a few years ago. He hadn't been told to recite it in some time, but it was still as fresh in his mind as it was at his graduation ceremony in Aabel Hall:

I am an American Soldier.

I am a Warrior and member of a team.

I serve the people of the United States and live the Army Values.

I will always place the mission first.

I will never accept defeat.

I will never quit.

I will never leave a fallen comrade.

I am disciplined, physically and mentally tough, trained and proficient in my warrior tasks and drills. I always maintain my arms, my equipment, and myself.

I am an expert and I am a professional.

I stand ready to deploy, engage, and destroy the enemies of the United States of America in close combat.

I am a guardian of freedom and the American way of life.

I am an American Soldier.

Had he quit? Had he left a fallen comrade? When others had spoken of his bravery and his heroism, he always thought about how afraid he had been that night. When he arrived at FOB Salerno, he had thought that his biggest fear would have been to be captured by the enemy who had no moral conflicts about how they would treat him. He had discovered that night as he kept his head low behind a rock sitting in his own blood as well as the blood of his friends that his biggest fear was failing them.

He remembered a low point in his recovery when he had become terribly frustrated with his failure to balance on his prosthesis. The next day he found an envelope in his room after physical therapy. It was from Tripp, and it simply said:

"Success consists of going from failure to failure without loss of enthusiasm." – Winston Churchill.

It was one of the countless times he had felt unworthy to be considered in the same group as Tripp and Torres.

David took time from his own grueling recovery to try to boost his spirits. Manny had jumped out of his vehicle without hesitation that night to try to protect his fellow soldiers. Now Manny was dead and David had to be his babysitter the next few weeks while everyone celebrated the heroism of Major Michael Reece.

He felt like he was walking on to glory while others were left behind. It was not the first time he had struggled with this dilemma. He sat in silence looking at the scar on his leg until the orange and pink hues on the eastern horizon foretold the impending sunrise.

*****

The echoing of countless fine leather shoes in the vast marble corridor allowed a degree of privacy for the two men in the midst of other public officials, reporters, tourists, as well as staff members. The tall, lean frame of Senator James Haxton strode with a regal confidence, nodding polite acknowledgement to those who took notice of him. Chip Johnson walked on his left side as he finished a conversation on his mobile phone. He tucked it into his inner suit jacket pocket and turned to the Senator.

"He's got it. Looks like he made the connection based on an Internet search regarding Sycamore House, and the old Wilmington article came up as a hit. I talked to Theresa Williams this morning and he had contacted her, as well as Dr. Phelps at Vanderbilt Academy. The broad strokes sound like it's a very positive piece, and he is giving us until mid-afternoon to make a comment if we want." He spoke succinctly and without flowering up the commentary, which was not only the Senator's preferred style but it served his purposes as well. "We should definitely make a comment but keep it brief, with deferment of credit away from you. I'll have a draft for you within the hour."

"Sounds good. I'm meeting Secretary Li for lunch, and let's touch base at the office when I get back. See if Sutton can be there too." He stopped and turned toward his staff member. "Remember, I don't want this to be a situation where we are breaking our arms trying to pat ourselves on the back."

"I agree. Trust me; you'll be happy with our statement."

Chip had already arranged for Sutton to be there since he spoke with him before the Senator. He gave Haxton the impression that he was talking with a source at the newspaper confirming that Weinrib had the story, when in actuality the phone had no one on the other end. When you're a campaign manager or communications director, handling your "principle" was as much a part of the job as interacting with the media. He knew how it needed to be played, but it would be an easier sell if the Senator believed it had been his own idea from the start.

Haxton was scheduled to be away from Washington in about a week and would be spending about ten days at his house on Figure Eight Island. Chip would probably be floating an idea of making an appearance in Asheville at the Sycamore House, but this wasn't the time to bring it up. He would let him bask in the warm glow of favorable press coverage, the most potent narcotic known for a politician. Once he began to see positive returns from this story, Chip would start Phase Two of the media campaign that would vault Haxton into the upcoming primaries as the frontrunner.

*****

Charlotte's favorite son and now war hero had a glamorous start to his sabbatical from work. After his early-morning rise and time with the dog, he made breakfast for Anna and the kids and drove carpool to summer camp. He then found himself alone, since Anna was uptown today at work. After about an hour of reading medical journals, he went for a run with Tiny, followed by a trip to the grocery store, where he stocked up on juice boxes and Lunchables, since school would begin soon.

Never one to enjoy being still, his restlessness took him into the yard, where he collected all of the family dog's gifts and put them in a garbage bag. *The life of a celebrity*...It was made all the more ironic as he saw Tiny take a huge dump in an area of the yard he had already cleaned. He didn't see staying grounded as being a big obstacle in the coming weeks. The front yard was a much easier task since the bulk of Tiny's outdoor time was in the back. He deposited his afternoon's work into the trash bin and walked down the driveway to get the day's mail.

There was the usual hodgepodge of junk mail, bills, and coupon collections among a few more personal items of correspondence. He had several cards addressed to him that were no doubt congratulatory notes from friends and close colleagues. There was also a thicker envelope from the Office of the Secretary of Defense that he had been told to expect, which would contain his itinerary for the days surrounding the upcoming presentation ceremony with the Commander in Chief. The final envelope was on personal stationary postmarked from Asheville, and the top of the return address said "T. Williams."

Michael came in the house and dropped all the mail except the letter from Asheville on the counter in between the kitchen and the den. He went through the back door and turned on the ceiling fan that was in the screened-in portion of the back deck. He dropped in a chair while Tiny filled up the couch beside him, and he opened the envelope.

Dear Michael,

I wanted to send you a note letting you know how proud I am of you. Not just for the things that have been on the news lately, but for the man you have become. Everyone here at Sycamore House has been excited to hear the news about you, and we are even happier that you have been able to recover from your injuries. You certainly look very handsome in your uniform as well.

Things here are going well. We have had some extra attention from reporters since the announcement of your award, and we have seen in increase in donations, which has been very nice. The children here are doing well, and we have added another full-time counselor to the staff as we have grown. We recently added two more rooms to the house, and one of the students at the local college helped us create a website. We have hung the large framed photograph of Charlie that you donated in the dining room, which is where I think he would have wanted it to be. It was very kind of you to do that.

You'll be happy to know that the child currently in your old room is doing well in school and has taken a liking to science; maybe he will become a doctor like you. His name is Travis and

150

we got him from Sylva where he had been taken from the home when both parents were incarcerated for selling drugs. So many lives have been destroyed by drugs, and many of them are people that were merely loved ones of others who became addicted. Some of our previous kids have been tangled up with them as well after they became adults. The Tyler boys had their troubles. Chris has seemed to have gotten away from that, but Darnell still struggles with addiction. There are many nights I worry I will get a phone call learning that something terrible has happened to him. Chris tried and tried to get him to come away with him, but he never would. Chris was at the coast the last time I heard from him, working odd jobs, and I'm happy that he seems to be away from drugs now. I've often wished that whatever light flickered to life in your spirit as a child would have done the same with them.

I want you to know that everyone here misses you and thinks of you often. I have loved and still do love you like you are my own child. Because of that love, I feel I should also be completely honest with you. I hope what I am about to write doesn't anger you. Maybe it will even be the thing that brings us together again.

I wish you would have tried harder to keep in contact with us here after you left for Chapel Hill. I have no doubt that your childhood still carries many difficult memories, and I have always defended your choice to make a clean break. But I feel like all the things that we had been through together and the relationships you had built here would have given you reasons to keep in touch. No one here is angry with your decision, but many including myself are confused and occasionally a little hurt by it.

As you know, most of the boys here have very little role models in their lives—especially men. I have always thought it would be a great help to have someone like yourself involved in these kids' lives, to show them that their possibilities are just as wide open as others who didn't have the challenges that they had. Chris and Darnell were really sad when you left, and it was very hard on them that you didn't keep in touch. I can't help but wonder if their lives would have been a little easier as young adults had they continued to have some of your influence in their lives.

Don't get me wrong, Michael. I do not think it is your fault that they had the troubles that they did after leaving Sycamore House. They made many bad choices that put them in bad situations, and they were their choices, not yours. You are not their father, and your contact may not have made any difference. But I always thought you should have tried harder. They always looked up to you.

I hope that, in time, our paths may cross again and that you don't think that my sharing this with you means that I have any anger in my heart for you. I love you as much today as I did the day you were brought to me as a child, and I will always be waiting for you with open arms should you ever want to visit. Remember that the Book of Romans says, "Welcome one another, therefore, just as Christ has welcomed you, for the glory of God."

I hope this letter finds you and your family well, and always know that you have a family here as well who loves you with all of their hearts.

I love you,

Theresa

The coolness of the tears on his face was a stark contrast to the warm summer air as he sat there for a while staring at the letter he had just read. He wasn't angry. He could never be angry at the woman who had played the role of his mother more than anyone he had ever known since the death of his own. Instead of anger he felt shame. He thought of Chris and Darnell and remembered their tears the day he had left for college, never to return. *I will never leave a fallen comrade...*

The screened-in area on the deck was beginning to give him a feeling of claustrophobia, and he felt his pulse quicken along with his breathing. He got up and walked outside, going across the backyard in no particular direction. The humidity in the air seemed to be rising precipitously by the second, and his legs felt weak. He reached the boat dock and began shaking, the air seeming to him like a wet oven. He barely had enough time to react when he dropped to his knees and began to retch over the side of the dock, spilling his breakfast into the water below. He wiped the vomit from his chin and the string of snot from his nose and sat back on the wooden dock boards, making an effort to slow down his breathing and prevent another wave of nausea.

She was right. He should have done more, and he owed them more than he had given to them since he had gone away. He made a promise to himself that he would reach out to her. It wouldn't begin to make up for his absence over the years, but it would be a start.

*****

Matt Weinrib opened his email account and saw a message from Chip that was titled "Official Comment." He clicked on the item to open it:

Matt,

I've attached the official comment from Haxton. Call me after you review it. He's fine with the interview as well, but it will need to be early morning at his office tomorrow before the day's session starts. He will certainly be asked about it tomorrow and wants you to have the chance to do your interview first.

The Senator and I both appreciate your professionalism with this, and I won't forget everything you did. You're a good man Matt, and I owe you one.

Chip

Matt grinned at the computer monitor. *You're damned right you owe me.* He filled out a small notched card with Chip's contact information, affixed it in the "J" section of his Rolodex, and moved it to the center of his desk. He was sure it already felt heavier than it did yesterday. He opened the attached document and read the comment, which was pretty much what he expected. It expressed happiness that someone had benefited from some of his charitable work, but it deferred all the credit to Reece himself. He grabbed his bag with his laptop, which contained the draft of his article, and headed away from the cubicle farm that was his work address to one of the actual offices that had a door and even a window. It was time to see the Political Editor.

*****

Michael and Anna finished packing up bags for Elizabeth and Charlie, including the stuffed UNC ram that Charlie slept with every night regardless of where that was. They each put

153

together an "entertainment bag" of books and DVDs for the ride to Washington, DC. They would be leaving in the morning with Walt and Tina, who were taking vacation time to show the kids around the nation's capital. They would meet back up with Mom and Dad for the White House ceremony. Keeping them calm before a trip with the grandparents was difficult, mainly because "no" was a word they hardly ever heard from Papa and Mimi.

Michael and Anna had reviewed the schedule that had been sent from the Pentagon: they would be leaving for Fayetteville tomorrow to spend two days at Ft. Bragg and then flying up to Andrews Air Force Base along with SFC Tripp and COL Tyson. There would be a reception at the Pentagon the day after they arrived, followed by the White House ceremony the next day, which would also be followed by a press conference and a reception. He would actually have a brief one-on-one chat with the President in the White House before the Pentagon reception. Michael had been informed that two full sets of Army Dress Blue uniforms had been put together for him on base at Bragg, and he would make sure the fit was good when he got there.

He had received the list of attendees at the presentation ceremony, including the ones he had requested to be there. It included Anna, Tripp, Giselle Torres, Tyson, Walt and Tina, Elizabeth, and Little Charlie. There would also be a few close friends that he had served with at FOB Salerno, as well as members of the medical and recovery team that had taken care of him while he recovered. There would be other dignitaries from the military and political world, including Secretary Dietz, whom he had really taken a liking to when they had met a few days earlier. He was friendly and easy to be around and seemed to have an exceptionally low capacity for bullshit.

He was happy that the roster seemed to be weighted in favor of military personnel instead of politicians. It hadn't taken him long after graduating at Ft. Sam Houston to know that he had made a good decision. He simply loved the Army and everything that it represented. His duties and deployments had allowed him to meet some of the most exceptional people he had ever known. He had also known soldiers who were young and without direction and sometimes in trouble before enlisting who had become admirable professionals sure of success either in the military or in the civilian world when they chose to leave the Army. He had formed bonds with others while deployed "downrange" that were more a brotherhood than a collection of friends. They had shared experiences in the ugly world of combat that others could never understand. Serving in the Reserves while having a separate civilian job and life had its challenges, but Michael was certain that his experiences in uniform had made him a better man. He felt what he had given to the Army paled in comparison to what the Army had given him.

They loaded the kids' bags in Walt's car and followed them to dinner at Firebird's restaurant in the Northlake area of Charlotte, which was about halfway between the West and Reece homes. After dropping off the ladies and the kids, Michael and Walt parked their cars and walked to the restaurant. Walt patted Michael on the back.

"You doing OK, Mike?"

"Yeah, I'm doing fine. It's still a little overwhelming, but I'll hit my stride."

"I know you will." Walt reached in his pocket and handed something to Michael. "Mike, this is my Dad's dog tag that he wore in the Pacific with the First Marine Division. He managed to survive two brutal years of combat, including Okinawa. He would never talk about his experiences with me or anyone else that hadn't been over there, and I know he struggled with bad memories for the rest of his life. I can't comprehend what it is like to be in situations like that, but I do know that he would have been proud for his granddaughter to have married a man like you. I want you to have this if you will, because you understand the significance of it far more than I ever will. I want you to know that Tina and I are very proud of you too, and this honor you will be getting will only allow the rest of the world to know what we already do."

"Thanks Walt." They embraced and headed into the restaurant, where Little Charlie had already gotten Tina to allow him to have a Dr. Pepper despite the furrowed brow of his mother. In the end, Anna knew that her parents would have to deal with the aftereffects of a big caffeinated soda in a young boy at their house, so she chose not to fight this battle. Elizabeth slid up next to Walt, who had absolutely no backbone when it came to his own granddaughter, and Michael had a feeling that Papa would be coaxed into going to the adjoining shopping mall after dinner.

They enjoyed a family dinner with lots of laughter and very little thought to the gravity of what would be happening in a few short days. The normalcy that had been absent for a while seemed to make a brief reappearance in their lives. Either no one had recognized him in the restaurant or they had respected their family privacy, since the only recognition of the specialness of what was happening to Michael came when the manager informed the table that the meal was on the house, in gratitude of his service, and he would never be allowed to pay for another meal at the restaurant again. Walt noticed the bottom portion of a US Marine globe and anchor tattoo under his partially rolled-up left sleeve.

They had their goodbye hugs outside the restaurant instead of by the cars, since Walt told everyone that Elizabeth needed to make a "couple of stops" in the mall before they left; she grinned like a cat with a canary feather peeking out of her mouth. Charlie was lobbying Mimi for ice cream, which was sure to be a successful effort. Michael and Anna made the usual parental last-minute instructions for the kids to behave and not argue with each other and then walked hand-in-hand to their car, enjoying the warm Carolina summer evening air.

The drive home was short, and they heard the bellowing bark of Tiny as the garage door started its upward roll. Michael kissed Anna, took Tiny for a short walk, and found two glasses of cabernet poured when he made it back. They sipped wine and watched a movie on the large, soft, leather couch in the den until the day and the wine began to make them tired.

Tiny stretched out in front of the couch for the night since Little Charlie's room was empty. Michael slipped into bed while Anna finished up in the bathroom. The slight moonlight silhouetted her as she opened the door, enough for Michael to see that she was wearing something silky and alluring. She slipped under the covers and into his arms and they shared a prolonged kiss. She ran her fingers through his short hair.

"You might belong to the Army tomorrow for a few days, but tonight you belong to me."

Their kisses became more passionate and purposeful as she rolled on top of him. She used her feet to push his gym shorts down his legs and off. She sat up and slowly pulled the silk short gown over her head, revealing her fit and naked body. She could feel under her that she was having the intended effect on him, and she bent down to kiss him again while he slowly moved his hips upward and they became one. They made love with no effort to conceal their vocal expressions of pleasure since the house was empty. Afterward, he fell asleep with his beautiful wife in his arms and enjoyed a rare but wonderful dream-free night of slumber.

CHAPTER 13

"If there are no objections, I think this would be a good time to call a two-hour recess. We will restart at one thirty. All in favor," the Chairman of the Senate Appropriations Committee said toward the microphone in front of him while looking to each side of him.

"Aye," was the collective response from the committee.

"This committee stands in recess." Senator James Haxton clapped the gavel in front of him, and the rustling of staffers and Senators began to fill the room. Today had been a hearing on the upcoming budget estimates for the Department of Health and Human Services. Overall, the hearing so far had been without contention, which was a fairly rare occurrence in this town, especially when it came to budgetary matters. He knew that would be different this afternoon when they would be discussing the proposed funding for several pilot programs across the nation that would provide contraceptive counseling to high school students on a one-on-one basis and would not require parental consent.

It would not be a productive afternoon session. Both sides had sent out their talking points to the masses via the media, more to stir up debate than inform. As with most circumstances in Washington, the talking points from both sides were long on rhetoric and fairly short on accuracy. Haxton had been accused of coming between parents and their teen children, and his associates had fired back by declaring the other side was participating in a war on young women. Being at the top of the Senatorial pyramid, he was able to stay above the fracas more often than not and let the junior Senators or staffers lob the salvos in the never-ending public perception war. He looked at the agenda and saw the list of those scheduled to speak this afternoon that had been chosen from each side of the debate. Their selection and what they intended to say was more for media highlights than actually aiding in the achievement of a solution.

He stood from his comfortable leather chairman's seat and headed to the Senators Only washroom. A junior staffer gathered his materials, as senior public officials should not be required to do something as common as carry their own things. He looked over his face and hair as he washed his hands and was met by Chip upon exiting.

He had already read the article in *The Washington Post* this morning and had done the face-to-face interview with the young upstart reporter at his office. His remarks were as vanilla and prepared as any such exchange in this town, which was fine with Chip. The morning's article had basically been a canonization piece on the Senator, and bland remarks in the interview would assure that the follow-up story would not alter that theme. The Senator had performed perfectly in the role of the benevolent leader who had used his status and wealth to lift up others so that they may bask in the warm light of American opportunity just as he had. He was consistently deferential when asked about his role in the life of Major Reece and said that the young man's achievements were the result of hard work and that the credit lied with him alone. The Senator was happy to see good things happen to good people and was overjoyed with the accolades Reece was receiving, but he himself deserved no credit. He exuded a sort of regal "aw shucks" attitude that the readers (i.e., voters) would absolutely love.

Chip had scheduled a press conference outside the hearing room "to discuss developments in the budgetary debate." He knew full well that there would be little if any questions on the bland drivel that had been discussed that morning, but the reporters would be aware of the *Post* story and it would be another opportunity to be mentioned in connection with America's feel-good story of the week. He watched the Senator's tall frame take his place behind the podium with the backdrop of young staffers and American flags behind him.

Haxton cleared his throat and bent the microphone holder to a more upward angle toward his face. "The Appropriations Committee hearings this morning were another fruitful step toward shaping a federal budget that will serve the needs of the American people and show the needed fiscal restraint that is expected by our constituents. I am grateful to my fellow committee members and our invited guests for their work this morning, and I look forward to a productive session this afternoon as well. I do have a few minutes to take a couple of questions if you have any."

Chip knew he would take as many questions as would be asked, as long as the subject matter would be this morning's *Post* story.

"Senator Haxton, Pete Frederickson, NBC News," was the remark from the reporter in the front who had timed his question to start a little sooner than the others. "There is a story in today's *Washington Post* that describes your relationship with an orphanage in your home state called the Sycamore House. This is also the home where Major Michael Reece grew up, who will receive the Medal of Honor this week. It suggests that you were influential in helping rescue the child. Do you care to comment?"

"First of all, Happy Birthday Pete," Haxton said with a smile. The reporter looked like he had been given a new puppy. "It is true that Major Reece lived at the Sycamore House starting at a young age. The details of his life that led him there I believe are private. It is also true that I have long had the privilege of supporting the Sycamore House financially and occasionally with my time. I have been honored to be the Chairman of the Board of Trustees for several years now. Let me be clear, the credit for the monumental achievements that Michael has attained is due to him and to the wonderful staff and volunteers at Sycamore House."

Chip grinned to himself when he saw the reaction of the reporter to the birthday wishes. He had alerted his boss to that fact this morning after learning that Fredrickson would be at the press conference, but the skill with which it was delivered by Haxton is what had won him every election he had ever been on the ballot. Working for someone as smooth as the Senator made his job a lot easier. He was also happy to hear him refer to Reece as "Michael," which was Chip's idea to subconsciously convey a personal relationship between the two of them without actually claiming one existed.

"Senator, Maggie Reaves from *Politico*. The story references a feature in a local newspaper that describes a much closer relationship between the two of you, and it includes a picture of the two of you together."

"I'm not saying that I didn't know Michael. I knew him well and I am very proud of him. He was an exceptionally smart child who gained a lot of success once he was brought to Sycamore House. I met him several times and even took him to my house on the coast to meet some alumni of my own high school who were very interested in having Michael enter as a new student. Alas, he chose another school in Asheville, which is also an excellent institution, despite our best efforts to sway the young man. This goes to show you that I can't get my way all the time…" This was followed by scattered chuckles from the reporters. "I just want everyone to understand that Michael is his own man. His achievements are extraordinary and should be celebrated, but they are *his* achievements, and for me to take any credit for his success would be a disrespect to his hard work."

Reaves raised her hand. "Senator, a follow-up question if you don't mind. Public financial records for the Sycamore House show that your monetary contributions have been substantial over the years. Do you plan to continue that support?"

"I certainly will Maggie. Look, I have been blessed with a degree of financial success that allows me to do things like this. I believe that those of us who have been fortunate have an obligation to help others who may not have had a fair shake in life." He grasped the sides of the podium and took a deep breath to let the audience know that he was about to convey something important. "As many of you know, I never had any children and I lost the love of my life to cancer many years ago. I try to support as many good causes as I can, but I won't deny that children's charities and cancer research have certainly been high on my list of attention. The Book of Matthew contains one of my favorite guiding principles: 'I tell you the truth, whatever you did for one of the least of these brothers of mine, you did for me.' Success brings responsibility, and I am just trying to do my fair share. That being said, Maggie, it wasn't my checkbook that made Michael the exceptional man he is. It was his own drive and hard work, and that is what we should be applauding."

"Senator, Will Stackhouse from CNN. Will you be going to the presentation ceremony at the White House?"

"I will not be going to the ceremony. That day is about Michael's heroism and the countless sacrifices of our men and women in uniform. I don't want my presence there to be any distraction from that."

"Terri Daniels from *USA Today*, Senator. Do you expect the issues of contraceptive counseling pilot programs to be discussed this afternoon, and do you feel that this will be an obstacle to gaining a majority for a budgetary vote?"

"I'm not sure if that will be discussed today, Terri, but I'm sure we can have a civil and productive discussion of whatever comes before the committee."

That was Chip's cue, and he stepped up to the podium microphone. "I'm sorry, but the Senator has other engagements he is due for."

Haxton raised his hand up to the reporters. "Thanks everyone. Have a good day."

When they had reached a safe distance from reporters and microphones, Chip patted Haxton on the back. "Jesus, sir. You are like Michelangelo up there sometimes."

"It's easy when it's true Chip."

The down-home humility that Haxton exuded on the subject was exactly what Chip wanted, but this would be an obstacle for the next phase of his plan for elevating his boss to the nation's most trusted and admired father figure. His next planned move would be a gamble that could potentially anger the Senator, but it could also be the cherry on the sundae in terms of PR gold.

*****

The Army Combat Uniform (ACU) was Michael's preferred military attire. It was the uniform of the deployed warrior, not to mention it was a hell of lot more comfortable than the others. His fondest memories in the Army were times where he was taking care of soldiers downrange, where you might not have the creature comforts in life but you were part of a brotherhood comprised of less than 1 percent of the nation's population. During those times, he wasn't "ribboned up" but was wearing his ACU—usually with a thin coat of dust all over it.

On the middle of his chest was a square patch with a golden oak leaf signifying his rank of Major. His right breast had his last name tab, and his left had "U.S. Army" over his heart. His left shoulder had the unit patch of the 332nd Medical Brigade, who he went to drill with one weekend a month, and on his right shoulder was the unit patch of the Eighty-Second Airborne. Soldiers could only "right shoulder" a unit patch if they had been deployed with them. Having a right shoulder patch was a symbol of "been there, done that" for soldiers in uniform. The only other attachment to his ACU was the Combat Action Badge, which was pinned on his upper left chest. Although he proudly displayed the Eighty-Second Airborne patch on his right shoulder, he did not have the Airborne badge since, he had not completed parachute training, which included five jumps at Ft. Benning, Georgia.

The Combat Action Badge is an oak wreath surrounding a bayonet and a grenade. Recipients must have been assigned to a unit where hostile fire pay or imminent danger pay is authorized, and the soldier must have been personally present and actively engaged with or being engaged by enemy forces and must have performed satisfactorily under the rules of war. It was a badge that the vast majority of Army physicians never received, and it was one of the many accolades that Michael had earned that night in Afghanistan.

As he pinned the badge on his shirt, he thought of a letter to the editor at the local paper that had been written in response to an article about his return home from combat. The author had claimed that Michael's actions had been inconsistent with his Hippocratic Oath that he had taken as a physician, which included the motto "premum non nocere": first do no harm. The letter writer followed that with a lecture on the evil of the actions of the US military and the call for all doctors to refuse to serve in combat. He was happy to see the following day a guest editorial written by the Chairman of the North Carolina Medical Board, Dr. Alexander Bradley, who eloquently explained that nothing Michael had done had been in violation of his duties as a physician and that the Hippocratic Oath did not exclude one from defending himself or others from those who meant to kill them, and it ended with a plea not to politicize the American soldier.

He made sure his uniform was squared away and put on his spare prosthesis on which he kept a combat boot. He tucked his wool beret in his right cargo pocket of his pants and grabbed his and Anna's bags to put in the truck. He got the usual approving smile from his wife when he came out of the bedroom. She made no mystery about the fact that, like most of the ladies, she really liked a man in uniform.

They gave contact phone numbers to Tricia's daughter Kristen, who would be staying at the house taking care of Tiny and checking the mail. The college sophomore thought it was a great gig to stay at a house much nicer than her meager apartment, not to mention that it earned her some extra cash. They gave a little love to the family dog and headed out toward Fayetteville and Ft. Bragg, dialing Tripp's mobile number as they pulled out to let him know they were leaving.

The drive to the southeastern portion of the state was pleasant, and they arrived at the Reilly Gate of Ft. Bragg in the mid-afternoon. It didn't take long to realize that he would be the focus of attention again as he pulled up to the post entry control point (ECP). There the Reeces were met by the Lt. Gen. Ray Brown, Command Sergeant Major Billy Danowicz, and Tripp. All three snapped to attention and gave crisp salutes as Michael exited the truck. He returned their salutes, feeling quite awkward being saluted by the two commanders of the entire post.

"Major Reece, Mrs. Reece, my name is Lieutenant General Ray Brown and I'm the commanding General here at Ft. Bragg. This is Command Sergeant Major Danowicz, and you all know Sergeant First Class Tripp. It is an honor to have you here as our guest."

Handshakes were exchanged, and Michael replied, "The honor is mine, sir. I appreciate all of you taking the time out of your day to meet me here. This is my wife, Anna."

Anna noticed the lingering handshake between her husband and CSM Danowicz, which was followed by an embrace. She kissed Tripp on the cheek and made the connection. "David, is he the one who wrote the letter?"

David nodded. "He sure is."

Billy Danowicz was nothing short of a legend in the Airborne Division. The grandson of Polish immigrants from Chicago, he had enlisted in the Army right out of high school and had risen through the enlisted ranks quickly due to his skills as a paratrooper as well as a leader. He had earned a Silver Star in the first Gulf War, for gallantry under fire, and had collected a second one in Baghdad for rescuing a fellow soldier from a burning vehicle while sustaining his own wounds in the process. He had a short but powerful stature, with a severely cropped haircut and a black patch over his left eye—another result of his heroism in Iraq. He had

164

graduated with distinction from both the Airborne and Ranger courses and was highly respected by anyone who had the pleasure to serve with him.

He was also the author of a long handwritten letter that had been delivered to Michael when he was starting the long road to recovery at Walter Reid Army Medical Center. It had arrived when Reece was at a low point. No one but Michael knew what the letter said, but Anna remembered that it had represented a turning point for him, and he kept the letter with him always during the long days of physical and occupational therapy. She still had not read the contents but knew that it remained folded in the family Bible at home; he would read it frequently. One man scarred by war had reached out to another and had really made a difference. Anna liked him immediately and rewarded him with a kiss on the cheek after they shook hands.

A staff member from the Provost Marshall moved their bags into a GMC Yukon and took their own vehicle to be kept at the command building. They would have their own driver and vehicle during their stay as "Distinguished Visitors." After bidding goodbye to Danowicz and Brown, Tripp accompanied the couple to the Sink Distinguished Visitors House on post. The beautifully furnished VIP guest house had an assortment of drinks and food along with a welcome letter from the Lodging Office. Outside, a light blue flag with the thirteen stars of the Medal of Honor flew by the front door. Michael felt overwhelmed at the attention and VIP designation.

"Well, Anna and I love the place," Tripp said with a grin and his arm around her. "But, where are you staying, sir?"

"Shut up," Michael said with a chuckle.

After unpacking and freshening up, they were taken to the post uniform store, where he tried on both sets of formal Army dress blue uniforms to ensure they were a good fit. Tripp reviewed Michael's DA 2-1 form, which chronicled his Army career and had a list of all decorations and badges that he had earned. This list was compared to the rows of ribbons on the left breast of the uniform to make sure they were accurate. He had no doubt they were, since a representative from Human Resources Command had contacted the uniform store and done the same a few days ago, but it was in David's nature as a Senior NCO to make sure everything was squared away as it should be. The ribbon rack had three rows of three ribbons each, and the fourth row contained his Purple Heart and Silver Star ribbons. The tailor made sure the neck line was symmetrical, since there would be a light blue medal draped around it in a few days.

Tripp nodded his approval after giving him the look over. "Nice collection sir."

"Thanks," Michael replied, although he knew Tripp's was far more extensive and, at least to Michael, far more impressive. He received a wink from Anna, who was very pleased with his appearance, although it was still hard for her to watch things like when they made sure the polished black left shoe was able to fit onto his prosthesis. He went back to the changing room to put his ACU back on.

David noticed the slight reflection of suppressed tears at the lower margins of Anna's eyes, and he put his enormous arm around her. "Hard not to be proud of him isn't it?"

"You're going to look after him through this aren't you?" Anna knew the answer to this already, but she felt her protective instinct toward her husband being awakened at the moment.

"You know I will. I know everyone sees him as a very loving and gentle guy, and I know he can be a little gullible sometimes, but believe me, he is one tough bastard when he has to be. I've seen it firsthand. But don't worry; I would do anything for that man. Between the two of us, we'll keep him clear of anything."

Anna went to the souvenir area of the store to look for something for the kids while David waited for Michael to come out. It was a fun tradition for them to look for some small gift for the kids whenever they traveled without them, although Anna thought they would probably have a car full of stuff from their grandparents when this trip was over.

Contrary to what many civilians think, a significant portion of uniform expenses for Army Reserve officers is out of pocket. There is a one-time four-hundred dollar stipend for this, but it usually doesn't cover everything required. All gear and clothing for deployments was provided by the Army, but the usual requirements for normal drill activities, such as ACU uniforms, PT uniforms, and boots, could easily exceed the stipend. Because of this, Michael knew that this would be a pretty penny today. However, when he got to the register at the store, he was informed that the uniforms were compliments of a grateful United States Army, and any other items purchased today were the personal compliments of General Brown.

"Don't argue with a General sir," Tripp said as he saw Michael about to protest this token of appreciation.

They thanked the staff who had helped him with the uniform and left the store. After loading the items in the Yukon, they decided they were hungry and would head back into the mini mall area where there was a food court. They invited Specialist Thomas Newton, their driver, to come with them. Michael told Tripp and Newton that lunch was his treat and he could make that an order if he had to. They offered no argument and took up position to Michael's left and slightly ahead. Through the parking lot Michael returned the salutes of the enlisted soldiers and junior officers that crossed his path. Anna noticed several double-taking and talking to each other after they walked by her husband.

The food court was similar to any other you would see in a small mall, with an assortment of eateries such as Burger King, Taco Bell, and Great Steak and Potato. Michael decided to take advantage of his adoration today and ordered a Whopper with Cheese with fries. Anna decided not to give him grief about it; hero or not, he did have high cholesterol.

Several soldiers at the Food Court recognized Michael and gave him words of encouragement or shook his hand. He even had three autograph requests, which seemed surreal. They enjoyed their lunch, and he decided to stop by the post barber to get a fresh haircut, since he would be addressing the Eighty-Second Airborne tomorrow and wanted to look sharp. They wound down the evening by having drinks at the Sink Guest House. Tripp had an apartment just outside Ft. Bragg, which was his assigned post, but he would be staying with the Reece family at their insistence. Besides, Michael said he wouldn't have anyone to drink bourbon with that night if Tripp didn't stay.

*****

Chris Tyler had spoken to his supervisor at Lowe's and explained that he had a family emergency back in Asheville and would need a few days off to take care of a few things. He promised to be back within a week, apologized for the inconvenience of a sudden request for time off, and promised to return as soon as circumstances allowed.

Blake Davenport was the floor supervisor and assured Chris that he would take care of getting his shifts covered. He knew Chris was a bit of a drifter with a somewhat checkered past, but he liked him a lot. Davenport had hired him after speaking with a local contractor, Jimmy Hardy, who had to cut back employees due to the sinking housing economy. Jimmy was well known to Blake, since he was a frequent customer who bought a lot of his materials from the store for his business. Jimmy was also a member of his church and someone who was respected in the small community of Shallotte. He had told Blake that he had let Chris go because of slumping business and not because he was a bad employee. He explained that Chris had been a hard worker who never complained and always showed up to work on time. Jimmy saw his employees as family and wanted to find something for Chris since he could no longer keep him on with his business. Hardy asked Blake to see if there was any work at the store Chris could do.

Having Jimmy Hardy vouch for someone certainly made up for any concerns about lack of experience or employment references, and Blake had hired him the next day. Chris had been exactly the person that Jimmy had described. He was hard-working and reliable, and he had shown an excellent knowledge base about building materials. Blake was a firm believer that you could be smart even if you weren't educated, and Chris was a perfect example of that. He had never missed a shift and never asked for any preferences when the schedule was made.

"Chris, it's not a problem. Rest assured, your job will be here when you get back," Davenport said. "Family should always come first. Call me if there is anything I can do for you while you're out of town."

"I appreciate it Mr. Davenport. I will let you know as soon as I'm back in town. I'll leave after my shift tomorrow, if that's OK."

Blake assured him that would be fine, and they shook hands. He didn't know much about Chris's past, but he thought it was likely that he had gone through some tough times. He didn't know what the family emergency was and it didn't really matter. Chris was a good man and a hard worker and would never use something as an excuse to slack off.

Chris left a voicemail on the phone number Darnell had given him and told him that he would be in town in a couple of days. He prayed that his brother was trying to stay clean since they had spoken on the phone. He also planned to reach out to Mrs. Theresa to see what would be the best option for getting and keeping his brother clean. One thing was certain: getting him the hell out of Asheville and away from his low-life friends would have to be part of the plan.

He stopped his lighter several inches from the unlit cigarette in his mouth as he noticed the tip quivering. He found himself fighting back tears. For the first time in as long as he could remember, he thought he had a real chance to get his brother back. Chris leaned against the gray brick of the backside of the building alone in the employee smoking area. His eyes closed with the unlit cigarette still in his mouth, he began to pray for his brother.

*****

The air was humid but not yet oppressively hot at the Airborne Corps parade grounds. Always one to be a little hot-natured, Reece was thankful that the uniform of this morning's ceremony was the ACU. He walked along a line of impeccably turned-out Airborne soldiers, along with General Butts, Secretary Winters, CSM Danowicz, Colonel Tyson, and Sergeant First Class David Tripp. This was the traditional reviewing of the troops that distinguished members would do with the unit commander on occasion. Reece suppressed a smile at the idea of him being the one to review the troops, as he always looked for the silent nod from Tripp that his own uniform was in good order.

Many of the soldiers looked very young to Michael as they stood in line snapping perfect salutes at the party of dignitaries walking by. He wondered if Manny Torres had been in one of these lines before that fateful night. The fact that the vast majority of the young soldiers he saw had right shoulder patches signifying a combat deployment was a sign of the times they were currently living in. He wondered how many of them would be leaving again in the near future.

They stepped up to the stage area and stood in front of their seats as General Butts went before the podium.

"At ease!" declared General Butts.

"Airborne!" was the collective response from the men below as they shifted to parade rest posture.

Along with the American, Army, and Airborne flags, a red flag with three stars reflecting the presence of the commanding general gently flapped in front of the stage. The Second Battalion (Airborne), 325th Infantry Regiment was the front and center unit of the audience, which pleased Michael since that was his unit downrange. Several other Airborne units stood in formation to the sides and the rear of them in the mid-morning sun.

General Butts welcomed those gathered and called for the presentation of the colors. The entire group of soldiers present snapped to attention in unison as the colors were presented. The Eighty-Second Airborne chorus sang the national anthem, and Michael remembered seeing them as a child in an elementary school performance once a long time ago. The group returned to parade rest positions as Butts returned to the podium.

"Today we are here to celebrate the recognition of one of our own. All of you present know the story by now of Major Michael Reece. He is not just a great soldier and a great American, but he is a great Airborne soldier."

"Hoooaahhh!" echoed from the men in attendance, eliciting smiles from all on the stage.

"He will be heading to Washington tomorrow to meet with our Commander in Chief and receive the Medal of Honor, which is the highest recognition that can be bestowed upon a soldier in the United States military. His heroism went far beyond the call of duty, and were it not for his actions, Sergeant First Class David Tripp would not be with us on this stage today. His quick and decisive actions reflect the best traditions of the United States Army, especially the Eighty-Second Airborne."

"HOOOAHHHH!"

"I now ask Colonel Greg Tyson to step forward for the formal reading of Major Reece's citation."

There were many shouts of admiration as Tyson stepped to the podium. He was a beloved Commander of his unit and had a long career of leading by example. He read the official citation in his booming baritone voice that made the microphone in front of him quite unnecessary. Thunderous applause followed, and SFC Tripp was called to the podium.

"My brother paratroopers, today we are all honored to stand with a man who has done us all very proud. I am the man that General Butts referred to who wouldn't be here today if it wasn't for the actions of Major Reece. I was with him the night described in the citation. There are many of you out there who have engaged the enemy, and there are many of you out there who have given life-saving aid to a wounded soldier. I stand up here with a man that did both things at the same time, all the while cut off from reinforcements and all alone. I remember his words of encouragement to me and his courage. I remember him pushing me behind cover while exposing himself to enemy fire. But more than that, I remember a soldier that I had grown to admire long before he did the things described by Colonel Tyson."

Tripp was an admired member of the unit who was still stationed there, and he had the rapt attention of the soldiers in front of him.

"I have had the privilege of getting to know Major Reece as a fellow soldier downrange and later as a friend. He is a man who felt the call to serve when it would have been far easier to enjoy his civilian life. He was willing to give his time, his skills, and even his life if necessary in the service of our nation. I have seen him perform miracles in the operating room with wounded soldiers, and I've also seen him painfully limp along the hallways of Walter Reed to check on fellow wounded soldiers while enduring severe pain of his own. I have seen him as a devoted husband and father. In short, I am honored to have served with him, and I am even more honored to be his friend. Today I am proud to present Major Michael Reese: friend, father, husband, Medal of Honor winner, but most importantly...an Airborne soldier!"

The parade grounds erupted with cheers and applause and "Hoooaahs." Michael was using all his abilities to fight back tears as he stepped up to the podium and returned the salute of Sergeant First Class David Tripp. He then embraced him as the brother that he had become...military protocol be damned. He faced the audience and nodded his gratitude. It was over three minutes before the cheers died down enough for him to speak.

"I am deeply honored and humbled at the words spoken here today. I want to thank everyone up on the stage today for treating my wife and I so well here at Ft. Bragg. I want to especially thank Command Sergeant Major Danowicz, who was an inspiration to me while I recovered from my wounds."

Applause and cheers along with chants of "Dano! Dano! Dano!" finally made the Command Sergeant Major stand and acknowledge the crowd who thought the world of him.

"I also want to thank my dear friend and brother Sergeant First Class Tripp who has taught me more about being a soldier than anyone I have had the pleasure of knowing. I know there are many of you out there today who know Sergeant Tripp and have served with him either stateside or downrange, so you will appreciate the fact that we have witnessed history today. Just a few moments ago, we heard the longest number of consecutive sentences ever said by him at an Army installation that didn't contain a curse word of some kind."

Colonel Tyson's booming laughter could be heard over the others sharing in the humor.

"I look out here today and see the faces of many whom I had the honor to serve with overseas, and I realize, with a heavy heart, that many of you will be going again soon. I am grateful to all of you who allowed me to stand among you and be treated as one of you. Your professionalism, courage, and skill will always be a source of great inspiration to me, and the memories of serving with you are things I will cherish for the rest of my life. I stand before you indeed honored, but truthfully also quite humbled given the fact that I am being celebrated for performing deeds that I have witnessed many of you out there do on almost a daily basis without all the ceremony and praise. Because of that fact, I want you all to know that when I receive this honor, I accept it as a representative of all of you, especially those who, as President Lincoln described, gave their 'last full measure of devotion,' oftentimes in lands far away and without the recognition of a public preoccupied with far less important matters.

"I have been asked countless times in the past several days what made me do what I did that night. If I were to be completely honest, I would say that I really don't know. Our training and, more importantly, our brotherhood condition us to make decisions that others will never understand. My fear of the enemy was far eclipsed by the fear of not doing everything I could for my brothers beside me. I would like to believe that I assessed the situation and saw that we were heavily outnumbered, and I made the conscious decision to protect my men and give the fight back to the enemy. In truth, however, I'm not really sure how much thinking I actually did. I simply reacted. I think that is why I struggle with the idea of me being celebrated for some innate specialness as a soldier. I stand before you today knowing that there is nothing inside me that has pushed me to do heroic things. I was simply put in a position to have to do things that could be dangerous or even deadly, and my training allowed me to do it.

"I am completely at ease with the fact that I am unabashedly ordinary. Any specialness that I have has been the result of the Army—more specifically, having the opportunity to work and live around soldiers like all of you. The transformation that can occur from experiencing the training and life of a soldier is hard to put into words, but I am a better man for wearing this uniform, because this uniform represents what the Army has given me, and it has been far greater than any service I have given back.

"I want all of you to know that whatever opportunities or ceremonies that are given to me from this point forward as a result of this award, today is what will mean the most to me. Today is the day that I get to stand among giants of courage and honor and know that I have been accepted as one of them. I remember waking up in Germany and coming to grips with the injuries I had sustained. I remember the crushing feeling of learning that one of my brothers had not survived. I remember feeling lost and inadequate for the job until Sergeant Tripp here appeared at my bedside. The joy I felt at knowing he would be OK was far beyond anything I could put into words, but there are many of you out there today who know exactly what I am talking about. The fact that he survived and recovered, and the fact that Colonel Tyson, a fine commanding officer by any measure, told me I had done a job worthy of the Airborne will always mean more to me than any medal that I will ever wear.

"I thank all of you for standing here in the heat today and making me feel like I have come home. I thank all of you for everything you do and what you represent. I thank all of you for accepting me as a member of your brotherhood, and I promise to always try to make you proud. If any of you are faced with what seems like an impossible situation in the future downrange, just remember that you are capable of more than you can possibly imagine. And if this middle-aged rear-echelon reservist can do big things, there are no limits to what any of you can do. I will always believe that God gave me life, my experiences gave me character, but the Airborne gave me courage. God bless all of you here today and anyone who will ever have the honor of wearing the Airborne badge. Thank you very much."

General Butts called the group to attention, and it was overwhelming to see several hundred of the finest the United States had to offer snap a crisp salute to him in unison. He returned it, shook the hands of all the men on the stage, and was grateful for the opportunity to walk among the at-ease soldiers below, exchanging handshakes, embraces, and back slaps. It was one of the greatest moments of his life.

The following day Michael, Anna, and David joined the rest of the official party boarding a VIP aircraft and took off to Andrews Air Force base just outside the nation's capital in preparation for his meeting with the Commander in Chief. The previous day's ceremony had lifted his spirits and given him perspective on the honor and responsibility he would carry as a recipient of this award, but in the recesses of his mind there was a sense of foreboding that no one around him would completely understand. He pushed it aside as he felt the faint rumbling of the air passing along the fuselage of the plane, holding Anna's hand in his own.

CHAPTER 14

Chris Tyler was thankful for the slight cooling of the air as he approached the foothills of North Carolina along Interstate 40 West. He was meticulous in the care of the engine of his old-model Chevy pickup, but it did not have air conditioning. The faster speed limits of I-40, which he had picked up in Wilmington, had helped create better air movement around the cab of the truck, but it hadn't been enough to prevent the perspiration that now dampened his back against the driver's seat. The slight incline in elevation had allowed the temperature to be about ten degrees cooler than it had been at the start of his journey, and he had about eight miles before the I-26 exit in Asheville.

He had left three messages on the cell phone number that Darnell had given him but had not gotten a return call in the past thirty-six hours. He had no illusions that his brother would have quit drugs cold turkey after calling him, but he knew it would be much harder to find him if he was strung out and God knows where in the city. He had decided against calling Mrs. Theresa until he had located his brother, and then they would go see her together to see what the next best step would be. Although they had not left on the best of terms from Sycamore House, he didn't know who else to ask about what to do.

He had played this role before. Since getting clean himself, he had tried to get Darnell to do the same. There had been everything from long talks to outright rejection of the idea in the past, but this was different. Chris had never thought his brother had reached rock bottom before. He had lived in that shit heap with the other degenerates and they found ways to enable each other's destructive habits for many years. When one was broke, one of the others had scored some cash by odd jobs or outright theft. They had all long ago decided that the drug stash of a roommate who was passed out was considered communal property, although this concept had resulted in multiple fist fights and the occasional brandishing of weapons. Secondly, Darnell had initiated contact with him this time, which was a first. He sounded desperate and sad and ready to make a change. Being a family member of an addict would create a foundation of cynicism that anyone in similar circumstances could understand, but Chris really thought this time was going to be different. He said a silent prayer as he smelled the pine and hardwoods in the breeze through his window.

*****

Chip was looking over Sandy Patterson's shoulder at the Senator's schedule for the upcoming several days, but his main focus was two days from now in the mid-afternoon. Currently Haxton was scheduled to meet with the Assistant Secretary of the Interior at two thirty and was supposed to go from there to the Trump National Golf Club to play eighteen holes with Brandt Gentry, who was an advisor (i.e., lobbyist) for one of the biggest financial firms in New York. This would be the trickiest part of his plan. Both of those items would need to be shuffled and without Sandy or the Senator knowing why.

"I can email the schedule to you if you need to look over it some more, Mr. Johnson," Sandy said to the man bending over her shoulder like a vulture.

"That's a great idea Sandy. Just shoot the next two weeks to me as soon as possible." Chip decided to ask for many days beside the one he needed to alter, to keep suspicions low. "I'll let you know if I need anything more than that."

He walked toward his office thinking of how this could be legendary among the Washington PR circle if he could pull it off, completely unaware that Sandy Patterson was wondering how hard she would have to throw her letter opener for it to wedge in this arrogant prick's back.

He settled into his supple leather chair in his office that advertised status both by its proximity to the Senator's but also by the size and décor. The area behind his cherry desk was adorned with the requisite framed photographs of himself with a multitude of Washington's biggest movers and shakers. Facing the desk, if one were to look to the left, one would see his diplomas and awards on what many called the "I Love Me" wall. The opposite wall was an ornately framed duplication print of a painting titled *Law Versus Mob Rule* by John Steuart Curry, which illustrates a judge protecting a man from an unruly mob at the steps of a courthouse. The original was on display at the Department of Justice, but reproductions were a common staple in the office of an attorney. Chip didn't reflect on the irony that he had never argued a case in a courtroom and that his job was essentially finding ways to manipulate the mob that was often the American public. The wall opposite of his desk had a framed 11' x 14' photograph of the Rotunda on the campus of the University of Virginia.

He dialed the mobile number of Brandt Gentry, Chief Advisor for Legislative Affairs for Haverston, Goldberg & Walsh.

"This is Brandt," Gentry answered on the second ring.

"Hey buddy, it's Chip Johnson."

"How's it goin', Chipper? What do I owe this pleasure?" Brandt said in his usual smooth voice that could sell an icemaker to an Eskimo. "I'm currently on the fourteenth hole at Congressional. You need to come out here with me next time."

"I need a favor, Brandt. I need to move a round with Haxton this coming Thursday to another day."

"Not a problem, my friend. Tell him I am at his service for whenever he wants to tee it up later on."

Chip leaned back in his chair and picked up his phone receiver, terminating the speaker phone function. "That's where the favor comes in. I need you to be the one that cancels it. I need to have him somewhere else that afternoon for something I'm working on, but he needs to think it's a coincidence. Can't really talk about it until it's over, but if you could do this for me I will owe you a big one."

Gentry's smile opened the curtains on his perfect white teeth as he reclined in the passenger seat of the golf cart. The beverage cart had come along the fairway and met the three Congressmen who completed the day's foursome. His drive off the tee was easily eighty yards ahead of the best one of the others. They had marveled at yet another great shot by him before stopping to get cocktails, compliments of his expense account, and flirt with the very attractive young woman who drove the refreshment cart around the course.

He had earned a bachelor's degree in finance while attending Arizona State University on a golf scholarship but had maxed out his post-collegiate golf career with three top-ten finishes, including a second place on the Nationwide Tour. He could never quite break through the barrier that was the PGA Tour and had become a featured sales representative for Callaway Golf Products. A chance meeting at a VIP reception at the US Open in Pinehurst with Thad Walsh had developed into a job offer with the New York financial giant. His natural sales abilities, love of golf, and unequaled talent for straight-faced bullshitting had made him a natural for the lead glad-hander that brought the company's messages to the nation's elected officials. Corporate memberships at all the area's best courses along with a staggering expense account had allowed him to live the dream while being paid far more than the Nationwide Tour or Callaway could dream of doing. His knowledge of the banking and finance industry along with a magnetic personality was just the recipe that Thad Walsh was looking for in his Legislative Affairs division.

He waved off the inquiry as to whether he needed anything from the cocktail cart while his smile continued to spread across his tanned, handsome face. Favors were the currency of Washington, if not the lifeblood, and he knew he was depositing one in his "for later use" account right now with a senior staff member of one of the biggest purse-string handlers in town.

"Not a problem. I will call the office later this afternoon and apologetically tell them I need to cancel. Let's get together for eighteen holes sometime soon or at least dinner...my treat." *That way we can discuss how you can pay me back.* "Your secret's safe with me."

"I appreciate it Brandt. Hit 'em straight out there today, and I'll call you soon to get together." Chip returned the phone receiver back to its home and drew a line through one of the two conflicting items on the schedule copy for two days hence.

Gentry tossed his Blackberry into the dash storage area of his golf cart and planned how he would tank the next couple of holes so as not to completely humiliate the rest of his foursome. He would still finish under par for the round and would take his three guests to dinner at CityZen restaurant at the Washington Mandarin Oriental so they could discuss over drinks how his employer had some excellent ideas of how to help the industry as well as how

178

campaign fundraising events could be put together for all of them...no strings attached, of course.

*****

Purchased by the United States government in 1942, the Blair House is primarily used to house foreign heads of state when they visit the nation's capital. It is located a short walk's distance from the White House and is managed by the White House Office of Protocol. Due to the absence of any official state visits occurring that week, the Reece family found themselves as guests there for the next three days. After getting a tour by one of the staff members, Michael was reading the plaque that honored Leslie Coffelt, a Washington police officer who had prevented the assassination of President Harry Truman, who had been living there at the time during a renovation of the White House. Unfortunately, Mr. Coffelt had sacrificed his own life while stopping two Puerto Rican nationalists from killing the President.

Boasting fourteen guest rooms and a full staff, it was far more home than they could possibly require, but the history that seemed to be around every corner was fascinating to both of them. They called Anna's parents and got very brief conversations from their kids, since they were busy getting everything they asked for from their grandparents. They would be staying in a hotel near the White House as well, by insistence, in order to give the couple a little time to themselves. They both felt a small degree of relief that their kids would not be staying here as they looked at the countless antique and priceless items that adorned every room. Little Charlie had never seen a banister that he didn't want to slide down...

Tonight was actually free, and Michael and Anna were going to go out to dinner like a regular couple. They had thought about simply eating at the Blair House, where there was a full kitchen staff to cater to their needs, but decided to be tourists tonight and keep their minds off all of the folderol around them, not to mention the fact that he would be meeting the Commander In Chief tomorrow in the White House Rose Garden the day before the presentation ceremony.

The Reeces enjoyed a romantic dinner at Firefly restaurant while they laughed about the three minutes they had to spend convincing the taxi dispatcher that they really were at the

179

Blair House needing a pick up. They strolled hand in hand around the DuPont Circle neighborhood afterward and then returned to the guesthouse. As he drifted off to sleep in the large four-poster bed of their room, he was sure that he was the first guy who had slept in that bed wearing frayed University of North Carolina gym shorts. Tomorrow the circus would officially begin.

*****

Chris Tyler marked his arrival in Asheville by visiting the home of his old pastor Billy Cash, who had also been his sponsor at Alcoholics Anonymous. He had taken up his open offer to stay at his home anytime he was in town. After embracing, they prayed together for the blessings of sobriety as well as for the location and rehabilitation of Darnell.

They both went to a local barbecue joint and caught up on each other's lives over sweet tea, barbecue, slaw, and hushpuppies. The food was good (in the South *barbecue* is a noun and not a verb) and so was the fellowship, but Chris knew that he had a tough job. Darnell would be hard to locate, and his desire for sobriety could have certainly faded over the past few days. Even though Chris had kept his demons away for some time now, he knew they would have a firm grip on his brother.

Before going to bed, he and Billy made a list of the places that Darnell could be found. It was long and Chris was sure that it wasn't remotely comprehensive, but you had to start somewhere. He tried the phone number again; there was no answer and the voicemail was full. As he closed his eyes and rested his head on the pillow, he told himself to focus on finding him before worrying about what the next step would be.

*****

Beverly Stafford waited for the response to what she had just told her boss and fellow staff members. Haxton's staff met every morning to share the progress on everyone's projects and responsibilities as well as the schedule for the upcoming several days.

"What do you mean 'it won't be ready'?" asked Haxton's budget consultant, Raymond Dockery.

"I thought it was for next week and I don't have the necessary figures. I can have it ready in three to four days, and I'll work through the weekend."

She hoped her pulse wasn't visible on her neck not to mention the flushing of her skin. She was not usually noticed at all at these meetings, especially when the Senator was present. Part of that was because she was a junior staffer who had only been there for about six months, but another part was because she was reliable with her tasks and responsibilities. She was not only scared of being seen as unreliable but worried about being caught lying. In fact, the executive summary on the budgetary recommendations for the National Park Service that she was responsible for was sitting in her desk right now.

Haxton wasn't visibly upset, but his disappointment was evident as he leaned forward, resting his elbows on the large cherry meeting room table. "Miss Stafford, you realize that without that summary I have nothing to discuss with the Assistant Secretary tomorrow. It makes us all look unprepared as well as uncaring about others' time."

"I understand, sir, and I'm very sorry. I promise it won't happen again."

"Jesus, Beverly," said Dockery. "Anyone can make mistakes, and I believe in everyone getting a free pass on their first screw-up. But you have just used yours, OK?"

"Yes, sir." Stafford cut her eyes toward Johnson, who looked bewildered at the revelation this morning.

Haxton leaned back in his chair and looked at Dockery. "Have Sandy reschedule the meeting and give our apologies. Don't sweat it, Beverly, it happens to the best of us."

Her face didn't conceal a large degree of relief. She was a hard worker and wanted to be known as a dependable member of the staff, not to mention she wanted to advance in her responsibilities as much as anyone else. She sat through the remainder of the meeting and made a point to stop by Sandy's desk to apologize for making the mistake. She offered to call the Assistant Secretary's office herself and explain the situation. Sandy waved her off and said it wasn't a big deal. Beverly was a fan of Sandy from the first day she came to work there, mainly because of her efficiency and talent but also because she tried to look out for the women staff members, who had to work a little bit harder to overcome the good-ol'-boy network that was still firmly entrenched in the Capitol Building. She thanked Sandy and headed to Chip's office.

He handed her an envelope that contained two hundred dollars that Hal Sutton had handed to him the day before. "You were great. Remember, this is not only for losing the report but also for not telling anyone about it. This gets out and I'll send your ass back to interning for your local county commissioner. That being said, I owe you one, and I remember favors."

"Don't worry and thanks." *Fuck you* were the words that were in her mind but not her mouth. Making ends meet as a junior staffer in this town was hard enough when you weren't one of the countless silver-spooners that roamed the halls here, and the mild rebuke she received for this perceived slip-up was worth the money as well as having the Wonderboy indebted to her to some degree.

Chip texted Sutton to let him know that the morning's plan had went off without a hitch, which caused "The Guvanah" to call Haxton's private line.

"What's up, Hal?"

"I've got an idea to set up a fundraiser while you're at Figure Eight, but I need to go over it with you in the next day or two to get the event details set up. You free for a late lunch tomorrow?"

"You always did have impeccable timing. I had two things fall apart for early tomorrow afternoon, so why don't we get together at the Senate Dining Room at around one thirty?"

Sutton smiled on the other end of the line. Getting someone to do what you wanted was nice, but making them think it was their own idea was even sweeter. "Sounds good. I'll see you tomorrow." He ended the call and texted "SDR 1:30" to Johnson's phone.

Chip read the text and made his next call to an extension at the Washington office of MSNBC.

"This is McLean," was the salutation of Rachelle McLean as she picked up her phone receiver at her desk.

"Hey, Rachelle, it's Chip Johnson. Interested in being lead-off tomorrow evening on your news broadcast?"

"Absolutely not; I prefer to trudge along in obscurity for the indefinite future." It had just the right amount of sarcasm to come off as friendly banter. She didn't like the guy personally, but he was solid gold when it came to a contact on the inside, and Johnson didn't make idle promises.

"I need you to be at the South end of the Capitol at two thirty with a camera guy. Have your cell phone handy, but that's all I can tell you. Trust me, you won't be disappointed."

"I'll be there. Thanks Chip."

She didn't hesitate. Whatever it was, it would be worth her effort. There were countless games played in this town, but officials and their staff knew better than to piss off members of the media on purpose. You got the media to do what you needed with armloads of carrots and left the stick at home. She called the video department, secured a cameraman for the following afternoon, and went back to work. Trying to decipher what it was all about would be a waste of time, and she would find out tomorrow anyway.

CHAPTER 15

The breakfast prepared by the Blair House staff was enough to feed at least a dozen people and included everything from pastries to cooked items, along with the offer from the chef to prepare any omelet requested to order for the three distinguished guests at the table. Anna spread vegetable cream cheese on a toasted bagel and cut her eyes at the virtual mountain of food on Tripp's plate.

"One day the cholesterol gods are going to catch up with you, David," she said in a half-reproaching and half-marveling way as she looked at "her men" bedecked in their formal Army dress uniforms with the coats hanging away from the table to avoid any unfortunate dribbling from the meal. It was hard to fuss at him too much when you could probably measure his body fat percentage on one hand.

"And when they do, I won't tell you anyway," Tripp said as he started to attack his Western omelet.

Michael pushed his food around the plate, trying to make it appear that he had eaten more than he had. There was a slight tremor in his hand. He felt Tripp put his arm around his shoulders.

"No need to be nervous, sir. It's not like you're meeting the President or anything," he said with his best Mississippi drawl and shit-eating grin. "Besides, breakfast's on me...I insist."

"You should eat, honey," Anna said in hopes of easing his nerves.

"I'm good. I'm a little nervous, but it's fine. Just don't have much of an appetite this morning." He pulled the napkin that had been stuffed in his collar as further protection for his uniform. He had already asked Tripp to make sure his ribbons were in the correct order and he hadn't screwed up anything.

They sat at the table exchanging small talk and funny stories and watched as it started to brush away the tension on his face. Anna went upstairs to make sure her makeup and outfit were as they should be. Both the men had remarked on how stunning she looked this morning, and with Anna one didn't have to exaggerate in saying such a thing. Michael liked that she wore very little makeup since she was so beautiful on her own. She wore a conservative maroon dress that was a hybrid of formal dinner and business attire and accented her dark hair and chestnut eyes superbly.

"When's your date getting here?" Tripp asked with a grin, further relieving his friend's uneasiness.

Michael laughed at his official "Protocol Escort" for the trip. "She's out of both of our leagues."

Minutes later, the three climbed into the government VIP GMC Yukon for the short ride to 1600 Pennsylvania Avenue. There was a White House Office of Protocol official in the vehicle, who briefed them about the itinerary of the morning. They would be met on arrival by the Secretary of Defense and the First Lady at the North Entrance to the West Wing. All of them would then meet the President, followed by Anna receiving a White House tour by the First Lady while Michael spent a few minutes with the Commander in Chief. In total, the visit would be less than forty-five minutes.

*****

The day had been less than fruitful for Chris and Billy. They had been to several of the places that Chris used to hang out with his brother, to no avail. He didn't know the exact location of the trailer that he shared with his "friends," which made it all the more difficult. They stopped by a car wash that Darnell occasionally showed up to with the hopes of earning a few bucks to get his next fix, but the supervisor said that he hadn't been there in weeks.

At Billy's suggestion, they had called the Sheriff's Department and the County Jail to make sure he was not being held at either location for anything; again the answer was negative. The day was further frustrated when Chris tried the cell phone number and it was answered by the man whom his brother had taken it from in the first place.

"I ain't seen him since yesterday when I got my phone back from that stealin' muthafucker. And if he takes it again, he's gonna get an ass-whoopin'."

"Do you guys still stay at the same place?"

"Yeah, but I ain't there right now so I don't know if he's there or not."

This didn't seem to be going anywhere, but maybe he could get an address. "Can you give me the address there and I'll go check myself?"

"Fuck you. I don't know who you are. If you're really his muthafuckin' brother, you should know where it's at. You could be a muthafuckin' cop for all I know."

"I'm not, I promise. I don't live here anymore and we haven't been in touch much. I just want to help him out. Could we meet up and I'll show you I'm his brother? I'll make it worth your while." Reasoning with him had far less chance of working compared to bribery.

"Are you a cop? You have to tell me if you are," was his reply.

Chris didn't have much faith in this guy's knowledge of legal protocols, but he was his only lead so far. "I'm not a cop. There's fifty bucks in it for you if we meet up and you give me the address where you guys stay."

There was a brief pause on the other end. "Meet me at the Krispy Kreme on Rankin Avenue tomorrow at one in the afternoon and I'll tell you."

"Can't we get together tonight?" Chris was frustrated with his only option being to barter with a goddamn crack head.

"No we can't. Tomorrow at the Krispy Kreme. If you are who you say you are and you have the fifty bucks, I'll tell you. Take it or muthafuckin' leave it. And by the way, if you ain't who you say you are, I'm going to seriously fuck you up."

"You got a deal," Chris told him and the line went dead.

Reverend Billy had listened to the conversation since Chris had it on speaker. "Looks like it's our best chance so far, brother."

"If he remembers to show up and doesn't try to shake us down. Piece of shit drug addict," Chris spat as he crushed his cigarette on the pavement with his shoe.

Billy put his hand on Chris's shoulder. "There is only one lawgiver and judge, he who is able to save and to destroy. But who are you to judge your neighbor?"

"Book of James," Chris said sheepishly as he remembered it wasn't so long ago that he was also a drug addict and it was Reverend Billy who helped lift him out of the darkness and stood by his side on his road to recovery. "I'm sorry. I just want to find him while he'll still letting us help him."

"My brother, you never need to apologize to me. I'll help you find him anyway I can. Just remember that the ugliness you see is the same hell you have dwelled in yourself. That is, until God bathed you in his light and his love. He now expects you to spread that light and that love to Darnell and maybe others as well."

They surrendered to the fact that little progress could be made until tomorrow and went to grab a bite to eat before the evening worship service at Billy's church.

*****

"You two clean up good," Secretary Dietz said with a grin and turned to Anna. "Mrs. Reece, it is an absolute pleasure to meet you. I would like to introduce to you all First Lady Lydia Danielson."

The First Lady stood to his right and extended a warm handshake to all three of them. "Gentlemen, it's an honor to meet you, and I am grateful for your service to the country. Mrs. Reece, I am grateful for all the sacrifices you make being a spouse of a service member." All of them seemed a little star struck as they shook her hand in succession.

Lydia Grier Danielson was one of the most popular First Ladies since Jackie Kennedy. After graduating with honors from San Diego State University, she spent several years as a social worker in Southern California in the Child Protective Services division, establishing herself quickly as a tireless advocate for the children she was charged to safeguard. She was not afraid to confront those who had failed in their primary roles as protectors and parents and had brought countless abusers to the attention of the authorities. It was through one of these cases that she met an upcoming prosecutor by the name of Paul Danielson, who had recently graduated from UCLA School of Law. What started as a few dates quickly blossomed into romance and marriage. They had stayed by each other's sides as Paul rose from prosecutor to District Attorney to Congressman and now President of the United States. They had enjoyed three daughters in their marriage, one of which tragically perished in 2001 in the World Trade Center, where she worked in an investment firm.

Their tragedy had become America's tragedy, and the late Amy Danielson became a symbol of all that was lost that day. Lydia had handled the worst nightmare a parent could have with grace and compassion and became an advocate for the children of those who perished that horrifying day. She wasn't a celebrity-telethon kind of spokesperson either. On the contrary, she spent countless hours at Ground Zero with the families as well as in their homes. She became the guardian of one ten-year-old boy who had lost both his parents in the collapse and eventually adopted him as their son. America not only healed alongside the Danielson family but fell in love with Lydia, who became the personification of strength and compassion. When Paul won the White House, many said the biggest factor was his wife, whose popularity crossed the lines of party affiliation, race, and age. The President had once joked that the biggest reason he had never lost an election in his career was because he had never run against her.

She led them to the Rose Garden, where the Commander in Chief was waiting for them. Both Michael and David popped crisp salutes, which were returned by the President. Introductions were made by Secretary Dietz.

"Mr. President, may I present Major Michael Reece and Sergeant First Class David Tripp of the Eighty-Second Airborne Division, and this is Mrs. Anna Reece."

"It's an honor to meet you, sir," Michael said as he shook the offered hand.

"Major Reece, the honor is most certainly mine. Would this be the same Sergeant Tripp that was with you that night?"

The President was an easy man to like. He didn't give the usual politician vibe of smiling at you while pilfering your wallet, and he seemed genuinely happy to meet them all. He had not served in the military during his career, but his brother had been one of the nineteen soldiers killed in Mogadishu in 1993 in the tragic mission that inspired the book *Black Hawk Down*. He had been a steadfast supporter of the military and their families throughout his political career and had received the votes of all three of his visitors today.

"It certainly is, sir. Sergeant First Class Tripp was with me the entire night. He is one of the best soldiers I have ever known, and I'm happy to have him as a close friend today."

President Danielson leaned in to the two soldiers and lowered his voice. "Is it true your nickname is Booger?"

Reece saw his friend do something he had never seen before: blush. "It's true, sir…Long story."

The President smiled. "I bet it's a good one." He turned to Secretary Dietz. "Mr. Secretary, I know you had a different itinerary, but I would like Sergeant Tripp to join us for coffee this morning, if that's OK with Major Reece," he said as he turned to Michael.

"Um, well yes, sir, it's fine with me, sir." He wasn't expecting the Commander in Chief to be asking his permission for anything today.

Secretary Dietz nodded. "That's not a problem, Mr. President."

The First Lady stepped forward. "Well, gentlemen, Mrs. Reece and I have some chatting and touring to do, so I will leave you all now." She stole one more look at Michael and David then looked at her husband. "Sorry, honey, but there's just something about a man in uniform," she said as she winked at Anna.

"I know, I know," the President said as his two guests blushed and looked like two junior high boys who had gotten the attention of the Homecoming Queen. "Gentlemen, why don't we sit down out here since the weather is so nice today?"

They agreed and enjoyed the unseasonable cool that had covered the nation's capital the past two days. Michael was surprised at the relatively small size of the garden, which only measured about a hundred twenty by sixty feet. The flowers were beautiful and the grass was manicured to a degree that would make the groundskeepers at Augusta National Golf Club envious. As they sat in cast-iron seats around a table in the garden that balanced the Kennedy Garden on the opposite side of the White House complex, an usher poured coffee in front of each of them. Coffee wasn't his drink of choice, but Michael would have drunk motor oil if that was what had been given him here.

"I hope everyone has been taking care of you and the families since you've been here," Danielson said as he passed the sugar caddy to Michael.

"Everyone has been fantastic, sir. The Blair House is quite impressive."

"The family is enjoying Washington?"

"Yes, sir. Our kids are with Anna's parents and we will be meeting back up with them later today. They arrived a couple of days before we did and have been seeing the sights. They'll be at the ceremony tomorrow along some other friends, sir."

He sipped the coffee to be polite and realized he still thought it tasted like asphalt. There was a slight rattle as he placed the fine china cup back in the saucer. The President smiled and put down his cup.

"I need a favor from the two of you. I realize I'm the President, but I'm not the Pope and I'm not royalty. There is no need to be nervous, and I assure you I am more impressed with the two of you than you should be with me. I know both of you are impressive soldiers, and I bet you're both impressive people as well. I've been looking forward to this for a couple of days, so let's enjoy each other's company without all the formality." He leaned back and smiled. "I can make it an order, you know."

"That sounds good to me, Mr. President," replied Michael.

"I'm on board with that, Mr. President," David chimed in right behind.

"How do you feel about all this, Major Reece?"

"I'm still a little overwhelmed. I'm trying to keep things in perspective and keep in mind all the others I have served with when I'm getting all this attention. The treatment and the kindness I have received has been beyond description, and I hope I can live up to it, Mr. President." Reece thought about reaching for the coffee but decided against it since the nerves weren't quite completely gone.

"Don't you think you have already lived up to it, Major?" Danielson seemed to sense a conflicted feeling as an undercurrent to the reply.

"Well, sir, I think I..." He fidgeted in his chair a bit. "I mean, I believe..."

Tripp leaned forward and set down his coffee cup, which looked like part of a doll's tea set in his massive and still partially scarred hands. "Mr. President, I hope you'll excuse me for butting in here, but what Major Reece wants to say right now is that he isn't sure he really deserves this honor. I have certainly tried to convince him otherwise, since I'm the one that pushed my CO to nominate him, but I'm not sure how much progress I've made with that." He looked at Michael. "I'm sorry for interjecting, sir."

Michael replied with a smile that told him an apology wasn't necessary.

"Hmmm." Danielson looked at Reece, then off into the distance, and then back at Reece. "Michael, I don't know if you are aware, but my younger brother was an Army Ranger. He died in Somalia on a mission that I believe he was sent on without everything that was necessary to succeed, by a man who didn't appreciate that ordering others into harm's way wasn't an abstract concept. He died fighting alongside his squad, and I know he would do it over again if he was given the chance. There were over a dozen men with him when he was hit, but it was him that was unlucky. It was his time." He pulled a patch from his inside suit coat pocket. "This is the Ranger tab that was on his uniform when he died. I have kept that with me every day since it was given to me by his squad leader, and it serves as a reminder of the incredible responsibility I have for the well-being of the men and women in uniform. He died with a dozen of his brothers beside him. You guarded and cared for two soldiers by yourself and fought off an enemy force when you had no idea of its size or when you would get any reinforcements. And, if I'm not mistaken, the man sitting with us today would be dead if it wasn't for you.

"The fact that you struggle with the praise you are receiving tells me that you are a good man, which makes me proud to know you. But don't mistake your humility with any doubt that you deserve this, Major. The things you did that night over there and the choices you made have merited the recognition I'm going to give to you tomorrow, but it's who you are as a man that will allow you to carry it with honor. I am certain the right man is getting this medal tomorrow and I know my brother would be as well."

Michael struggled for words. He felt guilty about some of the assumptions he had made about all politicians being snakes in thousand-dollar suits. The man sitting in front of him right now was one of the good guys, and he was proud to be serving under him. "I appreciate that, Mr. President. I will try my hardest to make everyone proud."

They stood and the President extended his hand to Michael. "I have no doubt that you will succeed in that, Major Reece. Why don't I give you the nickel tour, since we have a little time to kill until our better halves are finished? There's someone I want you to meet."

He took them into the Oval Office and introduced them to several of the staff members. They both noted the slight distortion of the images through the window behind the President's desk, which was due to it being bullet proof. As they walked toward the exit of the White House, Danielson stopped in front of one of the White House ushers.

"Major Reece, Sergeant Tripp, I would like you to meet Sergeant Major Clifford Thompson. He retired from the Army many years ago and joined his brother as an usher here at the White House. He served two tours in Vietnam and finished his career as a Jumpmaster with the Eighty-Second."

Thompson extended his hand and the two guests both shook it with reverence. Thompson's white hair contrasted with his brown skin, but there was no stoop in his posture. He stood with the ramrod straightness befitting a Sergeant Major in the best damned unit in the Army, thank you very much.

"You did good, sir. Airborne leads the way."

"All the way, Sergeant Major," Michael replied and turned to Danielson. "Mr. President, would it be too much to ask…"

"We have already gotten Sergeant Major Thompson a seat at the ceremony, Major Reece," replied the President.

"Thank you, sir."

They met back up with Anna and the First Lady, exchanged goodbyes, and were taken back to the Blair House, where Walt, Tina, Elizabeth, and Charlie were waiting for them. After hearing about the almost countless souvenirs courtesy of Mimi and Papa, Washington's newest celebrity and his "entourage" decided to have an opulent dinner of cheeseburgers and milkshakes from McDonalds.

*****

Just beyond the docks of Harbour Town Resort in Hilton Head, South Carolina, Drs. Gabriel Drake and Eric Daniels were sitting in the shadow of the famed lighthouse of the same name, sipping cold beer, and figuring out who owed what for the bets on the golf course earlier in the day. The gentle breeze carried the music from the bar to the outdoor tables along with the salty sweet smell of the coast. As they waited for their cheeseburgers, they chatted with others at nearby tables. Gabriel had already bought drinks for three different women at the bar, an activity he likened to casting your fishing line in the water until a good fish took interest.

Just a short walk from the bar in the Marina, *The Sculpted Lady* was being topped off with fuel and other supplies for the morning's departure to the island of Dominica in what had become a yearly tradition for the small group of friends at their hospital. The trip would include diving, drinking, and relaxing, not to mention large doses of bullshitting, with all the details already arranged by their local dive shop, Open Water Adventures. They would meet the others once they arrived at the island: Michael and one of the newer members of the diving group, David Tripp, who had to meet them in a few days due to a minor engagement in Washington, DC. Eric would be flying home with the others while Gabriel, who had become quite an accomplished captain of his favorite toy, would take about two more weeks cruising around the Caribbean.

Their burgers came and they ordered two more Coastal Brewing Company IPAs. When the tally was done, Eric had come out well ahead of his buddy on the golf betting, as was usually the case. He was a sight to behold on the tee box and was so sickeningly humble about it. Gabriel and Michael had often joked that sometimes they still hadn't reached his drives after two shots. Conversation turned to stories about previous gatherings of the dive club.

"Next time we'll have to have everyone go down on the boat together," Drake said.

The last time they had all been on the boat, Michael had dressed up in a pirate costume to go with his fake left leg and posed for a picture that hung in the dining area of the boat to this day, in a frame that read "Ahab Reece, Honorary Cap'n." This photo session had followed more than one beer, which went without saying. Their friend had always had an enormous capacity to laugh at himself, and that hadn't changed after his terrible injury, which put everyone around him at ease—a talent that Michael seemed to have with friends as well as strangers.

"That'll be a sight. We will have to have some sort of code of silence about that one after it's over," Eric chuckled. "I hope everything goes well in Washington tomorrow." Eric was a little down about his friend's sabbatical. It wasn't that he thought Michael didn't deserve the time off; he just missed his friend.

Drake picked up his microbrew and raised it toward Eric. "To Mike," he said as they clinked their bottles together. They were all looking forward to getting away and enjoying each other's company as the old friends they had all become.

194

CHAPTER 16

The East Room of the White House was adorned with alternating American and United States Army flags coming to the focal point of a light blue flag with thirteen stars, signifying the Medal of Honor, behind the elevated stage area. The sizable media contingent formed a semi-circle around the back of the room and the lateral portions. Seated were several Pentagon dignitaries in the third and fourth rows and the invited guests of Michael in the first two rows. They included Anna and her parents, Elizabeth, Reverend Webber with little Charlie in his lap, Tripp, COL Greg Tyson, and White House Usher and retired Sergeant Major Clifford Washington. He knew that each of these treasured colleagues would be there but was caught off guard when he saw every single combat medic that he had worked with at FOB Salerno present as well. His confusion as to how this was arranged was ended when he saw the sly grin and wink on the face of Tyson.

President Danielson stood behind the podium that displayed the seal of his office and was flanked by Secretary Dietz and General Shaver on one side and Secretary Winters and General Butts on the other. Michael had entered the room with the President and now stood ramrod straight on the stage to the President's right. Danielson cleared his throat and motioned for all to have a seat.

"Ladies and gentlemen, today represents one of the greatest privileges that are included in the office that I currently hold. Today I am allowed to stand with true greatness and courage and see those qualities recognized and rewarded. It goes without saying that the honor and bravery of the men and women in America's armed forces are unrivaled anywhere in the world, and it gives me great pleasure to recognize a man today whose humility belies the remarkable acts of valor that were conveyed to me by his Commanding Officer during the nomination process for this award.

"The Medal of Honor is the highest award that can be bestowed upon a member of the United States military. It was established in 1861 by then-President Abraham Lincoln to recognize uncommon acts of gallantry. The relative infrequency of these ceremonies should give you some idea of how special the circumstances must be in order to be considered for such recognition, and today's recipient, Major Michael Reece, is certainly emblematic of the qualities befitting a recipient of this award.

"It is customary for me to read the official citation of this award during my remarks, but those are included in your program today. I would like to share a version of what brought us all here today using the accounts that have been shared with me by his brothers and sisters in arms, as well as my experience meeting him and his beautiful wife Anna yesterday here at the White House. I certainly couldn't give you an appreciation for the gallantry displayed that night if I only had Major Reece as a source, since he is a man of upmost humility and makes every effort to distribute the praise to those around him. This, as many here in uniform already know, is one of the truest marks of a good soldier and a good leader." He turned toward Michael with a grin. "Unfortunately, Major Reece, as your Commander in Chief I will be lavishing praise upon you today, and you can't do anything about it." Several chuckles echoed around the room.

"On the night where Major Reece distinguished himself as nothing short of a true hero, he was returning from a humanitarian mission in a nearby village along with other members of his unit. They came under attack from a well-organized enemy force that disabled the convoy and wounded several members of the unit, including some fatally. At the same time, there was a separate attack on their operating base itself, preventing reinforcements from coming to the aid of the convoy. This left Major Reece cut off from his unit and looking after two seriously wounded soldiers.

"Under continuous fire by an enemy force that far outnumbered his own, he alternated between engaging the enemy to keep them away and rendering medical care to his wounded comrades. The cover from enemy fire was very limited, and he exposed himself to the insurgent force in order to protect his men from danger. This decision to expose himself to enemy fire resulted in his receiving a severe gunshot wound to his leg, which ultimately led to the loss of the lower half of his limb. His decisions and actions resulted in the survival of one of those severely wounded soldiers, who is here with us today.

"Sergeant First Class Jeff Harrison, who is also here today, was the first medic to treat Major Reece when reinforcements arrived from a nearby operating base. From his account, Reece was nearly unconscious from blood loss but refused treatment until he could relay information about the injuries of his fellow soldiers. He lost consciousness shortly after that and nearly died on the way to the operating base, whose medical team would work diligently to treat his injuries as well as marvel at the level of life-saving care he was able to give his comrades while engaged with the enemy.

"Far too many recipients of this award are not alive to receive it. I'm glad that his heroic actions didn't require his life, but by the accounts of those who were with him that night it is clear that he was willing to do just that if it had been required. Shakespeare said in *Henry V*, 'for he today that sheds his blood with me shall be my brother.' The attendance of many of Major Reece's brothers today is a testament to his standing among those who have had the honor to serve with him." The President looked toward Anna.

"So, without further rambling from me, I would like to ask Major Reece's family to join me up on the stage."

Anna and the kids stepped up on the stage and stood to the left of Michael. Danielson emerged from behind the podium with the medal in his hands. Michael brought himself to even more rigid attention than he had been during the preceding remarks.

The President faced him, holding each of the ribbon ends of the hallowed award in his hands. "For conspicuous acts of gallantry and selflessness above and beyond the call of duty, I hereby present to Major Michael Reece the Medal of Honor on behalf of the Office of the President, the United States Army, and a grateful nation."

He placed the ribbon around Michael's neck as the room echoed with a cacophony of camera flashes and clicks, followed by the applause of those assembled in the room.

As the camera clicks died down and the applause abated, little Charlie looked at his Daddy's new medal and turned to the President. "Does he get to keep that?"

197

Scattered laughter arose in the room, including from Danielson. "He sure does young man. He earned it, and I am proud to give it to him."

"That's pretty awesome Daddy." Michael was now at ease and had shaken hands with his Commander in Chief and smiled at his son's remarks.

"I think your Daddy's pretty awesome, Charlie," Danielson said.

The media gradually left the East Room to put together their respective stories or segments, and Michael took great pride in introducing the President to his guests, including the medics who had surprised him by being there. Michael told the President that the medics had taught him more about combat medicine than he could ever hope to learn in textbooks and seminars. He was proud to be among the people he was with and was beginning to feel a sense of relaxation now that the formality of it all was starting to end.

The President enjoyed the stories that the soldiers shared about their friend and could see their affection and admiration for him. He was very comfortable that the Army had made an excellent choice by awarding Reece this honor.

LTCOL Collins, Michael's PAO, was back with the family for this trip, and he gathered them together with the President to say their goodbyes.

Michael shook the hand of his CIC. "Mr. President, I want to thank you for doing this for me and all the Airborne guys. You and your wife have been very gracious to us."

"Major Reece, I assure you that I have gotten more from this than anyone. I want to thank you for your service and your bravery." He placed his finger on the medal that now hung from Michael's neck. "I have no doubt that his honor has found a more than worthy recipient. I also am grateful to your family, who has helped shape who you are and make their own sacrifices when you are away."

Anna smiled and took his offered hand. "That is very kind of you to say. We're very proud of him, and it was a pleasure meeting you and the First Lady."

Danielson turned to Collins. "Where do they go from here, Lieutenant Colonel Collins?"

"Sir, they will be going to the Capitol building for a short reception with the Congressional Veterans Coalition." The CVC was a group of Congressmen and Congresswomen who had served in the military before coming to Washington, including one who was still an A-10 pilot in the Air Force Reserves. They had worked it out with the Public Affairs Office, and Michael was happy to go and meet with fellow veterans.

"I'm going to the Capitol to meet with the Speaker of the House from here," Danielson said to the PAO.

Little Charlie tugged at the trousers of the leader of the free world. "Mr. President, do you ride in your helicopter when you go over there?" He was proudly wearing his White House lapel pin given to him by Sergeant Major Washington along with a lopsided Army formal dress hat that belonged to Tripp. As was true at most places he went, everyone there had taken a liking to him immediately, including the President.

"I wish I did Charlie. I do have a pretty cool big black car that has some neat stuff in it." He leaned down to the boy's level and spoke in a way that sounded like they were up to some mischief. "I tell you what. If it's OK with your mom and dad, why don't you and your sister ride with me, since we're going to the same place?" He looked up at Michael and Anna. "Would that be OK with you two?"

Anna's immediate thought was that there probably wasn't a booster seat in the Presidential limousine, but then again it was bullet-proof and was driven by a Secret Service agent trained in evasive driving…"That would be fine Mr. President."

"Fantastic." He turned to his lead Secret Service agent. "We can make that happen right?"

"Not a problem Mr. President," he said as he leaned his chin into his lapel microphone. "Bruin One en route to limo with two additional pax."

"Great. They will make sure we arrive at the same place. While you two gather your things, I'm going to show Miss Elizabeth and Mr. Charlie the Oval Office, and we'll meet up at the Capitol." He said it like they were coordinating a carpool to the neighborhood weekend soccer game, and the kids' faces were lit up like it was Christmas morning.

*****

There are several types of receptors in the brain that, when activated, cause cellular changes. The opiod receptors are activated by opium-derived substances such as narcotic pain-relieving medications and heroin. The delta receptors, when activated, promote cellular changes that produce analgesia or pain relief. The kappa receptors mediate the sense of euphoria that can come with many narcotic substances, especially heroin, which explains its extreme addictive potential. With repeated use of narcotics, the density of receptors at a cellular level changes, requiring higher doses of medication to achieve the same euphoric effects; this is the root of tolerance to a medication. Once these changes occur, the absence of the medication no longer returns a person to their baseline non-euphoric state but rather causes a pendulum-like swing beyond that, giving symptoms of agitation, nausea, and sweating among others; this is the root of narcotic withdrawal.

Darnell Tyler's opiod receptors were currently empty, due to the use of all of his stash and no money to buy more. He felt the wetness of perspiration in his armpits and forehead as he stared at the small circular cigarette-burn marks on the cheap plastic chairs of Green Mountain Pawn Shop. Willie Sampson, the owner of the seedy establishment, was currently not there, and he was the only person authorized to buy merchandise for the store. Darnell felt the volume of the television set in the front of the store was progressively increasing, further aggravating the pounding in his head. He felt the front pouch pocket of his hooded sweatshirt and made sure the bulge was still there. Inside was a Sig Sauer pistol that he had stolen from the glove compartment of a car in the parking lot of Biltmore Square Mall.

Willie did sell weapons at the pawn shop, given he had a permit to do so. His profit margin, however, was much higher with the stolen guns he bought from local criminals and sold in the back of the store. He would buy them for a fraction of their worth, taking advantage of the sellers' desperation for money, which they needed, no doubt, for drugs. Where the guns went or what they were used for after he turned them over didn't concern him. The high profits of his illegal gun trade helped him finance his frequent trips to the Jade Massage and Relaxation

200

Center, which was 10 percent spa and 90 percent whorehouse. As Willie debated which relaxation therapist would be servicing him today, Darnell sat in his store waiting for him to come back.

He would have liked to take the sweatshirt off except for the stolen handgun he had in the pocket. He didn't give a fuck about the newscaster on the television rambling on about politics and desperately wished they would turn down the volume. He started to feel the initial cramps in his belly that would continue to get worse along with the increased amount of saliva in his mouth, a preview of the upcoming desire to vomit that would arrive in about an hour if he didn't get his fix. *Why couldn't the fat fuck get his happy ending and get back here?* He remembered the last time he got "sick"; he actually shit his pants before his could get to his dealer to get more drugs. He looked up at the dusty clock beside the unbearably loud TV and decided that he would wait a little longer before he would think of something else to do get money.

As he rested the back of his head against the wall, all he could wonder was, Where the hell was his brother?

*****

The Congressional Veterans Coalition was a bipartisan group of elected leaders who had served in the military. They were consulted on all matters of legislation that would affect active military personnel or veterans. Woe to the official who pushed forward legislation that fell under this description and who didn't get the input of the coalition, which met weekly and was required to sit beside members of the opposing political party. They were fiercely pro-military and felt that their status as veterans gave them unique insight into military matters as well as a responsibility to advocate for their fellow Americans who had answered the call to serve or were still serving.

Each member gathered outside to welcome their guest of honor today for their weekly lunch meeting. They didn't expect to see the Presidential motorcade preceding the vehicle carrying Major Reece, but a staffer relayed the news that they had decided to ride together and that the Reece children were actually riding with the President at his invitation. There were members of the press gathered outside, since they were never allowed into CVC meetings; this allowed the members to be open with each other and leave their talking points at the door. No political topics were allowed except ones relating to the military.

Video cameras were lifted to shoulders and cameras brought to faces as the motorcade arrived at the Capitol Building, and they were soon rewarded with one of the shots of the day. Secret Service agents exited from the SUVs that were in front of and behind the Presidential limousine and gathered around the vehicle. The back door of the armored black Cadillac limo was opened, and the President emerged along with Elizabeth Reece who was all smiles. Charlie didn't follow and wasn't seen until the front door was opened. As usual, if something was on his mind, it was out of his mouth; Charlie had asked the most powerful man in the world if he could ride in the front seat where the cool radios were instead of in the back with him when they were leaving for the Capitol.

Charlie exited after an enormous Secret Service agent whose usually intimidating appearance was softened by an unconcealed grin as the young boy jumped out of the door and his small leather dress shoes made a slapping sound on the sidewalk. The photograph of the President holding the hand of Elizabeth Reece with his left hand and giving a high five to little Charlie Reece with his right became an instant hit for the following day's newspapers.

Farewells were exchanged between the Reece party and the President, and Michael was treated to a warm welcome by the CVC. Walt and Tina had come along as well and gathered the kids for a VIP tour of the Capitol Building while their parents went to the luncheon.

The food was blessedly unpretentious due to a CVC rule that nothing could be served at their meetings that wasn't available to service men and women deployed to combat areas. There would be some brief remarks after the meal, followed by Michael speaking to the assembled Representatives, but the real purpose was for the members to speak with their guest during the meal and congratulate him on his award. It was refreshing to be around so many politicians in such a non-political environment. The company was warm and the conversation easy. He was grateful for the complementary remarks from a Congressman from Wyoming who had been member of the First Marine Division in the First Gulf War. He shook hands with him and stood behind the podium.

"Thank you very much for your warm welcome here today, and thank you especially to Congressman Walker who was so kind with his remarks. To say that this day has been overwhelming would be an understatement of vast proportions. I have to say the highlight so far has not been actually receiving the medal but getting to see the medics I served with over there…many for the first time since coming home.

"This luncheon will also be a highlight, since I have been received so well by men and women who have served their country in uniform and now continue to serve in other capacities. I do hope one day that his room will become too small to accommodate the number of elected leaders who are also veterans. You all bring a needed and unique voice to our federal government, and, as a member of the military, I am very grateful for all of you taking the time to not only form this coalition but to advocate for the men and women who are in harm's way. As you know, members of the military have to be somewhat vocally subdued when it comes to political views, and it helps to have you all here to be our voice. My charge to you is to always remember what it was like when you served. Remember the highs and the lows. Remember the frustrations that you had with politicians, and strive to educate those who haven't been in your shoes so that they may understand the specialness of the military family's situation.

"Your kind words today mean more than I can express, for you know what it's like to be a soldier. Franklin Jones once said that 'bravery is being the only one who knows you're afraid.' Seeing the nods in the audience before me helps me believe that there are many who understand that this medal doesn't represent my actions that night as much as it represents the entire military and the excellence within it. Because of this, I will always carry this medal with pride, but will also carry it for the countless others who performed just as heroically without the pomp and celebration that I have gratefully received today."

Applause.

"I also make a request of you here today. I have no doubt that all of you are dedicated to advocating for the American soldier who is in harm's way. I ask you to also be forward-thinking and advocate for the soldier who has returned home. I do not feel that our system is prepared to handle the amount of men and women who will need not only physical care after the battle but also mental care. We are just starting to see the after-effects of many of the post-war conditions our military and veteran's health system will have to face for decades to come. I urge you to work diligently to make sure that we are funded and equipped to care for soldiers and veterans with such problems as post-traumatic stress disorder and traumatic brain injury. We also must educate to the public on these issues, along with giving the care needed to bring these men and women out of the debilitating combination of mental suffering from the disease itself and the shame of being affected.

"I, along with many of you here, struggled upon returning home with trying to put memories of humanity's capacity for evil behind me. Simple tasks such as driving and sleeping come with challenges I had not known before combat. I have been able to break free of these challenges with the help of friends and the tincture of time. That being said, to this day I continue to try to find a way to deal with the survivor's guilt that many a soldier has and very few are able to describe to others who haven't been downrange."

He felt a heaviness in the back of his throat and fought the wetness that began to form along his lower eyelids. He cleared his throat and willed himself to go on but knew he should wrap it up sooner rather than later.

"I thank you again for having Anna and I today for this wonderful lunch today, and I also thank you for what you do and who your represent. I assure you that I will do everything I can to make you and all veterans proud by carrying this medal with honor, and I will always stand ready to assist you in any way I can to help your efforts to advocate for our honored veterans."

Congressman Walker met him at the podium and shook his hand as the applause enveloped him from below the stage. Walker handed him a glass and held one as well as he leaned toward the microphone and asked all to stand.

"You honor us today with your presence, Major Reece, and we thank you for making the time to be here today. In accordance with a tradition of our meetings, I ask everyone to raise their glasses." Michael and the rest of the room complied. "Here's to us and those like us."

"DAMNED FEW!" was the response from the veterans/representatives in the room.

*****

Governor Sutton sat with Haxton as they discussed the possibility of a fundraising event in Wilmington in the next week or so. Allied Seafood, Inc. was a company based in the North Carolina port city that processed the bounty of local Atlantic fishermen and sold it mainly to restaurants but also some high-end grocery stores who longed for the fresh fish that could be put on a plane and sent all over the continental United States. They had enjoyed a competitive advantage over their South American counterparts, thanks to a tariff on imported seafood as well as the lengthy inspection process of international seafood that threatened the ability to get their product to the customers fresh. The tariff and inspections had long had the sponsorship of Haxton, partly because other nations were not as diligent at pursuing efforts to preserve the threatened fish populations. His main reason, however, for championing this cause was because Sam Ivey, CEO of Allied Seafood, Inc., was a longtime friend and big-time donor to any campaign efforts of James Haxton.

Ivey knew that the Senator was coming to Figure Eight Island in the next several days, and he wanted to host a fundraising dinner at Cape Fear Country Club in his honor. The fact that an exploratory committee had already been formed under the direction of Gov. Sutton with the purpose of being a launch vehicle for Haxton's Presidential campaign was no secret, and Ivey wanted to be remembered as one of the first financial backers of such an effort. His business was always in need of friends in high places.

The fact that this was an excuse to get Haxton in the Capitol Building for an entirely different purpose didn't change the fact that this fundraiser had to be handled carefully. Ivey was very popular with the Senator's environmental constituents because of his conservation efforts, but he was also known as a Grade A ball-breaker in negotiations with the local unions when it came to employee pay and benefits. It helped that Ivey was quite satisfied with his role as a successful "bundler" of campaign contributions who had the ear of his benefactor and never sought press attention for his campaign efforts, but Sutton wanted to make this a quiet gathering, simply because a Presidential run in the face of pissed-off labor unions was not a good way to start.

Sutton stirred two Splenda packets into his iced tea in deference to the admonishments he had received from his physician. Decades of campaigning in North Carolina politics made it impossible to avoid barbecue dinners, sweet tea, and potluck desserts. His profound political success also had made him forty pounds overweight and borderline diabetic.

"We're setting it up as a three-hundred-dollar-per-plate dinner for a couple hundred guests. The take won't be staggering, but several of the guests will be good friends to have in future efforts. Sam is covering all of the expenses at Cape Fear Country Club. He was hoping you would announce your intentions to run, but he understands it wouldn't be the right setting for that. But everyone knows that it's coming."

Haxton nodded as he pushed the salad around in front of him. "Sounds good. Who will be the point man on it?"

"Me. I figured I was going down a few days before you anyway. I'm going to play a round of golf with Sam when I get there at the club and we'll iron out all the details." He glanced at his watch. The plan was to leave when he felt the vibration of a text from Johnson, who was patrolling the hallways outside.

"Behave yourself down there. After that I wouldn't mind not having anything on the calendar for a few days. I would like to get some fishing in and just breathe the salt air a bit without any obligations."

"Sounds like a plan to me. I have to head out the day after the dinner. After your little rest, we are going to have to start making some concrete plans in terms of announcing and campaign staff. I'm arranging a meeting with the International Longshoreman's Union after that in case they catch wind of our event with Ivey." He handed the waiter his credit card as he passed. "My turn to treat."

*****

Rachelle was starting to get impatient. She leaned against the wall under one of the countless colonial-style paintings that adorned the Capitol walls. Jeff, her cameraman, played Words with Friends on his iPhone while the camera rested on the marble floor beside him. She checked her watch again. *If that little prick has sent me on a snipe hunt, I will rip his little balls off.*

Shortly after that thought, she saw Matt Weinrib loitering in the same area. After exchanging pleasantries, they soon figured out they were here on the same tip. It didn't bother her. The print-news dinosaurs couldn't hold a candle to the non-stop twenty-four-hour-coverage cycle that had been created by cable news networks. She would be already growing tired of the continuous loops of her scoop on television by the time he had his article somewhere in the *Post*. He wasn't a threat, so she felt no reason to be standoffish. There may come a day when she would need his help on something and she was too smart to make enemies for no reason.

She asked him about his story on the connection between Haxton and the medal winner with some degree of genuine admiration. She started to put two and two together and realized that Johnson was likely the source for the story. She admonished herself after thinking about the fact that he didn't even realize he was being used. After all, she was standing in the hallway of the Capitol with her thumb up her ass at the same person's bidding. *It's Washington; everyone uses everyone else.*

Her questions about his story had made him stand a little taller and even gave him the confidence to hint that they should get together for drinks sometime. Jeff made a token effort to conceal his amusement while still fiddling on his phone. Rachelle had just dumped the starting wide receiver for the Washington Redskins for being handsome but unbearably stupid. *Dream on kid, she is WAY out of your league.*

*****

The twenty-year-old Capitol staff intern walked out of the room that was occupied by the CVC and would soon be vacated. He put his cell phone to his left ear and scratched his nose with his right hand.

Across the hall, Chip watched the actions of the kid, to whom he had given fifty bucks that morning, and winked at him. He began typing on his phone.

*****

Sutton stood and started pushing his chair into the table. "I'll walk you back to the office, and then I've got to meet up with a few folks before I head outta town."

They walked out of the dining area and turned to the right to head down the marbled corridor that would put them in the direction of Haxton's office building.

*****

MacLean's and Weinrib's phones began to chime at the exact same time, denoting a text that was sent from the same person:

Reece will b heading down the corridor by u in about two mins. Follow them and have cameras r d. I won't be with them. You'll thank me l8r.

"Well, I guess that's our cue," Weinrib said as they pushed themselves off the wall.

"Guess so." MacLean showed the text to Jeff and they put their phones away and waited.

*****

The CVC meeting over, Walker offered to give his VIP guests a tour of the Capitol Building.

"Congressman Walker, there is a huge tour group down that way already. You might want to start the other way and work your way around, sir," said the young intern that was suddenly fifty bucks richer today.

"Thanks, Bret. Is that OK with you guys?"

"Neither of us has ever been here, so any direction will be new to us Congressman," Michael replied.

Anna was holding her husband's hand while stealing glances at the new light blue ribbon that hung from his neck. "Congressman Walker, it is very kind of you to do this for us. I know you must have a busy schedule and we are very grateful."

"Well, Mrs. Reece, you can show your gratitude by calling my Bill. That goes for both of you."

"As long as you call me Anna."

"Michael," Reece said, smiling at the very likeable Congressman from the state of Wyoming.

Their dress shoes echoed down the hallway as they started the tour. None of the three noticed Chip Johnson slip into a side room behind them, nor did they take any notice of the cameraman and two others who followed them at a casual, but not too far, distance behind them. They had to make frequent stops along the way as several politicians and staffers recognized Michael and offered their congratulations. The stress of the formalities behind him, he began to relax and enjoyed the company of a new friend as well as the best wife a man could ever ask for. He only wished that Elizabeth and Charlie were with them.

It was less of a tour and more of a conversation between new friends with occasional tidbits of knowledge shared about the building and the institution. Bill Walker was exceedingly likable and possessed an easygoing manner that seemed a complete contrast to many of his ever-smiling and ever-scheming colleagues. He shared stories with Michael about the liberation of Kuwait and his time as a nervous Captain in the First Marine Division. They hit it off immediately, and it warmed Anna to see her husband at ease and smiling when talking about his military experiences. There was a connection between soldiers who had seen combat that allowed them to have an understanding that others would never possess.

Immediately after that gratifying thought she felt an electricity to the air as the grip of her husband's hand tightened and began to perspire. He had stopped in his tracks and the look on his face was one she had never seen before. She wasn't sure if it was fear, panic, or surprise, but she was sure it was not good. Walker had seemed to notice the change in his demeanor as well. They both traced the path of his eyes, which were locked on a tall gentleman in a dark blue pin-striped suit walking toward them, a man who didn't see them yet and was accompanied by a more portly man who was returning his phone to his pocket. Then the tall gentleman saw Michael and registered surprise as well, coming to a stop only a few feet in front of them. Anna thought the temperature of the building had dropped ten degrees in the last few seconds...

CHAPTER 17

The brief period of silence seemed like an eternity as Anna sensed something was not right at all. She wasn't sure, but there might have been a slight tremor in her husband's hand. She reached her other hand across her body and placed it on her husband's forearm.

"Well, how about this?" Congressman Walker was familiar with the *Washington Post* story about the link between Major Reece and the man standing in front of them. "Good afternoon to you, Senator Haxton. I was taking Major Reece and his wife around the Capitol on a tour. I understand you know each other."

Anna's suspicions that this might have been choreographed evaporated as she saw a similar look of surprise on the Senator's face. The uneasiness of the encounter wasn't lost on Walker either, but she alone seemed to realize that something went beyond awkwardness. She sensed something from her husband that she had not quite experienced before. It wasn't simply surprise, since Michael had always been someone who could roll with whatever came his way whether it was anticipated or not. She wasn't sure if she was incorrect or she simply didn't want to realize what it represented. It seemed like fear. She thought she might not be the only one concerned when she sensed Tripp closing the distance between himself and their group.

Haxton seemed to regain mental focus after a brief silence. "Good afternoon to you as well, Congressman Walker. We do indeed know each other. Major Reece, it's great to see you again. Like just about everyone in the nation right now, I am very proud of your award as well as your many accomplishments in life." He turned to Anna. "I presume you are Mrs. Reece. James Haxton. It's a pleasure to meet you."

Anna shook the offered hand, followed by another.

"Governor Hal Sutton ma'am. It's an honor to meet you both."

No one except Sutton and possibly Tripp seemed to have noticed that this interaction was being filmed by the cameraman that had followed the Reeces down the hall.

"It must be pretty gratifying to see such a success grow from some of your charitable efforts, Senator," Walker said as he stood in between the two men.

Michael glanced at his wife and the subtle glaze of perspiration was evident on his forehead. *Something's wrong.* He seemed to be having trouble creating words to speak at the moment.

"It's gratifying to see anyone accomplish what Michael has, but it's because of Michael and not anyone's charity." Haxton smiled and nodded at Reece. "He is the reason he is what he is today."

"Umm, thank you, Senator. Good to see you again." Michael stammered out.

Anna was going from a feeling of uneasiness to alarm. She felt like she was watching fire trucks pass her by on the road, heading in what could have been the direction of her house.

She wasn't alone. Behind her, Tripp felt the tightly clipped hairs on the back of his neck stand up.

Haxton placed a hand on Reece's shoulder as the sound of a digital camera firing came from beside the video camera man. "I'm very proud of you, Michael."

There was no longer any doubt about it. There was a building tremor in the hand of her husband. Her alarm was now transforming into a protective instinct.

"Senator, would you like to join us for the rest of the tour? You have walked these halls longer than I have, and maybe you could catch up with an old friend," Walker offered to his colleague.

Michael hadn't moved or said anything other than his broken response to the Senator. Anna could see the fire trucks entering her neighborhood, on her street, with an ambulance in tow. She had never seen her husband this way, and Walker seemed to be noticing something was off as well.

"Wow. What are the odds? I promise you, this was not an arranged part of the tour, guys. Shall we continue?" Walker asked the Reece family.

The emergency vehicles were now slowing as they approached her house. There was a hint of smoke in the air. There was a dryness in Anna's mouth, and the look on her husband's face, however subtle, was triggering protective instincts for her family. "Gentlemen, I apologize, but with the lunch meeting going a little longer than we planned we have to meet up with my parents and get the kids." It was a lie, but she felt an overwhelming need to get her husband out of this building. The public officials around them responded with understanding smiles.

"Not a problem, Mrs. Reece. I want to give you both my card with my personal number on it. If there is anything I can ever do for you, please don't hesitate to call me anytime. Major Reece, it has been an absolute honor to meet you and spend time with you and your wife."

Michael seemed to be emerging from the place he had been the past couple of minutes and shook Walker's hand. "Congressman, it was my honor as well, and I apologize for cutting out of the tour early. I appreciate what the CVC is doing, and I mean it when I say I'm willing to help in any way I can. Good to see you again Senator Haxton." He shook the hands of the men around them making only sporadic eye contact and walked away from Walker, Sutton, and his old mentor.

Walker instructed his aide to let the Reece family's driver know that they would be coming out after they exchanged goodbyes. Michael and Anna walked hand in hand toward the exit, passing Senator Haxton, who was off to the side of the corridor speaking with a journalist while the same videographer recorded it. Anna noticed the reporter that had been taking the digital camera shots approaching them.

"Major Reece. Matt Weinrib with *The Washington Post*. Would you have a moment to speak with me?"

Anna decided to handle this one herself. "I'm sorry Mr. Weinrib, we are on our way to pick up our kids. Maybe another time." They kept walking.

Fuck. Right now, Rachelle was getting an on-camera interview with Senator Haxton, and Matt's target was leaving the building. He felt like the proverbial third wheel on an important date. The man's wife was very polite in her refusal, but instinct told him not to press the issue—an instinct reinforced by the look on the huge man in uniform right behind them.

"Not a problem, Mrs. Reece. Have a good day." He noticed her give a smile of gratitude as they walked away. He was 100 percent certain that the couple had no idea this meeting was going to occur, but the odd thing was that it didn't seem that Haxton knew about it either.

Weinrib saw McLean concluding the impromptu interview and noticed the man off to the side. It was former Governor Hal Sutton. He knew of their ties together from researching his article and also remembered that Sutton had been an active participant in virtually every campaign Haxton had been a part of, and now he watched him talking on his cell phone with a smile on his face. *Of course.* This dance had been choreographed, all right, but without the knowledge of either of the dancers. He put two and two together and decided to act on a hunch. He dialed a number on his phone.

It took several rings. "Hello?"

"Hey Chip, it's Matt," Weinrib said as he watched Sutton, who still had the phone to his ear but was no longer talking.

"Hey Matt...let me get off the other line," and there was a click.

Weinrib watched Sutton say a few brief words then drop the phone from his ear. His own phone clicked again at the same time.

"Hey Matt. Sorry about that. How did it go?"

"Well, I think Rachelle will owe you one, but not much for me. I tried to get comments from Reece after they got together but they were in a hurry to get out of there. She got the taped comments from Haxton, who seemed happy to talk to her."

"Well, what can I say? Rachelle is a hell of a lot better looking than both of us. Sorry it was a bit of a strikeout for you. I'll make it up to you."

"I'm guessing the Gentleman from North Carolina doesn't know about this little choreographed stunt." Weinrib decided to throw down a small gauntlet. *Goddamn right you'll make it up to me.* He wasn't blind to the fact that this wouldn't hurt a budding Presidential campaign one bit.

Chip smiled to himself and decided to play a countermove. "You guess correct, my friend. I'm taking a gamble here, but I believe people should know what kind of man Haxton is. I appreciate you hearing me out the other night and giving me the backbone to do it."

"Umm, well, no problem Chip. I'm always happy to talk things through with you. I think it was a pretty brilliant setup, actually."

Johnson was mentally patting himself on the back as he listened to the reporter on the other end of the phone. He had meant to puff him up a bit, but more than that he wanted him to feel a degree of responsibility for the setup. He thought of a quote by Adlai Stevenson: "Flattery is all right so long as you don't inhale." This eager guy was sucking it up like it was fine wine.

"Listen Matt, I know Rachelle got the better end of this deal. I will make it up to you...I promise. Listen, I gotta run, but I'll catch up with you later buddy."

Matt hit the end button on his phone as the other end of the line clicked. He was certain that there were two behind-the-curtain players in this drama—Chip and Sutton. Watching the two statesmen walking away, it certainly seemed that Haxton was angry with Sutton and the Governor was trying to get him to relax. Maybe he suspected it was as set up, or maybe he didn't want to step into any of Reece's spotlight. *Maybe this guy really is the real deal.*

*****

"Did you do this?" Haxton did not seemed pleased as he walked down the massive marbled corridor along with his long-time friend.

"Nope. Sometimes you're just lucky James." Sutton's reply was rewarded with a scowl. "Look, you were perfect with the interview afterward. You were deferential and came off as a proud and humble mentor. It will look great, and this is solid gold when it comes to campaign material."

"You know that we can't push ourselves into this any further."

"We won't. Any further questions about it will be met with a raising of the hands and distancing of yourself from his success. It will only elevate your status as the elder benefactor who wants the best for his underlings."

"I think we consider too much the good luck of the early bird and not enough the bad luck of the early worm," Haxton said, quoting Franklin D. Roosevelt. "Don't push it."

Sutton patted his friend on the back. "Agreed."

*****

Not to the surprise of either Billy or Chris, the true owner of the cell phone Darnell had used to contact his brother showed up at the Krispy Kreme over an hour late and was high. After going back and forth over how much money counted as being worth his while, he finally gave them the location and phone number of the trailer that was the occasional location of Darnell Tyler.

Predictably, the number was out of service when they called. Billy had to visit a member of his church who was currently a patient at Memorial Mission Hospital, and he agreed to go Darnell's house with Chris after visiting his sick parishioner.

*****

Henry Sallinger (the birth name of Hank Strickland seemed too pedestrian and common for a big-time player in cable news) had received instructions in his ear piece during the commercial break about the change in plans for his next segment. Not a single hair moved on his perfectly coifed head as he nodded to the comments of his producer. His two-hour show on MSNBC was primarily focused on the political comings and goings of the day. It followed the standard format of the host talking about an issue and its background, followed by commentary from two marginally respected hacks on each end of the political spectrum. His job was to

216

interject and steer the debate between the two guests of the show and offer his "impartial" additions at times. The fact that he had been the campaign manager of two Senators and one former Governor all of the same political party didn't seem to give anyone there pause about his objectivity.

The upcoming discussion on capital gains taxation was being pushed back to break in with a new story from Rachelle McLean. They had recorded a chance encounter between Senator James Haxton and the Medal of Honor recipient who had been honored at the White House earlier today. Haxton was a former mentor to the man when he was a child at an orphanage in North Carolina, and they had followed up the encounter with a brief interview with the Senator.

He was fed the introductory comments that he would say leading up to the live chat with McLean. Sallinger knew McLean and remembered how attractive she was. It was too bad she was a lesbian. (This assessment was based solely on the fact she had turned down his invitation for a late-night romp after the previous year's election coverage show. That she simply wasn't attracted in the least to the excessively hair-sprayed pompous ass-kisser didn't seem to occur to him.)

"We're back in twenty," was the cue from the producer, giving Sallinger a twenty-second warning before returning back to live broadcasting. He checked his hair and makeup in the small mirror he kept under the table top of his set and situated himself for the camera.

"In five, four, three..." The producer then showed fingers for two and one.

"And we're back. Thanks for staying with us. We are going to change course a bit in order to talk to MSNBC political correspondent Rachelle McLean, who happened to catch a chance encounter between two old friends...both of whom have been in the news a good bit lately." He swiveled slightly in his seat toward the large screen to his left, which showed the shoulder-up view of McLean with a "LIVE" moniker at the bottom-right corner of the screen. "Rachelle, what did you guys get to see today?"

"Well, Henry, we caught up with Senator James Haxton today after a chance encounter in the hallway of the Capitol Building with Major Michael Reece, who was awarded the

217

Congressional Medal of Honor today by President Danielson at the White House. Reece was the guest of honor at a luncheon put on by the Congressional Veterans Caucus and ran in to Haxton while on a tour of the Capitol, compliments of Congressman Bill Walker, who is the current Chair of the CVC. As you know, Reece grew up in an orphanage in North Carolina whose main benefactor is Senator Haxton. Their connections were chronicled in an article by Matt Weinrib of *The Washington Post* just a few days ago. Here is the footage of the encounter."

As the video was shown, Sallinger was on the other side of a split screen nodding thoughtfully while McLean had a few seconds before she was back on the live feed. She really liked the spunk of the *Post* reporter she had met earlier in the day and decided to throw him some props in her remarks. She didn't, on the other hand, share the same feelings for the pin-striped dipshit that was hosting the show right now. She remembered his drunken propositions the night of the election, along with his air of certainty that no woman could say no to the Henry Sallinger experience. She had joked with a colleague later that the only reason he wanted to kiss her was the alcohol had made him mistake her for an upper-level MSNBC executive's ass.

"Wow. I have to say, Rachelle, that the Washington cynic in me would say that this might not be as coincidental as we think," Sallinger said with his trademark Washington-insider smile.

"I certainly understand what you mean Henry. Although we were not able to get any comments from Major Reece afterward, I can tell you by the reaction of both of them that it certainly seemed to be anything but choreographed. That being said, this is certainly the kind of exposure one would want for a man who is the debatable favorite to win the Democratic Party's nomination for the next Presidential election. I did speak with a senior member of Senator Haxton's staff, who said unequivocally that this was a chance encounter and wasn't arranged by anyone." She knew that was bullshit, but it was how the game was played. "We were able to speak with the Senator immediately afterward, and here's what he had to say."

They flipped over to a full-screen broadcast of her interview with Haxton, then the screen returned to McLean, who recited the heroism and inspirational arc of the life of Michael Reece.

*****

Darnell watched Henry Sallinger segue to commercial on the television at the Green Mountain Pawn Shop. The combination of narcotic withdrawal and lack of sleep certainly was not helping him process what he had just seen. As he gradually emerged from his fog, Willie Sampson walked to the counter from the back entrance, still stinking of massage oils. Darnell stood up from his chair, still staring at the screen.

"Whatcha got for me today Darnell?"

Darnell turned to the owner with a look of rage. "Fuck you. I've been here for fucking ever waiting on your ass."

Willie stood at the counter in amazement as he watched Darnell walk out the door. He couldn't tell if it had been sweat or tears on his face under the hood of the sweatshirt. He shook his head at the obviously withdrawing addict and went back to his work. *He'll be back. No one else is going to give him cash for whatever the hell he stole this time.*

*****

Michael had not uttered one word through the corridor nor outside the Capitol Building, where Anna continued to hold his hand with a worried look poorly concealed on her face. Tripp was no longer keeping a casual distance from them and had the appearance of a family Rottweiler standing between the children and a home invader. They both sensed something was not right and both had absolutely no idea what it was.

They climbed into the vehicle. Anna looked at her husband and fought the urge to cry over something she didn't understand. "Are you okay baby?"

Tripp was just as confused, and his career Army NCO vocabulary came out, which was something that didn't usually happen in the presence of Anna. "Sir, what the fuck happened back there?"

Michael kissed Anna's cheek. She could still feel his trembling, although it seemed to be less than earlier. "I'm fine…I'll be fine. Look, I'm going to need to talk to you both about

219

something, but this isn't the place. I'm sorry I kind of zoned out back there. I'm going to need some time to figure how to explain this to you guys, but I promise I'm not in any danger anymore."

The unconscious use of "anymore" hung in the air as Tripp and Anna glanced at each other. Tripp's face showed more confusion than alertness now in the safety of the vehicle, while Anna seemed to be simmering a quiet but growing anger.

Tripp put his hand on top of the interwoven fingers of the Michael and Anna. "Any way you want to handle it. I'm here for you both."

The rest of the ride to the Blair House was a quiet one, but Michael seemed to be recovering his bearings and losing some of his tension. He looked at his wife and winked.

"Nice audible you called back there to get us out of the building. Everything's going to be fine."

*****

Billy and Chris pulled up to the trailer on the outskirts of Asheville that matched the address that had cost them fifty bucks. Judging by the grass height underneath them, the two busted-up cars in front had not been operable for quite some time. There was the sound of a television coming from the inside, but no one answered the door when they knocked several times.

Although it was more than a small risk to enter a home inhabited by users/dealers, Chris decided to do just that. The inside was an absolute wreck, with trash, dirty dishes, and drug paraphernalia scattered everywhere, and the place smelled like shit from a combination of the overall lack of any upkeep as well as something else.

Chris turned to Billy. "Do you smell something burning?"

"Maybe but it could be spoons," Billy replied, referring to the spoons heroin addicts used to "cook" the drug in water before injecting it. Billy noted that the television from the far bedroom was on a cable news channel, which struck him as odd. "Anybody back there?" he yelled toward the bedroom. No response.

As they approached the last room, the burning smell intensified. It was not the charred chemical odor Chris remembered from his own times as a user. It was something different.

As they reached the door, they saw two feet spread out on the floor in front of the television. Startling a heroin addict from his sleep was a good way to get jumped or worse, so he walked to the door softly. What he saw in the room brought a horror that made him fight the overwhelming urge to vomit. Instead he just screamed.

On the floor sat his brother, with his back against the footboard of the bed. The front of his t-shirt was a dark crimson from the blood that had poured from his mouth, some of which had congealed there, as if his mouth was full of wine-colored jelly. His eyes were grotesquely swollen and blue, while the top of his head had been blown open like the ruptured peak of a volcano, explaining the crimson spatters on the ceiling above him. By his right hand was a Sig Sauer handgun containing the spent gunpowder residue that was the origin of the burning odor. In his left hand was a folded piece of paper that said "Chris" on the outside.

Billy held his friend as the screams turned to sobs. He said a silent prayer for his friend's brother and hoped that God would have mercy on him for performing such a horrible sin as suicide. He thought of a verse from Revelations and said, "He shall wipe away every tear from their eyes, and death shall be no more, neither shall there be mourning, nor crying, nor pain anymore, for the former things have passed away."

After Chris began to gain some semblance of self-control, Billy stepped into the narrow hallway to call the police. Chris knelt down beside his brother. He quietly wept some more, then noticed again the note in his brother's left hand. He took it and unfolded the paper, some of which was spattered with blood as well. The message inside was short and had not been distorted by the blood:

You know why.

They never had to pay a price for what they did.

221

I'm sorry. It's not your fault.

Always your brother, D

He folded the note again and put it in his pocket. He kissed his twin on the forehead, not giving a damn about the blood that was getting on him. "I'm sorry D." He felt the cold blood now on his check, and he believed he had more on his hands. "I'm sorry I didn't get here a little sooner."

CHAPTER 18

Michael awoke precariously balanced on the extreme edge of the mattress on the antique four-poster bed at the Blair House, requiring him to grab the bedside table to keep from falling off. The fitted sheet under him was drenched from perspiration. Only the distant sound of the grandfather clock in the hallway encroached upon the silence in the room. He told himself that the shaking was from almost falling out of the bed, but he knew that it was more likely from the place that sleep often took him and from which he had just escaped. He was unsure if his screams from slumber had actually occurred in real life as well until he rolled over to look at the other side of the bed and saw Anna sitting up against the headboard. The invading moonlight through the window was reflected on the tear trails on her face.

"I'm sorry baby. I almost rolled off the damn bed, I guess," was his hurried reply to discovering her awake. He knew even as he said the words that they were going to be inadequate to explain away tonight's disturbance.

"He hurt you, didn't he?" Anna said as she vacillated between sadness and anger.

Michael's poorly concealed nightmares had been present from the time they first shared a bed. She had assumed that they arose from growing up in an abusive home before being rescued, but recent events suggested she was probably wrong.

God had blessed her with two of the greatest parents anyone could wish for, and she felt like she could never understand the hell that Michael had escaped from in his childhood. Because of that, she had allowed him the illusion that she was unaware and never let him know that his struggles would frequently awake her as well. The anger she felt was partly at herself for realizing she may have been wrong all along, but most of it was at the fact that someone may have brought more horror to her husband's already horrible childhood.

"What are you talking about?" Michael felt a panic that he imagined an animal would feel when he realized he had no means to escape something unpleasant.

She placed a hand on her husband's cheek and spoke to him while her lip still quivered. "Sweetheart, if you don't want to talk about it, I will understand. But don't lie to me. You know what I'm asking you."

There was no way out. He tried his hardest to think of anything that could explain away the series of events that had brought his wife to ask him that question. There was a searing burn in his throat from rising stomach acid and an abrupt increase in saliva production as he fought his body's attempts at retching. The shaking that had been abating began to return with vigor, and he felt a flushing warmth travel across his skin. The tears came as he began to stand.

"I...I can't breathe," he choked out as his breathing became rapid. The room began to collapse on him and he felt an overwhelming need to escape. He started to hop to the chair that held his prosthesis ten feet away, but the world seemed to be spinning around him and he fell to the floor, his fast breathing changed to whispered sobs.

She leapt from the bed and ran around to the other side to help him...to hold him...to protect him. He didn't need to say anything now. She knew. At that moment, everything came together and funneled into one conclusion. The nightmares, the avoidance of returning back to his roots, his silence about much of his young years, and his constant fear about the well-being of his own children. She simply held the man who had been her rock and her best friend since she had met him while he unsuccessfully tried to compose himself. Their entire married life, his presence had given her a constant feeling of love and safety. He was the man that evil couldn't break, the flower that grew from the scorched forest floor. Now she held a man that she realized had been broken long ago and had never completely mended. The image of the man whom she had just met a few hours ago flashed into her mind. *You son of a bitch.*

There was a building sense of panic and guilt intruding into Michael's existence at the moment. The life he had worked so hard to build seemed to be in danger of being repossessed by the demons of the past. He had seen his education as the best bet to escape the horrors of poverty and victimization, and along the way he had found the woman who now held him as he cowered on the floor. She had made him believe that God had finally smiled on him and sent him an angel who would give him love and hold his hand as he continued his exodus from the bondage that had been his childhood. He felt he had returned the favor by not being honest

224

with her about the most horrific details of an early life of abuse that had led him into the clutches of pure evil. Now she knew that he was more damaged that she had ever known, if not broken all together.

"I'm so sorry, Anna. I'm so sorry."

She tightened her embrace of him. "There is nothing to be sorry about, Michael. I love you. I love you so much." She turned his face to hers. "If you think there is anything that could change that, you're wrong."

She had always wondered how so much could have been thrust on just one person, as a child, and it had often saddened her. After that afternoon's chance encounter, she now had an image that seemed to personify the ugliness that had tried so hard to destroy the man she loved. She no longer felt sadness. She felt hatred.

She spent the rest of the night listening to her husband open up about a man who had taken an interest in him for what he believed to be the desire to mentor him and show him opportunities that could be his with hard work and dedication. He had been shepherded into educational opportunities as a young man he would never have hoped to enjoy from his meager background. Shortly after being accepted into Vanderbilt Academy, with tuition compliments of The Honorable James Haxton, he learned that the doors that had been opened to him had a price.

The overwhelming majority of child victims of sexual abuse keep their struggles hidden from others. Feelings of dependency, indebtedness, fear, and shame are often barriers to seeking help. Michael had them all. Haxton made him keenly aware on repeated occasions that his education, his home, his food, and his chance at a better life were all dependent on being in the continued good graces of his benefactor. Haxton was a pillar of the community, with accolades from the worlds of business, politics, and charity. Michael was the filthy orphan that had been given a new life. Who in God's name would believe him if he told? Who would he tell? Everyone in his life that he trusted was in some way dependent on the charity of Haxton. What would happen to him? What would happen to Sycamore House, and would he be able to stay there? Who would pay for his education?

What resulted was a life where all those around him saw him as the apple of a benevolent mentor's eye, when in reality he was simply a toy for another's amusement and pleasure. He channeled all his efforts to succeed in school and make others proud, which he did without fail, but only he knew that it was his desperation to prop up a withered sense of self-worth that had been completely crushed by his supposed savior. Haxton had been masterful in convincing Michael that his chance at a good life as well as any chance for the Sycamore House to stay in existence was all dependent on his consent and his silence; this alone would buy his eventual escape and the survival of Sycamore. He decided that he was unworthy to expect his rescue to be more important than the people around him that had given him shelter, love, and hope.

He silently and obediently went to "mentoring sessions" at Haxton's home in Asheville or his getaway on Figure Eight Island, where he was treated as nothing more than a receptacle. On one hand he felt worthless for being a victim of such deviance, and he felt deceitful on the other for misleading those who cared for him unconditionally. And he felt the same deceitfulness had followed him away from Asheville...

"I didn't know how to tell you. I just wanted to bury it forever." His tears had evolved into almost a detached numbness as he shared the details of the darkest times of an already dark story. "You were everything good and different than what I had known, and I didn't want to poison it with this. I thought you wouldn't have me if you knew...I'm sorry."

Anna squeezed a little harder the hand she had held since the beginning of his story. "I love you for who you are, Michael. Where you came from doesn't change that." Her tears had ebbed as well, and she mainly listened with quiet horror. "I don't know how you have carried this all this time without letting anyone know."

"You're actually the second person I have ever told, Anna."

One name leapt immediately into her mind. "Charlie."

"I told myself that I was worried it could happen to someone else, but it may have been that it had finally eaten its way to the surface and I just couldn't take it anymore. I told him one night after I had helped him clean up after dinner. We sat outside the back door of the kitchen that he used to use to go smoke until I guilted him into quitting. I told him that I was ashamed and didn't know what to do. Haxton was in town again and I was afraid he was going to come get me again. And I had reached my breaking point. I was going to run away but wanted Charlie to know it wasn't because of anything at Sycamore House. I thought I had it all figured out, but I was just a stupid kid who was panicked. I told him I would finish school wherever I wound up and would send him a letter whenever I got there." Michael actually chuckled. "It was idiotic, but I was sixteen."

"What did he do?"

"He told me I wasn't going to go anywhere. If Haxton called the next day, he would figure out some reason I couldn't go. He was so angry...I could tell, but he stayed calm. He promised me he would help me work out a plan and would have my back no matter what. All he asked was to promise that I wouldn't do anything crazy like running away that night. He was starting to cry, and I was too, but he said if we didn't come back in someone would come looking for us and find us crying behind the kitchen and ask what was going on. He hugged me and told me he loved me more than he could imagine loving a child of his own."

"What happened after that?" Anna asked but feared what the answer was going to be.

"He died," Michael replied with his lip starting to quiver again. "He died that night in a car accident. The next day, I can't tell you how close I came to killing myself. I took it as a sign that it was a secret that wasn't meant to be told. Haxton took me to Figure Eight the next day. Nothing happened there and he promised he wouldn't touch me again. He told me not to make any rash decisions and, for the first time, he threatened me. He said if I ever told anyone about what he had done, he would destroy me. He said he would close down Sycamore House and would convince everyone that I was crazy, and he reminded me how everyone saw him as a great human being and it wouldn't be hard at all to make me look like an unstable battered kid who was as ungrateful as I was insane. He promised that he would give me money for college and even after that. I was so relieved that it was going to stop that I agreed to never tell anyone and promised myself that I would do anything to get out of there and never come back."

"Did he know you had told Charlie?"

Michael shook his head. "No. I think the sight of me being so unhinged about Charlie made him worry I might talk to someone. I think he decided to cut his losses and cover his behind. Whatever it was, it was the beginning of my escape. I didn't want to break away from everyone like I did, but I didn't want to jeopardize the home and their jobs." He looked at Anna briefly then back at the floor. "I know what you want to ask me and the answer is no...I don't. I have worked hard to get away from that time and I want to leave it behind me. I have found happiness, and I think I've earned the right to keep it in the way I choose. I'm gonna tell Tripp about it at some point, but after that I would like to bury it forever at least as much as I can."

Anna rested her head on his shoulder. Although he wouldn't have minded at all, she didn't feel right offering an opinion on how to handle this. "I'm sorry this happened to you Michael. I love you honey." Her response had felt terribly inadequate to her, considering the gravity of the revelations from their conversation.

"I love you too. That's all I needed to hear."

Horrible memories are never pleasant to revisit, especially given the amount of effort he had exhausted to hide them. Nevertheless, he still felt a sense of catharsis and, to some degree, relief that there was now literally nothing that he hadn't shared with his wife. They sat beside each other on the edge of the antique bed and watched the sun rise over the nation's capital. Neither of them had ever looked more forward to going home than they did at that moment.

Anna went to shower and get ready for the day, while Michael put on his Army PTUs for a date with David. They met outside the Blair House and went for a run that took them first to the Capitol then down the National Mall, passing first the Washington Monument and the reflecting pool and ending at the Lincoln Memorial. They sat at the steps under the watch of he who Michael felt was the most courageous man that his beloved country had ever produced and caught their breath—Michael taking a good bit longer than Tripp to do so. They sat in silence for quite a while, just watching the other joggers and dog-walkers framed in the background of the gossamer wisps of fog that rose from the reflecting pool.

"You OK, buddy?" Tripp broke the silence while still watching the awakening city in front of them. "I've never seen you flustered like that before. You don't have to tell me anything or talk about it if you don't want to. I just want you to know that I'm here for you no matter what."

Tripp deserved an explanation for the day before and his devotion to Reece was without question. It was time. Reece spent the next twenty minutes opening up to his friend as the morning sun burned away the last wisps of water vapor escaping from the reflecting pool while Tripp listened in silence vacillating between sadness and rage at the suffering his friend had endured. Opening up to his wife only hours before made narrating it again easier to do without breaking down. They sat together in silence for several minutes without either one feeling the need to fill the quietness to avoid discomfort; one of the truest marks of a close friendship. Tripp patted the back of his friend and sniffed away the tears that had not been allowed to escape his eyes. "I'm sorry, Mike."

"You and Anna are the only ones in my life that know about this. I don't think I'm going to do or say any more about it again after today and I'm just going to try to move on with my life. I might need to talk it out with you some more in the future, but right now I just want to try to leave it behind me. I think I've earned a little bit of normal for a while."

"Whenever you're ready brother." He tossed his water bottle into a nearby trash can. "You think you can make it back to quarters or are you too fucking old and fat?"

It was perfect. If there was anything he needed right now, it was a little bit of normalcy from his friend without all the formality and ceremony that had been part of their past several days. "There's the Booger I know." He squirted the remainder of his own water bottle directly on Tripp's crotch. "Oops, looks like you pissed your pants." And with that, he started his run back to Blair House with his friend giggling beside him.

After a brief farewell get-together with a few Pentagon representatives, the entire Reece family was reunited and driven to Reagan National, where they boarded a flight to Charlotte, with Tripp catching a quick connecting flight to Fayetteville. In a few days, he would be back with Michael for their diving trip. He would find out that his schedule would allow plenty of time with his friend in the next several weeks, since General Butts had received a phone call from the Commander in Chief explaining that it might be a good idea to let SFC Tripp be available to the newest MOH recipient during this time of adjustment. The CO of the Eighty-Second Airborne made sure that any responsibilities Tripp had coming up were covered by others and was given carte blanche for activities with MAJ Reece for the near future. David also didn't know that a letter of commendation from the President of the United States had been added to his personnel file as well.

*****

Dr. Alexander Bradley dictated his initial findings as the technician sutured the skin flap back into place on the deceased patient's head. State law required an autopsy for deaths that occurred outside of medical supervision, but this would be a fairly short dictation, given the cause of death was blatantly obvious. He brought the dictation microphone toward his face.

"Patient is a thirty-one-year-old black male. Injuries are consistent with a medium-caliber gunshot wound to the head, with the entry wound being in the hard palate and exit wound being in the posterior region of the sagittal suture, approximately three centimeters from the lamboidal suture convergence of the skull. There is a catastrophic loss of brain matter out of the exit wound. Based on burn signatures inside the oral cavity as well as along the skin fold between the first and second digits of the right hand, it is concluded that the gunshot wound was a range of less than two centimeters and was self-inflicted. Gross inspection of the liver shows signs of fatty infiltration and possibly early cirrhotic change consistent with possible alcohol or other illicit substance abuse. Blood and urine specimens were obtained for toxicology studies and will be added when available. End of dictation. Dr. Alexander Bradley, Chief of Pathology."

Bradley along with everyone else involved with this case knew the cause of death within three seconds of looking at the patient, but rules were rules, and if an autopsy was required it would be given the meticulous care that all cases received from him. He made sure the blood and urine specimens were properly labeled, along with representative biopsy specimens from various organs that would be prepped in formalin solution for microscopic evaluation. He thanked the pathology technician for his assistance and looked with satisfaction that the Y-shaped chest-to-abdomen incision was being closed with care. An autopsy was a fairly brutal invasion of the deceased's body, and Alex felt it was important to close it with as much care as you would with a living patient after a surgical procedure.

He signed the papers releasing the body to Crawford Funeral Home, and Alexander Bradley, MD, FCAP, Chief of Pathology at Blue Ridge Regional Medical Center as well as Buncombe County Medical Examiner and Current President of the North Carolina Medical Board, moved on to the next part of his day.

*****

Jack Pulaski sat at the bar at The Banana Leaf, which overlooked the Dominica Marine Center in Port Rosseau. His roaring belly laugh echoed through the establishment as he sat with several of the locals that he knew very well. He was an American but had permanently moved to Dominica in 2005, where he had started Clear Water Excursions, which in only a few years had come to be regarded as one of the best scuba diving operations on the island. He had about an hour before his clients would arrive at the marina and tie up for several days of diving, and he insisted on greeting new clients personally if at all possible.

Jack, or "Pully" as everyone knew him, was someone that you wouldn't forget even after one encounter. His trademark loose-fitting tropical shirts couldn't hide the fact that he was, by anyone's definition, a massive collection of muscles. His friends would joke that they could watch a movie projected on his back if he wore a white shirt. The slight graying at his temples and speckles of white in his chest hair were the only things that would give you a hint that he was almost fifty years old. His commitment to staying in peak physical condition had resulted in his appearance changing very little in the past two decades, with the exception of his decision to say goodbye to his mustache in surrender to a better-fitting scuba mask. He wore no jewelry and preferred flip-flops and cargo shorts wherever he went. The only decoration that could be seen on his body was a tattoo of an eagle perched on an anchor with a trident and pistol. It was known as the Special Warfare Insignia or the "Budweiser," and it denoted someone who was a Navy Seal.

Put simply, to know Pully was to love him. He could talk to anyone...and talk for a long time. If you had spent more than about ten minutes with him, people watching your conversation would think that you were lifelong friends, especially due to the frequent ear-splitting laughter he was known for around town. He always preferred to hang out with the locals and brought his customers to bars and businesses owned by local families instead of large international chains. He gave scuba lessons to local children for free and was always the first in line to support charitable efforts aimed at helping the island and its people. If Master Chief (Retired) Jack Pulaski had an enemy in Dominica, no one had been able to find him.

Pully was all smiles as he kicked back in his chair and watched a cricket match with a few of the marina workers in the bar. Smack talk is the universal guys' sports language all over the world, and the men critiqued the match and picked on the misfortunes of each other's teams in between pulls on bottles of Kubuli Beer. The former Navy Seal was probably more excited about this week's dive party than about any he had ever had.

The guys at Open Water Adventures in Charlotte had referred him several groups in the past. The positive feedback Joe, the owner, had heard from his customers upon returning home had motivated him to continue to send more Charlotte-area divers to Pully. He had gotten a heads-up that one of the incoming divers was none other than Michael Reece who had just received the highest military honor that existed. Pulaski had a framed Navy Cross hung in his dive shop that he received for actions with Task Force K-Bar in Afghanistan in 2002, where he had exposed himself to enemy fire on purpose to divert attention away from the evacuation of a wounded team member. He had seen Reece's coverage and read the citation, but he was going to meet the man this week. He also was looking forward to seeing the prosthetic fin attachment the guys at Open Water had made for Reece in order to continue to dive.

He had visited the marina supervisor's office before coming to The Banana Leaf and had offered him a little something extra for a prime dock spot for *The Sculpted Lady*, which was often the lubricant that got things done with officials on the island. It wasn't as much corruption as it was simply a way of doing business ingrained in the trading culture of the Caribbean. It didn't bother Pully in the least, because people here remembered when you had taken care of them and were, more often than not, happy to return the favor when you were in a pinch. Something as simple as letting some employees of the Division of Tourism use his boat for taking photographs had made him the number-one recommendation by them when cruise

232

lines asked the DOT whom they would recommend for their disembarking passengers interested in getting a little diving in. He saw this island as his home now, and he truly loved the people here, so he fully subscribed to the idea of "when in Rome."

His cell phone rang and he chatted with the Port Master, who told him that the yacht was approaching and had requested port clearance. He planned to meet up with the Customs and Immigration agents, who were old friends, and make introductions. He ordered an iced bucket of Kubulis for his soon-to-arrive clients and bid goodbye to his buddies at the bar. "I'll catch you guys later," he said as he shook their hands.

The owner of The Banana Leaf, waved to his friend from behind the bar. "Bring your friends by tonight, mon."

"I just might do that my friend," Pully said as his massive frame eclipsed the door on his way out to the docks.

CHAPTER 19

Very few of the attendees at Victory Assembly Church of Christ knew the young man who lay in the closed casket under Reverend Billy Cash's pulpit, but that didn't matter. He was one of God's creations who had fallen and needed the power of their prayers, and that was reason enough to be there. About a dozen remembered the departed's brother when he would come to services before he had moved away. Brother Billy's own mother, a constant presence at this house of God, sat beside him holding his hand as he stared at the floor seemingly oblivious to the words being delivered from the pulpit.

Billy didn't have much use for the formality often seen in church services. He had often said that Jesus was a poor carpenter who didn't need silk robes and golden jewelry to change the world forever, which was the reason Billy stood before his congregation now with a shirt and tie and a simple satin sash around his neck.

"We weep today for a young man in whom many would see imperfections. But, my brothers and sisters, are we not all imperfect when compared to the Almighty?" There were affirmations and nods throughout the church. "There are no imperfections, no matter how great, that would change the fact that we are all children of God. We see the presence of Satan every day in the form of temptation. His desire to lead us astray is always near, and he will prey on the weaknesses that we all have. We have all fallen before when battling Satan's overtures, and that's what makes us all a common race of frailty. If not, we wouldn't need the unwavering love and devotion of our Lord."

He had already spoken about Darnell's life and shared stories of his struggles as well as stories of his brother's devotion. He now wanted his audience, especially Chris, to see Darnell as a man who had more in common with all of them than they would care to admit.

"I want you to see the face of Darnell in the brother or sister that needs your help. The brother or sister that needs your love. The brother or sister who needs God's knowledge...And I want you do be the one who gives it to them." He wiped his brow with his cotton handkerchief that he pulled from his right pants pocket. "It is a terrible place to be, where you feel you have nowhere to go. Satan's treachery can make you become even blind to the always-present choice of our Lord Jesus Christ."

He looked up at the audience over his reading glasses that he used to read his sermon notes. "God is all powerful, is he not?"

The church members affirmed his question with vigor.

Billy nodded. "Yes he is. Yes he is. But he created us in His image, and with the gift of life comes the responsibility to reach out and help our fellow man! When you see someone running low on hope, I want you to be that one who stops. I want you to be that one who puts a hand on their shoulder or two arms around them. I want you to be the one who kneels with them and asks God for His guidance!"

He paused and saw his flock nodding under the drone of the wobbly ceiling fans above them that were losing the battle with the summer heat.

"We are but imperfect beings made in the image of the Almighty, but it is our choices that help us achieve righteousness. Here are the things I ask of you today, my brothers and sisters. One, I want you to pray for our brother Chris here today so that God may help heal his heart and vanquish his sorrow. Two, I want you to rejoice for his brother Darnell who watches us now in the arms of God. Finally, I want you to commit yourselves to being the righteous one who takes the time to help the next Darnell you see out there. Let us do more to be our brother's keepers!"

The church members voiced their agreement with Brother Billy and offered their praise to God.

"Let us end our gathering today remembering the words from Titus...'He saved us, not because of works done by us in righteousness, but according to his mercy, by the washing of regeneration and renewal of the Holy Spirit.' I thank you all for being here today to celebrate brother Darnell's reunion with God Almighty and to pray for brother Chris as he struggles to carry on after tragedy."

The church members came up to Chris and offered their prayers and hugs while the choir sang about the blessings of God. He thanked them for their kind thoughts and stayed until everyone who so wanted had the chance to speak with him. He embraced Brother Billy and thanked him for everything but said he needed some time alone and told him he would be going back tonight. Billy told him to call anytime to talk and to be strong and resist the temptations to use again. Chris promised he would never go back to that again and walked out of the church, as the representatives of Crawford Funeral Home collected Darnell for a quiet burial with no ceremony. He truly was grateful to Billy for his kind words and sharing of the Gospel, but he had another biblical quote in mind as he left the church, this one from the Book of Romans:

For he is God's servant for your good. But if you do wrong, be afraid, for he does not bear the sword in vain. For he is the servant of God, an avenger who carries our God's wrath on the wrongdoer.

*****

Cape Fear Country Club was a private institution where membership was by invitation only. Inside the expansive white-columned clubhouse, tables were arranged on the ornate blue carpet and fine silverware clinked against dinner plates that fed supporters who had paid three hundred dollars for a seat at this event. Wilmington's polished upper crust had gathered to dine and talk with the Honorable James Haxton, Senior Senator from North Carolina and likely soon-to-be candidate for President of the United States.

The featured speaker, introduced by Sam Ivey, offered remarks about the need for stronger regulations for the protection of coastal wetlands, which were short and sweet. He was followed by Governor Sutton, who introduced the crowd to the newly formed Coalition for the Common Good and explained to them how they could take the opportunity to be some of the first donors to an organization that would champion the ideals that America desperately needed, i.e., it would help start to fill Haxton's White House campaign war chest. Sutton insisted that this announcement should be in the last part of the evening, since it would give everyone the chance to take advantage of the open bar, which always loosened financial inhibitions. All guests who made a paltry donation of at least two thousand dollars would be recognized as members of The Cornerstone Club. What that would bring the donors in the future was unspoken but understood: *you can say you were with him from the beginning.*

The number of guests who had answered Sutton's challenge to give was better than expected. Each one got to pose with Haxton for a picture, followed by warm handshakes and the usual platitudes and driveling small talk before being guiding by a staffer back to the crowd. After sending off the last of their guests, Haxton now sat at the table with Ivey and Sutton, swirling glasses of Scotch.

"Better than expected. We should take in about a hundred thousand when it's all counted up," Sutton said. "I think this is a good sign that donors will be very receptive to your candidacy. Sam, we appreciate you putting this together."

"It was my pleasure Governor," replied Ivey.

Sutton raised his glass to one of his election sugar daddies. "Well, it's the least you could do after whipping my ass on the golf course today."

Haxton and Sutton agreed to start getting serious about campaign planning next week. The first item on the agenda would be where to make his announcement. Tentative plans were to announce the formation of an Exploratory Committee in a few weeks and officially announce his candidacy further down the road. The first of the two announcements wouldn't personally involve Haxton and would simply be released to the press. Sutton had a few suggestions about where his official launch could be announced, but Haxton only gave him a cursory comment and said they would talk more later. He was exhausted and was looking forward to getting to Figure Eight alone for a few days.

Both men thanked Ivey again for his generosity and hospitality and promised to be in touch again soon. Sutton was headed to the airport and back to Washington for some work with the lobbying firm. Haxton climbed into the hired Lincoln Towncar, in which the driver would deliver him to his large waterfront estate. He called his DC office and said that he was "out of the loop" for a few days and would accepts calls only if there was an emergency.

*****

Mahatma Gandhi once said "man's happiness really lies in contentment." The man that, just a few days before, was on national television being honored by the President of United States could not have agreed more. He sat on his couch with his son's sleeping head in his lap and his daughter leaning against him under his arm. Little Charlie's feet were draped across Anna's lap, and his steady quiet snores announced that he had surrendered before the end of family movie night. Never far from Charlie, two hundred pounds of family dog were stretched out on the floor in front of the television.

Despite the unexpected uprooting of horrific memories that occurred in Washington, he couldn't help but feel that a pressure valve in him had been released...and for the better. He had felt some degree of shame about the relief he had felt when he realized that none of what he had hidden had affected Anna's love for him one bit. She was the purest love he had ever known, and her reaction and her unflinching support should not have been a surprise. He lifted her hand that was interlocked with his own and kissed it and was rewarded with her resting her head on his other shoulder.

His journey had been long and hard, but he was happy with the destination. Michael believed that perspective was one of the greatest things a man could give to himself, and he took stock of his current life while he sat in his living room. He had a family that any man would have felt lucky to have. He worked with colleagues who pushed him to continue to improve and had patients who were grateful for his devotion and care. The United States Army had given him the opportunity to build relationships that were more fairly described as brotherhoods and a pride of service that was worth the time it required—it was even worth half a leg. He was financially secure and could afford to live in any neighborhood in the area. He loved his spot on the water and he was blessed with neighbors who cared about him long before he was famous.

There had been many times in his youth when he had questioned his faith and had found himself wondering how an all-loving God could allow such misery to visit one child. As he kissed the top of his daughter's head, he had decided that he and God were all square. Many considered a man to be the sum of all of his experiences, and Michael had no doubt that his childhood had shaped many of the decisions he had made to this point. But his past wouldn't define his self-image anymore. The burden of secrecy had been lifted, and he pledged to himself that many of the demons that had followed him would be set down and left behind. Haxton was his past, while his present and future surrounded him in his home. It was an easy choice.

He began to feel a heaviness descend on his eyelids and tilted his head back against the couch, confident that no evil would corrupt his dreams tonight. Tomorrow, he would leave with his friend to the Caribbean, where he would share his past with one more person before letting the warm tropical waters wash away the remaining stains of betrayal and exploitation forever.

*****

Preston Gates leaned against the counter at Causeway Café, chatting with the employees as he poured sugar into his morning coffee. On Fridays he treated himself to an omelet here for breakfast, since there wasn't a better place for a morning meal in Wrightsville Beach. Unfortunately, today wasn't Friday and he had been cutting back on his calories due to his belt feeling a bit more snug of late. Coffee and a toasted bagel would have to do for the policeman here in the popular beach town on the southern coast of North Carolina.

Preston had grown up in nearby Wilmington and graduated from John T. Hoggard High School. From a young age, he had always wanted to be a police officer. He had been accepted in the training program in his home town and had served in the department for two years before the opportunity to join the force in Wrightsville Beach. It wasn't an increase in pay, but it meant fewer night shifts, which was attractive to the newly married officer with plans for a family soon. His supervisor hated to see him go but told Preston's new employer that they would be gaining an extremely likable young man who performed all aspects of his job with dedication and skill.

In a short amount of time, Preston had gotten to know the year-round locals in town. He insisted that having a good relationship with the people you serve makes your job easier, but his good relationships were more a reflection of his friendly personality and professionalism. Bill McLamb, owner of North Island Marina, was one of the locals that Preston had gotten to know quite well, so when he got a call from dispatch that Bill had reported some stolen property, he finished his coffee, said goodbye to the staff and regulars, and made the short drive up North Lumina Avenue to see what was going on.

"How ya doing Preston?" Bill asked as the officer came into the marina office.

"Not bad Bill. What's going on this morning?" Preston shook his head as the owner lifted the coffee pot toward him, offering a cup.

Bill pointed out the office window toward the docks. "Someone stole a boat last night."

"Any chance the owner took it out before sunrise, Bill?"

"Nope. I called him this morning and he was still at home and hadn't given the keys to anybody. Goes without sayin' he was pretty pissed." Bill shook his head. "Never had a boat taken in over twenty years. Don't want it gettin' around that this ain't a safe place to keep your boat Preston."

Officer Gates patted his friend on the back. "Well, let's go take a look buddy."

They walked out onto the floating docks where tenants could rent "wet slips" to tie their boats up and not have to wait in line at the local boat ramp anytime they wanted to go out on the water. The last slip on the row sat empty.

Bill pointed to the vacant area. "Right there. Triton 240 LTS. Paul White owns it. You know Paul, don't you?" Preston nodded. "Petey was working security last night and said he didn't hear anything, but who knows if the son of a bitch was actually awake during his shift."

Preston squatted down and looked around the slip. Nothing seemed to be out of order, and there were no cut pieces of line around. The owner still had the keys, but Preston knew it was much easier to hotwire an ignition on a boat like this than a car. He found out from Bill that the boat had a two-hundred-fifty-horsepower outboard engine, which meant it could be taken out on open water without any problem and wouldn't be confined to the Intracoastal Waterway.

Bill didn't have a code-entry security gate and relied on Petey Mitchell to provide security during the night. Preston didn't fault his friend's disparaging remark about his security man. Petey had been a backseat guest in his police cruiser on two occasions: once for public intoxication and another for marijuana possession. Unfortunately, there were no security cameras to review either.

Bill called Petey in to talk with Preston. The watchman didn't really have anything of substance to offer, and Preston left to go talk with Paul White, who owned the stolen saltwater fishing/recreational boat. He made a stop at the Kwik Mart that was next door to see if any of their security cameras caught any part of the marina, but no such luck.

Paul gave him all the registration and license number information, and Gates headed to the station to file a stolen property report. He thought there were two likely outcomes for this: either it would turn up in the next day or two, tied up somewhere none the worse for wear after some local young kids had taken it for a joy ride, or they would never see it again. It wasn't exactly the Antwerp diamond heist, but it was a crime, and Gates took his job seriously. Not to mention that the owners of both the boat and marina were friends.

CHAPTER 20

Michael floated weightlessly as he stared down a sea cliff that plunged over a thousand feet straight into the ocean. Achieving perfect neutral buoyancy at a drop-off like this is as close to diving nirvana one can achieve. One of his old dive instructors had described it as like skydiving while on LSD. Sponges and coral of every color grew to claim every square inch of exposed sea rock available, while seahorses and scorpion fish danced lazily around the vibrant garden of marine life that was called L'Abym, just off the island of Dominica. There was no sound except the low rumble in his regulator when he exhaled and the echoing hiss of inhalation. There were no cell phones, no pagers, no bullets, no operating room delays, and no dog poop to scoop. It was, put simply, perfection.

Pully swam in front of him and pointed to his eyes with his index and middle fingers and then pointed them a little further along the sea wall, telling him go look at something with him. The former Navy seal swam forward and Reece followed the dive leader, who had three neon tape stripes on his tank to make it easier for his group to find him underwater. Every diver had a "dive buddy," and Tripp followed them about twenty feet behind.

They were treated to the sight of a lionfish that floated at the wall under a slight outcropping of a coral fan. It wasn't like the ones one could get for their home saltwater tank at the pet store. It was about a foot across with its fins spread out, and simply floated there, staring back at the bubbling aliens that stared at him. A slight swishing sound announced the launch of Pully's spear gun, and they watched the triple-pronged tip pierce the fish, followed by a brief fluttering of fins before it went completely still. Although its origin is debatable, this species has become the nuisance of the Caribbean. Due to very few natural predators, the population has exploded across the region and threatens natural species. In order to protect the marine life that is indigenous to the reefs, divers are allowed to kill lionfish when they encounter them.

Pully produced heavy-duty scissors and, with gloved hands, clipped the pronged and venomous fins off the fish and handed the body to Michael. It was surprisingly soft to the touch compared to the spiny fins. He let it go in front of him and used a front kick of his fin to send it several feet in front, where a large grouper inhaled it and then casually swam away. Divers were trying to teach native predator fish to not only eat the lionfish but also to hunt them. They had made strides with getting species like the Oscar to eat them when fed to them, but very few had been observed to actually eat live ones themselves. Everyone believed that this was the ultimate solution to controlling the lionfish invasion.

Tripp and Reece saw several other specimens with their fins clipped in a mesh bag attached to Pully's buoyancy control (BC) vest. He made a circling motion in front of his stomach, producing the universal "yummy" sign, then used his fingers to mimic the swimming motion of a diver's legs, pointed further down the wall, and led the way to the next discovery.

Michael's diving prosthesis was not only an engineering achievement but also a labor of love. The guys at Open Water Adventures back home had spent countless hours perfecting it as a gift to their client and friend who had returned home from war missing a fairly important part of a diver's body. The stalk of the prosthesis was made of aluminum that attached to a hard rubber foot-shaped tip that fit perfectly into a diving fin. The biggest challenge had been to find a way to keep the cupped upper portion that fit over Michael's stump from coming off, since gravity would not work in their favor when they were under the surface. The solution had been what they called Michael's "garter belt"—three meshed straps that went from the "cup" upward and attached to snaps that had been installed to his BC vest. It had been given to Michael at a welcome-home party at the dive shop, and then the guys had spent hours in the pool with him to get the weight distribution and buoyancy of it just right. Reece was grateful that he would still be able to enjoy one of his favorite hobbies, but he was touched to the point of tears that the guys at the dive shop had put so much effort into something for the sole purpose of getting a friend back in the water with them again. Michael's first diving trip with his new prosthesis was featured in *Dive* magazine, and the dive shop had received an award recognizing ingenuity and dedication from the Wounded Warrior Foundation. It had been the subject of many baggage inspections, and it was one of Michael's most prized possessions.

Eric and Gabriel were paired up behind them, along with a newlywed couple who had rounded out the seven-person dive party. The ever-mischievous Dr. Drake couldn't help but have a little fun with the young couple by telling them with a straight face, right before they entered the water, that Michael had lost his leg in a shark attack at this very dive site. He let them sit there breathless for a few seconds before he couldn't hold in his laughter any longer. Drake then said that all drinks were on him when they got back from the day's trip as a means of recompense for what all his buddies called his "jackassery."

Once this dive was complete, they would spend their required "surface time" returning to the island for a light lunch, then it was back to the boat for a short drive to Rodney's Rock, the second and more shallow dive of the day. Pully was an exceptional dive operator. He took good care of his clients both above and below the surface but did it in a way where they didn't feel smothered and were allowed to explore with as much or as little freedom as they wanted. His boat was in impeccable condition, which was reflective of his former career as an operator in the most elite naval unit the world had ever seen. He didn't mind if his clients had one beer or cocktail during the lunch break, but he never partook in alcohol while doing his job.

At the end of the day, they returned to the dock, where they would leave their dive equipment for the staff to clean and service and get ready for tomorrow's one-dive day. Gabriel had suggested not doing a morning dive on the second day in anticipation of the drinks and good times they expected to have that night. The entire dive party went to a small tiki bar that was next to the dive shop so Gabriel could honor his pledge of buying drinks. The four men were invited to have dinner and drinks with Pulaski after they cleaned up on Drake's boat. They enthusiastically accepted, since they enjoyed their dive leader's company as much as he did theirs.

Gabriel had rented a condo beside the marina where they showered and changed into to island casual clothing. They met Pully back at *The Sculpted Lady* and had drinks and small talk as they watched the sunset along the western horizon casting pastel hues in the sky. Pully wanted to hear the story that got Reece the Medal of Honor, but he had "seen the elephant" and knew not to ask. Those stories are offered, not solicited. He had found out that he and

Tripp had stomped on some of the same dirt patches, and they exchanged stories and talked about common acquaintances.

A full day of diving tends to build an appetite, and they left the boat and headed to The Carib Wood, which had been recommended by Pully, who knew the chef. The restaurant was less than a ten-minute walk from Drake's docked yacht and had both an indoor and outdoor seating area. The men chose to dine under the sky, given the gentle Caribbean breeze with temperatures in the low eighties now that the sun had gone down. They perused the menu, which changed daily due to the chef preparing what he had bought from the fishermen's market each morning. They kept to the local beer, which they had all taken a liking to, and enjoyed it straight from the bottle as any self-respecting man would insist.

"I took the liberty of having an appetizer made for us which will be out in a little bit. I think you'll like it," Pully told the table. He saw the collective thumbs-up of the group, which had proven to be very low maintenance thus far.

He had walked to the restaurant chatting with Tripp, discussing some more of their shared locations of action, and had found all of the guys a pleasure to be around. He had found Reece to be soft-spoken and easy to get along with, and it wasn't hard to figure out that his three diving companions, although very different men with varied backgrounds, cared a lot about their friend. He had sensed a degree of protectiveness from them as well. The former Navy Seal and leader of men believed that you could learn a lot about a man by how his friends treated him, and he was impressed so far.

Chef Ricky brought out a large platter of small fish fillets with smaller individual plates for the group. "Please enjoy, gentlemen. Compliments of the house."

The fish was quite tender and had been sautéed to perfection with what appeared to be a small amount of oil infused with citrus of some type. It went perfect with the beer and seemed to gain the approval of everyone present.

"Damn, these are fantastic Pully. What are they?" Drake asked their host.

"It's the lionfish that we speared today. People don't tend to think about eating them because of their appearance, but the meat is excellent. I usually bring whatever I kill to Ricky, who really knows how to cook 'em right."

Drake wiped his hands after eating another piece. "They're perfect. How long have you been out of the Navy?"

Pully took a drag on his beer and leaned back. "I retired after getting home in 2003. I had been in for twenty-four years and thought it was becoming a younger man's game. I also knew that if I renewed, I would be more in the command side of things and not really going out with my men much anymore. I have been blessed with some excellent commanders in my career, but that part of it didn't appeal to me. My last tour was with a group called Task Force K-Bar, and we were some of the first on the ground in Afghanistan. We did some crazy shit, including rooting some of those fuckers out of their own caves. I didn't think I would ever serve with a better group of guys, so I thought it was the perfect time to retire. I had a fair amount of money put away and had planned to own a dive operation whenever I left." He waved his hands around referring to the surrounding area. "I had been here before and really liked the diving, and I love the people. I wasn't meant for the American suburb life, and this seemed like as good a place as any to start my second career. It's worked out well. I make pretty good money and I get to meet a lot of different people."

"Do you miss it? The life, I mean?" Tripp asked his new friend.

"Every day, brother. Every day. That being said, I know I made the right decision. I wouldn't have been doing the duties that I had gotten used to and loved. Plus, seeing guys you know get hurt or killed starts to break you down a little bit each time, and I knew that there would be a lot more of that for a while to come." Pully raised his bottle in the air. "To those who didn't come back."

"Here, here," was the reply from the group.

"Major Reece, how about you? How are you doing with your new celebrity status? What was it like that night?" Pully asked as the main entrees were being put on the table. "And I ask

246

you this with the complete understanding that you may not want to talk about it, and that's OK with me, sir."

Michael looked at Tripp, who gave him a subtle nod. *It's OK, he's one of us.* "Well, for starters we're not in uniform, Master Chief, so let's drop the formality. My name's Michael, and I don't drink beer with anyone who won't call me that."

Pulaski raised his bottle. "You got it."

"I'm kind of hoping the celebrity stuff will die down after a while. I'm on a sabbatical from my civilian job, but at some point I have to get to back to work. My job's pretty demanding in terms of my time, and I have a family that needs me, too." He looked down and started to pull on the corner of his beer bottle label as he transitioned to the second part of the question. "As far as that night, what it was like for me was terrifying. I was scared out of my mind. I just got lucky that they thought there was a bigger force than two wounded troops and a terrified reserve soldier. I just didn't want them to get to my guys...I couldn't let that happen. I spent every minute of my deployment being protected or isolated from danger, and all of a sudden I was in a situation where the ones who protected me were in danger. It wasn't that I was afraid of dying, it was just that I was afraid of failing them," he said as he nodded toward Tripp. "They never failed me."

"I don't think we were lucky that they didn't come after us," Tripp said after Reece paused. "I think they didn't come forward because in between saving my ass he was giving them fucking hell. He shoots pretty good for an officer." Tripp and Pully laughed out loud at that.

The dinner was as fine a seafood meal as they had ever had, and they stayed at their table enjoying each other's company as the dinner crowd transitioned to the bar crowd. Conversation was easy and relaxed and helped no doubt by continued reloads of beer. Daniels and Drake were fascinated with Pully's stories, and Tripp knew that the ones he couldn't tell were probably way more interesting.

"Next round. It's my turn to buy," Reece said as he rose from his chair.

Pully raised his hand up in the air. "Sir, don't you know that a Medal of Honor recipient is not allowed to pay for drinks when he is with other soldiers?"

"Master Chief, don't you know that you have done countless things far braver than me that you can't even talk about and no one will ever know? I got this one…my pleasure."

Daniels got up as well. "I'll help you with them." Drake was already at the bar talking with a pair of quite attractive customers. That left Tripp and Pulaski at the table.

The Navy man lifted his chin toward the pair walking to the bar. "He seems like a good man, Sergeant."

Tripp nodded as he lifted the bottle to his mouth. "The best."

"I saw the feature on TV about his upbringing and his connections with that Senator. This isn't some political push-through where he's cashing in on some high-end Washington connections is it?" He heard the scrape of the plastic chair against the wooden deck and saw the Army man standing over him.

"You ever ask me that again and I'll kick your fucking Navy ass across the deck and back, motherfucker!"

Pulaski raised his hands. "I thought so Tripp…just had to know. No offense intended, and your reaction tells me everything I need to know. My apologies."

Tripp sat down and slapped Pully on the back. "No problem brother…I know we have all known some that climbed the ladder on their ability to lick boots, but he's not one. He's as real as the real deal gets. I know he talks about how scared he was, and I believe him, but let me tell you this: that night…before I lost consciousness…that guy was as cool as a fucking cucumber. The reason he limps around on that goddamn peg leg is because he drug me and Torres behind the only cover we had and left himself exposed. He alternated between treating us and using my weapon to keep those assholes back, and he never showed the least hesitation or fear. Medics said that when they got there he was about to buy the farm from blood loss. Even then he refused treatment until he could tell them about our injuries and what we needed. It damned near destroyed him that Manny didn't make it, but he would've died if he had been hit at the fucking entrance to the hospital...his wounds were just too bad. He set up college accounts for Manny's kids, which he doesn't know that I know about. There isn't *anything* I wouldn't do for that guy. I'm the one that pushed my CO to put him up for it."

"To the real deal, Tripp," Pulaski said. They clinked their bottles together and finished their drinks as Daniels and Reece approached with refills.

Drake dropped back in his chair as well. "Jesus, Tripp, you're killing me. Those women let me buy them two drinks before I realized they wanted me to introduce them to you the whole time. What do you think? Let's go over there and maybe I can get the leftovers."

"No way, my friend. This is a guy's weekend and I'm not leaving my wingman."

The men drank and talked away the rest of the evening, and it became evident that it was good planning to not have an early morning dive the next day and also to have a short walk (or stagger) back to the boat. Pully crashed with the group, as he also had fallen victim to too much local brew. As he laid his massive frame on the couch in the den of the impressive yacht, he looked at the prosthetic leg that had been taken off and leaned against the wall near Reece's bed. That night, he had met friends of this man from both the military and civilian worlds. They had come to know him in very different circumstances but all obviously cared deeply for him, and it had nothing to do with the ribbon that had been placed around his neck several days ago. Pully realized that he felt the same.

*****

Sandy Patterson had long been the primary blocking force between the Senator and the legions of people who wanted some of his time. She was the primary decision maker of who got in and who got diverted to a lesser functionary when it came to unannounced visitors or unexpected phone calls, and she had developed a good feel of what needed his personal attention and what could be handled by others; it was a rare occasion when Haxton said she had made the wrong call.

This morning, however, she was unsure what the right decision was. Paul Timmons, Governor of Iowa, wanted to speak with the Senator about a joint appearance in about two weeks. She had gotten the message relayed to her from Wilmington that he was at his Figure Eight Island home and didn't want to be bothered unless it was absolutely necessary. Sandy wasn't part of the campaign team on staff, but she wasn't ignorant of the fact that her boss was probably the leading contender for the party nomination in the upcoming Presidential election, and all roads start in Iowa. Timmons was immensely popular in his state and, to her knowledge, he had not contacted any other likely candidate about appearing together. No, this was not something that could be farmed out to a staffer, and she decided that Haxton needed to be called.

She dialed the number of the house on the island and was greeted with the answering machine after five rings.

"Senator, it's Sandy. Governor Timmons wanted you to call him about a possible joint appearance next week. I'm sorry to disturb you, but he needs an answer by tomorrow. I will send the phone number to your cell phone and will call you there as well. Again, sorry to disturb you, but I thought you would want to know about this opportunity." She terminated that line and dialed his cell phone number, where she got his voicemail as well.

This was a bit unusual, but she also knew he would go for runs around the area and occasionally would go on fishing charters where cell phone reception could be tenuous. She left the same message on the cell phone inbox and went back to work...

...unaware that behind the wooden door to her left, Chip Johnson had received the same call about the joint appearance with the Iowa Governor and was on the line with Governor Sutton.

"We have to jump all over this, Governor," Chip said into the phone. "Getting in before anyone else with Timmons is a huge score. It sends the message that Haxton is his guy and it will be very hard for him to swing to someone else later on down the line. I know we have until tomorrow, but we need to reply as soon as possible. You and I both know Timmons likes to feel the love, and he knows this is a big bone to throw someone early in the game. I don't want to give him the chance to call Merritt or Sears and we have to watch one of those assholes grinning alongside him while we wonder what happened."

"You're preaching to the choir Chip, and I promise you that the Senator will see the magnitude of this as well," Sutton replied on the other end of the line. "Give him a call and see how he wants to go about it. Stress that it's important to call Timmons personally. We also need to have a little prep time before the event to go over his responses to questions on ethanol subsidies. He will certainly be hit with those. Our position isn't exactly parallel with Timmons's, but we need to respond in a way where we don't undercut him while his is standing right beside Haxton. That would totally fuck up any chance of his endorsement before we are even out of the gate. Give him a call and call me when you hear back and I'll do the same if he calls me first."

"Sounds good Governor." Johnson was thinking that one of the first withdrawals from the funds raised in Wilmington would be to fly him to Iowa for an advance meeting with Timmons's staff.

He dialed Haxton's cell phone first instead of the house line. He was a player, and insiders called directly to the personal cell...

"You have reached 202-..."

Chip left a message reflecting his thoughts on the Iowa opportunity and then dialed the house number.

"You have reached 910-..."

Chip simply left a message asking the Senator to check his cell phone inbox and get back to him as soon as it was convenient. He called Timmons's Chief of Staff and let him know he would contact him as soon as he heard from the Senator and that he, Chip, would plan to fly in to go over details personally. He knew that Timmons was doing a poor job of hiding the fact that he coveted the VP slot in the future party ticket. Unfortunately for him, he wasn't even on the first page of the list of potential candidates put together by Johnson...but he didn't have to know that. *Sorry Governor, you are not in a swing state and, after the primary, you're really not much use to us.*

He pressed Sandy's intercom line.

"Yes, Mr. Johnson."

"Sandy, I may be flying out to Iowa in the next couple of days. I'll keep you posted, but I may have to juggle around a few appointments." He didn't need her to help him with that, but he wanted her to know that he was already aware of the call from Timmons too.

"OK, Mr. Johnson. Would you like me to get one of the girls from the office pool to help you with that?" Two could play this game.

Chip frowned as he stared at his speaker phone. "No, that won't be necessary right now, Sandy. I'll let you know. Thank you." He made sure to click off the line before she had the chance to do the same.

*****

Officer Gates knew that he was a relative newcomer to the police field, but he could hardly imagine even the older veterans of the force had had anything like this.

He had received a call from one of the vacation rental companies on the island. One of the rental properties on the waterway was undergoing its weekly cleaning between tenants, and the cleaning lady had called to say that there was a boat tied to the dock that she had never seen before. The company had called the family that had just checked out that morning to ask if they had brought a boat down for their two-week stay, and they had replied that they didn't have one. They then called the owners of the home, who informed them that their boat was in dry storage in Beaufort.

Ronnie Blackman, the son of the rental agency's owner, was sent over to look into it. When he arrived, he found the boat tied securely to the dock with no apparent damage. There were no keys in the ignition, and there was a note addressed to "North Island Marina." Blackman called back to the agency, and his father Jim called over to the marina. He gave Bill McLamb the registration number, and Bill matched it with the missing Triton.

Bill headed over to the rental property while Jim called the police department. Preston happened to be the one on duty at the time, promised to meet them there, and asked that no one board the vessel until he arrived. Now he stood inside the boat literally scratching his head at what he found.

He agreed with Ronnie that the boat had no damage. The only apparent change in condition was that the gas tank was now about one-third full. What had surprised everyone, however, were the contents of the envelope.

Inside was sixty dollars, along with a note which read:

Dear sir,

I have left the boat along with this note with the hopes it will get to you quickly. I apologize for any problems I caused by taking it and here is some money which I hope will make up for the trouble I caused as well as the gas I used. I did hotwire the ignition but didn't do any damage. Very sorry.

It was not signed, and it was written in regular ballpoint pen on the back of a fuel receipt that had been in the storage area under the wheel. There was a faint smell of cleaning fluid, which had probably eliminated any fingerprints that may have been left behind.

Gates let Bill come on board, who quickly put the wires used to start the engine back under the console in the proper place then used the key he had brought and was happy to see that the engine started with no problems. He also looked around and agreed that there was no damage.

"I guess he had a change of heart or an attack of conscience."

They called the owner of the boat and told him about the recovery and the lack of any damage. All agreed that, short of any appearance by the culprit at the station with a full confession, there wasn't anything else to do but drive the boat the less-than-one-mile distance back to the marina, where they would always have one heck of a peculiar boat-thieving story to talk about in the future.

Preston kept the note, and Bill promised to give the money to the boat owner, along with two months' free rent to make up for the inconvenience.

*****

Champagne Reef is one of the more popular dive sites in Dominica. The hot springs under the sea floor cause bubbling jets to rise around the ever-present seahorses and frogfish. Pully had suggested that they make this a night dive, not only because of the relative crowds that are at the popular site during the day but also because of the sea life that wasn't as easily found during the day.

The dive leader had cracked several Cyalume light sticks, in which hydrogen peroxide mixes with diphenyl oxalate to cause the dye in the tube to fluoresce. Each diver had one tied to their regulator first stage, which would allow all the divers to be accounted for under the surface. The first stage was chosen due to its behind-the-head location, which would not interfere with the diver's night vision. Pully had three different colored sticks attached to his rig so his clients could pick him out from the others in case they needed his assistance. For a little comic relief, the group had tied four sticks to Michael's diving prosthesis, like a Christmas tree, and Pully could see the linear array of them moving rhythmically about thirty feet in front.

They used small underwater flashlights to keep their bearings while minimizing the disturbance to the marine life. The sea floor came alive with crab and lobster walking among the vertical bubble fountains. The current was very light here, which allowed the divers to hover over interesting sites for as long as they wished. The area was occasionally altered by a strobe-like flash of light as Daniels took photographs of their findings on what was their last dive of the trip.

When the first diver reached the agreed-upon 500 psi air level on their dive computer, they all ascended slowly to a depth of fifteen feet for their mandatory three-minute safety stop. All four of the friends held on to the anchor line during this time while they watched Pully perfectly suspended at the same depth without holding anything, due to his experience at achieving neutral buoyancy with the slightest of adjustments. After that they surfaced and climbed onto the boat one at a time under the watchful eye of their dive leader, who was always the last to leave the water in case any of his group had any difficulties.

With the anchor pulled they headed back to the marina to drop off the dive party at the yacht. They would drop lines and head toward home in the morning at a leisurely seafaring pace, making a couple of stops along the way. Eric and Michael took the dive suits and BC vests up to the condo to wash the salt off of them before going home, while Pully helped the others secure the other gear on the boat. There were no tanks, since they were supplied by the dive operator, which made transporting their gear a much safer undertaking.

Michael and Eric returned with the dripping webbed bags of cleaned dive apparel and draped them on the deck of the boat to dry overnight in the gentle Caribbean breezes. Goodbyes were exchanged between the men and their dive leader, and Drake handed Pully an envelope with a hefty gratuity for the Navy Seal and his co-workers, always a sign of a grateful group for a fantastic diving experience. Pully gave them a few of his business cards to share with anyone at home that might be coming to the island and asked Tripp and Reece to walk him to his own boat.

"Master Chief, I want to thank you for the best diving trip I have ever been on," Michael said to Pully as he shook his hand.

"I agree," said Tripp. "No bad at all for a Navy puke."

"Gentlemen, the pleasure was all mine. You guys are pretty good divers and a blast to hang out with, even though my hangover the other day was pretty rough." This comment elicited a few empathetic chuckles. "I want you to have this sir," he said as he handed another business card to Reece. "On the back are my email and my personal phone number. If there is ever anything I can do for you, I want you to call. The pressures of being a highly decorated soldier can be a pretty heavy burden sometimes, and I know you struggle with survivor's guilt. I know this because I did, too...still do in fact. It will never go away, but you learn how to deal with it. I know the memories of that night were not good ones, but you have to know that you did everything you could and you absolutely deserve the attaboys that you're getting now. Anyway, I'm available twenty-four-seven, and don't hesitate to call me for anything."

Somehow the handshake that followed seemed inadequate for the moment, and the two decorated soldiers shared an embrace. Reece didn't have the words to say what he wanted to, and Pully's look told him that none were necessary.

The hulking old sailor turned to Tripp and shook his hand. "You look after this guy Sergeant."

"Always, Master Chief," Tripp replied.

They parted ways and Reece and Tripp boarded the yacht, where the others had already opened both of them a cold Kubuli for their post-dive bullshitting session.

*****

The bulk of the day had come and gone without a phone call. Chip had pictures of an antsy Gov. Timmons in his mind and was getting anxious himself. He had swallowed his pride and asked Sandy if she had heard anything yet, praying that she hadn't in fact heard from their boss before he had. She told him that she hadn't heard anything either. He called both numbers twice again.

He punched the speakerphone line and dialed the mobile number of Felicia Sumpter, who was one of the lower-level staffers from the home office that had traveled to Wilmington to help set up the fundraiser a few nights ago. Felicia picked up after the second ring.

"Felicia, it's Chip up in DC. How are you doing today?"

"I'm doing great, Mr. Johnson," she replied. Chip never got tired of hearing staff members call him Mr. Johnson.

"Have you gone back to Asheville yet?" he said as he mentally crossed his fingers.

"No, sir. I had a few vacation days accrued, so I stayed in Wilmington to visit some friends from college. I ran it through the office for approval." There was a nervous tone to her voice, like a kid who was being accused of skipping class.

"Oh, not a problem Felicia. It's actually great that you're still down there. I need a big favor from you."

"Anything, Mr. Johnson. I'm happy to help. What can I do for you?"

Chip could hear the same eager-beaver tone in the young staffer as he had experienced in his conversations with Weinrib. "I've got an urgent message for the Senator, and his phones are on the fritz. He's at his house on Figure Eight Island, and I was hoping you would be willing to go over there and relay the message to him. It could be a big thing for future campaigns, and he'll be thrilled to hear about it." The last sentence was more of a dangling carrot to give her thoughts of being remembered fondly by the fledgling Presidential candidate.

She was enthusiastic about the errand, and Chip relayed the information about Gov. Timmons. He instructed her to call him on his cell phone as soon as she was able to meet with him. "You're really saving our butts up here, Felicia."

In Wilmington, the young staffer ended the call and walked out to her car. As she did, she wasn't sure her feet were even touching the ground.

CHAPTER 21

Felicia Sumpter reached the guarded bridge that allowed access to the private island that was popular with both wealthy North Carolinians as well as well-heeled celebrities. Haxton's Washington office had called ahead and security let her through, after checking her driver's license to confirm her identification. She drove her Honda Accord down Bridge Road then took a right down Beach Road South. Her drive toward the southern point of the island was flanked by million-dollar-plus homes on each side, of various coastal pastel shades and with clever names like "EcstaSea" and "Salt Heir." She would snort at the pretentiousness of the place if it wasn't for the fact that she wanted to be part of it so bad.

At the very end of the island she turned into the long driveway that led to the eight-thousand-square-foot waterfront home of her boss. The expansive cedar-shingled estate rose in the distance of the elongated lot that straddled the point of the island with the Intracoastal Waterway on one side and the white sand beach on the other. She noted the green Range Rover that Chip had told her was a vehicle he kept there, and there were no signs that he had any company. She smelled the salt air and listened to the distant sounds of gulls as well as the swaying of sea oats in the breeze as she walked to the front door. She rang the bell three times over a period of about three minutes, with no result, then circled the house to the back, where Johnson had told her to check in case he was on his dock that reached out into the waterway over the marsh or was practicing on his custom-installed putting green in the backyard. No signs of him at either location.

It was when she decided to try knocking on the back French doors that she saw something that sent an icy shot into the pit of her stomach. One of the doors was about a third of the way open and moved slightly back and forth with the breeze coming from the water, and inside she saw a footprint on the bone-colored tile floor. It was blood red and was accompanied by others that made a trail coming from the interior of the house to the very door she stood at currently.

She reflexively turned around to look behind her to see if the boogey man himself was standing there, but she only saw the waving marsh reeds divided by a wooden walkway that led to a boat dock in the distance.

"Senator Haxton, are you home?" She called into the house with an audible tremble in her voice.

Nothing.

"Senator? It's Felicia Sumpter from the Asheville office."

Still nothing.

She wasn't sure what was the best thing to do next, but she was certain what she didn't want to do was go inside the house. She briskly walked back around the house to her Honda, looking side to side for anything out of the ordinary, got in, locked her doors, and quickly dialed her cell phone.

"This is Chip," said the voice on the other end.

"Mr. Johnson, it's Felicia Sumpter."

"Oh, hi Felicia. Did everything go OK?" Chip asked with an upbeat tone.

She felt like she was in a vacuum and noticed that she was starting to sweat from the summer heat as well as the events taking place around her. "Umm, no sir...not exactly. I went to the front door and got no answer, so I went around back like you said. He wasn't in the back yard or on his dock that I could see, so I went to the back door. It's part of the way open and no one is answering and...and there's blood on the floor. I called for the Senator twice through the door but no one answered. I didn't go in, and I have to tell you Mr. Johnson, I'm a little scared right now."

It hadn't hit him yet. "Did you say blood ?"

"Yes, sir. There are several footprints on the floor and it looks they were made with blood."

The temperature of the room in his office seemed to drop several degrees. "Did you find him inside?"

"No, sir. Like I said, I didn't go inside. I really don't want to either. I'm not sure what to do, but I'm starting to freak out a little bit." The tremble in her voice was obvious to both of them.

"OK…umm…OK. Look, I want you to stay there, and I'm going to call the police to come out there." Chip's world seemed to want to start spinning, and the likely explanation was starting to sink in. "Can you do that Felicia?"

"Yes, sir, but I'm going to back out of the driveway into the street if that's OK. I'm a little scared being here on the property."

"Well, umm…OK, that's fine, Felicia. I'm going to call the police and I will call you back."

"OK, Mr. Johnson."

He punched the line dead. For all the times he wanted everyone here to see him as in charge, he had no desire to be the only person coordinating this. He punched the intercom line. "Mrs. Patterson, could you come into my office? It's kind of an emergency."

Sandy got up from her desk, certain that it meant he needed something from her; it was the only time he respected her enough to call her Mrs. Patterson. She was somewhat taken aback when she walked through his door and saw the sweat droplets forming on his pale forehead. He held his phone in his hand halfway between the console and his face, and he looked like a monster had just crawled out of his bedroom closet.

"Chip, is everything all right?"

He relayed the information that he had received from the terrified junior staffer to her. "I'm not sure who to call."

Sandy felt a growing panic in her own chest. She put a hand to her mouth and forced herself to think clearly. "We need to call the New Hanover County Sheriff's Department. I'll take care of that. I know the Sheriff and will try to get him on the line." She tapped her fingers on her lips while she continued to think of what the next steps should be. "You call Ms. Sumpter back and talk to her until the authorities arrive and tell her not to go inside the house." And with that, she turned on her heels and walked out of his office to make the call to the Sheriff's office.

*****

Sheriff Eustace Porter had served in his current job in New Hanover County for the past thirteen years. He was currently heading down Beach Road toward the southern point of the island with a deputy following in a cruiser behind him. He had decided not to turn on the siren and disturb the area and arouse unneeded curiosity. He was well aware of the owner of the house he was heading toward and had been informed by Mrs. Patterson about what the young lady at the scene had discovered. He had brought one deputy in the off chance that there was still some sort of troublemaker on the property, but he wanted to limit the number of people in case he discovered a crime scene where forensics would need to be performed.

A man with a smile as broad as his waistline, Porter hadn't had a serious challenge in an election in New Hanover County in a decade. He was a beloved member of the community, a deacon at his church, and a man who had long shunned the corruptive temptations that could tempt a Sheriff in the South. Despite his folksy demeanor and humble origins, he was also in possession of a sharp legal mind and was known in law enforcement circles as a straight shooter who didn't screw up investigations or contaminate crime scenes. He was also known for working well with local police departments and the North Carolina Highway Patrol and for not having any interest in petty turf fights over jurisdiction. On top of that, he wasn't afraid to ask other agencies for help if he thought it would aid an investigation.

He pulled up to the entrance to the Senator's driveway and saw a late-model Honda Accord parked on the side of the road with a young woman inside who put down her cell phone and exited the car when she saw their cruisers. He introduced himself, got her name, and took note that she was clearly shaken. He asked her to walk the route she had taken on arriving at the house with him, which she did all the way up to the partially open back door.

"Senator Haxton? It's the Sheriff's office. Are you home and may we come in?" said Porter in his booming baritone Southern drawl. No answer. "If anyone else is in the house, it would be a good idea for you to let us know now so no one gets hurt." He turned to his deputy. "You stay here with Ms. Sumpter and I'll take a look inside."

He reached into his back pocket and took out two blue shoe covers that one would see in a hospital. He pushed the door all the way open, using his shirt cuff instead of his fingers, and took two steps into the house with care not to disturb any of the bloody shoe prints on the tiled floor; he noticed that it was only a left shoe making the marks.

The first room was a large living room with light blue walls adorned with black-and-white photographs of Haxton with friends and paintings of a coastal theme. Near the door were a pair of flip-flops and a pair of topsiders. He decided to follow the shoe prints instead of going room to room. He peaked around the edge of the arched entrance to the next room, a large foyer which served as the base for an enormous waterfall staircase that led to the second floor. Off to the left was the entrance to another room, with wooden wainscoting and what was probably hardwood flooring. He couldn't be sure because it was covered by a large dark tongue of viscous material coming forth out of the room and onto the marble. He slowly walked toward the room, avoiding stepping in any of the blood, which increased in amount the closer he got to the doorway. When he reached the entrance, he saw a man on the floor lying on his back with his knees bent under him splaying his lower legs to the outside of the rest of his body. His head was the closest part of his body to the doorway.

There was a single hole in the man's forehead, with a good portion of the back of the head completely blown out. There was purplish darkening on the back of the neck and the parts of the legs and that were the closest to the floor, due to the blood pooling to the lowest portions of the body. The arms were behind the upper body in a way that made Porter quite certain that they were tied up in some way. The eyes were open and stared vacantly with dilated pupils toward the ceiling, and the face was ghastly pale with discoloration of the upper eyelids and a cut beside the left eyebrow. But Porter knew that face. It was Senator Haxton, who appeared to have been executed in his own home.

He pulled the radio microphone that was attached to his upper left shirt toward his face and pressed the activation button. "Mills, this is Porter."

The deputy outside did the same. "This is Mills. Go ahead."

"We have a one-eight-seven. One victim so far. Instruct Dyson, Smith, and Chavis to head this way to help secure the scene. Tell them no lights. I'm comin' out."

Porter carefully turned around and retraced his steps to the back door. He stepped back outside and removed the shoe covers.

"Ms. Sumpter, we are going to take you back to where the cars are parked, OK?" Porter said to the young woman who stood with her arms crossed to help control the shaking.

"What did you find in there, Sheriff?" Her lower lip had begun to quiver.

"Why don't we get back to the road and then we can talk, all right?" Porter said as he raised his arm in the direction of the road. People who receive shocking news can become very emotional. Very emotional people can do odd things such as lose control and contaminate a crime scene. He had to coax her back to the vehicles before giving her any more information.

"OK," she said while both Porter and Deputy Mills could see the moisture forming along her lower eyelids.

They walked back to the vehicles, and Porter sat her in the back seat of his cruiser, facing out the door with her feet outside on the pavement. Mills had opened his trunk and removed a large roll of yellow caution tape. The burly lawman squatted down to get to eye level with the woman, who was becoming more shaken by the moment.

"Ms. Sumpter, did you say you worked for Senator Haxton?"

"Yes sir. I work in his office in Asheville, but I came to Wilmington to help coordinate a fundraiser he had there a few days ago. Mr. Johnson called from Washington and asked me to come by since they couldn't get the Senator on the phone about something. They asked me to bring him a message about contacting the Governor of Iowa, and that's how I wound up here." She looked down at her feet. "Mr. Porter, could you please tell me what you found in there?"

Porter actually had met Haxton on a couple of occasions and was familiar with his story. He knew that he was a widower and didn't have any siblings or children, so essentially there was no reasonable next of kin to notify, and he sensed that the young lady in front of him was coming very close to coming unglued.

"It appears that Senator Haxton is dead inside the house, Ms. Sumpter. I'm sorry to tell you that, and I know this is very shocking news." He saw her shoulders start to shake up and down, and the tears were finally released. "I'm going to need to take a statement from you today before you go, but there are a few things we have to do here first. Are you going to be OK to wait here for a little bit while we check out the rest of the house?"

"Yes sir," she said as she nodded thanks to the big man, who handed her some tissues. "Would it be OK if I called my office?"

"That won't be a problem, but could I ask that we wait to do that until we have checked the rest of the house and make sure there isn't anything else? Also, would it be all right if I spoke with them first and then hand the phone to you?" He received a nod of approval.

The three other deputies that had been summoned had arrived, and Porter instructed Deputy Connie Chavis to stay with Felicia and Tim Dyson to cordon off the property. He then gathered at the back door with Mills and Smith.

"I want the two of you to clear the first floor. Mills, you go to the right, and Smith, you go to the left. I want you to make sure there are no perpetrators in the home and no other victims, and that's it. Don't touch anything and don't go in the first-floor office where the body is. Do you two understand?" Both of his deputies nodded. "I'm going to check out the victim again and then clear the second floor. Yell if you find anyone and call on the radio if you find any other victims. All right, get to work." He handed them both shoe covers and put fresh ones on himself, and they entered the house.

Porter stood over the body again in the office. Upon returning, he had noticed an electronic chirp that repeated about every fifteen seconds and discovered it belonged to the answering machine on the desk in the same room; it blinked the number nine, reflecting the new messages. He was pretty sure Haxton's hands were bound behind him, but he wouldn't dare move the body until the forensic team arrived and had already decided to request the assistance of the FBI as soon as the house was cleared, due in small part to the amount of forensics involved but in large part to the identity of the victim.

He stepped to the base of the stairs and began walking up to the second floor. He was almost certain that no bad guys were in the house, but you didn't make assumptions in police work—especially a homicide investigation. The stairs were hardwood with a strip of beige carpeting in the middle, and he was immediately grateful for the color choice. Every fourth or fifth step there was a barely perceptible dark maroon spot in the carpet: blood. As he reached the upstairs hallway at the top of the steps, the flooring was hardwood again. He brought out his flashlight and held it at floor level, sweeping the light back in forth until he found the next drop of blood. He moved to each drop and repeated his flashlight exercise until he had identified a trail that led to the master bedroom. He called Smith and Mills upstairs to clear the other rooms while minding where they stepped (he had marked each drop he had found with a post-it note on the floor).

Luck was on his side again as the expansive master bedroom was carpeted wall-to-wall with beige. He noted the bed was made and there wasn't any sign of a struggle, just like the rest of the house. He marked the trail while thinking about the cut on the eyebrow of the victim. The trail seemed to stop in the middle of the floor between the plush king bed and the wall. He was certain he was missing something. Someone had come up to this room after blood had been shed. There wasn't a meandering trail of blood. It had lead straight to this point, and there had to be a reason for that. Nothing seemed disturbed or damaged. He kept looking around for anything. Nothing was under the bed. The bedside table contained nothing out of the ordinary. He traced his inspection over again, and that's when he saw it.

One additional small drop of blood was mere inches from the wall. He approached the area and saw a portrait of Haxton and his late wife hanging just slightly askew. He put on a latex glove and touched the picture. To his surprise, the picture was not hanging at all but mounted on the wall with two hinges behind the right side of the frame; the fact that the left side was pulled slightly away from the wall had given it the subtle appearance of crookedness. He used the tip of his pen to "open" the picture from the wall, and he found himself looking at a wall safe that was slightly open. He used his pen again to open the safe door further and saw that whatever had been inside was no longer there.

This wasn't just a murder. It was a robbery. A robbery committed by someone who knew about the existence of this safe and likely what was inside. He decided it was time to call the FBI and, now that the house was cleared, he ordered everyone out.

*****

Having a personal bathroom attached to your office was one of the marks of being a top-tier member of a Senator's staff. Always one to covet superficial symbols of status, Chip was, however, currently more grateful for the perk for another reason as he wiped away the vomit from his chin. He stood on wobbly legs and turned to the sink to brush his teeth and splash water on his face.

He had received the call from Sheriff Porter followed by a conversation with Sumpter, whose composure was close to going away completely. She would be heading to the Sheriff's office to make a statement and would be taken home after that. He had told Sandy, who, understandably, was quite distraught and had went to Haxton's own office to try to collect herself and contact whatever distant relative she could find to notify. After that, he had called for staff to gather in the conference room for an urgent meeting, followed by a rather rapid run to his bathroom to empty the remnants of his lunch into the toilet below him.

He collapsed more than sat in his desk chair and stared forward. The staff was gathering in the conference room, but he had one more call that he needed to make. It took him three tries to dial the number correctly due to the shaking of his hands.

"American Alliance for the Middle Class; this is Mary Phelps. How can help you?"

"Ms. Phelps, this is Chip Johnson from Senator James Haxton's office. I need to reach Governor Sutton. I understand he is there today. I'm afraid it's an urgent matter," Chip said, trying hard to sound different than he felt at the moment.

"One moment please, Mr. Johnson; I'll see if I can locate him for you," was the pleasant reply from the receptionist at one of the many Political Action Committees (PACs) who listed

Sutton as a consultant or board member. The "hold music" allowed one to hear a loop of their most recent commercial, urging the viewer to "call your Congressman and tell them to vote against taking away victims' rights in the courtroom." Sutton had no part in the organization's efforts other than glad-handing elected officials and finding out what their support would require. He had just arrived from North Carolina this morning.

"Mr. Johnson, I've located him and will transfer you."

"What's up, Chipper?" Johnson heard after a click and ring in his earpiece.

"Are you somewhere private?"

"I am," Sutton replied as he sat down in front of his desk with the office door closed. "What's going on?"

Johnson fumbled for the right words. "Governor, I don't know how to say this, so I'm just going to say it. Haxton is dead."

A brief silence followed. "What did you say Chip?"

"Haxton is dead. He was found murdered at his house on Figure Eight a couple of hours ago. He was shot in what may have been a robbery. The local sheriff is there now and they are requesting the assistance of the FBI. I don't have anything more than that right now."

There was silence. Chip allowed him a chance to let it sink in. He heard the faint squeak of his office chair as Sutton leaned forward and rested his head in his hands on the desktop. "Jesus Christ, Chip. You don't know anything else?"

"That's all I have right now, Governor."

"Wait, you said it looked like a robbery. Why do they think that?"

Chip had to think for a moment. "The police said it appeared that something was taken from the—"

"What?" Sutton interrupted. "What was taken?"

"They didn't say. I'm going to meet with the staff, and then I was planning on going down there. Sandy's a wreck."

"They didn't say what was missing? Are you sure about that? Do you know if any of his family has been contacted?"

Chip was a little confused about his fixation. "No, I mean yes, they didn't say what was missing. Sandy was going to try to contact some family members, but he really doesn't have any relatives that are even remotely close to him."

"I know. I'm the executor of his will and have power of attorney if he is incapacitated. I'm leaving now. You call me immediately if you hear anything else. You got that? Anything."

"Of course...I mean I'll call you if I hear anything." Sutton clicked off the line.

Why is he getting all shitty with me? Chip brushed aside the thought as soon as he had it. The man's best friend was dead, so he deserved some latitude right now.

Chip stared at the speaker for a moment and remembered that he had to meet with the staff. He thought it was best not to make Sandy come to that. He walked across the central reception area of the office suite and headed into the conference room. He saw a gathering of confused faces. His description of what he had found out caused many there to gasp or begin crying, then he told them he was leaving for Figure Eight Island immediately and would try to keep the office updated. He parted with one request.

"I think it would be best if we keep this to ourselves for the moment. I understand that it will get out and probably get out quickly, but Mrs. Patterson is trying to contact relatives right now and let's give them the chance to find out that way instead of on TV news."

He had worked in communications and public relations in Washington for several years now and he knew the game. He looked at the approximately two dozen faces in the room and was certain that at least one would tell someone within ten minutes of leaving the meeting. It was just as likely that someone would tell a reporter within the hour. It couldn't be helped, and there was no need to keep harping on it because it would happen anyway. He called the number for Sheriff Porter on his way to his car and let him know that Governor Sutton was on his way and that he held power of attorney for the Senator.

It struck him as he sat down in the driver's seat of his car that at no point had he felt sadness. He had alternated between panic and confusion, and he told himself that it was because of the shock and not because he was mainly concerned with how he would find a new star on whom to hitch his wagon.

*****

Several minutes prior to Johnson's departure from the Senate Office Building, Sutton had climbed into the back of a Lincoln Town Car owned by the PAC. He looked at the driver. "Do you have GPS in this thing?"

"Yes, sir," replied the driver, who had been told to get a car ready for Governor Sutton immediately.

"We are going to Figure Eight Island in North Carolina. I want you to get there as fast as this fucking thing can. Don't worry about speeding tickets or anything like that. I know it's a long trip, but that's the way it is. If you have a problem with that, you need to get another driver here right fucking now. Otherwise, we need to get going."

The driver was taken aback but had been told that he would taking Sutton somewhere fairly far away, and the amount of overtime pay he would receive was just fine with him. "Not a problem, sir. He punched in the location in the dash-mounted GPS system and pulled out into DC traffic. He figured he had free reign to go wide-ass open, and he didn't waste any time building up speed. He hoped his eagerness would impress his passenger, but the old man was already on his cell phone talking frantically, which wouldn't change for almost the entire trip to the North Carolina coast.

*****

Delta Airlines Flight 488 inbound from Atlanta Hartsfield Airport was asked to remain in a circular holding pattern above Wilmington International Airport. Below them, a twin-prop engine plane carrying Special Agent in Charge Meredith Scott and Assistant Special Agent in

Charge Mitchell Frierson, both of the Charlotte Field Office of the Federal Bureau of Investigation, landed at the airport.

Both of the agents had received their "oh shit" call earlier in the day from Sheriff Porter, who had given a brief summary of what had taken place at the coastal home of the now late Senator James Haxton. Special Agent Scott had actually worked with Porter on a kidnapping case three years ago and had a high opinion of the man. With this crime, he had kept the number of personnel inside the home to a minimum and had taken great pains to avoid corrupting the crime scene. A special forensics team was already in the air en route from headquarters in Quantico, Virginia, and all agents from the small Wilmington field office were already on scene.

After speaking with Porter, Scott had spoken personally with the Director of the FBI, Sam Purser, who had in turn spoken to the President. It would be an understatement to say that this had the interest of a lot of important people. The two agents walked to the waiting Sheriff's department vehicle which would take them to the crime scene. Frierson checked his smart phone to see if the media had gotten wind of what would be one of the most publicized murder investigations in quite some time and, to his surprise, nothing was on the cable news websites yet.

CHAPTER 22

When tutoring young upstarts in his field, Chip taught that there were four basic reasons that people leak information to the press in politics. The first reason is perceived nobility. They believe that the information *should* be given to the public despite efforts to conceal it; they tell themselves they are acting as crusaders for truth and openness, and the greater public good would be served by bringing said information to the light of day. History is replete with examples of such motivation, both of actual honorable outcomes as well as misguided foolishness. Johnson would usually give as an example to his audience Julian Assange, founder of Wikileaks. Whether he was viewed as a beacon of openness and truth or a possible sex offender with an authority problem depended very much on the eye of the beholder.

The second motivation is good old-fashioned greed. Washington insiders as well as members of the media were very familiar with "I have something you want...how much is it worth to you to have it?" Despite the beliefs of the general public, this is the least common motivating factor for leaking information. Former FBI man Robert Hanssen would be the parallel Chip would draw for this example. Hanssen sold countless secrets, including the identities of agents, to the Soviets for vast sums of money. "He wasn't a Communist, he just liked expensive shit" was one of Chip's favorite phrases about the man who now sits in solitary confinement in a Supermax federal prison in Colorado and likely will for the rest of his life.

Third is the desire to harm or at least sully the reputation of someone or something. There is no dream of the good of the people or exposing evil to righteousness. Anyone in politics knows that this is not only common but often considered good campaign strategy. Usually the only person who benefits is the one who wants harm brought to someone else, often because of a betrayal either imagined or real. A non-political example given by Johnson is the story of a Washington socialite who discovers that her husband has been having an affair. In addition to initiating divorce proceedings, she auctions off her husband's various penile lengthening products that he has bought over the years.

The final example is by far the most common motivation in the confines of the nation's capital: ego. Oftentimes there is no real end goal of releasing non-public information other than showing others that you know something they don't. In a town where one's status is often measured by the level of privileged information one is privy to, this is often the Washington equivalent to the proverbial pissing contest. It is one of the reasons that secrets have a very short life in politics. Even if the person receiving the information gets no real value from possessing it, it makes the gabber seem in the upper echelons of whatever organization they are part of at the time. The usual result of this kind of exchange is that the person who got the information finds someone else to tell, to make them seem in-the-know as well, which often makes that recipient seek someone else to tell for their own validation. The information currency in these events can be anything from gossiping about how many wine bottles are in a neighbor's recycling bin to when an elected official will announce a policy change. In essence it is nothing more than gossip used to inflate a fragile sense of self. It requires no stretch of the imagination to conclude that politics is full of Napoleons who were never breastfed. Chip probably never even thought that many of his "disciples" thought of him when he spoke of this kind of caricature. Four motivations summed up in four categories: chivalry, greed, malice, and ego.

There were just too many people that already knew for it not to happen. He had his satellite radio tuned to CNN Headline News when he heard the announcement that they were stopping whatever story were doing currently to report some breaking news. As soon as he heard that, he was pretty sure what was coming next.

"CNN has received unconfirmed reports that there has been some sort of break-in at the coastal home of Senator James Haxton of North Carolina. This includes reports that Senator Haxton may have been injured during this robbery attempt. This is being reported as occurring at his house on Figure Eight Island, which is a private island on the North Carolina coast, near Wilmington. Haxton is the Chairman of the powerful Senate Appropriations Committee and is considered a likely frontrunner for his party's nomination for the upcoming Presidential election. We repeat: these reports are unconfirmed, but we have learned from more than one source that there has been a robbery at the coastal home of Senator Haxton and that he was there at the time and may have been injured during the break-in. We will pause for a quick break and be right back."

As if on cue, Chip's cell phone began ringing, and he saw the caller ID showed one Matt Weinrib. He didn't answer but noticed he was receiving others every few minutes from many of his media contacts. His aversion to talking to them at the moment wasn't going to change the fact that they were going to continue to call. He was the Director of Communications for the Senator and knew that it would fall on him to control the message to whatever degree possible, especially since he had instructed the staff at the Washington and Asheville offices to give no comment on any inquiries about the Senator today. He activated his car's Bluetooth speaker and called Sutton.

"I thought the fact that the island is private would buy us some more time, but the local NBC affiliate has got a fucking helicopter over the house right now. You can see multiple police cars there, and they're close enough to see that there is police tape around the property," Sutton said upon answering, without even saying hello. "I spoke with Sandy and she has been able to contact his cousin in Arizona, and she let the police know that as well. I think we have to put out a statement—a brief statement—saying what has happened. Keep it simple Chip. I mean real simple."

Chip was nodding to his windshield as he listened. "OK, I'll put out a statement saying we regret to announce so-and-so and we ask for privacy at this difficult time and have no further comment. Something like that." He took a deep breath. "Jesus Christ, Governor."

"I know what you mean, Chip. I'm about an hour away, so call me when you are getting close." He ended the call.

Chip dialed Rachelle MacLean. *Sorry Matt, this is the big leagues.*

She answered on the first ring, and it was clear she had seen the caller identification. "Chip, what the fuck is going on?"

"OK, Rachelle. You're the first person I called. This is for general AP release and will be our official statement so grab a pen." She told him she was ready. "It is with profound sorrow that we report the death of Senator James A. Haxton, who was killed during an apparent robbery at his home on Figure Eight Island. We have no further comment at this time and ask that Senator Haxton's family and staff be given some privacy and time to deal with this tragic loss."

There was a solid ten seconds of silence on the other end.

"Holy shit, Chip," she finally responded. "What the hell happened?"

Jesus, it's never fucking enough with these guys. "The statement is all I have, Rachelle. I will touch base with you when I can, but I don't have anything else,even off the record, right now. Listen, I'll give you twenty minutes before you have to release the statement to AP to report the scoop, but no more. I mean it."

"No problem, thanks. I'm really sorry for your loss, Chip."

It hit him a second time that he seemed to be devoid of grief, but put it aside. "Thank you Rachelle. The clock starts now."

She ended the call, got up from her desk, and literally ran to the studio. She used her cell to call her producer as she went and told her she needed to be on the air in five minutes max and it would have to be without makeup or prep; she gave him the reason in two terse sentences. He told her to go directly to the side commentary desk where she would pick up the broadcast when they returned from commercial break, and then he followed with his own "Holy shit!"

The news organization was used to a frantic pace, so Rachelle's assistant was waiting for her. She fitted the small microphone on her collar and threaded the wire beneath her jacket under her arm to a wireless transmitter clipped to the back of her waist. The assistant applied a quick few brushes of makeup base to her face, but there wasn't time to do anything more. Luckily, MacLean wasn't one who required a lot of touching up. Behind the glass in the director's studio, an assistant typed up the statement for release across the AP ten minutes after they were the first to officially announce the death of one of America's biggest political figures. They also had access to the live helicopter feed from the local NBC affiliate, which they planned to run split-screen with MacLean.

*****

Anna crossed over the curving bridge that spanned the Intracoastal Waterway at Holden Beach. Both kids stared at the DVD monitor that was currently playing *Madagascar*. The audio was beamed to the wireless headphones that insulated them from the outside world, while their mother had decided to enjoy the simple pleasure of quietness for the last two hours of the drive from Charlotte. Just the simple act of crossing this bridge seemed to wash away the cares and stresses of the world at home, and she smiled to herself as she saw the town gazebo pass underneath her as the bridge started its downward decline toward the small coastal island near the North Carolina/South Carolina border.

They had purchased a home here several years ago after falling in love with the small beach town that seemed to shun the pressures of development and tourism. Settled between Oak Island and Ocean Isle, it boasted a fishing pier along with several small family-owned shops and restaurants. Visitors who needed a dose of bustling crowds and tourist traps needed only to make the forty-minute drive south to Myrtle Beach. Holden had stubbornly held on to its small-town Southern charm and slow pace, which were two things Anna and her husband cherished about their time on the island.

She drove approximately three miles down Ocean Boulevard West until she reached the "guardhouse" that marked the entrance to the West End development. This was a private part of the island that required anyone to check in with the security guard that occupied the small hut in the middle of the road. The "security force" of West End was made up of several older local women who worked shifts and called the police if anyone insisted on entering who didn't belong but who couldn't do much else since there was no actual gate.

Anna stopped and chatted with Lydia, who was currently at the guardhouse. They both asked about each other's families, and Lydia said how proud everyone was of Michael.

"Michael not with you this time, honey?" Lydia asked.

"He's coming. He was on a trip with friends, and they get back tomorrow to Wilmington and they're going to drop him off here," Anna replied.

"Hey Miss Lydia!" came from the lowering back driver-side window.

"Well hey there, Charlie. How're you doing, sweetheart?" She pulled out two lollipops and handed them to the young man, who gave one to his sister. "You gonna come visit me here tomorrow before you go out on the beach?"

The pathway access to the beach the Reece family used came right by the guardhouse, and Charlie always stopped by to say hello to whomever was there. The fact that they had lollipops didn't hurt either.

"Yes ma'am. I'll show you my new bucket."

"It's a date honey." She turned to Anna. "Let me know if ya'll need anything."

"We will. Great to see you, Lydia."

Anna drove less than a quarter mile, turned right into their cul-de-sac, and pulled into their driveway. Like most homes on the island, it was on pylons to protect against flooding. She pulled under the house and the family went up the stairs carrying what they had brought for the upcoming week. There were two stories mounted on the supports with a classic inverted floor plan popular on the coast, where the bedrooms were on the first floor and the family room, dining room, and kitchen on the second, where you could enjoy a more elevated view. The house backed up to the marshy area leading to the waterway which divided Holden from the mainland. They had a small boat dock that Michael hoped to use for an actual boat one day but which currently served as the place where they would grill or watch the kids try to catch crabs on the ends of strings using chicken necks as bait.

Anna unpacked the clothing and put away the groceries she had purchased at the local Food Lion on the way in. She brought a glass of wine and a book out to the screened porch area that overlooked the marsh, where she could keep track of the kids, who were running down the planked walkway that led to the dock. She frowned as she heard the chime announcing a text message, wondering if it was something related to work. She was pleasantly surprised to see it was from a neighbor, and the message simply said "turn on the news."

*****

The red camera light came on, letting Henry Sallinger now that they were back from commercial. He looked into the lens with a grave face.

"We are back, and I'm now going to hand it over to MSNBC Political Correspondent Rachelle MacLean with an exclusive development in our coverage of the break-in at the coastal home of Senator James Haxton. Rachelle…"

MacLean appeared on the right side of the screen while the left half was occupied by live helicopter footage from Figure Eight Island. "Tragic news has come forth in relation to the developing story on Figure Eight Island. MSNBC has now confirmed that Senator James Haxton of North Carolina was murdered in an apparent home invasion. This has been confirmed by senior officials in the Senator's office. We have also received a statement from the Senator's staff, which reads…"

Rachelle read the statement Chip had given her while the production booth changed the banner at the bottom of the screen to read "Senator James Haxton Confirmed Dead." Simultaneously, they sent the statement out on the wire for use by other media outlets.

Rachelle continued, "It was well known that Senator Haxton was considered one of the most likely candidates to achieve the party nomination in the upcoming Presidential race. He was a widower, his wife passing away from cancer several years ago, and they did not have any children. The thoughts and condolences of everyone at this network go out to the family and friends of the Senator."

The screen had now been filled with a chest-up official photograph of Haxton, over which MacLean's audio was laid.

"This marks the first time a United States Senator has been killed while in office since Senator Robert Kennedy was assassinated at the Ambassador Hotel in Los Angeles during his Presidential campaign run." MacLean was receiving frantic tidbits of information in her earpiece from the production booth. "Initial information suggests that this was simply a home burglary attempt, and there is nothing currently to suggest that the Senator was specifically targeted. Henry..."

Sallinger slowly shook his head. "Thank you, Rachelle. Obviously shocking and tragic news. Once again, sources confirm that Senator James Haxton of North Carolina has been murdered in what looks like an attempted home invasion. We will be right back to discuss this further."

*****

Anna was uncertain how to feel about what she had just watched. She realized that a historic tragedy had occurred, but she also knew that the dead man had visited horrible acts upon the man she loved more than anyone in the world. The one word that kept creeping into her mind was "karma," and she wondered if she should feel guilty about feeling that way about someone who had been murdered.

She then realized that the bulk of the coverage was coming from the Wilmington affiliate, which was less than an hour north of where they were currently. She picked up her phone again.

"Hello?"

"Gabriel? Is that you? It's Anna," she asked the man on the other end of the call.

"Hey good-lookin'. Hang on one minute," Drake was saying over the static-riddled call. "Mike's down below—"

"No, I need to talk to you, honey. Are you guys coming in later today?"

"Yep. We'll be pulling alongside in about eight to ten hours, I should think," he told Anna.

"Where are you going to dock at?"

"Wilmington Marine Center is the plan. I'm only tying up long enough to drop the boys off and then I'm off again," he said, referring to his upcoming two-week trip around the Caribbean.

"I need a favor Gabriel."

He didn't know what it was, but he recognized a certain gravity to her tone. "Sure Anna. What can I do for you?"

"Have you been watching the news?" she asked.

"Nope. We've been enjoying a blissful break from technology and your modern world, my dear." *Something's wrong*, a voice started to tell him in the back of his mind. "Anna, is everything all right?"

"Everything's fine sweetheart, but I need you to dock in Southport. I can't really elaborate any more than that, but I need you to do this favor for me. We'll talk more later about it. Do you think you can do that?"

"I'll be happy to, Anna. Anything else I can do?" He didn't feel like it was appropriate at the moment to pry into the reasons behind it anymore.

"No. I know the boys were going to rent a car in Wilmington, but I'll come pick them up. Just call me on my cell when you're about an hour away, and I'll meet you there. Thanks, Gabriel. I'll talk to you in a few hours."

"No problem Anna. Bye."

He hit the end button on his phone. Like just about anyone who had met her, he was a big fan. She was not one to put others out, so when she asked a favor, he did it without question. The boys were on the back of the boat kicking back and enjoying the weather, so he took the opportunity to turn on the satellite-linked television in the captain's area and tune it to CNN. There was only one story being covered, and he was pretty sure that Anna's request had something to do with it. He made a call to Wilmington to cancel his dock and fueling plans and then called Southport Marina to make alternative arrangements.

Anna sat her phone down and looked out at Elizabeth and Little Charlie playing on the dock with the audible laughter of children coming up to the back porch. She immediately thought of the often-used image of a young Michael Reece walking on a similar structure with the Senator during the time the story broke about the connection between her husband and the recently deceased. *Enjoy your time in hell, you son of a bitch.* No, she decided. She didn't have to feel conflicted at all about not mourning the death of one Senator James A. Haxton.

*****

The number of security guards at the private bridge that was the only access to Figure Eight Island had been increased due to the virtual circus of activity in the past several hours. No one without an island access decal or clearance from the town's rental agencies was allowed across, with one exception. The Communications Director from Senator Haxton's office had called ahead to make them aware of the upcoming arrival of Governor Hal Sutton. Not only was Sutton a close personal friend of the Senator, the man had explained, but he was also the executor of Haxton's will as well as the family's attorney-in-fact. He was not to be delayed at the bridge.

Due to the advanced call, the black Lincoln Towncar was given a temporary access placard to display on the dash and was waived through. The driver drove directly to the scene of the crime, receiving directions from his passenger.

Sutton had called ahead and Sheriff Porter met him at the street, where the Lincoln stopped. The two men shook hands.

"I understand the two of you were very close friends, Governor. I'm very sorry for your loss," Porter said to the new visitor.

Sutton nodded as he looked at the ground for a moment then seemed to get his composure back. "I appreciate that, Sheriff. I appreciate you meeting me, and I certainly don't want to keep you from other work here. I don't want to be any trouble."

"Not a problem, sir. The FBI has taken over the forensics side of things, at my request. They have much better resources, and I would assume that scrutiny over how long the investigation takes will be a lot higher than your average one. They've already completed their work in the house and the grounds. They didn't seem too hopeful about getting a usable fingerprint, and there was no murder weapon found on the premises." Porter hesitated a bit before going on. "There was, as you know, a fair amount of blood at the scene, and we assume that most of it is from the victim, but there were samples taken at several locations with the hope that maybe the perpetrator left some as well. They are flying that evidence to Washington where they can have a much quicker turnover with DNA analysis, and we should know by tomorrow if any of the samples don't match Senator Haxton's blood type. I was surprised that there are no security cameras on the premises, given the status of the owner of the property, but I assure you that we're doing everything we can to get answers and an arrest as soon as humanly possible."

Sutton placed his left hand on Porter's upper arm. "I have no doubt you are, and it made me feel more at ease knowing you are one of the point men with the investigation. You're top notch around here, Sheriff. Is there anything you need that you're not getting?"

"No, sir. The FBI Wilmington Field Office is fairly small, but the SAC from Charlotte and her staff flew in several hours ago. They have been nothing but helpful and professional."

The ex-Governor gave Porter a grateful smile. "That's good to hear. If you hit any walls, I hope you won't hesitate to call me. This old Governor might still have a little clout around here."

"I certainly will, Governor. I have surmised that the two of you spent a fair amount of time together. Would you have any idea of anyone who would wish him harm?" Porter raised his palm up to Sutton. "Of course, if you would rather wait to talk about this, I completely understand."

"Well, I can't say anyone in particular comes to mind. As you know, he was very well known and was being talked about as a possible candidate for the Presidency. There are all kinds of crazies out there, but I can't be more specific than that. I will certainly ask around with the staff and relay any information I get." He was rewarded with an appreciative nod. "You said it looked like it was a robbery?"

"Yes, but not a usual smash and grab kind of home invasion." He gestured toward the house, inviting him to walk with him. "Forensics is done, so I am happy to take you to the house if you would like, sir. The Senator has already been taken to the Medical Examiner's Office, but I must warn you that there is still a fair amount of blood, so if you would rather not, it's not a problem."

Sutton shook his head. "No, I would like to go inside if I could. I might help you identify anything that's missing. I've spent a lot of time here."

"That would be great, Governor. As I was saying, the target of the robbery seemed to be one thing. There were several obviously highly valuable things the perpetrator would have had to walk by, and they weren't taken. Based on some blood trailing, it seems that the Senator was taken to a certain location in the house before he was killed. Thus far, to our knowledge, there was nothing else taken from the premises."

As they came around the corner toward the back entrance to the house, there was a woman in a nylon FBI jacket standing near the door talking on a cell phone. She was barely over five feet in height but had the look and mannerisms of an absolute professional. Sutton could see her badge clipped on her belt just above her left front pocket of her business slacks and a 9 mm Beretta attached on the other side. She saw the two men approaching and told the person on the other end of the call that she would call them back.

"Governor Sutton, I'm Meredith Scott, Special Agent in Charge at the Charlotte Field Office. I am very sorry for your loss, sir." She shook hands with him and gave him one of her cards. "I assure you, we will be working round the clock to get answers as soon as we can, and feel free to contact me if there is anything you think would add to the investigation. I wrote my personal cell number on the back."

"I appreciate everything that you are doing here, Agent Scott. I have upmost faith in everyone's abilities, and I appreciate you offering the help of the FBI in this matter."

"Sir, jurisdiction is a little murky here. Since there is not obvious evidence of a terrorist motive for the murder and there are no signs of any kidnapping, primary oversight would belong to the local law enforcement agents. I made the decision, however, that given the scope of the investigation as well as the significant resources available to Special Agent Scott, to request that the FBI take the lead role," Porter added.

Scott nodded toward the Sheriff. "We appreciate the confidence of Sheriff Porter, and we're happy to do that."

"I've never been a fan of turf wars in crime investigations, and I've been nothing but impressed with Scott's agents from the beginning."

Sutton appreciated the Sheriff's lack of ego in the matter, which can be hard to find in law enforcement sometimes. "Would it be too much to ask for one of you to walk me through the area?"

"Not at all, sir," Scott said. "As I'm sure Sheriff Porter has told you, the forensics part is complete, so there is no harm in that. Sir, did he mention—"

Sutton nodded. "Yes, he told me that there is still plentiful evidence of violence, and I'll be fine. But I appreciate you preparing me."

The two law enforcement professionals walked him along the first-floor area that concluded at the office area where there was still no small amount of blood on the floor.

"Governor, the cause of death was a single gunshot to the forehead, but it appeared that the Senator had been struck in the head at least once prior to this. There was a small gash on his left eyebrow, which we believe was the source of blood droplets that led upstairs to the master bedroom. The actual gunshot was at a range of no more than eighteen inches and probably much less given the fairly small confinement of powder burns at the entrance wound. Sir, at any time you would like to stop or take a break..."

She was given a dismissive shaking of the head in reply.

"OK, as Sheriff Porter had suspected, his hands were bound behind his back with a zip tie and he was on his knees when he was shot...very much like an execution instead of a burglar being surprised by a home owner. Sheriff Porter?"

Porter guided Sutton out of the office and toward the stairs leading to the second floor. "I noticed blood droplets leading upstairs and followed them to the master bedroom." He led the group up the stairs to that location. "The trail seemed to end in the middle of the floor here until I discovered another droplet near the wall under this photograph, which is how we discovered the safe." He pointed to the open door that had a fine, dark, dusty coating from the forensics team's attempts to obtain fingerprints. "We really don't have any idea what was in the safe, but..." Porter noticed that all color had left the Governor's face and he seemed a little unsteady on his feet at the moment. He put a hand on the man's shoulder to steady him. "Sir, I'm sorry. I know this must be very difficult for you, and I can brief you on the rest later."

The Governor looked at him vacantly for a moment and then seemed to recover his bearings. "Thank...thank you, Sheriff. It's just a little overwhelming. I will let you get back to work. I appreciate both of you taking the time to talk to me. I...um...left my number with the Sheriff's office and don't mind any of you calling for anything." He shook hands with the two officers and told them he could show himself out.

*****

Anna reached for her cell phone as it chimed the melody of "Hark the Sound of Tarheel Voices." Her love for her alma mater was just as strong as her husband's, if not stronger.

"Hello."

"Anna, it's Gabe. We are about an hour from the marina, but the owner is arranging for a rental car to be there so we can drop off Mike at your place. After that, Eric is going to drop me off back here and David in Fayetteville on the way back," he said over a much-higher-quality connection now that he was closer to the mainland.

"That's great, Gabe. I appreciate you changing things around. Have you guys seen any of the news since we talked?"

Bingo. "I have, but they've been on the back deck hanging out. I take it this has something to do with the murder near Wilmington and all the circus going on?"

"Something like that. Look, if there's a way to not tune in until you guys get here, it might be a good idea. I'm sorry, Gabe. I don't mean to be cryptic, but it's a little of a touchy situation."

"Hey, if you're being cryptic, you're doing it for a good reason. I'll do my best to keep the outside world outside for just a little longer."

"Thanks sweetheart. I'll see you in a little while." Anna ended the call and leaned back in her chair. Despite the fact that, at times, his immaturity and boorishness could be maddening, she realized that Drake was a dedicated friend to her husband, and that's what made her love a guy she could have strangled if she didn't know him better.

She had moved to the front porch, where Elizabeth and Charlie were riding their bikes with some of the other kids in the cul-de-sac. They were blessed that several of the families that owned homes on this street had kids of similar age, and many of them were here enjoying the last bit of summer before school started back. The cul-de-sac was set off from the main road that could be a little hectic for bike-riding children, and it allowed for the perfect gathering place for kids to be kids in between sessions playing in the smooth white sand of the beach about a hundred yards away.

She felt like she knew her husband probably better than anyone except for Charlie Potts, who passed away many years ago. That being the case, she didn't have the faintest idea how Michael would react to this news. Then again, it didn't really matter. She would be there to support him regardless of what, if anything, he wanted to do.

She never even considered being angry at the fact that he had decided to keep that part of his life a secret from her. She sensed both confusion and uncertainty when he finally decided to let it out, but the prevailing emotion she had seen in him was shame. He hadn't kept her in the dark because he didn't trust her; he had done it because he was humiliated. There was the sexual aspect that had shamed him, but also the fact that he had allowed someone to victimize him repeatedly and over such a long period of time. Michael didn't possess size on the scale of someone like David, but he took care of himself, and he certainly wouldn't be someone you would pick in a group as a guy you could mess with and not pay a price for it. The weight of manipulation and fear, however, can overcome many things, and his subjugation to his tormentor was due more to mental control than physical.

She had sensed a turning point after his revelations to her about his past. Michael seemed to have reached a point where it was OK to move on to the rest of his life, and he had a mission now to provide and care for his family, not to mention protect them. The painful excision of his personal terror had been the first step in truly escaping it. It wasn't an instant break, and she was sure that the nightmares would take a while to go away if they ever did, but she had been convinced that better days were ahead for him. Now Anna wasn't sure if what happened on Figure Eight Island would help him gain further distance from his past or if it would reach out from the grave to try to pull him back to hell. But whatever direction it took, she would be standing by his side.

CHAPTER 23

People of blood type O-negative are considered universal donors, since red blood cells of this variety do not express the "A" or "B" proteins or the surface protein known as the Rhesus factor. Because of a lack of these structures on the cell layer, they will not elicit an adverse immune response from patients who have antibodies against these three most common red blood cell surface proteins. This is the type of blood used for transfusions where there is no time to perform proper cross-matching, usually for a patient who has suffered severe blood loss and is in a life-threatening situation. It is for this reason that it is the most needed blood in banks across the country. It is also the blood type of one Senator James Haxton.

Nik Patel had spent the first five years of his career as a lab technician at Kaiser Permanente while finishing his Masters in Forensic Science at the University of California-Davis. He had received a bachelor's degree in biochemistry at Stanford, and, much to his parents' chagrin, he decided against medical school in order to pursue his childhood dream of working in forensics. His impressive academic credentials, along with a likable personality that served him well in school and job interviews, had helped him secure a job with the vaunted FBI Laboratory in Quantico, Virginia. He had quickly built a reputation as being rock solid and meticulous and had never had an issue that complicated an investigation or a prosecution.

No one at the lab was surprised when he was chosen to be on the forensics team for the Haxton case. His current task was ascertaining if any of the forty-two blood samples taken at various locations of the crime scene belonged to anyone other than the victim. Systematic as always, he started by testing to see whether any samples were type A or B or were positive for the Rhesus factor. If the blood was O-negative, it didn't guarantee that it belonged to Haxton, but if it wasn't, you had a hit. Despite the fact that this investigation had immediately moved to the front of the line, DNA testing was slower.

He was currently working on sample number 31 and, as he had for the previous thirty, he diluted a portion of the sample and added a solution that contained antibodies to both A and B proteins as well as antibodies to the Rhesus factor. He drew some of the concoction up in a small pipelle and transferred it to a glass microscope slide, where he viewed it at 100X power. Unlike the previous thirty samples, he saw clumping of the red blood cells in his eyepiece which resembled small clusters of grapes. If this was O-negative blood, no antibodies would have found and attached themselves to their "match" antigen, causing the clumping together that he saw with this sample. As was his custom, he immediately repeated the test with another pipelle of the sample to confirm the same results. Satisfied that it was an accurate result, he picked up the phone.

"McPherson," was the greeting he received on the other end, by Dr. Randall McPherson, team leader for this case.

"Dr. McPherson, it's Nik. I have a hit on blood sample number thirty-one. I had reproducible clumping when mixed with A/B/Rh solution. I will start narrowing it down further but wanted to let you know," Patel told his supervisor.

"Thanks Nik. Good work. I'll be down in a few minutes."

McPherson hung up the phone and grabbed his white lab coat off the hook on the back of his office door. He took the steps down to the second floor where Patel was at his lab bench and confirmed the results microscopically as well and separated the rest of the sample into three containers: one for DNA testing, one for further blood typing, and one for evidence for any later use that might be needed for the case. It wasn't that he doubted his colleague, but this was the FBI Lab and this was one of their biggest cases in recent memory. Nothing was left to assumption.

He thanked Patel, who began working to identify the exact blood type of the sample, and went back to his office to call Special Agent Scott. She wrote down the information that he relayed to her and repeated it back to make sure no mistake had been made in her transcription. Scott thanked Dr. McPherson and consulted her evidence log after getting off the phone. Blood sample #31 had been taken from the inner handle of the back door of Haxton's house. McPherson had assured her that it would be immediately taken for DNA analysis, and the search for a match would begin. They both knew that the usual turnaround time of several weeks wouldn't apply in this case.

Scott relayed the information to Special Agent Frierson as well as Sheriff Porter. The latter wouldn't be directly involved with the forensics side of the investigation, but she felt it was professional courtesy as well as a sign of gratitude to the man who invited their team to join the case with nothing but a pledge of complete cooperation. To date, it was the first real lead from evidence they had. There were no fingerprints that proved to be useful, the only matches being to Haxton himself and his housekeeper, and no security cameras anywhere near the home. The land the home sat on was expansive, so the neighbors had not seen or heard anything unusual. They had interviewed all the security guards who had worked the bridge entrance for the past week, and that labor had also refused to bear any fruit. She remembered having high hopes for the bridge personnel, since access to the island was much more limited than most locations, but, as is often the case, the most promising sources of information turned out to be total blanks.

Given the position, influence, and relative fame of the victim, the possible murder motives were too numerous to count, not to mention that it could simply be a random home invasion that went terribly wrong. Scott, however, didn't believe that was the case. The limited evidence she had pointed to the killer wanting something very specific. The perpetrator had simply ignored several highly valuable items in the office alone. There were no signs of struggle which could have forced the killer to leave before he could gather all of the things he wanted (she thought of the perpetrator as a "he" since they were almost always male in these circumstances), which made her believe he had one, possibly two, objectives. First, he wanted whatever was in the safe. The second objective could have been to kill Haxton, but that was less certain. So many questions remained.

But now she did possess a piece of information she didn't have before her call from Dr. McPherson. Someone other than Senator Haxton had shed their blood inside the home. She couldn't say with absolutely certainty that it was the blood of the killer, but it was very likely to be the case. If not, it would certainly belong to someone who had some explaining to do. She looked at her phone when it chimed, signaling a received text message.

Blood Type: A Positive; DNA analysis begun. Formal report faxed. –McPh.

She placed the phone back in her belt holder just beside her FBI badge. She had already ascertained that the housekeeper's blood type was O-positive, and she was already considered a highly unlikely suspect given the fact that she was almost seventy years old and no more than 110 pounds; as well she was utterly devastated upon hearing the news of Haxton's death. That left at least one other person in the house recently.

"Who are you, Mr. A Positive?" she said to herself while sipping on what seemed like her millionth cup of coffee since arriving on the coast.

*****

The Sculpted Lady had pulled alongside at one of the outer docking areas of Southport Marina. Drake had used the marina many times before and had a good relationship with the owner, who had arranged for car rental agents from Wilmington to bring a full-size SUV to the marina with the promise that the owner would drive him back personally. Docking fees, fuel, and other items for such a large boat were a nice profit for the man, and he strived to keep his customers happy and coming back. After securing the boat and receiving an entry pass to return to the property, the men got in their rented Ford Expedition and made their way to Highway 17 South toward Holden Beach.

Drake kept the conversation lively to negate the need to turn on the radio which could bring news from Wilmington. It wasn't hard. The men were all good friends and had added several new stories over the past several days to relive. The plan would be to drop off Michael at Holden and visit for a while, then Drake would return to the boat while Daniels would then head home to Charlotte by way of Fayetteville to drop off Tripp at Ft. Bragg.

As they headed west on Ocean Boulevard, the air had the hint of salty decay that was often present from the canal and waterway areas on the island during low tide. They were delayed a few minutes at the guardhouse at the entrance to the West End development so

Michael could catch up with Patty, who was currently staffing the post. She offered him congratulations on his award and told him how proud the town was of him. The final tenth of a mile in the cul-de-sac included a bicycle escort from Little Charlie, who peddled as fast as his small legs could, bouncing the frame from one training wheel to the other. Anna was waiving from the expansive front porch area and Elizabeth was dribbling her soccer ball around the front yard, collecting sand spurs on her socks as she did so.

Michael was rewarded with big hugs from both of the kids as he climbed out of the truck, followed by a longer one from his wife. Anna kissed the cheeks of all of the guys as they came into the front yard and asked if everyone had enjoyed the trip. Charlie was already perched on Tripp's massive shoulders and Elizabeth was opening the bag with her souvenirs from Dominica. Tipped off by Drake when they loaded the truck in Southport, Tripp asked the kids to take the men to the boat dock out back while Michael took his bags up to the house alone with Anna.

"Did you have a good time, honey?" Anna asked as they walked up the steps to the front door. "Sit on the swing with me a minute before we go inside."

Michael didn't know what it was but sensed that something was afoot, so he set his bags down on the porch and sat down with her. They began to unconsciously rock back and forth on the swing in the same way one sways slightly side to side when cradling a baby in one's arms.

"What's up Anna?"

"Haxton is dead, Michael. He was murdered on Figure Eight Island in an apparent break-in while you boys were on your way back here." She gripped his hand a little tighter. "I didn't know how you would feel about it and didn't want to spring it on you in front of everyone."

He stared forward for a while, and she could see him processing what he had just heard. There was no outward display of emotion. "He was killed?"

"Yes. They don't know who did it, and it seems to be part of a burglary attempt. The Wilmington area and Figure Eight are a madhouse right now—"

"That's why we went to Southport instead," Michael interrupted.

"It is. I called Drake and told him to come there." She read his mind and answered his question before it was asked. "I didn't tell him about that. I just told him it would be crazy there and if you were noticed you might be bothered by reporters because of your past connection with him."

He swayed on the swing with Anna for a while in silence. "Fuck him. I'm pretty sure where he is right now, and I'm not going to let him occupy any more of my thoughts," he said while still looking out toward the blue horizon of the Atlantic Ocean in the distance. "He has taken enough from me, and I sure as hell am not going to let him take anything from the grave." He turned to face his wife and kissed her. "He was my past. You and the kids are my future."

It was a relief and, to some degree, a shock. She had worried that this might traumatically bring back troubles that he had finally made a big step in putting behind him, but it seemed that it was helping him gain further closure. His somewhat cold detachment about the death was a little surprising. It wasn't that she felt he should be sad about the news, it just wasn't like him to react in such a matter-of-fact way. But then again, this wasn't usual news, was it? It really didn't matter why he reacted in the way that he did, she decided. If it got him closer to putting down this part of his past, it was fine with her. His next remark surprised her even more.

"I think I need to tell Gabe and Eric," he said as he turned to his wife. "It gives me a small circle of confidants about it in case I need to talk about it. After that, I plan to close the book on this and never open it again if I can help it." He patted her hand. "Is that OK with you?"

"Of course it is honey," she said. "I can't possibly understand how it feels, and whatever you think you need to make it easier to move on is fine with me."

They got up from the swing together and walked holding hands around the house to the boat dock.

292

"Eric and Gabe? I need to talk to you two about something," Michael told his friends quietly as Little Charlie was giving a lecture on the best way to catch crabs off the dock.

Tripp took the cue and asked if Elizabeth and Charlie would like to go get ice cream before he had to leave. As always the response was enthusiastic, so he patted his friend on the back and piled the kids into Anna's car, pledging to be back in about an hour, once again reminding Michael and Anna that the man's hulking presence belied the fact that he was one of the most sincere and gentle souls they had ever had the privilege of knowing.

Michael and Anna sat on the back porch with Eric and Gabe while the sun began to show its red hues as it set over the Intracoastal Waterway on the western horizon with the homes of Ocean Isle in the distance. Both men sat with mouths agape as Michael explained his dark connection with the recently deceased Senator Haxton.

"Besides Anna and David, you two are the only ones who know this," Michael said as he concluded his narrative about his past life. The message was implicit...*I don't really want anyone else to know either*. "I'm ready to move on from this, and it's a part of me I don't want the kids to ever know...at least not until they're much older. I just wanted you to know so it wouldn't seem strange with me being pretty detached about the death of someone who just about everyone else thinks was a father figure to me."

Unsurprisingly, they both pledged to keep the information to themselves and offered to help any way they could at any time he needed. Tripp returned, and they all enjoyed each other's company for a few hours before Michael's three diving companions had to leave to go to their respective destinations. Drake gave his satellite phone number to them in case they needed to reach him on his Caribbean odyssey, and they all shared embraces before leaving.

*****

Pete Riddle had gotten a text as a heads-up that he might need to get down to the coast on short notice, so when he got the confirmatory call a few hours later he had already packed everything he would need and made his way from his home in Garner to I-40 West toward Wilmington. The heat and humidity had reached mild misery levels of late, so he had driven down with the windows up and the air conditioning on. His Pullman suitcase was in the back seat of his Jeep Cherokee and contained four days' worth of clothes and toiletries. He patted the inside pocket of his sport coat to confirm that his wallet and passport were in their proper place. The briefcase on the passenger seat contained yet another set of identifications, all of which were completely fictitious but would only be revealed as such by a very sharp professional with several hours on their hands to investigate.

Riddle had been born in rural North Carolina to a tobacco-farming family between the two small farming towns of Coats and Angier. His family members had farmed tobacco, soybeans, and cotton for generations and were respected members of the community. Pete was the first and last born of his parents. A heart condition discovered in his mother shortly after his birth had come with the recommendation against future pregnancies. The long, hot summer days picking tobacco, meant to instill a strong work ethic, had actually made him determined not to make a living as a farmer.

Mediocre grades and lack of direction had not given him a lot of options in terms of colleges, so he spent a year after high school working on the farm and trying to decide what he wanted to do with his life, all the while showing his parents a less-than-impressive work ethic. After a year, his parents gave him the option of making his career on the family farm or going to school...or moving the hell out and getting a job. He placated their frustrations by enrolling in Wake Technical College and moving into an apartment in Raleigh with a high school buddy whose ambition and direction were also not stellar.

He and his roommate spent a year having a great time on Hillsborough Street at the local bars where students from North Carolina State University would hang out. It was during this year that Pete found a vocation at which he was quite talented: selling weed. Raleigh had several colleges filled with young adults with a yearning for partying as well as extra spending money from home. In less than eight months, he had a regular customer base that was growing every day along with a growing supply network. He had struck up supply deals with growers in nearby Harnett and Cumberland Counties, who used isolated patches of fertile land near the banks of the Cape Fear River along with liberal payments to the local Sheriff to produce bumper crops of marijuana that didn't have to be smuggled in from abroad.

By the time his parents discovered that he hadn't sat in a single class for an entire school year at Wake Tech and cut him off financially, he was banking twenty-five-thousand dollars a month, which he split with his roommate and fellow entrepreneur. He told them he didn't want the farming life and promised to keep trying to find what career would light his fire beneath. He told them he had found a job that allowed him to afford to live in Raleigh and apologized for his dishonesty about school. Although frustrated with his seemingly shiftless ways, neither parent had any suspicion that his was an up-and-comer in the area's drug trafficking industry...and they never would. Less than a year later, both his parents were on a commuter flight coming back from a trade show in Lexington, Kentucky, that unexpectedly plunged into a forested area two miles short of the runway at Raleigh-Durham International Airport due to an unforeseen wind shear from an early summer storm front.

The collapse of the tobacco industry was yet to come, and Pete found himself the sole inheritor of several hundred acres of prime farm land. This did nothing to ignite his desire for a career in rural North Carolina agriculture, and he instructed the family attorney to auction off the land as soon as feasible. The probate period of the estate was quite brief given that there were no liens on the land and the family home had not carried a mortgage in several decades. A small percentage of the sale price of the land and the family home went to balances on a few pieces of farm equipment that had been financed and some more to attorneys' fees, and, after estate taxes, Pete Riddle walked away from his parents' deaths with over six hundred thousand dollars.

Young and now ambitious, Riddle saw this as an opportunity to expand into more profitable ventures. His marijuana network now had selling operations in all the college towns of the Triangle area, and he had added cocaine and heroin to his inventory. His old roommate, who had formed a habit of sampling their product too much, found early retirement by way of a shotgun blast to the head followed by dismemberment in one of the many rural marijuana fields, with subsequent employment as food for the enormous catfish in the Cape Fear. This marked the first murder Riddle had participated in as part of his business, but it was by far not the last. He was somewhat surprised at how little emotion he felt when he aimed the shotgun at the back of his longtime friend's head and exploding it like a putting a firecracker inside a watermelon.

The decision that marked his transition to the big time was when he invested in prostitution. What began as petty use of cocaine-addicted customers as hookers in truck stop parking lots grew into high-priced call-girl operations in the city of Raleigh. He began to cater to the rich and influential of Raleigh society, which included everyone from business executives to prominent politicians. Although not educated, Riddle was far from stupid and realized that most of his clients, no matter how devious or depraved their preferences, valued their standing in society and their image over everything. Initially this irony was a source of amusement for the young criminal entrepreneur, but later on he began to see it as an opportunity.

Hidden video equipment, Riddle found, was not only fairly inexpensive but easy to install in ways that were hard to detect. Compilation of an expensive video library of Raleigh's rich and influential was an undertaking that was ever growing. Although occasionally used for blackmail, its main purpose was insurance. It was hard to fear retribution or prosecution when one had thousands of hours of high-quality footage of all of the sick and perverted habits of several state legislators, the Raleigh Deputy Chief of Police, prominent businessmen, several pastors, and, his coup de grace in terms of potential legal entanglements, the District Attorney of Wake County, Hal Sutton.

As his enterprise grew as well as his wealth, he sold off his drug operations and focused entirely on prostitution. He "employed" all types of people to serve the needs of his clients, including college co-eds wanting to earn occasional easy money, sex slaves who were paying off their transit from whatever shit hole they had fled, young attractive gay men who performed for money or to pay off past drug debts, and the occasional minor who had been kidnapped and sold into what could only be described as the biggest living hell that one could imagine. They were used for as long as they were useful and then cast aside if they were lucky but killed if they were a threat.

Very few clients knew about others and would have been shocked to know that neighbors, partners, friends, and even pastors were part of the debauchery. They were also blissfully unaware of the non-consensual video recordings kept in Pete Riddle's vault. They were only made aware of these if there was the potential for trouble. High members of society were harder to kill off than the wayward prostitute—people would miss them—so the threat of death wouldn't carry much weight if it was unlikely to be carried out. Besides, exposure for what they were was a far greater penalty than death to these superficial egomaniacs. If a client had decided to give up their debauchery or had an attack of conscience, Riddle would sit down with them and wish them the best...and show them a snippet of footage that they would do anything to keep out of the light of day. Riddle described what happened next as the "departure fee." The video would never be let out of its secure location if two conditions were met: 1) the client would pay an often substantial monthly fee, in cash, to Riddle, and 2) the client never mentioned to anyone else that the video collection existed.

One spring day, Riddle sat with a certain DA Hal Sutton who stared open-mouthed at the video in front of him. He had been recognized as the rising star of North Carolina politics and was taking the advice of others to enter the Lieutenant Governor's race that year. He had informed Riddle that he was moving on to higher office and had made "more discreet arrangements" to satisfy his appetites for unconventional fare. Riddle was not a fool and knew that Sutton was a huge prize in terms of arranging the departure fee. He was a prominent politician, well-respected in the community, and very wealthy. Instead of a monthly fee, Sutton and Riddle agreed on a one-time payoff that totaled seven figures. The pimp was pleased with the huge windfall, and the future Governor was happy that there would not be any future payments that would have to be carefully hidden from his family, the media, and political foes.

Sutton was angry over being had and putting himself in a situation that could have ruined him, but he was still ever the opportunist. He thanked Riddle for offering such discreet arrangements to bring closure to "this chapter in our relationship" and told him he was impressed that he had the balls to shake down such a prominent figure who would have no choice but to come clean on his sins if he were ever caught. The message was clear: *If I go down, I'll take your ass with me.* In a few short words, he had impressed upon the pimp that it would be much to his own benefit to protect Sutton as much as Sutton had protected him over the years from prosecution. His former client was about to be the biggest beau at the banquet when it came to state politics, and he wasn't afraid to play a little dirty if he needed to as well.

By the time he had reached the age of thirty-five, Riddle had accumulated enough wealth that he "retired" from the active workings of his escort service. He continued to make money in payments from other criminals who had benefited from the network he had built, but he no longer had any direct involvement in things that could cause him future troubles. It was around this time that he found another career in the underbelly aspect of politics. He became a faceless independent contractor who could either find or create compromising information on men that others wanted to discredit, blackmail, or even get rid of. He had remarked to friends that despite his life in criminal activities, he had never met a true sociopath until he started working with professional politicians. Now in his fifties, he still did the occasional jobs for men of power, mainly for the handsome fees that they brought but also because he couldn't imagine doing anything else.

He grabbed his briefcase out of the passenger seat and headed into the hotel and up the elevator to a hotel room pre-booked under a fictitious name. This wasn't where he would be staying (he had a taste for luxury accommodations), but it was where he would be getting his instructions.

He knocked lightly on the door and saw the small dot of light behind the eyehole darken briefly before it was opened. He nodded at the man who opened the door, walked into the small suite, and sat on the sofa facing the man seated at the desk chair beside the bed.

"Always good to see you, Governor," Riddle said.

"Good afternoon, Mr. Riddle," Sutton replied before turning to the man at the door. "Tom, could you give us a minute please?" The larger man gave a curt nod and left the room without comment.

"How may I be of service to you, Governor?"

"I'm afraid an old ghost may have come back to haunt me, Mr. Riddle. As I'm sure you have heard, my dear friend Senator Haxton was murdered several days ago."

Riddle nodded. "I heard."

"The police and the FBI really don't have much of an idea who did it. Not much in the way of evidence was left at the scene, and they seem to be spinning their wheels at the moment." Sutton looked at the floor while swirling his scotch in its glass tumbler.

"Governor, I have done many things for you in the past, but please understand I'm not a private investigator. I mean, I could ask around to some associates to see if they have heard about anything, but I don't really have the resources or expertise to do much more than that." He shifted in the sofa, starting to realize that he might have driven all the way there for nothing. "I'm sure there are many private investigators out there that could help you out, and you wouldn't have to worry about...well, being associated with them."

Sutton looked up from his drink. Riddle couldn't help but notice that he looked like shit. He appeared ashen and sleep-deprived. Throughout his political career, Sutton had a poker face that always made his opponents guess what was really on his mind. None of that was apparent at the moment. He looked afraid.

"I don't need someone to find out who did it. I know that already. I need someone to find him...and find him really fucking quickly."

Riddle leaned back in the sofa again as the light came on in his head. "Oh, I see. I'm gonna guess that you don't want me to drop him off at the Sheriff's office when I find him, right?"

"That is correct, Mr. Riddle. The man who killed Haxton broke into his home and stole something before he shot him. I need what he took, and then I need him to disappear forever. Do you understand what I require of you now?"

"I do."

The men spent the next twenty minutes discussing what Sutton knew about the killer and possible places he might be found. What was taken from the Senator's safe wasn't described, but that didn't matter. Riddle would get that information from the man when he found him; he was pretty sure what it was anyway. He decided to high-ball it a little bit and quoted a price of two hundred fifty thousand plus expenses. The Governor agreed without hesitation.

A few minutes later, Riddle pulled out of the hotel parking lot on the way to the Hilton Wilmington Riverside. Whatever was going on, it had Sutton shitting his pants sideways. That could be good and bad for Riddle. Good in the sense that he was obviously willing to pay big money to get this job done, but bad in the sense that he wanted it done yesterday and didn't seem to care that the world's largest and best-funded investigative organization would be doing everything they could to find the guy first.

Riddle had never seen the Governor as rattled as he was in the hotel room. Telling someone to kill another man certainly could cause anxiety in anyone, but Riddle was certain it was more than that. Besides, it wasn't the first time he had made such a request to him.

*****

Chris Tyler had stayed over his shift on purpose. The Contractors Desk had its busiest times in the early morning and just after lunch. There were very few visitors to this particular counter about an hour from sunset, as most contractors were heading home for supper. End-of-shift reports had already been done, and he sat at the counter alone in front of the computer.

As with most plans, the initial steps receive the bulk of the analysis and thought, with the later parts having an ever-increasing range of uncertainty and error. Chris had neither a telephone number nor an address for the customer he was looking up, but he was sure of the identity. He had watched the same man purchase a salt water boat lift kit from around the corner, ducking behind a large stack of plywood over a year ago. Chris had possessed no desire to speak to him and kept out of sight to avoid being recognized.

To his surprise, there were four hits that matched "Reece, Michael." A quick review of the purchase histories of each hit soon revealed the one who had purchased a do-it-yourself boat lift kit. The phone number had a Charlotte area code, but the address was Holden Beach. It seemed the best of very few options. He hit Print Screen and took the paper with him to the employee break room, where he clocked out from the last shift he would ever work at the store. He slid an envelope under the door to Blake Davenport's office on the way out.

CHAPTER 24

John Galsworthy once said that "the beginnings and endings of all human undertakings are untidy." The past few weeks had given Michael no shortage of things to reflect upon and adjust to, many of which were unexpected. The virtual buffet of memories both recent and distant gave him a lot to choose from and analyze as he ran along the sidewalk of Ocean Boulevard—exercise for which he was currently grateful.

He had long recognized the importance of regular exercise for maintaining good health but also for keeping in shape for his duties in the military. Running was one of the purest forms of aerobic activity that countless people across the world had developed a dedication to if not an obsession with in pursuit of fitness and improved times and distances. Michael was not one of them. He had often said that his favorite part of the run was the end. He had long recognized its utility but sought distractions to help him ignore the monotony and fatigue he associated with it. He had become a connoisseur of anything that would take his mind off what he was doing and how much farther he had to go, using anything from music to counting lines in the sidewalk.

His gait was still unorthodox and off-balance due to his prosthetic leg, but he had made incredible strides in a relatively short time. His biggest adjustment had not been balance but enduring the process of toughening the skin pressure points on his stump, gradually taking away the painful blisters and occasional bleeding that had been commonplace in the beginning. Even before his injury, he had never had the seemingly effortless approach to running that he saw in his wife and Tripp, but he soldiered on in the interest of better health.

The music in his ear buds began to decrescendo as he began to think about recent events. Today he had employed his iTouch to enjoy the musical distraction not available when running on an Army installation. The quote by the English novelist certainly rang true to Michael, but he had to admit that the end was shaping up to be much tidier than the beginning. There wasn't an obvious moment that he could point to at which his relationship with Haxton crossed from guidance to exploitation, but rather it seemed to have been a process so subtle that by the time he realized he was in a situation that was terribly wrong he felt hopeless to escape. The way the older man had cultivated a feeling of reliance on his good graces had been a gradual form of enslavement that never required shackles. This was compounded by the burden of shame that far outweighed the physical pain of molestation. There was no doubt that the beginning of that phase of his life had been untidy indeed.

There had been times in his childhood that he had felt cursed even before he really knew what the term meant. His memories of physical abuse as a young child had taken him from one evil to another, and he started to believe that it was his purpose in life to suffer, often at the folly of others. Even the flashes of goodness and unconditional love like Charlie had been too brief and had often come to abrupt and tragic ends. He had credited one thing that had lifted him out of the belief that he was destined for torment: God. After all, God had sent him Reverend Earl Webber and Anna. Michael had no doubt that his young life would have ended with suicide after Charlie's death if it hadn't been for Webber, whose guidance had allowed him to make it long enough to find not only a life outside of Sycamore but eventually Anna as well.

Time and the gradual belief that there could be guiding forces in one's life that didn't require pain in return had led him to what he had seen as an exodus similar to that of Moses. Where the Jews of old had found Mount Sinai and eventually Canaan, Michael had found a family and a circle of friends who cared for him for no other reason than he cared back. This was the reason that he had a framed print of *Israelites Leaving Egypt* by David Roberts hanging in his office. While he certainly didn't think his journey from exploitation had shared the same significance of the prophet, he felt a debt of gratitude to God for eventually releasing him from his own bondage and he saw helping others and being a good man as his own personal shibboleth.

Now his pharaoh was dead, and he could find no compelling reason to revisit the reasons for his own enslavement. He had moved on and had a family to provide for and protect, and he was satisfied that he had been able to build an identity that was strong enough to hold up without requiring the contribution of his earliest and most difficult foundations. In short, life was good now, and it was time to leave the blackness of his past behind.

Two short beeps of a car horn pulled him out of his current mental exercise as one of the locals waved and drove by in the other direction down the main artery of this small coastal island. Many of the year-round residents knew he had a place here, and most knew him personally. He had no doubts that his would probably be his permanent address after retirement one day, given his love for the town grew larger every time he came here. The people here were yet another example to him that there was no shortage of goodness in this world despite his decidedly slanted early life exposures. He waved back to the car as it passed and actually took out his headphones for the final mile in order to enjoy the salt air and sounds of the gulls overhead. He smiled to himself as he thought of another quote, this one by C.S. Lewis: "there are better things ahead than any we leave behind."

He waved to the guardhouse as he passed and finished the final quarter mile with a fast pace. He grabbed a bottled water from the outside garage refrigerator and enjoyed the cool sensation in his throat and stomach as he drained it. He walked up the steps to the back door and saw Tiny lift his head up from his slumber on the couch. He had shown little interest in accompanying Michael on this early morning run.

He gave a mocking shake of the head toward the massive dog. "Lazy," he said in reproach. He was rewarded with the tail wave that was symbolic of a dog's unconditional happiness at seeing his friend again.

He walked back out the sliding glass door with Tiny, who went off to take care of his morning particulars and then met Michael back on the boat dock. He lay down on the wooden surface beside his owner, who sat with his legs (both real and substitute) dangling over the edge. Reece wrapped an arm around his massive chest and watched the early morning sun slowly climb higher from the eastern horizon.

In a little while the rest of the family would be getting up, and he looked forward to a casual day that would mark the beginning of a life unencumbered by the past. For now, he would enjoy the stillness, completely unaware that the occasional local driving by wasn't the only one watching him this morning.

*****

304

The morning sun was low in the sky still, and the ocean breezes made it pleasant as Tyler sat in his truck. He had been parked in the small parking area of the western-most public beach access area on the island. He had planned to simply watch the entrance to the West End development today to look for his old housemate but was pleasantly surprised when he had seen him run right by him heading back to his house. He could recognize his face easily, but the prosthetic leg had given him a heads-up from a hundred yards away.

He had slid low enough in his seat to hide the profile of the back of his head while still being able to look out his window in order to make sure it was really him. The close encounter had left no doubt, and now he had to map out the next step, which would be tricky.

West End was private, and he couldn't just drive up to the house. He would be stopped at the guardhouse, and he would have to explain where he was going and why. Even if he just drove straight through without stopping (there wasn't a gate), the authorities would be called, and that wouldn't do at all. It was an uneasy feeling when not only the execution of the plan was uncertain but so was the plan itself. His gamble, he decided, would depend on the beach access just on the other side of the guardhouse. He pulled out of the parking lot and went to his small house for probably the final time before moving on to a location he hadn't quite worked out yet.

*****

A few hours later, a gentleman strolled into the Lowe's and stood at the customer service desk. He wore frayed jeans and a pocketed t-shirt he had purchased at a thrift store the night before along with a used pair of working boots. He smiled generously as the attendant asked how she could help him today.

"Good morning, ma'am. I purchased an order of sheet rock several weeks ago, and I need to get more. I worked with a Chris Tyler last time, who was very helpful. Is he by any chance here today?" Riddle asked with his best eastern North Carolina drawl.

"Let me check for you dear," the attendant said as she picked up the phone and called an extension for another area of the store.

"No problem. Thanks for checking."

She hung up after a brief conversation and looked up at the customer. "I'm sorry, sir. He is supposed to be here but hasn't arrived for his shift yet. Can I get you someone else to help you with your order?"

"That's OK, ma'am. I've got a few more errands to run and I'll stop by a little bit later if that's OK," Riddle said. He was rewarded with a friendly nod. "Thank you very much."

He wouldn't be back, as he was sure would be the same for Mr. Tyler.

He flipped open the prepaid cell phone he had purchased under a false name the day before. He had one text message in his inbox, which had Tyler's address, taken from one of Sutton's pals in the NC Department of Motor Vehicles. He would be meeting up with a former associate from his Cape Fear days who would be helping with Riddle's current job, and that would be their next stop.

*****

The Combined DNA Index System (CODIS) is not, contrary to popular belief, a storage bank of DNA samples from criminals. CODIS is simply a software product maintained by the FBI that allows comparison of DNA markers between national, state, and local DNA databases. This allows DNA that has been obtained at a crime scene to be compared to known sample characteristics to not only help match DNA to a particular person but also to link several crimes to the same DNA profile, indicating a repeat offender. The actual repository of the DNA information itself is called the National DNA Index System (NDIS) which can have DNA profiles entered from laboratories at levels ranging from national to actual municipalities, and CODIS is simply the software that performs the match searches.

CODIS searches are performed on a weekly basis with reports generated to any submitting agency as well as any agency that possesses a sample that generates a match. Profiles in the database can be forensic samples, arrestee profiles, suspect profiles, as well as profiles of unidentified human remains and missing persons. Set locations on the chromosomes of a sample are compared, and at least ten of the genetic locations must parallel to be considered a positive match.

The analysis and sequencing of the predetermined chromosomal locations from the door handle specimen at Haxton's home had been completed in record time at the FBI Laboratories and was currently being uploaded into the NDIS. This case was special and would be referenced in the CODIS software before the next scheduled weekly run. The relative paucity of physical evidence that had been recovered from this particular crime scene meant that the investigative team for this case had high hopes for this particular search. In case of a match, there was a list of several people to be notified immediately, each of whom had their own personal phone trees for disseminating the information further.

Special Agent Scott received a text from the Field Office updating the progress of the DNA analysis. She had plenty of work to do but felt like the investigation itself was treading water at the moment. She had hit dead end after dead end, which was not uncommon in an investigation, especially a homicide. This fact, however, was not understood by members of the media, Haxton's staff, and other higher-up political figures that were questioning why there wasn't any new information. Sometimes these questions were directed to her, sometimes to her boss, and many times they were pontificated out loud by morons in front of an eager media audience.

There had been a brief moment of excitement when they discovered that the small BP station had a security camera that caught every car that passed by on the way to the bridge off the island. Resolution had been good enough to make out license plate numbers. Unfortunately, searching the plates of every car that left the island for the eight hours following the estimated time of death had turned up nothing. It was if the perpetrator had parachuted in, committed the crime, and flapped his wings to fly away.

Scott's thoughts kept returning to the safe like an itch that she couldn't scratch. The blood trail that had been discovered by the Sheriff as well as the fact that nothing else had been taken from the house seemed to indicate that the motive for this murder had something to do with what was inside. The person behind this crime was either willing to kill someone to get inside that safe or was willing to kill someone because of what they found in it. She had the how and the when of this crime but was getting nowhere on the more important who and why.

*****

Chris had packed up most of his clothes as well as a few other things he couldn't leave behind and placed them in a large duffel bag he used to use when he would go on several-day trips while on shrimp boats. He was a man who didn't have a lot of luxuries, so the bulk of his worldly possessions didn't require a lot of packing space. He had about eight hundred dollars he had put away over time, part of which he placed in his wallet and the rest in his backpack, which also contained the gun that his brother had used to end his life with, his Holy Bible, as well as a bulky padded shipping envelope that he had taped securely closed.

He took a deep breath and looked around to make sure he hadn't forgotten anything. The house was small, but it was his. He had made a good bit of repairs, much to his landlord's delight, and always kept it clean and in order. The life of an addict and criminal was long behind him, and he was proud of the modest but clean life he had built. The turnaround had been a result of recognizing how his life would end if he continued the path he was on and his decision to contact Billy Cash. Under Billy's guidance, he had found sobriety and God, and from that day forward he had become known as a quiet but hardworking man who hadn't even raised his voice to another to anyone's recollection.

Reverend Billy had helped him realize that there was goodness inside him and Darnell and that the choices that they had made to that point in their young adult lives, although poor, were a reflection of a life where they had been victimized by others who had surrendered to the influences that came from parts other than Almighty God. The shame of their past had made them feel unworthy of God's grace, and they had sought a life of sin. Billy had quoted the Book of John early in his intervention with Chris and said, "If we confess our sins, he is faithful and just to forgive us our sins and to cleanse us from all unrighteousness." The realization that he was still God's child and had a right to a good life like any other had given him a completely different outlook and, with that, a determination to change. The grip of drugs on his brother, however, had been too tight, and the transformation that Chris had embraced had not taken a strong enough grip on Darnell.

Chris had stayed in contact with Darnell as best he could, but it was sporadic at best. When the call had come this most recent time, there was desperation but also resolve in Darnell's voice, and Chris couldn't help but think that his death had come at least partly due to his delay in getting to Asheville. The note gave him more than just an explanation for his death, but also a challenge to bring some sort of reckoning for past abuses. That reckoning had come in a form other that what he had planned, but it was sufficient nonetheless.

Haxton's death, though not mourned, had not been part of his original plan. His knowledge of the area coupled with the "borrowing" of a boat had allowed him access to Haxton's remote property. Darnell's gun and a firm crack across the eyebrow had convinced the Senator to give Chris what he sought. He had planned to leave Haxton tied up with a note explaining what he had done to them and allow the authorities to make a decision on his fate from that point forward. Unfortunately, powerful men often cannot resist the temptation to pronounce their importance even in the direst of circumstances, and Haxton, unaware of Darnell's recent passing, informed Chris that he was a respected and powerful man and no one would believe accusations from the likes of Chris or his criminal, drug-addicted brother.

The declaration by Haxton had released a rage that had been kept dormant for some time. A rage created by victimization, betrayal, and the recent loss of his brother that was no longer willing to remain inside. Chris wasn't even fully aware of his decision until he stood over a man who had lost possession of a good portion of his brain matter. He could still remember the smell of spent gun powder as he saw the faint helical strand of smoke rise from the end of his gun. Time seemed to have stood still for a moment while he stared at his victim, unable to process what had occurred. His ears had a faint ringing from firing the gun in such a small room, and then he realized that things that are loud can be heard by other people. He gathered what he had come for and made directly for the back door, unaware that his left shoe had stepped in the edge of the growing pool of blood on the floor and marked his path, which ended as he hit the centipede grass of Haxton's backyard.

He had been relieved that nothing had linked him to the crime to this point, but he was certain that would change. Murdering a man of such fame and power would mean there would be a lot of people wanting to find the person responsible...and find him quickly.

The mapped-out portion of his plan had ended with the pulling of the trigger, and he found himself in the "winging it" portion now. The best option now seemed to involve putting his trust in someone he had grown to hate over the years. He was still working out the details of this next step, but he was quite certain that disappearing would have to follow. He loaded his duffel and backpack into the passenger side of his truck and pulled out of his short driveway, stopping further down the gravel road at the mailbox of his landlord, where he put an envelope for the rest of the month's rent and a note thanking him for renting to an unknown drifter and informing him that anything left behind was his to keep.

He pulled out onto the rural highway heading back toward the coast, unconsciously placing a hand on the backpack to ensure that its contents were still there.

*****

"Fuck, that's him, Pete," Randall McCray said as he pointed to an older-model pickup truck that had just pulled out of the gravel road they were heading toward.

"Put your goddamn hand down, you fucking moron," Riddle barked as he yanked his associate's hand back down. He focused on the person in the truck as he passed in the opposite direction, taking care not to turn his head toward him. In the rearview mirror he noted the first three letters of the truck's license plate, which matched the plate registered in Tyler's name. "I think you're right."

Riddle waited until the gentle curve of Rural Route 17 took the truck out of their line of sight before performing a U-turn to pursue at a distance. He gave another disapproving look to Randall as he sped up until he could see the vehicle of interest ahead of him at a distance of about a quarter mile. He would have preferred to do this alone, but knew it would likely require more than one person...especially if there came a need to dispose of a body.

Randall McCray was currently between prison terms, in the sense that it was a matter of "when" and not "if" he would return. He wasn't overly bright and had a temper that was legendary, but he also had two characteristics that suited Riddle right now: he would do anything for a price and was completely without a conscience. His expertise at illegal horticulture had been how he had initially come to know Riddle. Growing up in rural Lillington,

310

North Carolina, he had spent a lot of his childhood years exploring the woods around the Cape Fear River that meandered through the county. He had worked summers in the tobacco fields and had picked up the foundations of successful crop growing in that area of the country. It was that experience that helped him develop a profitable enterprise of growing marijuana in remote areas near the river on land that didn't belong to him but was rarely if ever visited by anyone. The damp and slightly acidic soil had been perfect for his product, and he used a collection of friends to process the crop and move it along the river to predetermined areas at which buyers could purchase in bulk.

It was an efficient system in the sense that, if a field was discovered, the land wasn't in his name. The fact that more than one completely innocent landowner had been charged with growing a prohibited substance with intent to sell was never something that bothered him in the least. The biggest hassle of his work had been the multiple small-time dealers he had to work with on a regular basis to move his product. He lived under constant worry that some dipshit pusher would get picked up and offer up him as a way to get out of possible jail time. There was one small-time pot dealer who had drifted to the bottom of the river in pieces after threatening to give his name to the police after a dispute over price. He didn't advertise that this had happened, but he didn't discourage the spreading of such information to other dealers as a deterrent to causing any trouble for him.

The answer to this problem had come in the name of Pete Riddle. Initially a modest buyer of McCray's product, his business model had been so successful that he approached Randall about being the exclusive buyer of anything he could grow. He offered 10 percent more than he got from the others and had a well-organized group of people who could pick up large quantities at one time, therefore limiting the number of times Randall would have to actually be present with the contraband for a delivery. Riddle had bought him six pontoon boats engineered with an eighteen-inch-deep storage area under the entire square footage of the false floor, allowing easier and stealthier transport.

This could have been the point in Randall's life where he relaxed and simply enjoyed the substantial profits of his business venture, except for one thing: McCray loved to drink, and when he drank he loved to fight. What he lacked in fighting skills he made up for in willingness to do whatever it took to beat the other guy. Whatever it took could mean anything from using weapons on an unarmed person to using his "posse" to help him make it a decidedly unfair fight. Misdemeanors involving public intoxication, disturbing the peace, and simple assault blossomed into felony assault, oftentimes involving a deadly weapon. Despite his numerous trips to prison, he never gave up any information about his marijuana operations, partly because he wanted to preserve the business and mostly because he was certain that Riddle would have him killed without hesitation.

As Riddle had graduated to the prostitution business, McCray's success had waned, mainly due to his drinking and frequent incarcerations. Again, Pete Riddle had been the answer to his problems; he had kept him on as an enforcer and all-around do-the-dirty-work kind of guy in the organization. The money he was paid was enough to keep him quiet and, for the most part, out of trouble. The amount of drinking he had done was deeply reduced after a conversation laying out the consequences of it affecting his work for Riddle, and now he simply enjoyed a decent living for not a lot of work. There was an understanding, however, that whatever Riddle asked him to do was to be done without question. McCray had agreed to these terms for two reasons: he enjoyed having a steady financial income, and he recognized that, unlike his own hot-headed alcohol-fueled bravado, Riddle was a cold-blooded son of a bitch who would follow through on any threats with lethal efficiency.

He now sat somewhat cowed by the admonishment of his boss while he watched the truck ahead in the distance as it merged onto Highway 17 South. Randall was dying for a cigarette, but his companion didn't smoke and he knew better than to ask if he could in his car. He laid his right arm on the bottom of the open window and let the sun warm his brown skin that had multiple old scars from work in agriculture as well as the occasional bar brawl when he wasn't the only one carrying a knife. He slid the base of his seat further back to accommodate his over-six-foot frame.

"What do we do when he stops?"

"It depends on where he stops and if anyone is around," replied Riddle. He had two instructions: get back what was stolen from Haxton's house and get rid of the man ahead in the truck. If the man was unfortunate enough to stop somewhere with no observing eyes, he hoped to accomplish both. "Don't do anything unless I tell you to. I have to talk to him before we get rid of him. Is that understood?"

"Got it," McCray responded. He had a six-inch folding knife in the back pocket of his baggy jeans, and there was a silencer-fitted 9 mm Ruger in a compact holster attached to the bottom of each of their seats with Velcro. In the trunk of the Crown Victoria—rented with false identification—were two tarps, duct tape, and chains with attachable weights. There was nothing to do but follow at a distance for the moment.

*****

The short walk to the beach was never as simple as you would think if you have two kids. Anna was applying sunscreen despite vocal protests from Elizabeth and Charlie on the deck while Michael loaded the "beach wagon" on the ground level. Two years ago, he had purchased a wagon that was fitted with large knobby tires that could roll through loose sand, which he still claimed as one of the best purchases he had ever made. He loaded four folding beach chairs, buckets, shovels, a small cooler, snack bags, four towels, and two boogie boards into the wagon. Ever the engineer, he had attached a PVC cylinder to the back to hold their folded beach umbrella.

The rest of the Reece crew came down the steps and he stole a peek of Anna as she followed the kids. There was no doubt about it, she looked damn good in a bathing suit, and it was always one of the things that made going to the beach great. Charlie jumped on the back of the oversized wagon holding on to the umbrella pole like a fireman as was his usual custom. They walked the short distance out of the cul-de-sac and were equal distance on each side to the periodic planked walkways that went over the protected dunes and sea oats to the white sands of the beach. They didn't even discuss the choice and turned toward the one to the left that was near the guardhouse...and lollipops. Charlie leapt off the back of the wagon as they approached the guardhouse and Hazel opened the door. He paid the price of a hug and was rewarded with a Dum-Dum lollipop, with Elizabeth doing the same. The parents stopped briefly to catch up with Hazel and then headed toward the sounds of the waves, Charlie's flip-flops as slapping as he ran along the walkway.

It was a beautiful day, and Michael and Anna set up their umbrella and chairs close to the water line as the kids grabbed their boogie boards and ran to the water. The horizon was a straight line of blue-green ocean, broken by the occasional shrimp boat. The Holden Beach pier sat to their left in the distance, and Ocean Isle sat across the point to the right. A gentle breeze came in off the water from the south. Life was good.

*****

Chris had two things to worry about currently. He sat in the same parking lot near the western end of Holden and had watched the Reece family make the trek to the beach after a brief stop at the guardhouse, and it was time to make a decision as to what to do. That was his first problem. The second was he was certain that he was being followed. He had attributed to paranoia his suspicions of a man pointing to him from another car when he had left his home, until the same vehicle appeared in his rearview mirror shortly after and had remained there the entire way here. It had pulled into a house close to the lot he was in, which could have explained it being on the same route, except that the house looked completely vacant and no one had gotten out of the car for over twenty minutes.

He had initially worried they were cops, but he had seen the rental agency sticker on the back of the car, which he thought would be highly unusual for an undercover police car. He had watched the car when it had initially passed him by before parking under the rental home nearby. There was an older white man driving with what appeared to be expensive sunglasses, who hadn't turned his way as they passed, and a younger black man in the passenger side that appeared to be close to his own age. The temptation had been too much, and the passenger had turned to look at Chris in a way meant to look casual but wasn't quite the same. Chris was also sure that it was the guy who had pointed at him many miles ago near his home.

It didn't change what he had to do next, but he wasn't sure how he was going to get away after it was over. He thought it was still possible he was being overly paranoid, but it didn't seem very likely anymore. Either way, he was pretty sure he would be certain in a few minutes.

He exited the truck and slung his backpack on his shoulders. After reaching into the back of the truck to grab a folding lawn chair, he headed across Ocean Blvd. and walked up the public beach access walkway. His sunglasses concealed the fact that, although his head faced forward toward the ocean, his eyes were firmly fixed on the car parked under the rental house to his right. The two men were discussing something, with both of them periodically looking his way. Chris looked back toward the parking lot and was thankful there were several people hanging out there waiting for friends and sharing beers, some throwing Frisbees in the open area next to the parking lot, which meant it was highly unlikely that the two men could break into his truck while he was gone. Besides, the important things were currently hanging from his shoulders in the backpack.

Heading right once he emerged onto the sand, he went about a hundred yards before seeing the Reece family. There was no division on the beach between public and private, and he was free to walk anywhere he wanted. He unfolded his chair and tried to look as casual as he could. He alternated between watching the Reece family and the beach access he had just used. It didn't take long. The younger man from the car came onto the beach from the same access and was trying a little too hard to look relaxed. He had no chair and no towel and wasn't wearing swim trunks. There was no doubt anymore. The mystery man didn't stay very long and soon was leaving the same way he came, lifting his cell phone to his ear as he went.

Whatever was afoot, it didn't change what his next step had to be. The men that were following him didn't seem to be police and that made him worry even more. Michael was sitting under the umbrella with his wife while the children were playing in the water. There were enough people on the beach that Chris didn't have to worry about standing out, and he waited, using his sunglasses again to hide the fact that his eyes were mostly fixed on one family. As he sat there, he began to think of his exit plan. He was under no illusion that the two men that followed him had anything other than violent intentions, and he needed to put some distance between himself and them as soon as possible.

Fortune smiled upon him after about half an hour, when it appeared that the kids had coaxed the Reece mother to come in the water with them. He got up from his folding chair, shouldered his backpack, acted like he was hunting for shells, and began to walk toward Reece.

*****

Despite his often staggering success at adapting to life with a prosthetic leg, handling himself in surf was not something he had really come close to mastering yet. The kids didn't seem to mind, but he felt a slight pang of guilt as Anna went in the water with them and he remained in his beach chair. He returned his attention to his e-reader and didn't take any notice of the man who approached until he sat in the sand beside him.

"Hey, Mike, it's been a long time," Tyler said after sitting down in the sand.

It took a few seconds for the man's identity to register. "Chris? Is that you?" He had a fifty-fifty chance of guessing correctly between Chris and his brother, since they were identical and it had been a long time.

"In the flesh," Chris said as he looked out into the water. "How you been?"

"I've been doing all right...This is quite a surprise Chris."

Anna saw her husband speaking with someone who had sat down beside him. It wasn't anything unusual, since her husband could strike up a conversation with about anyone, and he didn't seem bothered at the moment, so she went back to playing with the kids.

Chris took off his sunglasses and looked at Reece. "Look, Mike, I know we haven't talked in a long time, and I'm sorry to surprise you like this. Darnell's dead and I need some help from you. If you hear what I have to say and don't want to, I understand, but I think you owe it to me to hear me out."

"Darnell's dead? What the hell happened, Chris?" Reece was trying hard to catch up with what had just dropped into his life.

"I'll tell you all about it but not here. I want you to meet me on the pier in thirty minutes and we can talk. I need you to come by yourself." He pulled the padded envelope out of his backpack and put it in Michael's lap. "I need you to keep this. Open it up after we talk, and I'm gonna trust you to do the right thing with it. I think you know what's in here."

316

The last sentence hung in the air for a moment, and the most perplexing thing was that Michael had no idea what was in the envelope. He looked at Chris, then at the envelope, and then back at Chris.

Chris stood up. "Will you meet me there, Mike? I'm in a pretty tight spot and I won't ask you for anything else after this, but you need to hear what I have to say. After that, it's up to you what you do. Will you come?"

"Of course I will." He looked to the water. "I just need to tell Anna that I've got to go and I'll head that way."

"Don't tell her what you're doing, all right?" Chris pointed to the envelope in his lap. "Put that somewhere safe while you're gone, and then it's up to you what you do with it." He turned and walked away.

He still didn't have the slightest clue what was in the envelope, but someone that he hadn't seen in many years had dropped abruptly into his life and seemed to be in some sort of trouble. His brother was dead and he had turned to him. There was a sickening feeling as he stared at his new possession, but he knew there was only one choice he would make. He got up and walked toward the water to let his wife know that he had to run to the pier for a moment. He didn't like withholding anything from her, but wanted to respect Chris's wishes until he had a chance to speak with him.

*****

Riddle lowered the binoculars from his face. He had climbed the steps up to the main level of the house he had parked under after being satisfied there were no signs of a tenant. The covered full-width balcony that was so popular for oceanfront homes here had given him good concealment. He didn't have the slightest idea who the guy was that Tyler had spoken with, but they had gone their separate ways and he knew Tyler had to return to his own vehicle. The only two things Riddle seemed certain about were that they knew each other and Tyler had given him something before they parted.

317

He saw that Randall was already back in the car, and it struck him how much he favored Tyler: same height, same color, both fairly slim. He made a mental note about the fact, as it could come in handy in the future, and got back in the driver's seat, placing the binoculars in the center console.

He turned to McCray. "He'll be coming up the access in a moment, so get ready to move."

As if on cue, Chris came walking up the wood-planked walkway that was elevated about eighteen inches over the sand, rising and falling to follow the contour of the dunes underneath. He had the folding chair in his left hand and the backpack was still draped on his shoulders. He looked forward as he walked, showing no signs that he had suspicions of being watched. He crossed the street at the crosswalk, and instead of going directly to his car he approached a group of twenty-something kids and had a short conversation. It didn't appear that they knew each other, and the fairly muscular young man he spoke to seemed a little quizzical at their conversation at first. But something was exchanged between them, and the man nodded and climbed into his oversized 4x4 Ford pickup truck, along with another friend of similarly impressive size.

"We'll wait for him to pull out and get about a quarter mile away before we go. You have the binoculars ready, but be fucking careful with them and don't make it so obvious. And if you point again I'll break every fucking one of your fingers," he said to Randall without looking at him.

Randall started to retort but thought better of it and placed the binoculars in his lap. They both watched Tyler pull out of the parking lot and head east toward the access bridge to the island. Pete started to mentally count to thirty, but at twenty his entire rearview mirror was filled with large knobby tires with chrome rims and the lower half of a white truck. Two bulky guys with sleeveless shirts got out and opened the hood. Pete had a pretty good idea what was going on and was pondering what was the best—

"Hey man, get the fuck outta the way!" Randall had already got out of the car and was handling challenges head-on, as was his custom.

318

"Take it easy, buddy. We've got a funny noise in the engine and we need to check it out," one of the men with the truck responded. "Just give us a minute."

Randall kept walking toward the two men and was starting to reach into his pocket. "I'm not going to give you a fucking minute. Get the fuck outta the way."

"Listen, dude...you need to relax before I smack the shit outta you."

All three heard a voice come from the Ford rental sedan that had a steady and measured tone. "I'm sorry for my friend, gentlemen. We don't want any trouble, but my friend is right about one thing." As he came around the rear corner of the car, the two men saw that he was holding a gun. "We are in a bit of a hurry and need to be on our way. So I would be very grateful if you two fellas would get back in your truck and let us leave." He glanced down to the Ruger in his hand. "There really isn't any reason for anyone to get hurt today."

The burly driver of the truck realized that the hundred bucks the black stranger had given him a moment ago for this wasn't worth getting shot over. He raised his hands up to his shoulders as he looked at the older man with the gun. "Hey, no problem buddy. We'll move...not a problem..." He and his friend backed up, climbed into their truck, and pulled away.

The exchange had been brief, but it had been enough. Riddle went east along Ocean Blvd. as fast as he could without drawing attention, but it didn't take long for the men to realize that Tyler was gone. They crossed the bridge and pulled into the Main Street Grill, where he had a phone call to make.

CHAPTER 25

If there had been a gathering of more important political figures in Asheville, no one could remember when. There seemed to be as many media satellite trucks as limousines outside the Cathedral of All Souls. The funeral service was attended by a virtual who's who of national and local politics, including leaders from both political parties, not to mention the President of the United States. There was a live broadcast of the service by a single camera team that was available to all networks in the interests of not creating a circus-like atmosphere within the unique architecture of the Episcopal house of worship.

The Bishop presided over the service from a pulpit that was elevated over the polished mahogany casket that had been draped with the North Carolina state flag flanked by a framed picture of the deceased. A moving eulogy had been given by former Governor Hal Sutton, and hymns had been sung under the lead of the massive pipe organ, including "When the Roll is Called Up Yonder," the one currently playing as the casket was taken out of the church toward a hearse that would carry it to a private burial service attended only by the members of the small Haxton family.

When the trumpet of the Lord shall sound,

And time shall be no more.

And the morning breaks eternal bright and fair;

When the saved of the earth shall gather

Over on the other shore

And the roll is called up yonder,

I'll be there...

Sutton's mobile phone in his suit jacket pocket began to vibrate. He had checked on three separate occasions to ensure that it wouldn't be the embarrassing source of noise during the service, but now wasn't a time he could be unreachable. The chorus rose toward the vaulted brick and wooden ceiling, and he knew he would be able to check the voicemail momentarily.

Let us labor for the Master

From the dawn till setting sun,

Let us talk of all His wondrous love and care;

Then when all of life is over,

And our work on earth is done,

And the roll is called up yonder,

I'll be there.

As the echoes of the organ faded and all of the attendees were folding their hymnals, Sutton's phone began vibrating again. Either two different people had called in succession by random chance, or someone really needed to speak with him.

The Bishop held out his arms to the congregation. "All prayers for our departed friend…now go in peace in the service of our Lord."

The various friends and dignitaries began filing out of the church, shaking hands with each other and showing just the right balance between sorrow and strength. Sutton watched the majority of the political attendees immediately flock to the waiting receiving line of media members like moths to a bright light. While the bustle of activity on the beautiful church grounds occupied most people's attention, he went around the corner to a wooden bench probably designed for meditation, prayer, and reflection and pulled the phone out of his pocket.

Both calls had come from the same number. The second call had produced a message, so Sutton hit play and held the phone to his ear.

"Governor, it's Pete. I need you to call me as soon as you can." The staccato click that followed signaled the end of the short and to-the-point message. Sutton pushed the number to return the call.

"This is Pete."

"It's Sutton," the Governor said.

"Sir, we saw Tyler leaving the address you gave us and we followed him to Holden Beach. He parked in a public beach access parking area, and there were a lot of people around." Riddle volunteered this information to give a reason why they hadn't scooped him up right then and there. "He stayed in his truck for a while like he was waiting for someone. Anyway, he went out on the beach and I had Randall follow him while I watched from farther away. He met up with a guy. I mean, a guy was out there with his family, but he talked to him alone. They didn't talk for too long, but the important thing is that he gave him something. We weren't close enough to be sure, but it seemed to be something that would fit the description of what you're looking for." Riddle paused and took a breath. "The thing is, sir, we lost Tyler. When he left the beach and pulled out of the parking area, a truck blocked our exit for long enough that by the time we were able to get back on the road he was gone. I'm sorry about that, sir. We were planning to head back to Tyler's house to see if we could catch him there but wanted to update you and see if that's what you wanted us to do."

Sutton cursed under his breath. "Tell me about this guy he met up with on the beach."

"Not a whole lot I can tell you. He left through another beach access that leads to a private development here. I couldn't drive in to follow him because there's a guardhouse that takes your name and license plate number when you go through. He said something to who I assume was his wife and headed off the beach. He had whatever Tyler had given him, I'm sure of that." He wanted to give *some* positive news since he didn't know shit about the new person in the mix. "He was a white guy. I can't really guess on his age. Oh, and he had a fake leg." Riddle heard silence on the other end.

322

Sutton had the sudden need to go to the bathroom. He looked up at the front courtyard of the church at all the influential people there shaking hands with each other and talking to the media. For decades it was a group he had relished being a part of and enjoyed the status and privilege that came with it. He had went as far as he had ever dreamed in politics, and when he had retired as Governor he had kept the influence and gained the staggering wealth that came with being a mover and shaker in the private world of political horse trading. The last five words he had heard on the phone made him realize that he was in real danger of losing it all...and more. He feared the consequences that seemed to be pursuing him with vigor, threatening his notoriety, influence, and access to the ultimate grown-up table in the world of politics. Most of all, he enjoyed being special. He loved the feeling of being "more" than the next guy...whatever adjective followed the "more."

He followed the long line of limousines waiting for their VIP occupants to the end of the paved road that was visible, and he stopped on another type of vehicle. Parked there was an Asheville Police Department cruiser that was there for security and traffic control. It was a stark contrast to the waxed and buffed black chariots of luxury lined up in front of it. It was stout and utilitarian, and it seemed like it was waiting for him...waiting to take him as far from the life the other vehicles represented as one could possibly go. He felt the tingling of perspiration forming on his forehead.

"Sir... you still there?" Riddle interrupted his train of thought from the earpiece of his phone.

"Yeah, I'm still here. Look, I want you to rent a car for Randall and put him on finding Tyler. I want you to stay with the other guy. I'll text you some information about him. I need you to find out if he has the package, but don't make any other move on him than that. Do you understand? I'm going to send you someone who can help you. The directive for Tyler is unchanged, but tell your hotheaded friend to use some discretion."

"I got it," Riddle replied, receiving only a click in response.

Sutton pulled a handkerchief from his pocket and wiped the sweat away from his face. He walked toward his own waiting limo, and there was no way to bypass the waiting media.

"Governor Sutton. Do you have any updates on the investigation? What will you do next?" There were several reporters vying to land the question that actually got answered first.

He calmly showed them his palms, summoning the cool demeanor of an important man in charge that he was so talented at. "I don't have any update on the investigation, but I have full faith in the excellent work being done by the FBI as well as the other supporting agencies involved. These things take time, you know, and I don't want to impede their work by badgering them for information. I have no doubt that they will bring the person who did this unspeakable crime to justice." He took a somewhat theatrical deep breath before going on. "As for me, I'm going to take some time away for a bit. As you know, it has been quite hectic since this horror occurred, and I need a little time to deal with my own grief. Now that James has been laid to rest, I think I can do that now. I understand you all have a job to do and you do it very well, but I would appreciate being allowed a little of my own privacy for a while." He was able to manage a convincing, albeit completely fake, quiver of his lower lip. "Thank you, everyone."

"Thank you, Governor," the closest reporter replied.

He climbed into his limo, raised the privacy screen, and once again dialed his phone. He had a short conversation and followed it up by dialing David Heinberg, the current General Manager at the luxurious Grove Park Inn and an old friend.

"This is Mr. Heinberg, how can I help you?"

"David, it's Governor Sutton. How are you doing today?"

"Oh, Governor, how good to hear from you. Please accept my deepest condolences for the loss of your friend. He was a valued member of our community and we all mourn his passing. I know he was a good friend of yours, and everyone here will have you and the Senator's family in their prayers," Heinberg replied

"I appreciate your kind words, David. I was hoping to get a little privacy for a few days to work out things by myself after all the craziness. I know it's short notice, and I completely understand if you don't have anything available—"

Heinberg politely interrupted. "Think nothing of it, Governor. Our Presidential Suite is actually available, and we will make it ready for you. Please accept it compliments of us as a token of our sorrow for your loss."

"Are you sure, David? I don't want to make any difficulties for you," was Sutton's completely counterfeit response.

"Governor, it is always our pleasure and honor to have you here. I will have the suite ready for you within the hour and will let the staff know that your privacy is our utmost concern." Retired or not, Sutton was still a highly influential man and sat on the board of many organizations that often needed a venue for junkets and conferences. Heinberg was actually a very kind and sincere person, but he was also a savvy businessman.

"David, your kindness is overwhelming and I won't forget that. I will be there in a couple of hours. I will have one guest arriving named Landon Pierce. It's all right to allow him straight up when he arrives."

Heinberg assured him everything would be in order and waiting for him, and the two men ended the call after some additional flattery and butt kissing. Sutton lowered the privacy window of the limo and instructed the driver to stop by Christianson, Reaves & Polk where, as executor of Haxton's will, he would pick up a certified copy to review, after which he would go to the Grove Park to have a meeting of an entirely different manner.

*****

Michael parked his 4Runner in the Holden Beach Pier parking lot. What used to be a large arcade twenty years ago is now a short-order restaurant with a counter and tables where locals and pier visitors can get breakfast in the morning or burgers and sandwiches later in the day. There is still a small portion of the indoor area devoted to the sale of beach items and fishing gear for one of the dwindling number of fishing piers left on the North Carolina coast. Fishermen angle for flounder, spot, mackerel and whiting along the pier as it stretches out into the surf, but beachgoers who want to take a walk on the hurricane-shortened pier have to fork out the kingly sum of one dollar.

The pier and adjacent rental apartments and campground have been family owned since 1959, and it was one of Michael's favorite places on the island. The grill had delicious country breakfasts that made his cholesterol-minding wife frown and some of the best burgers around. Tasty, unpretentious food aside, what he really loved about the place was the people. From the family owners of the establishment to the fishermen to the visitors, the place brought back memories of simpler times when friendly conversations with strangers and telling stories with absolutely no regard for the time was commonplace. The usual smile on his face when he walked to the front door, however, was absent this time, given the confusion and shock of the past hour.

He went through the usual offer to pay his dollar to walk on the pier, followed by the usual refusal to charge him for it. He shook hands with the owner and pushed open the door to the pier after hearing the buzz announcing that the lock had been deactivated. The ocean breeze intensified as he walked up the gradual ramp that was the first quarter of the length of the pier, bringing him to about twenty five feet above the sand and eventual surf. As he reached the part that was over the water, the benches on each side were about half occupied with the day's fishermen, who cast their weighted double-hooked lines in the water and occasionally brought up spots and sand sharks. The further he went along the old wooden planks that made up the surface, the reels became bigger and better equipped for the larger marine species such as mackerel.

He saw the back of Chris's long-sleeved t-shirt in an unoccupied corner at the end of the pier, where it became a rectangular-shaped deck area. Michael had spent many an hour here just sitting and listening to the surf or watching the kids lean against the railing, tossing pieces of biscuit into the water and delighting at the fish who would surface to snatch up the offered snacks. He sat down next to him on the other half of the fishing bench and simply looked out into the water in silence for a few seconds, not knowing what was the right thing to say. Finally, Chris broke the silence.

"Thanks for coming Mike," he said, not diverting his eyes away from the horizon ahead.

"No problem, Chris. I have to say that I wasn't expecting this at all when I got up this morning. What's going on?"

"Before we go any further, there are a few things that I have to know." He turned to Michael and the look wasn't an overly friendly one. "First, I need to know if I can trust you, and then I need to know why the fuck you just bailed on us when you left for college and never lifted a fucking finger to call us or anything."

The words hung there and stung much more than the salt that was in the brisk ocean breeze coming across the pier. Michael didn't have a shred of doubt that Chris deserved an answer, but he didn't know how to begin. The accusations in his questions were entirely justified based on what the man across from him knew—or, more aptly, what he didn't know. Both of the twins had been like little brothers to him, and walking away and not keeping contact had been the most gut-wrenching part of his exit from Sycamore. He knew they had both felt like he had abandoned them, and he wasn't sure if they were wrong.

He looked back out at the ocean. "I, uh, it's really complicated, Chris. I had to agree to leave and not keep contact, or bad things could have happened." Reece hoped that his response would be sufficient, but as he said it he knew it wouldn't be. "There were things that were happening there that were not good. I was told that if I tried to keep in contact, then the future of the house might be in jeopardy. Also, I had to get away. I don't know if I can tell you about it, but you have to trust me that I had to do it. I didn't want to leave like I did, but I didn't have a choice."

"Bullshit. There's always a choice, and I don't *have* to trust you at all," Chris said. "I'm just going to be straight with you, and then you can tell me how I'm wrong. If I'm not wrong or you won't tell me the real truth then I came to the wrong person, which means that I'm fucked. I'm in some real trouble right now, and I don't really have anyone else to turn to that might understand."

"Why are you in trouble, Chris?"

"I ain't ready to get to that yet. My theory is that you were the golden boy back then at home. You got a lottery ticket to get outta there with a full ride to school, and you took it. You had to leave behind a lot of people who'd been there with you, but the prize was too big to turn down. You took a shit on us—especially me and Darnell—and made a deal with the devil. And all of the success and awards and other bullshit you have now have been you spending the rest of your life trying to buy your soul back. You figure if you surround yourself with enough people who will tell you what a great guy you are and that your fucking farts smell like perfume, you'll forget what you did to get there."

He turned back to face Michael.

"Tell me I'm wrong. Better yet, tell me how I'm wrong, or I'll walk away and you'll never hear from me again. I'll deal with this trouble the best I can, but I deserve to know, Mike. Darnell deserved to know too."

Michael stood up and draped his arms over the railing, with his back to Chris, mainly because he didn't feel worthy to face him at the moment. He needed to know what happened to Darnell, and whatever trouble Chris was in, he deserved his help, which meant he had some explaining to do.

"You're not wrong...you're not wrong, Chris." He thought about Haxton and figured *he's dead now anyway*. The only thing that could keep him from explaining himself to Chris would be shame and cowardice. "But the reasons I did it are not what you think."

He took a deep breath and braced himself. He thought the best thing to do was to get it out quick before he chickened out.

"Haxton was...he wasn't a good man, Chris. He, um, did things to me that to this day very few people know about. He molested me for years and made me keep it a secret. When Charlie died, I think Haxton was really worried I was going to rat him out." He turned around and leaned his back against the railing and looked at Chris. He was trying really hard not to lose it. "You remember that I was getting close to being done with high school then?"

"Yeah," said Chris.

"Haxton promised me that he wouldn't ever touch me again after that, but he also said that if I told anyone what he had done, he would make sure that Sycamore House was shut down and every single one of the kids would be thrown to the wolves, not to mention everyone who worked there would be out of a job. The other condition was that when I left for college it

328

had to be a clean break and I couldn't come back or contact anyone again." He turned back to look out into the horizon. "What was I supposed to do? You two were the closest things I ever had to brothers, and what were the chances that they could find a place for you both...a good place for you both where you wouldn't be split up?"

Chris had to give him that. "Not too good, I guess."

When Michael faced him again, it was clear he was losing the battle not to break down. "Can't you see, Chris? I did it for you guys and everyone else there. I didn't want to do it, but I didn't think I really had a choice. Everyone might be angry at me...hell, they might even hate me, but at least I'd know they were in a good place and not kicked out into the street. I hope you understand, and I hope you can forgive me, Chris. But even if you don't, I don't think I would do it differently if I had the chance to do it again."

In what was one of the biggest reliefs that Michael had felt in a long time, Chris stood up and embraced him. Several inches taller, Chris felt the man's tears absorb into the front of his shirt. He had been wrong, and only now did he realize that Michael had also lived in his own hell during his time at Sycamore.

"I'm sorry, Chris. I'm really sorry. Please forgive me."

Chris held him tighter. "I'm sorry too, bro. I'm sorry too. I had you all wrong, and I owed you more than assume that you'd been selfish. There ain't nothing to forgive. I hope you'll forgive me for not trusting you were a better man, and I hope you'll forgive me for putting you in a tough spot."

Michael was getting control of his emotions, and the last sentence had made him remember the circumstances that had brought them back together. "You're like family to me, Chris. You can trust me to do anything for you I can."

The both leaned forward on the railing again after Chris looked around to make sure that no one was giving them any unwanted attention and they were out of earshot from anyone else there.

"Mike, I'm going to tell you some things straight up. They are probably going to shock you. What you do with what I tell is up to you. I'm going to trust you because I really don't have anyone else."

Michael patted him on the back. "You can trust me, Chris."

There was no preamble or buildup. He wasn't one to waste time building a story into a crescendo before the big reveal. "I killed Haxton, Mike."

Reece looked like he had received an electric shock. "What!?"

"I killed him in his house a few days ago. I broke into his house hoping to get what I gave you earlier today." He shrugged his shoulders. "Some things happened, and I ended up shooting him in the head. I had no intention of killing him, but I'm not sure I feel bad about it…even less now."

"Jesus Christ," was all Reece could muster for the moment.

"I'm pretty sure that the police or the FBI don't have anything that points to me yet, but you've seen the news. They have everyone trying to find out who did it. Sooner or later, they're going to find something that could lead to me." Chris paused and thought about his words. "Look, Mike, I'm not telling you to help me get away with it. I know killing is a sin, and I will face God's judgement when the time comes. But I don't want to sit in jail for the rest of my life or be killed by the government. That being said, somebody knows, and they're following me. I know that they're not cops…No, that's not right. I'm almost certain they're not cops. They have had a couple of chances to snatch me up, but I've been careful not to be anywhere that's not around other people. That makes me think that they want to catch me but they don't want anyone to see them taking me, which means…"

"They're bad people." Michael finished the thought for him.

"That's right. And I'm pretty sure they mean to do bad things to me because of what I took." He made a self-reproaching grunt. "I know that puts you in a tough spot, Mike, and I'm sorry."

"Tell me the rest, Chris."

He nodded. "Right. Well, I was afraid they might get to me before I could unload it, and then this was all for nothing."

"What was all for nothing?" The sense of foreboding was not subtle anymore. "What did you take?"

Chris put his hand on Michael's shoulder. "I'm not going to tell you, Mike. I want you to see for yourself and then you'll understand. What you do after that is up to you, and I trust whatever you decide. I think it's God's will now."

He hugged his old friend one more time. The embrace reminded Reece of one of the few joyful things from his childhood. His brother was back in his life and, more importantly, he had his brother's forgiveness.

"Listen, I gotta get out of here. I parked my truck behind an RV over there in the campground so the guys following me would think I left. Take this." He handed a folded piece of paper to Michael. "This is a cell number where you can reach me anytime. I'll try to update you where I'm at when I can. If you don't hear from me for several days, you can probably assume they got me."

It seemed like Chris was about to leave, and Michael felt a panic. There was so much more he needed to know in order to decide what to do next. "Who, Chris? Who is after you?"

"Just look in the envelope and I think you'll figure it out." He hesitated before he went on. "I have a question for you, Mike. Did you tell Charlie Potts about this?"

Michael looked dumbstruck. "Yes. Yes I did. Why?"

"I don't think he died in a car accident. People will go to great lengths to keep their secrets safe, brother. I think I really need to get moving, Mike."

The world was starting to spin. Mike grabbed Chris's arm. "You didn't tell me what happened to Darnell."

331

This time it was Chris pausing before he gathered the words. "You weren't the only one, Mike." He hugged his friend who just had too much to process at the moment. "I love you, bro. I'm sorry I didn't have more faith in you. I'll call you when I can."

Michael saw him walking away back down the pier. He was enraged that he wasn't sure what to do next.

"No! I've got an idea."

*****

The Presidential Suite at the Grove Park Inn is often referred to as the Bob Timberlake Suite since the spacious living area is adorned with his paintings and furniture of his design. Sutton had come to the realization that it was going to take more than two drug-dealing dipshits to accomplish what he needed. After learning that Riddle and his partner had lost Tyler and that Michael Reece could be involved as well, he knew it was time to call a professional.

The amenities of the luxurious suite didn't disappoint and, without having to ask, the bar had been stocked with several brands of high-end scotch and other spirits. He finished pouring two iced tumblers of Glenlivet and turned to hand one of them to his guest. He sat down on the sofa, facing Landon Pierce across the coffee table. Sutton raised his glass to his friend.

"To good health."

"Cheers," replied Pierce as he took a small, polite sip.

Landon Pierce was essentially a private investigator. His specialties were locating people who often didn't want to be located and finding out things about people they didn't want discovered. To those that didn't know him (including the IRS), he was the owner of a small security consulting business called Stillwater Security Consultants. One would never find a single advertisement for the company, a business card, or any marketing activity whatsoever. Pierce was Stillwater, and his clientele was made up exclusively of people who had been referred by other clients. They all had common characteristics: they were powerful, they were discreet, and they had a lot of money to spend for his services.

The majority of his personal wealth, estimated in excess of ninety million dollars, was earned investigating embarrassing histories of prominent political figures at the behest of well-funded opposition campaigns. That being said, they were far from the only ones who had used and paid for his services. His clients spanned from corporate CEOs to mafia bosses to South American drug lords. Although he was not in the killing business, he had no illusions about what the fates of many of the people he located were. He would often compare himself to a well-trained Springer Spaniel who would find the bird hiding in the brush for the hunter and simply point them out. What happened to the bird after that was not his concern, and he made it clear that it would not be told to him either. Pierce insisted on being detached and ignorant of the business ends of his searches.

He was not a man of many words and detested small talk. "What can I do for you today, Mr. Sutton?"

"I have someone I need located." Sutton slid a manila folder across the hand-carved wooden coffee table. "The information is fairly meager but should be sufficient. Inside is the name and secure phone number of who to contact when you locate him. There may be one or even two other people to locate after him, one of which is the man's brother. I won't know if I need to locate them until I have gained information from the first contact. This will be the last contact we will have with each other on this matter, and all future conversations will be with Mr. Riddle, whose phone number you have in the folder. His last known sighting was in the Wilmington area."

Pierce stood without even looking at the contents of the folder. "Very well. My fee structure will be similar to what it has been before. Good day, Mr. Sutton." He shook hands and left without another word.

Sutton had used Pierce's services on several occasions and had never been disappointed with the results. The fee would be on the far side of generous but worth it. Besides, money wasn't even on the list of concerns for him in this matter. Long ago, he and Haxton had set up an untraceable account based on the Isle of Man for discretionary use in matters such as this. The balance was well in the eight-figure range and had always been accessible by both of them independently. It had been used rarely in its lifetime, but Sutton would have no hesitation to drain the entire account if it was required to settle this matter.

This was a race and nothing more. He knew he had a huge advantage on the FBI, since he was already almost positive who had done this and why. That being said, he had to find him and deal with him before his opponents could even identify him if at all possible. The sooner he closed this matter, the less likely his link would be exposed by anyone who didn't already know. It was worth paying big money for...It was worth killing for.

He finished his scotch, grabbed the tumbler across the table, and leaned back, contemplating the ramifications of not succeeding, which made him quickly drain the second drink.

*****

Anna waited behind the house as the sky was softening from a lowering sun. She had received one of the strangest calls from her husband that she could remember, asking her to have the kids occupied upstairs and to meet him behind the house. As he had requested, she had opened the door to the right-side garage under their cottage, which housed a 1990 Toyota Land Cruiser that they kept at the beach to tool around the island. It was regularly serviced and kept in the garage when not in use to protect it against the harsh effects that salt air can bring. She saw Michael's truck pull into the driveway and pull around to the back of the house where nothing but a mile of marsh and Intracoastal Waterway had a direct line of sight.

Her second surprise was seeing a man sit up from the rear floorboard when the truck came to a stop. He appeared to be a few years younger than Michael and seemed to be more than a little nervous, and she realized it was the same man that she had seen with her husband on the beach a few hours ago. Michael got out after grabbing the receipt for an 8' x 10' storage unit in nearby Supply that he had rented for six months, paid in full up front, which now concealed one Chevy S-10 pickup owned by Chris Tyler. The only other stop they had made before coming to West End was a Bank of America ATM where he withdrew $1000 (the maximum allowed withdrawal per day from a teller machine) from both his checking and savings accounts and gave it to his companion over his protests. He kissed his wife and turned to the taller gentleman exiting the back door of the truck.

"Anna, this is Chris Tyler. He lived with me at Sycamore House," Michael said to his wife.

Anna remembered that some of the few stories that he would tell about his time there involved the Tyler twins, about whom he obviously cared a great deal and missed very much. As was her way with people that she knew were special to her husband, she stepped right through his offered hand and hugged him.

"It's good to meet you, Chris."

She was one of the most disarming people ever to walk the earth, and Chris's initial surprise was quickly replaced by comfort. Michael smiled to himself, as he had seen it countless times before.

"It's good to meet you, Mrs. Reece," Chris replied.

"It's Anna. From what Michael has said about you, you're more like family than a new acquaintance."

"Do you have the keys, honey?" Michael was rewarded with a nod from his wife. He took them and handed them to Chris. "He's going to take the Cruiser for a while. There's a lot to explain, and I will, but he's got to get going."

He turned back to his old friend. "It's gassed up and up to date on everything from service to registration. Keep me posted on what's going on when you can, and I'll touch base with you, too, OK?"

Chris nodded and Anna could tell that there was a lot of emotion under the surface of both men in front of her that wasn't going to be contained much longer. He and Michael shared a long embrace and Anna could see tears in her husband's eyes.

"I'm sorry bro, and I love you," Chris whispered.

"Me too brother, and you've got nothing to be sorry about."

Chris hugged Anna again. "It was nice to meet you, Anna. I hope we can see each other again and catch up a little better than this."

Anna nodded and kissed him on the cheek. "I'm going to hold you to that, Chris. I want you to be careful out there." She had no idea why it had occurred to her to say the last sentence, but something told her she should.

Chris started walking to the garage and paused. "Mike, I don't know. Do you know what this means for you if I take this? I don't want to put you—"

"I don't want to hear it. I'm here for you no matter what," Michael interrupted.

They both watched Chris pull out of the driveway, and Michael called the guardhouse to let Hazel know someone was leaving with his truck to get serviced. He knew he would be waived through without a question.

"I promise I'll tell you what is going on, but I have to look at something Chris gave me first."

"OK, baby," Anna responded. She was worried but didn't really know why yet. The explanation would come in due time, and she would wait until it did.

CHAPTER 26

Like many homes built on the coast, Michael's had an "owner's closet." Since many second homes are used as rental properties as well, one of the closets is equipped to be locked and inaccessible to anyone who may be a temporary occupant. This allows owners to keep items such as sheets, toiletries, and other things they can use without the worry of others using or taking them. He used his key to open the door and reached behind several rolls of paper towels where he extracted the large padded envelope. After taking it to the master bedroom that was located alone on the third level, he opened it.

Inside were two discs, neither of which had a label of any type. There was no indication if the contents were audio, video, or some other type of data. Further inspection revealed nothing else inside. With equal parts uncertainty and dread, he simply stared at them for a couple of minutes. He remembered Chris's words on the pier: "Just look in the envelope and you'll figure it out…"

There they sat in his lap, beckoning him to investigate further. He knew what he had to do, but he was quite sure that whatever was on the discs in front of him, they were going to bring back unpleasant memories or possibly get him further involved in aiding a fugitive. The self-rebuke came almost instantly as he reflected on how his two concerns were about how things would affect him and not Chris.

Anna saw him come down the stairs and kiss the foreheads of the kids who were enraptured with the latest episode of *Phineas and Ferb*. He grabbed his laptop off the counter dividing the living room from the kitchen area and showed her the two discs in his hands.

"I'm going down to the dock for a few minutes," he whispered to his wife after he kissed her. "We'll talk after we get them to bed."

"OK, baby," she said as he went through the sliding glass door and down the steps.

Aside from the occasional distant boat motor, the collisions of the marsh reeds in the gentle breeze were the only noises he could hear. Twilight was about to surrender to night, and the exposed oyster beds under the support poles of the walkway showed that it was low tide. As the laptop completed its startup, Michael said a silent prayer asking God to help him handle whatever these discs would reveal with the honor that he should.

He sat on a bench chair on the dock and made sure there was plenty of battery power on the Hewlett-Packard computer that rested in his lap. After the boot-up was complete, he inserted the first disc into the loading tray. The computer then offered suggested programs to use to view the contents of the disc, and, based on what it suggested, Michael could tell this was a video file, which for whatever reason was the option he had dreaded the most. He selected Windows Media Player, and a viewing window popped up which he maximized to fill the screen.

When the image came to life, he recognized the room as Haxton's master bedroom which he, unfortunately, had seen several times. The quality was poor, which suggested that this had been converted from a VHS cassette. A few seconds later, a young black child walked in front of the camera. Michael recognized him as Darnell Tyler instead of his brother because of the eyebrow scar; he was around the age of eleven. He seemed to be listening to someone, but there was no sound. He checked to make sure his own computer wasn't muted, but it seemed that the video either never had sound or it hadn't been copied over on this newer medium. What happened next brought a sickening feeling of familiarity.

Darnell began to undress slowly in front of the camera. Michael barely had enough time to pause the video before leaning over the side of the dock and ejecting the contents of his stomach. Several dry heaves followed after his stomach had nothing left to give, and he collapsed back in his seat. He had been told several times to slowly undress while Haxton watched, which only brought more humiliation, before his director would approach him and expect Michael to do his perverse biddings. The only difference was that there had never to his knowledge been a camera present. He sat looking at the paused image on the screen and felt the burning on the roof of his mouth from the stomach acid that had so recently assaulted it.

338

He ejected the disc without viewing anymore and inserted the second one. It began virtually the same, except this time it was Chris. It wasn't just the shared features and appearance of identical twins that made them look alike. It was also the look that Michael knew too well. It was a mixture of shame and fear. The shame from simply being there and existing under the mercy of someone who came under a banner of trust and mentorship only to reveal themselves as pure evil. The fear came from what would follow...the humiliation and the physical pain of parts of his body being used for another's perversity. When it was over, he would always be sent away to dress. That was when the tears would come, while he cleaned himself of the blood and whatever else had polluted him before dressing.

He paused it at a similar point and was unsure whether to go any further. He knew what would happen next, and he really wasn't interested in revisiting any more than he already had that night. Something, however, was telling him not to eject the disc. In front of him was evidence of two friends...more like younger brothers...that had suffered a fate he knew well. Although he had made a decision long ago that he believed was done to protect them, he now realized all he had accomplished was to abandon them. Chris had turned to him and entrusted him with these, and, whatever followed on the disc, he owed it to them to see it all.

He swallowed the bitter accumulated saliva that had pooled in his mouth and hit Play. He was pretty sure what would follow. Haxton would come out from behind the camera in order to be serviced by the terrified child he looked at currently. Sometimes, he remembered, Haxton would already be naked, and sometimes he would make Michael undress him, further adding to the humiliation.

The screen briefly lost focus as the back image of a man came in front at a much closer distance and walked to the shaking child, who now stood at the foot of the bed completely naked. The man was still dressed, but something was different. Something was wrong. Foreboding changed to shock as the camera gained better focus and the man turned enough to make his face visible. It wasn't Haxton...it was Sutton.

More of their conversation on the pier made sense, but things also were more complicated. If it had been Haxton, he would be watching the debauchery of a man who was no longer alive and whose behavior was certainly no surprise to Michael. Now there was a very powerful and influential man that probably knew that something had been stolen that could destroy him...and that something was now in Reece's possession. Two more things that Chris had said now seemed to reemerge in his mind: "somebody knows, and they're following me" and "people will go to great lengths to keep their secrets safe." The latter made him think of Charlie Potts. Somehow the fact that more than one person was involved in such horrible acts made it more plausible that maybe Charlie's death wasn't as straightforward as once thought. He put the building rage aside for the moment and thought about the three people in the house behind him. *People will go to great lengths to keep their secrets safe...*

As he walked into the house and headed to the small office room, he thanked God that Anna was so good about keeping and organizing the family photographs that they had taken over the years. He opened the desk drawer and found what he was looking for—a ten-pack of blank writable discs. He made a copy of each disc that Chris gave him and locked the originals back in the owner's closet. The newly made copies were put in his laptop case, and he decided he could use a drink. After pouring a bourbon on ice, he sat down on the floor in front of Anna and watched a rented Disney movie with the family that he had difficulty giving even the smallest amount of attention to. His wife watched him gaze right through the television screen, absently patting the side of their massive family dog, and wondered what had happened in the past several hours.

*****

Craig Chambers was in the middle of his shift at North Charlotte Memorial and was currently buffing the floors in the control desk area of the surgery department. He had been with the Environmental Services department for only three months and enjoyed the two p.m. to eleven p.m. shift because it allowed him to take his two kids to school. This had been a gift of necessity rather than generosity from his ex-wife, since her job started early in the morning. The past two years of his life had been marked by one bad deal after another, and he had been lucky to catch this job when he did.

The Charlotte area had not been spared by the housing market collapse, and Craig had lost his job in home construction just two months before his wife had decided to leave him. She had cited "a growing distance between them," which he translated it to "You're broke and I'm screwing someone else." The past year had been a series of odd jobs where he could find them, with no benefits and very little pay, all the while falling further and further behind on child support payments until she had threatened to petition to limit his already meager visitation with his kids. An old co-worker had given him the heads-up about the opening for a housekeeping staff member at the hospital, which including benefits after ninety days. His ability to take the kids to school along with the promise of putting them on his health insurance in three months had bought him a reprieve, but he was having trouble even making the minimum payments on his debt and was a month behind on the rent. If better days were coming, they weren't coming fast enough.

It didn't take a lot of convincing when a man approached him in the parking lot at the end of the last shift and offered him a thousand bucks for what would amount to ten seconds of work. The man said he was a reporter who wanted to ask someone for an interview but wasn't allowed to do it on hospital property. He promised to never reveal Craig's involvement and gave him a hundred dollars in advance to think about it, with the balance to follow if he actually went through with it.

He scanned the empty operating room area as he edged the circular floor buffer closer to the control desk. The last surgical case had finished over three hours ago, and there was no one around and wouldn't be for a while as long as no urgent surgical cases came through the Emergency Department, and even then staff would be called in from home. One last scan around the area convinced him that it was all clear.

He kept the buffer running as he walked around the side of the counter to the desk area that was usually occupied by the surgical unit coordinator. It took him less than a minute to find the Rolodex on the left-hand side of the desk near the phone. He thumbed to the "R" tab and quickly wrote down the cell phone number under "Reece, Michael Dr." and resumed his floor work. Three hours later he was walking away from the reporter, who met him again in the parking lot with enough cash to cover this month's rent as well as over half of his delinquent child support payments. Less than a minute later, the same number was texted to the cell phones of Hal Sutton and Landon Pierce.

*****

Anna held the glass of wine that Michael had insisted he pour for her about twenty minutes ago. After hearing what her husband had to say, she decided it was time to take a rather large sip. He had told her everything, starting with his unexpected visit on the beach by his old friend and ending with the DVDs that he had watched (and insisted that she didn't) and copied. The kids had been put to bed over an hour ago, and he had poured the wine after making sure that both were asleep. As she tried to digest the information, it felt like she was trying to run a hundred-meter dash in knee-high mud.

"So he killed Senator Haxton?" she asked after several minutes, wanting to make sure she really heard that part right.

"That's what he said, and I have no reason not to believe him," Michael replied.

She hesitated. "Michael, you know—"

"I know what you're going to say. I'm not saying what he did was right, but even I can't really put myself in his shoes. I know this affects all of us, but I have to help him. I think there are people out there who are willing to do bad things to him to keep him silent. What he took could destroy someone who is very powerful, and I imagine he is willing to do a lot to keep that from happening."

"Why not tell Chris to turn himself in? If bad people are after him, he might be safer in custody, honey."

Michael shook his head. "Because he made it out. He navigated the hell he was in and made it out. And, he made it out without a golden ticket. That hell tried to return and he fought back. With what he's been through, that shouldn't come at the cost of his freedom or maybe even his life."

Anna put her hand on his. "Do you believe him about Charlie?"

"I don't know. Even he said that he wasn't sure. He just said that Sutton had made some veiled reference to him one time when convincing the twins to keep quiet. Chris was sure that Darnell killed himself, but he said that he had big suspicions about Charlie." Michael took a deep breath and shook his head as if to dislodge that fear for a moment. "I promise you this: I will find out one or the other, and someone will be held responsible for that if it's true. But right now I have to focus on Chris."

"Honey, I need you to keep in mind that the thing that Chris took that could get the attention of a lot of bad people is now in this house. What happens if they find out that we have it?" Anna saw that her question had jolted her husband.

Michael felt a burning in his stomach as well as a heat flush in his face, similar to the sensation one feels when the car in front of them suddenly hits their brakes unexpectedly. It was the word "we" in her question that made him realize the scope of what was going on. He looked toward the two bedrooms where his children were sleeping and then back his wife's face. Without even thinking, he looked to make sure the lock on the back door was engaged.

"I think we should go home tomorrow. It would be better if we were around more people that we know...I don't know if that makes sense, but I think we should."

Anna couldn't put her finger on it either but she felt the same way. "Why don't we get our things together so the only thing left to pack in the morning will be the kids' stuff?"

Michael agreed and it took only a few minutes to get everything ready to go since a lot of things one would usually pack stayed at the house to be available whenever they came down. They sat together with his arms around her on the coach until she fell asleep.

After lying in the bed staring at the ceiling for two hours, Michael realized the futility of remaining there. He plodded down the steps and rechecked the door locks for the umpteenth time, then peeked in Elizabeth's room to make sure all was well. He was thankful that her face showed the peace that comfortable sleep brings. Next he peeked into the other part of the "Jack and Jill" bedroom configuration where, dwarfed by the two-hundred-pound Great Dane in the bed as well, Little Charlie lay sideways with his arms stretched over his head and his legs draped over Tiny's chest. Michael was certain that he had made no noise, but he watched the dog raise his head from the bed and look his way. Once Tiny was satisfied that everything was as it should be, he rested his big jowls back on the bed and went back to sleep. It was almost comical how protective that dog was with his son, but he certainly wasn't complaining right now.

343

After leaving just a small crack in the door, Michael went downstairs to his truck that Eric had dropped off for him before meeting Gabriel on Hilton Head Island what seemed like a million years ago. He cringed slightly when he hit the unlock button on his key fob, producing the staccato chirp that announced that the alarm had been deactivated. Opening the passenger door, he reached into the glove compartment and brought out his Heckler and Koch P30 pistol. He pulled out the ten-round magazine and, for the first time since he could remember when not at the shooting range, slapped it into the handle slot, making sure that the safety was on. Michael spent the rest of the night getting sporadic episodes of sleep on the couch with the pistol tucked under the middle seat cushion.

The sun was beginning to crawl over the horizon when Michael heard the clicking of large paws across the kitchen hardwood flooring. The dog's head was well above his, which rested on the couch. The time interval before his first face lick was quite short.

"Hey, buddy. How are you this morning?" Reece said as he rubbed the top of his head. "Want to go outside?" Tiny responded by walking toward the sliding glass door.

He paused halfway to the door, remembering there was a loaded handgun under the seat cushion of the couch. He retrieved it and clipped the Blackhawk molded belt holster to his cargo shorts, allowing his loose golf shirt to conceal it. As Tiny trotted off to take care of his morning constitutional, Reece found himself looking around the yard to ensure there were no signs of anything disturbed or out of place. He felt the pistol press against his flank and chuckled at his paranoia, but then remembered the old saying: just because you're paranoid doesn't mean they aren't out to get you. He jumped when he heard Tiny barking, until he realized he was merely pestering a crane that had perched on the dock to take in the morning sun.

Seeing the emptiness of the left-side garage where the Land Cruiser used to be gave him the temptation to call Chris and get an update, but he decided against it. His friend would have enough on his mind and didn't need to be bothered just twelve hours after he had last seen him. He decided he would call him when they arrived in Charlotte later today. Upon returning to the house, Michael found Charlie awake and sitting on the living room floor in his University of North Carolina pajamas manipulating the remote to find the Disney Channel. Tiny sprawled on the floor behind him, and Charlie took his usual position of using the dog's chest as his backrest. Michael kissed him on the top of the head and started making some breakfast for everyone.

"Hi, Daddy," Elizabeth said as she shuffled out of her bedroom and into her father's arms.

"Morning, sweetie. Waffles OK for breakfast?"

"OK," she replied as she went to the living room to enjoy the morning's edition of *Sponge Bob Square Pants*. Anna soon followed and gave her husband a grateful kiss on seeing the coffee was already brewing. After breakfast, Anna took the kids for one last walk on the beach while Michael packed up the kids' clothes and squared away the house. Both he and his wife agreed that it was a good idea to head back home, but he wondered if they were being overly suspicious. But even if no one was aware of his part in the evolving drama, he was sure that Chris had tough times ahead, and Michael felt a little too isolated here on the coast to be able to come to his aid if necessary.

Four hours later, the kids were back from the beach and had washed the sand away from their legs in the outdoor shower. Anna loaded the kids in her car while Michael put the rear seat down in his to allow Tiny to lounge during the four-hour ride to Charlotte. They made their traditional beach departure stop at Provisions Company for shrimp burgers and onion rings and made their way to Highway 74 West toward home.

The Reece caravan made its way northwest passing by the towns of Whiteville, Lumberton, and Polkton on the way to their Mountain Island Lake neighborhood. But, unbeknownst to Michael and Anna, the convoy was made up of three vehicles, the third being a rented Ford Explorer driven by Pete Riddle.

*****

Landon Pierce was by no means a dim-witted man, and he knew that a big reason for his success was his substantial intelligence. That being said, he was also aware that his early willingness to find and pay people in organizations with access to information was instrumental in creating the network of informants he now enjoyed. His love for efficiency led him to give up searching for someone each time he needed something and instead to find people who were willing to enjoy a small regular retainer fee with the promise of generous payments when they performed tasks on an as-needed basis. There were certainly times when he needed something and didn't have an "insider" within an organization, like in the case of Craig Chambers, but more often than not he was able to rely on his network of under-the-table consultants who worked in organizations that ranged from the IRS to internet service providers—or in this case Southcomm Wireless, who was the provider of mobile phone services for the Reece family.

After obtaining the cell number from the hospital employee, he called his "consultant" at Southcomm and within an hour had the billing address, Anna's mobile number, as well as the promise of a daily report of all calls and texts sent and received from both. If the time came to track him down, Pierce didn't think Reece would be a hard person to locate, but he was betting, based on the information he had been given about him meeting Tyler on the beach, that the two men would contact each other. Once that occurred, he would have the mobile number of Chris Tyler, and he had another consultant in mind as to what to do with that information.

Pierce sent an electronic transfer of money to a predetermined account number that belonged to his consultant at Southcomm, with the understanding that more would come if the daily reports produced more fruitful information. He had already tasked someone to keep an eye on the known address for Tyler; no activity whatsoever had occurred, leading Pierce to believe that Tyler wouldn't be returning to that location anytime soon. More as a proactive strategy than anything, he planned to devote a little time to finding out about the other Tyler brother just in case he became a more prominent focus in the future.

He had been provided with Darnell's birth date, social security number, and last known address. There was no landline telephone account in Darnell's name, but he was able to find one that matched the address. He placed a call to the number he had found, which quickly revealed that Darnell didn't live there and hadn't for several years. Next, he started up a program called Chunnel, which had been custom-designed for him and very expensive but worth every penny. It burrowed like a tapeworm into countless repositories of government documents and used names and other identifiers as keywords to find matches in reports such as arrest reports, tax returns, property purchases, and many others.

He entered Darnell's social security number, name, and birth date and set the program to work. As the program searched, it would look for patterns of locations or addresses which would allow it to narrow down its search as it went. There were times that these patterns would veer the search toward the wrong person with similar associated keywords, but this was rare and easily rectified. The only drawback was, due to the massive size of the databases the program would mine, searches could be a several-hour affair. This was compensated for by the fact that it was linked to his smart phone and would send him messages about possible patterns that he could either instruct Chunnel to pursue and ignore, thereby minimizing the chance of a "wrong turn" and also allowing Pierce to leave his computer while it did its job.

Satisfied the program was off and running on its current task, Pierce grabbed his gym bag and left for an afternoon workout. He would receive a text alert on his phone when the search was complete and would even have the option of viewing the results that way as well.

*****

The past several days had left Chip Johnson feeling like he was a highly talented sea captain who had lost his boat. He had kept busy with press releases related to Haxton's funeral and well as consulting with MSNBC and Fox News, who were both doing one-hour specials on the Senator's life and career. But the funeral was now over, and there wasn't much left to do on the documentaries either. He had grieved in public like everyone else, but in essence Haxton had been a vehicle of opportunity for Chip.

He had left other employers in the past few years, mainly due to their coattails being rather diminutive compared to those of a likely future President. His departure had not really been ugly, but to return might risk being told he was not welcome anymore, or worse, that he was having to slum with them again. Prospects for advancement within his former employer's structure would be limited, secondary to the well-supported suspicion that he would jump ship for a better deal in a New York minute.

All this had left him anxious and uncertain, and his current phone conversation was not helping things at all.

"Look, I think we need to be more active in the process, Governor," Chip said to Sutton. "The current Governor will look to us for guidance as to who to appoint, and I think it will be more than just professional courtesy. I think we have a real opportunity to help decide who gets the nod."

"You might be right, Chip, but it's not a big deal if we wait for a few days. If he announces it too soon after the funeral it will look like he had been working on it since before Haxton's body was even cold." Sutton had enough on his plate right now, and the current Governor's attention in this matter was going to have to wait.

Chip shook his head while he sat in his room at the Sheraton-Downtown Asheville. He had remained in town after the funeral mainly to get together with the man on the other end of the line and start making a plan for who would fill his former boss's office until the next election, and now he was getting blown off.

"I disagree, Governor. I know he won't announce anything yet, but you can be sure there are others who will be bending his ear about this, and I think we are being naïve to think he isn't making a short list. I think we are risking missing the boat on being able to put in our two cents' worth." Johnson felt like he was in the Twilight Zone. There weren't many better seasoned politicians than Hal Sutton, and he had to know that what he was telling him was true.

"You just need to relax for a few days, Chip. I'm a little busy right now, and it won't kill you to wait a few days before you start looking for your next date to the dance."

What the fuck was that? Chip silently said to himself. It was a cheap shot. Sutton had been around long enough to know that this was how the game was played. Chip knew that Haxton and the Governor had been friends for a long time, but it wasn't like Sutton wasn't also expecting to get a big lift of stature from a Haxton presidency. He was acting strange, and Chip felt the person who had the most to lose by his dicking around was himself. Sutton had reached his career goals and had planted his flag on his personal mountaintop, but Chip was far from his.

"Well, when can we get together?"

"I don't know right now! Jesus Christ, Chip, I have other things I'm taking care of too, you know. Do you already have someone in mind? Is that why you're so amped up about this right now?"

Chip took a breath. This had the potential to get heated, and he was running out of sugar daddies. "I have an idea, but I need to do a little digging first. Since you're busy, let me do a little discreet research and maybe we can talk in a few days." It was time for a little smoothing over. "Look, Governor, I know this has been a rough time for you with you losing your best friend and all, and I'm sorry if I was pushy. You get done what you need to, and I'll touch base with you in a few days."

"It's OK, Chip. I'm sorry too. That sounds good to me. Just make sure the digging you're doing is discreet."

Sutton might need him for PR stuff later, and maybe whatever he wanted to do would get him out of his ass for a few days. He didn't want to take any chance that Johnson would catch wind of what was causing him to have heartburn twenty-four hours a day right now. Besides, he was afraid that current Governor Jim Wade was likely to appoint his dipshit nephew, the current State Senator from Pitt County. The kid was a moron but knew how to shovel out the pork when it was budget time, was sharp in an interview, and had impeccable hair.

"Give me a call in a couple of days, and I promise I will get this higher on the priority list."

"Not a problem, Governor. Talk to you then."

Chip ended the call. What he was considering would be considered almost sacrilege to seasoned politicians, but it just might work. He packed up his Pullman and suit bag, checked out

349

of the hotel, and headed east on Interstate 40. If he could pull this off, it would be one of the best sales jobs of his career, and he had done a lot of them.

Meanwhile, Sutton didn't even have time to devote any thought to his conversation with Johnson before his phone rang again. This time it was Riddle. After making sure Riddle was in an area where no eavesdropping could occur, he asked for an update.

Riddle was sitting in the parking lot of a fast-food restaurant on Highway 74 after watching the Reece family pull into a produce stand east of Wadesboro. The kids were taking a needed potty break while Michael was treating himself to some of their famous peach cobbler and ice cream.

"OK," Riddle began. "I couldn't get a line of sight to his house yesterday, but I came back to our location just outside his neighborhood before sunrise. I saw the wife and kids go to the beach...he wasn't with them. After they went back to the house, the whole family left the neighborhood, and I could see suitcases in the car. They stopped for lunch and headed west on what would be the most logical way to get home, if that's what they're doing. I called the wife's work number, and they told me that she would be at the beach for the rest of the week. They're still about an hour away from Charlotte, and they're currently taking a little pit stop for what looks like a bathroom break."

"Why the hell did you call Mrs. Reece's office?" Sutton demanded.

"Relax, Governor. I told them I was a client and was trying to reach her. It was a hunch and it paid off."

Sutton was confused. "What do you mean?"

"Look at it this way: I follow Tyler to the island, where I see him meet up with Reece. I clearly see Tyler give him something, and they part ways. Immediately after that, Tyler disappears. His wife's office said they were out of town for the rest of the week, but the day after Tyler and Reece meet, the whole family is bugging out and heading home." He still didn't think Sutton was getting it, but then again Riddle had much more experience watching people try to get away with something. "Look, from his reaction I don't think Reece had any idea that

350

Tyler was going to meet up with him on the beach that day. He gives him something and all of a sudden the whole family is changing their vacation plans. I would bet my life savings that whatever it is you are looking for…Reece has it now and not Tyler. I think you can focus your search on him rather than Tyler."

Sutton thought about the information in silence for a moment and couldn't argue with the logic. He popped another antacid in his mouth before speaking. "I think you're right, but have your guy keep looking for Tyler. My instructions on him are not changed."

What Riddle didn't understand was that it didn't matter if Tyler still had the package or not; he still had the knowledge of what it was. Not to mention that, if he was apprehended, it wouldn't take an investigator very long to start trying to figure out what kind of motive Tyler could have had for what he did.

"Keep your eyes on Reece and don't lose him. I need that package back, Pete, and we're running out of time."

"I got it," Riddle replied before ending the call.

Sutton felt as panicked as he had when Sheriff Porter had shown him the empty safe on Figure Eight Island. For Sutton, it wasn't just the sexual satisfaction of what he did that he enjoyed but also the power he felt over another human being who was completely helpless to do anything but bend to his will. He enjoyed it so much that he had decided to record an episode or two for more private reflection. Young Chris Tyler had dressed and come out of the bathroom, still wiping away tears, a little quicker than Sutton had expected. He hadn't quite finished putting the tape away in the safe in the bedroom. He hadn't worried about it at the time, since the kid didn't know the combination or anything. But he was worried now.

Haxton had insisted on keeping the tapes at his place on the island since it had been made in his bedroom and, therefore, could be linked back to him. Initially, Sutton thought it was really so Haxton could use them to amuse himself whenever he wanted, which didn't bother him since he had access to the house whenever he wanted as well. Later, Sutton suspected it was done to keep him aware that there was damning evidence of his activities in Haxton's possession. Politicians always like to have insurance against other politicians—

especially ones that know the sins of the other. Either way, he realized as he stood with the Sheriff at the scene of the crime that day that there were only two people that had seen that safe besides him, and one of them was dead downstairs. That was when he knew who had killed Haxton and why and he was afraid the FBI was going to find that out too.

Tyler was the easy part of the equation. He was a drifter with a history of drug use and crime. He was a bit of a loner and wouldn't be missed by many and certainly not by many important people. Reece, on the other hand, was different. Not only was he a well-known member of his community, but now he was a national fucking celebrity. Making Tyler disappear wasn't a big challenge, but Reece was. Sure, it could be done if absolutely necessary, but the chances of getting away with it were much lower. Reece was an educated man with a family. He had a lot to lose if something went bad, and that was what Sutton decided to exploit. Haxton had done some terrible things to him, but if Reece had kept it secret for this long maybe it was because he wanted it to remain that way. Haxton was dead and Sutton had never touched Reece (his friend had always claimed him as his own personal toy), so wouldn't it be better to just let this all go away? He had a few carrots to dangle in front of Reece to make him see reason and would only talk about the stick if he had to. Time was running out, and it was a gamble he was going to have to take.

CHAPTER 27

As with any good neighbor, you can't just pop in and pop out. Michael found himself leaning against the counter in Seth Katz's kitchen while Charlie and Will Katz were running up the stairs to trade Pokemon cards. Seth was a fairly successful defense attorney in Charlotte, and, having been neighbors for many years, the two families had become close friends. Seth had been collecting the newspapers and mail for the Reece family while they were gone and Michael had come to pick it up. They had lost count of the number of nights that one of their sons had spent the night at the other's home, not to mention times spent carpooling or vacationing together. Their families had become so close that Seth's oldest son Jerrod had insisted the Reeces sit in the family section at his Bar Mitzvah last year.

Anna and Elizabeth were still unpacking at the house with both the alarm on and a two-hundred-pound dog lurking around the house, allowing Michael to not feel overly rushed to get back. The two friends caught up with each other's lives, and Katz filled Michael in on his observations from the first preseason game of the Carolina Panthers, to which they shared season tickets every year. Reece was not discouraging the continued small talk since he was procrastinating on something he had never done before, and that was lying to his neighbor and friend. Finally he realized that it had to be done, and it was time to pinch his nose and get it over with.

"Seth, I need a favor from you," Michael said to his friend in his kitchen.

Katz shrugged his shoulders. "Sure."

"The Army arranges all the interviews and things I have to do so reporters are supposed to go through them if they want one." The deceit had a bitter taste as it went over his tongue. "That being said, there have been a few that have tried to shortcut the process and come to me directly. I think I've seen a few kind of stalking me."

His friend chuckled. "Michael Reece, followed by the paparazzi. You're like a Kardashian now."

"Yeah, who would have ever thought? Look, you know I'm a pretty private guy and protective of my family. Could you kinda keep an eye out around here and let me know if you see anything out of the ordinary or anyone that doesn't seem familiar?" Michael gave an embarrassed shrug. "It's probably nothing, but would you mind?"

"Not a problem, buddy," Katz responded.

Not long after that, Michael was headed across the Katz yard with an armful of mail and Charlie in tow waving back to his buddy. He hated the dishonesty, but he didn't want to involve anyone he didn't have to in the true nature of his paranoia, and his motivation was protecting his family, which any man could understand.

He dropped the wad of mail on the elevated counter in the kitchen and, based on the phone conversation Anna was having, pizza delivery was on the dinner menu. After stuffing his phone in his pocket, he headed out to the backyard accompanied by Tiny. He took his familiar seat with legs, both real and manufactured, dangling over the edge of the dock just above the gentle lapping of the water against the wood, and sent a text to the number that Chris had given him:

Back home in Charlotte. Let me know you're ok when you can.

The message left the phone and found its way to the nearest tower and then onward to its destination. It would soon be displayed on Chris's phone and on the daily report Landon Pierce received from his contact at Southcomm.

*****

The skyline of Charlotte was just south outside of Chip's hotel window after checking in to the Hilton Garden Inn near Northlake Mall. He decided on the casual look of khaki pants and a blue button-down shirt for what could be one of the biggest coups of politics done on the fly. The ride to the address on his rental car's GPS was less than ten minutes, and he pulled into the driveway with about an hour of daylight left in the warm late summer day. He had gotten the address from his office in Washington and hadn't told anyone what he was up to.

After taking a deep breath, he rang the doorbell and heard the distant baritone bark of a very large dog. Michael Reece's face appeared through the partially opened front door with a look of part confusion but mostly suspicion.

"Can I help you?" Reece asked his visitor.

"Dr. Reece, my name is Chip Johnson. I'm very sorry to bother you at home, but I have something to discuss with you. I'm the Director of Communications for Senator Haxton." Chip rushed to finish after seeing a decidedly unwelcoming look from Michael. "I have to tell you up front that no one from his office knows I'm here or what I want to talk to you about, but I think it's something you should hear. I just ask for about fifteen minutes of your time, and if you don't want to hear anymore, I will leave without another word."

This was about as expected a visitor to his home tonight as a spaceship landing in his front yard. A short appraisal of the man at his front door didn't reveal anything threatening. Maybe he knew something about who Haxton really was and was having an attack of conscience.

"Fifteen minutes. You can meet me around back on my deck." And with that the front door closed.

Chip had expected many reactions, but this wasn't one of them. As he sat down on the deck after shaking hands with Michael, he thought it was very telling that he was not wanted inside the man's home. *Maybe this was a bad idea.*

"I have to tell you, Dr. Reece, I'm not feeling like you're happy with my surprise visit tonight, and I apologize for the intrusion again. I really don't mean any harm, and I hope that after our conversation you will feel differently about me."

Reece showed no emotion of any type. "Don't take it personal, but you're down to fourteen minutes. I'm not a big fan of politicians."

355

"Believe it or not, Dr. Reece, neither am I. That's one of the reasons I came to see you today. I have a proposition for you, and I simply want to know if you're interested or not." Chip leaned forward, resting his elbows on his thighs as he began his pitch. "Again, in full disclosure, I am here on my own, and no one else knows I am speaking to you about this. In other words, if you say no, it will end here.

"As I am sure you are aware, the Senator was extremely proud of you when he heard about your award, as we all were, and insisted that we stay out of the story about your accomplishments because he said they were yours and no one else deserved the credit which, I have to tell you, as essentially his public relations director I was decidedly unhappy about. No matter, it was what he wanted, and in hindsight I have to say it was the right and honorable thing to do."

Michael leaned back in his chair. *Well, there goes my attack of conscience theory. He obviously doesn't have a clue of what kind of piece of shit his boss was.*

"As you know," Chip continued, "there was nothing more important to Senator Haxton than serving the people of this state. He considered it his mission every day to—" He stopped in mid-sentence as Reece put his hand up.

"Look, Mr. Johnson, I'm not really interested in hearing a packaged canonization of the Senator. Maybe I missed it, but I haven't heard you get to this proposition yet, and you're running out of time. I know we don't know each other, so let me clue you in to the fact that I'm not a big fan of how things are done in Washington," he said with an unhidden tone of impatience.

"Exactly, Dr. Reece! That's exactly why I'm here today!" Chip saw a door crack open and he meant to exploit it. "Believe me, I know exactly what you mean. I'm there every day and I see the inner workings of how things get done…or maybe, more accurately, how they don't get done. Senator Haxton's death, while horribly tragic, gives us an opportunity to get someone to take his fallen torch and carry it with the honor that most politicians these days have forgotten. That's where you come in, sir."

And there it was. With those final two sentences, it was becoming clear to Michael why this pencil-necked little shit was sitting on his deck and taking up his time.

"I'm going to save you some time and effort right now, Mr. Johnson. If you think I'm interested in being some cheerleader for a guy you want to take your boss's place, you are sorely mistaken. As I'm sure you know, I'm a registered Independent, and I chose that because I don't particularly care for most politicians of either side, and I care even less about being a poster boy for one. I'm sorry, but you have wasted your time."

Michael started to stand to walk his visitor to his car, but the man was pleading with his hands to say just a bit more.

"No, Dr. Reece, I want *you* to be Senator Haxton's replacement. You are *exactly* what Washington needs, and the fact that you don't like politics is why. The Governor will appoint someone to fill the vacant seat for the remaining three years of his term until the next election. I want to suggest that you be that person. I know I'm probably getting low on time here, but just give me a few more minutes to explain why."

Michael's silent consent was given more by shock at the suggestion rather than actual interest. If someone had given him a hundred guesses as to why Mr. Chip Johnson had come to his house today he still wouldn't have come up with this. He almost was starting to look around for cameras and a crew from some practical joke show.

"Dr. Reece, the fact that you are shocked at the suggestion makes me even more certain that I have the right person for the job. I know politics is a foreign subject for you, but that's where I come in. I know Washington, and I know how to make this happen. What you represent is sorely needed up there, and I know that most good people like you would never consider running for office because of your disdain for what politics has become."

He leaned back in his chair to let it sink in for a moment. This was his chance. He took somewhat of a theatrical breath and began again.

"By my watch, Dr. Reece I have about five minutes left. Let me use them to explain why I think you would be an immensely popular choice to be the next Senator from North Carolina..."

357

Chris Tyler nearly collapsed in the bed at the Clarion Hotel in east Asheville. He had slept very little in the past several days, and the combination of confiding in someone and gaining some physical distance from the coast had bled away a lot of accumulated stress. Tomorrow he would figure out what his next step was, but for now he felt relief. That relief was helped by Michael's text. Part of him worried that Michael would view the videos and decide he wanted nothing to do with this whole thing, and he would either get a call urging him to turn himself into the police or he would simply call the authorities himself.

Thinking back to their interaction after they opened up to each other, he realized he was wrong to think that. After all, Michael gave him two thousand dollars of his own money as well as one of his cars with little or no expectation of getting them back. He felt guilt at the incorrect assumptions he had made about him. Not long ago, he had buried his brother in this very town, but he felt like he had found another who had been lost for far too long. No matter how difficult life could get, it would be a bit easier knowing that there was at least one person who had his back.

He activated his phone and texted the words "I'm ok. Will call tomorrow if I can." He got up and opened the bag from the local Walgreen's where he had bought some toiletries and a six-pack of bottled water. A hot shower had made him feel human again, but he barely had the energy to kneel at his bedside, where he prayed for God's guidance and forgiveness and the safety of his friend before crawling under the covers and surrendering to the exhaustion that had finally caught up with him and demanded satisfaction.

*****

"Special Agent Scott," Meredith said after grabbing the vibrating phone from her belt.

"Ma'am, this is Brian Baxter with CODIS. I was told to update you if there was any change in our analysis of the door handle blood spatter in the Haxton case," the supervisor said.

Scott bolted upright in her chair in the conference room of the Wilmington Field Office of the FBI. "That's correct, Mr. Baxter. What have you got?"

"Well, Agent Scott, this is very preliminary, but we may have a possible match on your sample. A more detailed confirmatory analysis is being done right now which should be complete in a couple of hours, and we hope to have a name for you at that time if it is still a match."

He waited as the agent digested what he had said. He was always jealous that the DNA side of criminal investigation didn't get its due credit, and on many occasions he found himself having to explain simple DNA concepts over and over again to some Ray Ban-wearing, pistol-waving pain in the ass in order to convey his results.

"Do you have a name for this potential match, Mr. Baxter?"

"No, ma'am. It's strict policy not to release any names before confirmatory testing. I'm just letting you know that we have a possible," Baxter replied.

Scott scrunched her face at the voice in her ear. Far too much coffee, far too little sleep, and no leads in the investigation were taking their toll.

"So you called me to say that you might have something but don't know yet?"

She regretted it the minute she said it. She wasn't the only one getting pressure on this case, and this guy had probably been instructed to call with *any* updates, and he wasn't about to get chewed out for waiting until the test was confirmed.

"That's correct, Agent Scott. I was told to keep you up to date. I promise we are working as fast as we can on the confirmation." There was a subtle edge to his reply.

The tone had changed, and she had deserved a little irritation from the man on the other end. It was time to make nice. "Of course. I'm sorry about that remark, Mr. Baxter; it was uncalled for. I appreciate you doing everything you can, and thanks for letting me know. Call me anytime."

He was at a loss for words for a moment. Lab types had always been treated like second-class citizens by the field agents, and it may have been the first time he had actually gotten an apology from one. "Not a problem, Special Agent Scott. No apology necessary, and I'll let you know when I have something more concrete."

After ending the call with Baxter, she picked up the phone, called Mitch Frierson, and told him that they may have a match on the DNA and to be ready to travel within a couple of hours. He sounded even more fried than she was. He was an outstanding Assistant SAC and had tried to handle as much of the bureaucratic bullshit and calls from people who had nothing to add to the investigation and only wanted to be updated or complain about the lack of leads, thereby freeing her up for more productive work.

She felt guilty at her lack of production, when a lot of her time had been spent staring at a large grease-marker board where they had diagrammed the known details of the case for hours on end looking for something she had missed. She felt like she had bilked the taxpayers out of the money she had used to rent a room at a nearby hotel, since she hadn't been there since checking in and grabbing a quick shower before returning to the field office. Leaning back in her chair, she wanted so bad to give up the struggle against sleep for just a few minutes, and another cup of coffee would surely finish off any lining of her stomach that might still be left. Getting up to pace the room, she noticed Frierson standing in the doorway.

"Meredith, I am closing the blinds on this glass and I am closing this door. The staff has been made aware that there might be a DNA match forthcoming and to be ready to move. If you do anything but sleep until the DNA data is confirmed, I will personally come back in here and shoot you. Do you have any questions, Special Agent Scott?" His trademark smirk was still there despite his own obvious exhaustion.

"No questions at all, Mitch."

She sat back down in the chair and leaned her head back against it while her assistant twisted the rod closing the blinds of the small window that led to the field office hallway and closed the door. In the short seconds it took for her to fall asleep, she promised to work as hard as she could after this case was finished to make sure that Assistant Special Agent in Charge Frierson became Special Agent in Charge Frierson very soon.

*****

He used some leftover fast food napkins to press against his nose, tilting his head back as much as he could and still see to drive. There had been at least some relief when he had looked into the rearview mirror and found that all his teeth were still in their proper place. Never had a conversation went so wrong, so quickly. Chip waived off the concerned look of the hotel desk clerk as he came through the automatic sliding doors and headed to the elevator.

His blue Brooks Brothers shirt was only fit for the trash, due to the blood on the front and the grass stains on the back. The bleeding from his nose had stopped, and he now held the filled thin plastic ice bucket bag against the left side of his face. The room was no longer spinning, and he played back the last part of his conversation with Michael Reece.

"You are immensely popular right now and represent the kind of person everyone wishes would hold this kind of office. You don't have any debts to pay to any donors who got you there, and you care about others far more than you care about yourself. You have a beautiful family and you're a respected doctor. I've done some homework on you, Dr. Reece. You give a LOT of money to charity but never want any recognition for it, and you are respected by your colleagues. In our last telephone poll we did from my office, we asked over a thousand people their opinions on different policies and the Senator's job performance. This was the day after you ran into Senator Haxton at the Capitol, mind you. We put in a favorability question about you. Guess what? Not only did over ninety percent know who you were, but you had a higher favorability rating than the Senator has ever had in his career, and he's pretty popular with his constituents. Oh, and don't even get me started on how we could use this Medal of Honor thing to our advantage—"

It was at that moment that Reece had stood up and pulled him out of his chair and sent him backward over the deck railing with one terribly hard punch. After that, the man looked down on him from the deck and told him he had less than a minute to get in his car and get the hell out of there. He didn't really look to be in a mood to debate the plan, and Chip high-tailed it to his car and driven back to his hotel to treat his injuries. He had never been in a fight in his life, including his younger days in school, but was pretty certain this was what it felt like to get your ass kicked.

Chip just couldn't understand. The title of United States Senator was something that *anyone* would give their first born for, and he had offered the possibility of that to Reece on a silver fucking platter. Was the man just too dumb to realize what a gift this was? Despite all of his bullshit lines tonight about knowing how much Washington is broken, Chip couldn't understand that there were things far more important than prestige in politics. All he knew at the moment was that if he didn't find a new horse to back and soon, he might have to find work outside of Washington and have to work and (gasp!) live among the "constituents" that political types so often extol in public but mock and despise in private.

Now he seemed to be in the position of having to let the process play out with the appointment and pray that his past PR exploits as well as the patronage of Sutton would be enough to either remain in his position that he currently held or possibly jump ship to a better opportunity. Hopefully, the swelling of his face would go down before he actually had to meet with Sutton, so he wouldn't have to explain the horrible miscalculation he had done tonight. He had banked on some hometown guy who spent his spare time as a knuckle-dragging weekend warrior who didn't understand the importance of elevation to the major leagues of power play, but he realized that even doctors could be stupid.

*****

It had only been about two and a half hours, but they had been spent in glorious slumber. Agent Frierson had called Baxter after leaving the conference room and asked him to call his own number when it came through instead of Scott's. It had given her twenty extra minutes of rest before he opened the door again to wake her. On the table he placed a plastic Target bag which contained a toothbrush, toothpaste, washcloth, soap, and contact lens solution. From his other hand, he put down a deli sandwich with a pasta salad and Snapple.

"We've got a name. They're getting the plane ready, and we leave for Asheville in about twenty minutes, which gives you enough time to freshen up and get some food in you. I'll brief you on what I know on the way to the airport." With that he winked and walked out of the room, no doubt to try to freshen up a little himself.

She looked at the shopping bag and then the meal in front of her and seriously thought of naming her next child after him. She would need to be on her A-game for the next phase of this investigation, and he was making sure she would be. "You're the best, Mitch," she said to his back as he waved back at her on the way to the men's room. "I don't deserve you!"

Frierson smiled at her last remark. He hadn't forsaken his own nap and run those errands to try to get in his boss's good graces; he had done it because he admired the hell out of her. She was second to none as an investigator, and she took care of her people. The FBI was one of the most established good-old-boy networks still in existence, and Scott had broken through by being just as good as or, more often than not, better than her peers. He knew that there was monumental pressure on her from multiple directions to wrap this up quickly, but he also knew she wouldn't even consider taking a shortcut or doing something half-assed in order to placate anyone above her pay grade.

The Assistant SAC looked over the limited information he had in the folder as he took a dump. He figured it might be the last chance to do it in a while, and the small twin-prop plane they would be taking to the western part of the state didn't have an enviable throne room. Picturing his current activity versus the image everyone thinks of when they hear the words "FBI Agent," he couldn't help but snicker. He reminded himself to call Porter as a professional courtesy before leaving for the airport.

CHAPTER 28

The software was part rip-off and part augmentation of Google Latitude. The original application was a way for cell phone owners to sign up for a locating service that didn't require a GPS-enabled phone, and then one could build a collection of "friends" where you could see where they (or more specifically their phones) were located at any given time. Carla Tibbert had taken what had been a popular phone feature for socially mobile friends and suspicious spouses and taken the next step.

Although her IRS returns listed her job as an IT Consultant at a large insurance company, her main source of income was enhanced by pirated software that she designed and sold to whoever needed it. She had designed programs that could invade a personal computer and capture private information such as emails, financial records, or even embarrassing photographs, and she had designed programs that could erase selected items from other computers through their own ISP.

Probably her biggest creation so far though was a program she had nicknamed "Black Drone." She had taken the concept of mobile phone social locator applications and designed a way to install them on someone's phone without their consent...or their knowledge. After that, anyone with the administrative software could track the affected phone's location from their own laptop or mobile phone. It had taken her less than three days to complete the program after breaking down the code of more legitimate and ethical applications, but she had sold it to Landon Pierce for fifty thousand dollars.

Pierce's "consultant" at Southcomm had installed the drone part of the software on his workstation computer long ago. It was hidden into the code of a benign part of the regular operating system and was essentially undetectable by anyone looking for it. To open the program, he clicked on the fictional "Stat Analysis" icon in the Accessories portion of his PC. A small window appeared with a single unlabeled data entry slot. The young man simply typed in the phone number that had sent Reece a text, and it was now available as a "friend" to the administrative software that was in Pierce's personal laptop as well as a secure desktop PC at his home.

The "drone" data was accurate to a distance of about five hundred yards and used Google Maps to give Pierce a visual reference of where Tyler's phone was currently located. There were several restaurants, businesses, and hotels in the footprint of possible precise locations. After noting that the location did not move for over two hours, he ruled out a restaurant and felt that it was likely one of the three hotels located at the interstate exit. He made a list of the three hotels and emailed it to Riddle, who used the information to dispatch McCray west as fast as he could go.

Pierce put the likelihood that this particular phone belonging to Tyler as greater than 90 percent after reviewing the two texts that had been exchanged between the number and Reece's phone. He had also forwarded the information gained from his Chunnel software, which found a death certificate for a Darnell Tyler who shared the same birth location and date as Chris, essentially eliminating one of the three people Pierce would have to track down. Riddle texted Sutton a cryptic message relaying that McCray was en route to Asheville and also the date of Darnell's death, which he noted was before the death of Haxton.

*****

Sutton received the text right after getting off the phone with Sheriff Porter. He knew that the FBI was now on the way to arrest a man that was buried in a cheap coffin in a poorly maintained cemetery just outside the mountain town. This was a fact that he was sure wouldn't take the investigators very long to figure out as well. The real question was how long it would take someone on the team to figure out that the deceased had a twin brother, an identical twin brother who had the same DNA as Darnell but who had never been arrested for an offense that warranted a sample from the inside of his cheek being placed in the DNA database. Sutton wasn't sure, but he didn't think it would be as long as he would like.

He paced in the living room area of the suite at the luxury getaway that had become his prison. His future schedule—actually his future in general—would be determined by the fate of Chris Tyler. He cursed his perversions for getting him into this mess but cursed McCray and

Riddle louder for their slow pace at taking this sticky variable out of his current life equation. Then there was the more challenging issue of Reece.

A horrifying picture of Reece handing over the discs to the authorities or even the press was running through Sutton's mind. The steady but slow infusion of scotch could not prevent the shiver that went through the former Governor as he pictured what his fate would be if either of those things happened. Time was a luxury that he was expending far too quickly with far too few results, and bolder action was needed. There was no way around it, the time had come to take a gamble and offer a carrot to the good doctor.

*****

Seth Katz was taking the family dog for an early morning walk and noted a Ford Explorer parked on the side of the street just outside the subdivision entrance. The driver seemed to be consulting a map when Seth passed by but didn't roll down the window to ask for help. Initially he didn't think anything of it, but as he continued to walk he remembered his conversation with his neighbor about keeping an eye out for anything unusual.

It seemed a little odd that someone would be on a neighborhood road and lost at just after six in the morning. Also, if the man was lost, why didn't he ask for directions or help from a man who was walking his dog and obviously lived in the area? As he walked along the curvature of the road that took the vehicle out of his sight, he decided that if it was gone when he came back, the man was probably just what he appeared to be: lost.

Fifteen minutes and a mile of walking later, Seth came around the same curve but in the opposite direction. There it sat, not an inch from where it was before. Either the man wasn't lost at all or he was the dumbest map reader in the history of maps. Seth decided to try a little secret agent stuff and activated the camera portion of his iPhone, placing it to his ear with the camera lens facing his right and acting as if he was involved in a normal phone conversation.

Providence smiled upon him further when his dog decided to take a leak right when they were even with the mystery vehicle. Trying his best to align the phone for a good shot, he clicked away at the driver's window across the street, where the man was still consulting his map. Once the dog was done, he walked on, pretending to conclude his conversation. His pace the rest of the way home was a little more brisk, and he opened his photo gallery immediately upon entering the house.

"Hot damn," Seth said when he saw that four of the six pictures had gotten a pretty good shot of the man's face. He uploaded them to his laptop in order to get a bigger view and saved them to his hard drive. He studied them further and noticed two things that didn't add up with the lost driver act. First, the map clearly said "Wilmington" in the top corner, which was over two hundred miles away, and second, there was a pair of binoculars in the passenger seat. *Gotcha*. Seth realized that maybe his friend wasn't being overly paranoid after all.

*****

"Buncombe County Office of the Medical Examiner, how may I direct your call?" It was a pleasant surprise that it was actually a real human being on the line rather than a recorded directory.

"Good morning," Michael began, "this is Dr. Michael Reece and I'm trying to reach Dr. Bradley."

"One moment, Dr. Reece," the operator replied.

Alex Bradley had been a huge help to Michael as he had struggled with his actions in Afghanistan and how it affected his status as a physician who had taken the Hippocratic Oath. The current director of the North Carolina Medical Board had been patient and reassuring to Michael and had informed him that he and the board felt that his actions were performed in the defense of his life and the lives of others, including two men who would be considered his patients, and in no way did they betray the principles laid forth in the oath. He even drafted a proclamation saluting Reece for his service and sacrifice and stating that they were consistent with the high professional and moral standards of the Board. Michael had felt the same but had been very relieved to hear someone else declare it too.

"Michael my friend!" blared from the earpiece. "How in the world are you? By the way, congratulations on your award. I can think of no one who deserves it more."

"I'm doing good Alex. Thank you for that. I'm calling because I need a favor if it's possible. I certainly understand if you can't, though."

"You know I'll be happy to do anything I can for you, buddy."

"I need you to review an autopsy that was done a long time ago but in your county. The name is Charles Potts. He was in a motor vehicle accident." Reece gave what specifics he had, which were the date of the accident and not much more.

"OK. I can do that. What am I looking for?"

Michael hesitated for a moment but decided that honesty was not only the best way to answer the question but it was something he owed Alex for being a good friend and colleague.

"Alex, he was kind of my mentor as a kid...more like a father. I have come across some information that makes me a little concerned that he may not have died by accident. I really don't have anything more specific than that, and I guess I'm just looking for information to set my mind at ease. Look, I know it's a weird request, and I understand if you can't do it, Alex."

"It's not a big deal, Michael. But remember it was a good while back. I can read the autopsy report and see if there were any radiographs done, but that's probably all that's there to look at. Give me a few days and I'll give you call. How's the family doing?"

"Thanks, Alex. Everyone's doing well. Getting used to the extra attention, but life is good. Give my best to Sandra and the kids."

The men said goodbye to each other, and Michael fervently hoped that the next time he heard from Alex Bradley it would be to hear that Charlie's injuries were completely consistent with a random car accident. It was just a lingering question that he needed reassurance on and would pursue no further if the science didn't support such a worry.

The house was oddly quiet at the moment, as Anna and the kids, despite Michael's worries, had just gone to the mall to pick up some clothes for the upcoming school year. He was usually banned from shopping with his daughter, due to his complete lack of a spine in those situations—a condition that Elizabeth was becoming more and more aware of as she grew older, which made Anna think with horror of a teenage daughter with a credit-card-carrying father who was a complete wimp.

The original discs were in the family safe that was bolted to the floor of the office room, and the second copies were wrapped in plastic and stuffed in the bottom of a large plastic container of Christmas decorations in the attic. He sat down into the soft leather cushions of the family room couch and decided to enjoy the first minutes of peace he had enjoyed in several days. The awakening of his mobile phone made it a very brief respite.

"Hello?" Reece said as he hit the answer button on the touch screen.

"Dr. Reece?"

"Speaking," replied Michael.

"This is Governor Sutton. I believe you have something that belongs to me."

*****

As had been the routine the year before, finding the right clothes for Elizabeth's back-to-school needs had involved seven different stores, including two that received repeat visits, and countless trips to the dressing room with gut-wrenching debate and contemplation. Charlie's had involved one stop for three pairs of blue jeans and one stop at the sporting goods store for shorts and sports-themed shirts—all in all a fifteen minute endeavor, compared to the three hours for Elizabeth. They now sat at the food court, surrounded by shopping bags, while the kids had ice cream and Anna had Starbucks. In other words, a win-win situation. Charlie's speed in completing his treat made the two ladies wonder if he had ever actually tasted the ice cream he had put in his mouth. Anna sipped her café mocha and Elizabeth rolled her eyes as her younger brother went up and down the escalator over and over waiting for the ladies to finish.

It wasn't long before the recurring discussion of why Elizabeth couldn't have a mobile phone, which Anna had estimated to occur approximately a thousand times in the last few weeks, reared its head again. Elizabeth's arguments bore the common themes—all of her friends had one and she would be the odd one out, etc. Anna's counterpoints involved responsibility and what the actual need for one was. What was a shock to no one was that the discussion ended in yet another stalemate.

Anna smiled, as she was thankful that these discussions didn't end with the stomping off and door-slamming that was sure to come when the teenage years arrived. She got up to gather the bags and call Charlie to come along when the smile left her face. Charlie wasn't there. The predominant emotion was irritation, as she expected to see him on the floor below, running around the chairs despite him not telling his mother that he was going to do it. Irritation became confusion when there was no sign of him there either.

She began to walk around the food court, scanning the area. Confusion was becoming worry. After sending Elizabeth downstairs to look for him, she half-walked, half-ran to the bathroom area in case he had needed to make a pit stop. Decorum lost to a mother's worry as she pushed open the door to the men's bathroom…no Charlie. Worry was now changing to fear. She called out his name as she walked across the dining area again toward the escalator. Looking over the edge of the railing, Elizabeth made a shrugging gesture indicating she had not seen him either.

Anna's mouth was dry and her stomach was churning. She grabbed the arm of a nearby security officer and described her son quickly and asked him to look upstairs, then took the escalator down, leaping two steps at a time until she met up with her daughter. Rapid looks down each end of the long middle thoroughfare showed no signs. Fear had now become panic. She fought the quiver that was beginning on her lower lip as she began to yell his name with no regard for whether she was making a scene. She ran one direction and reversed course when her search had borne no fruit, the welling of tears distorting her vision somewhat.

Elizabeth saw the raw terror in her mother's face, and she was now crying as Anna desperately asked shoppers if they had seen her son. She heard the overhead announcement that if a Charlie Reece was in the mall, he should come to the food court or any customer service desk, his family was looking for him. Elizabeth was now calling out for him also between her sobs, and still nothing. She could barely keep up with her mother as she leapt back up the steps of the escalator with no care that she was bumping into to shoppers along the way. The tears were coming freely now, and there was an intense burning on her face that had come from the burst of adrenaline that had been released.

Her calls for her son were now screams, and Elizabeth was starting to completely come apart at the sight of her mother on the verge of losing it until a familiar sound made both of them turn their heads.

"Mommy!" Little Charlie called out from less than ten yards away, standing with a gentleman near the food court.

Anna ran in full sprint to him and dropped to her knees and hugged tight enough that he began to squirm.

"Ma'am, is this your son?" the gentleman asked. "I heard the announcement and saw that he was alone."

"Yes...yes he's my son," Anna stammered as she tried to gain self-composure again. She felt as if she had just run a marathon as the adrenaline began to fall in her body and an enveloping sense of relief and exhaustion came over her. "Thank you, sir...thank you very much." Elizabeth now held on to her brother as well as she snuffed heavily, also trying to stop crying. Anna stood and shook the man's hand. "I can't thank you enough. I don't think I have ever felt more terrified."

"That's OK, Anna. I'm just glad you are all back together now," replied the man. He appeared to be in his fifties but still in good shape.

"I am too. I...Wait. How did you know my name?" Anna asked the stranger.

The man looked at all three of the Reece family in succession slowly and with a smile. "It can be such a relief to have your family when you were worried you had lost one. There's nothing more precious than family, and I can tell that keeping them safe is very important to you, Anna."

His gaze was on her now, and it didn't convey warmth. Some of the flush in her face was beginning to return. Something was not right here. "I'm not sure I heard what you said, Mister...I didn't get your name."

"That's right, Anna; you didn't. You make sure these little ones stay safe."

His gaze turned to the security guard who was walking in their direction and explaining into his walkie-talkie that the boy had been found. The man looked back down at Charlie and spoke to him.

"I'm going to leave you with your mommy now, young man, but here's a prize for being such a brave fella." He handed him a small round pin and looked back into Anna's face while still talking to Charlie. "You have to be careful these days."

He took one more look at the approaching security guard then turned on his heels and walked away, quickly disappearing into the gathering crowd who had come to see the source of Anna's commotion.

The exchange had left her terribly confused, but she was certain that he had meant to send her some kind of message and he was far from simply being a good citizen. She felt a sudden overwhelming desire to get to the safety of home, although she wasn't quite sure why.

"Look, Mommy, I got a prize," Charlie said to her as he held up his pin.

She looked at the old-fashioned round pin, noting the hinged needle that was on the back allowing one to attach it to his or her lapel. When she flipped it over to see the front, it all made sense, and there was genuine fear inside her now. It read:

SUTTON FOR GOVERNOR

She put the pin in her pocket, took both her children's hands, and walked as quickly as she could without running out the exit to her car, leaving all the shopping bags at the food court table they had been at only minutes before.

*****

There was silence on the other end of the line. Although he was fairly certain Michael was in possession of the discs, there was still a chance that he wasn't and therefore wouldn't have any idea what he was talking about. It would be the best of all possibilities, since he could focus only on Tyler.

"I'm sorry. My Governor is Jim Wade. I'm not aware of a Governor Sutton," was the rather terse reply after the pause.

Uh-oh. "Touché, Dr. Reece. I guess I should have said 'former Governor.' Title debates aside, I'm pretty sure you know who I am. Would I be mistaken in making that assumption?"

Sutton kept a cool tone. Reece's snippy reply made him even more certain that he was not only in possession of the videos but knew what they contained. An adversarial confrontation, however, would not serve his purpose.

"You assume correct, Mr. Sutton."

"I thought so. I would like to return to my first statement, Dr. Reece. I have reason to believe that you have something that belongs to me. It is something that I would very much like to have back. It is an item of a personal nature. Would this be an assumption that is incorrect?" His words were measured and calm in the hopes that the man he was speaking to would listen to reason.

Michael reflexively looked out his front and back windows as he held his phone to his ear. "Well, Mr. Sutton, I would agree that I have something that is of a personal nature to you, but I'm not sure I agree it belongs to you."

Fuck! "Why don't we agree to disagree on the matter of ownership for now, Dr. Reece? It would suffice to say that I would very much like to have what you possess, even if you might not agree that it is my property. It is something that I would be willing to be very generous about ensuring that it is returned to me with discretion." He took on an almost professorial tone in his conversation. "Dr. Reece, sometimes the unpleasantness of the past doesn't need to be made the unpleasantness of the present. I am in a position to offer things that could be very enticing indeed to both you and Mr. Tyler to keep such things in the past. I would be happy to discuss this with both of you, but I don't have a way to get in touch with Mr. Tyler. Would you happen to have a way for me to contact him that you could share with me?"

"Yes on having a way to contact him, no on sharing it with you," Michael replied. He wanted to tell the man to go fuck himself and hang up the phone, but he needed to know what he was up against. "Speaking for myself, I am pretty enticed by life just the way it is."

Sutton chuckled like he was catching up with an old friend. "Fair enough, Dr. Reece, fair enough. Do you think, however, that Mr. Tyler is happy with his current situation right now? It seems to me a little presumptuous to speak for the both of you, if you don't mind my saying so. I know he has had his struggles in the past, both personally and financially, and I had heard that his brother had passed away recently as well. I certainly don't want to be presumptuous myself, but don't you think the possibility of never having a financial worry for the rest of your life would be something you should at least discuss with him and make sure it wasn't something he would want? Again, I don't mean to speak for him, but I know I would certainly want to know of such an opportunity if the roles were reversed."

"Mr. Sutton, I don't think you should speak so casually about the roles being reversed. That is just an observation, but it's also a warning," Michael said through gritted teeth.

"Very well, Dr. Reece. I'm not asking you to agree with choices I have made in the past, and I'm not asking you or Mr. Tyler to forgive me. I do want you to know that I have changed, and, with the help of my faith, I am committed to leading a better life." Sutton knew that Reece regularly attended church and thought that this remark might help his case, bullshit though it was. "After all, Dr. Reece, forgiveness is one of the basic foundations of our faith is it not?"

"So is atonement for your sins, Mr. Sutton."

"Absolutely...absolutely it is. That leads me to my point. I will not waste your time with some sort of sales pitch, Dr. Reece. I am prepared to offer you and Mr. Tyler five million dollars each for the discreet return of the property we have discussed, no strings attached, with the exception of the assurance from the both of you that the contents of the discs will never be discussed with anyone nor the circumstances of my relationship with you, Chris Tyler, and Darnell Tyler. It would not be hidden money but would be presented as a gift from the estate of

Senator Haxton for achievements of two former Sycamore residents. In case you were not aware, Dr. Reece, I am the executor of the Senator's will and estate." He sighed. "So there it is, Dr. Reece. That is my offer to you and Mr. Tyler. I ask that you discuss it with Mr. Tyler and let me know if these terms are acceptable. You may reach me at this number with your answer or if you have any further questions. There is no need for any unpleasantness on anyone's part because of the unfortunate events of the past few days."

Reece didn't miss the veiled threat in the final sentence. "I will speak to him, Mr. Sutton, but I hope you understand that unpleasantness can go both ways. Good day."

He ended the call, and only then did the shaking begin. This was a powerful man who could lose everything based on what was now in his possession, and worse, that powerful man knew Michael had it. Once again, Chris's remark about what people will do to keep their secrets safe chilled the room a few degrees. *What the hell do I do now?*

His silent pondering was interrupted when his phone yet again started to ring. His biggest fear was that it would be Sutton again, since he was unsure he could hide the shaking in his voice now that the conversation had sunk in. Much to his relief, the caller ID revealed a familiar name and number.

"Hey, Seth," Reece said to his neighbor.

"Hey buddy. Listen, I am probably just being the very amateur secret agent man, but there was a guy parked outside the entrance to our street for over a half hour just sitting there. He was looking at a map, but when I came back by walking the dog I noticed it wasn't even a map of Charlotte. Plus he had binoculars in his seat. It's probably nothing, but I snapped a couple of pictures of him. I just looked outside and he's not there now, so maybe he was just lost. It just seemed a little out of place. I took the picture on my phone and I was going to send it to you."

Michael was walking to the bathroom to get an antacid. "Absolutely...that would be great. You're right, it's probably nothing, but I'll keep it in case I see the guy again out there."

"No problem, buddy. I'll send it right now. By the way, if the *National Enquirer* offers me some cash to dish some dirt on you, can I interest you in a bidding war for my silence?" Seth loved razzing his buddy a little when the chance came.

"You know how cheap I am, Seth. I wouldn't have a chance." His attempt at sounding cool and funny was pretty poor. "Hey, I gotta run. I'll give you call later, OK?"

"All right, Mike. Talk to you later," Seth said and got off the phone.

A few moments later, the phone chirped, announcing an incoming message—the three photographs. Michael studied the image of the man and was quite certain that he had never seen him before. His willingness to blow it off as nothing was significantly diminished after his conversation with Sutton. He emailed the pics to his account so he would have a copy on his laptop for future use. After opening up the Hotmail account on the kitchen counter laptop, he opened the pictures using his media player and kept the image on the screen. He wanted to show it to Anna when she got home in case either one of them saw him again.

As if on cue, he heard the garage door opening, followed shortly after by his family coming in the door. It was obvious that both Anna and Elizabeth had been crying, and Little Charlie was very quiet and seemed shaken as well. His wife put up her hand to tell him not to ask yet.

"Kids, can you go upstairs to the playroom? I need to talk to your dad for a couple of minutes," Anna said in a voice that was still very shaken.

Michael walked with both the kids to the base of the staircase and kissed both of them on the top of the head. It struck him as a little strange that his son was holding Elizabeth's hand all the way up instead of his usual mission of running up the steps faster than anyone else who might be with him. His suspicion that something was very wrong was confirmed as he turned around to see his wife staring pale-faced in horror at his laptop screen, where she saw the face of the man who had just cryptically threatened to harm her child less than twenty minutes ago.

*****

"You fucking moron!" Sutton wanted to throw his phone out the window. "Didn't I make it very fucking clear to simply keep an eye on him and not do a goddamned thing?"

"Look, I'm sorry. You said you would call and I hadn't heard anything." Riddle was trying to calm Sutton down. "One of the last things you told me was that we're running out of time. I only followed the car because it was the one he was driving yesterday. When I realized that it was his wife and kids, I decided to follow them a little while. The opportunity presented itself and I decided to take a little initiative. No one heard the conversation we had, and I left before security got there. I think you're making too big a deal out of this."

"Well stop thinking then, you fucking retard! I just called Reece and tried to fucking reason with him to turn the package over for a payout. I don't think there's a chance in hell he accepts that proposal now that you went and threatened his goddamn wife and kids!" Sutton threw his drink tumbler on the ground. "Jesus fucking Christ, Riddle!"

The man was coming unglued, and he knew far too much about Riddle's own enterprises to be unglued. "Listen, you need to calm down. I'm sorry for acting without your direction, but we can't undo that now. Besides, this might push him to accept your terms, almost like good cop bad cop. If he thinks about it, he'll probably think he has a choice between a big check and possibly something bad happening to his family." Pete had no idea if that was the case, but it was possible, and he needed to get Sutton to chill the hell out.

"It might also make him march right out of his house and go to the police station or the goddamn media. Did you consider that? This is not some fucking weed pusher that you need to be afraid of you. This is a respected member of the community as well as a goddamn war hero." Sutton thought for a minute and realized that this would probably change everything and not for the better. "You are to stay close to him and not do a fucking thing more than that unless I tell you to. I've got enough people making my life too complicated right now and I don't need another one. Do you understand what I'm telling you?"

"I understand, but—" was all Riddle was able to get out before the line went dead.

He was a man used to browbeating others, not the other way around. He figured this would go one of two ways: either Reece would be scared shitless about something happening to his family and agree to Sutton's terms, or it would make him reject them outright with plans to nail the Governor to the wall by his balls. Pete knew if it looked like the latter, he would probably be asked to make Reece and possibly his family disappear. He was ready either way, but if that fat old fuck barked at him like this again, he was going to have to explain that Reece wasn't the only guy that had information that could cause him problems. *If you didn't want your life to be complicated, you shouldn't have stuck your dick in young boys.*

He decided to head to the airport and change rental cars since his surveillance days weren't yet over. If he appeared in the neighborhood so soon after the mall incident in the same car he had been in earlier, he risked being sighted. Pete knew how to take care of himself, but he had no desire to have to explain himself to the police.

*****

Michael was no longer a man full of fear. Rage had become the predominant emotion enveloping him. He had listened to Anna's recounting of the events at the mall, including the revelation that the man Seth had seen loitering outside their neighborhood was the same one who had toyed with kidnapping his son. The old campaign button had made the message very clear: cooperate or this could become painful for you and the ones you love.

He rolled the button around in his hand and tried desperately to shake away the mental pictures of his son being in the hands of someone like Hal Sutton. The list of the things he had to do began with keeping his family away from harm; everything else was secondary, including his own safety. The security and comfort that was his home had evaporated in a matter of hours, and he no longer felt like this was the best place to be. While Anna went upstairs to pack things for the kids, he dialed the Fort Bragg operator.

CHAPTER 29

"I'll let you guess what my answer is," Chris said in his phone as he sat in a booth at Burger King.

"I knew it would be, but I didn't want to assume anything. It's my answer too."

Michael had relayed the offer put forth by Sutton. What slim chance there had been for him to consider it had vaporized after the incident at the mall. Chris's response was what he predicted, but Reece figured that if anyone had earned the right to decide such a matter, it was him.

Chris was disgusted but not surprised at Sutton's tactics, but it did make him feel somewhat guilty at essentially forcing Michael's involvement. "How're you doing, Mike?"

"Pretty shitty, but I guess it's better than you. Listen, I think you need to change locations every now and then. It's obvious that it's more than just Sutton who is involved, and I would imagine he is going to be gunning for you just as much as me. I've got a few things to take care of here and I'm going to call you back in about an hour. I'm not going to ask much from you, Chris, but I need you to pick up when I call no matter what, and I need you to go along with what I tell you. You trusted me before, and I'm going to need you to trust me again. In the meantime, I want you to stay moving. Once Sutton knows we can't be bought, he is going to look to silence us. Promise me you'll do that."

"I will. Where are you right now?" Truth be told, Chris didn't want to get off the phone. It was nice to talk to someone, and he had made very little headway in what he was going to do next. A lot of it would depend on what Michael decided to do with the discs.

"Give me an hour or so and I'll call you and we will talk about where we go from here. I have some ideas, but I have to get a few things in order first. You just find a new hotel room for now." Michael didn't want to let on, but he was absolutely terrified that Chris was in real danger.

"OK, man, I'll do it. Talk to you in a little bit," Chris replied and ended the call.

Michael put his phone in his pocket as he stood underneath a dogwood tree in the front yard of the Sink House. It hadn't been very long at all since the Reece family had been distinguished visitors at this very home on the grounds of Fort Bragg, and here he was again. Only this time he was more like a refugee than an honored guest. Inside, Anna was unpacking after the four-hour ride from Charlotte. There was a military police officer standing post at the front door and another in a vehicle on the street. This was on top of the fact that they were on a United States Army installation that controlled access to the grounds. Despite all of the events of the day, Michael was pretty comfortable with the idea that his family was safe here.

Tripp came out of the front door and whispered something to the MP nearby, who nodded curtly and remained at his position. He patted his friend on the shoulder as he came out on the lawn to check on him.

"Colonel Collins spoke with General Butts, and the house is yours as long as you need it. The two MPs are going to stay outside tonight, and the Provost Marshall has been briefed on being pretty tight-assed about who is allowed on post. There are MP vehicles a block away in every direction, and anyone that approaches this house will have to explain why they're here."

Michael nodded mainly because he was unsure he could keep his composure if he spoke. Less than five hours after he had reached David on the telephone, Tripp had pulled into his driveway with Colonel Tyson and two other men from the Eighty-Second that he had never met but who had obviously been told that one of their brothers was in danger along with his family. They had been exceedingly friendly and helpful around the family, but their physical appearance and the way they carried themselves would convey only one message to outsiders: don't fuck with us. They had arranged for the family to stay at Sink House as long as they needed, and it was made clear that whatever they required the men and women of the 82nd would find a way to provide. A hand-written note from General Butts was on the coffee table when they arrived, which included his home and cell numbers. No one but Tripp knew any details beyond the fact that someone had threatened Reece's family and they were being followed, but it was all they needed to know to come running.

Tripp squeezed his shoulder slightly. "Look, nothing is gonna happen to them here. No one can get within five hundred feet without some serious fucking guys wanting to have a little talk."

Staring at his feet, Michael was trying to find the right words. "Look, David…I…um, what I mean…"

"You don't need to say anything, sir. I'm glad you called me."

"No," Michael said. "Not sir. This is not a sir kind of moment. Thank you, David. I will never be able to say how much this means to me. You know you're the best friend that I ever had, don't you?"

Reece was many things, but he had never considered himself a tough guy—…especially compared to the guys he had worked with in the Army. He was having a tough time holding it together, but it was important that his friend knew how much he meant to him.

"It's my honor, Mike."

They followed with the classic hug and back slap that was common among men. Tripp had joked once that it was still manly because, even though you're hugging a guy, you're kind of hitting him, too.

They walked into the house, where Michael needed to discuss something with Anna that would not be well received at all.

*****

Riddle was getting a little nervous. Getting another rental car had required going to two separate agencies, since the first had nothing but compact models—which wouldn't have been real conducive to abducting one or more persons, a real possibility, in the near future. Those two trips along with getting something to eat and picking up a few essentials at a local Target had kept him away from Mountain Island Lake for almost eight hours.

He had been to two separate locations near the neighborhood, waiting for a sign of the Reece family, then had driven by the home three times over a period of several hours. There were no signs of activity or even occupancy at the house. Further waiting had made him start to wonder if, instead of them running an errand or going out for a meal, they were gone…and wouldn't be coming back for a while.

He was not aware that they were currently two hundred miles away on a secure Army installation surrounded by military police, all of whom had a copy of the picture Seth Katz had taken of him the day before, furnished by David Tripp. Nevertheless, he was beginning to think the Reece family had shaken him loose. The prospect of calling Sutton and telling him this was about as appealing as taking a good ass-kicking, so he decided to go another route and enlist some assistance. He called Pierce to see what magic he could work.

Pierce already had Reece's cell phone number and sent an encrypted email to his consultant at Southcomm to assign the Drone software to it, while still tracking Tyler's phone as well. Once the software traced the first call made from the particular phone, it could continue to track its location by its "pinging" signal triangulated from the three closest cell phone towers (Tibbert was working on fixing the glitch so it could start tracking immediately without waiting for the first call to be initiated). He assured Riddle that he would have a pretty good fix on Reece as soon as he made his next call.

Nervous or not, he would wait for Pierce to work his magic with the cell phones before making a call to Sutton. Their last conversation hadn't been an enjoyable experience, and there was no reason to poke yet another stick at him. He was getting a little tired of Sutton treating him like some lackey on his staff. He had often compared their relationship to the United States and the Soviet Union at the height of the Cold War: both superpowers would have loved nothing more than for their enemy to disappear from the planet, but both sides were aware that there was no way to make such a wish a reality without an Armageddon-like retaliatory strike in return. It was called MAD—"mutually assured destruction." Lately it seemed that the Governor had forgotten the "mutual" part of their uneasy association.

*****

382

"No," had been Anna's to-the-point reply to her husband's words. Her face showed a look of part confusion and part fear. "You can't do that, Michael."

The married couple was joined by Tripp as they sat in the living room of the Sink House. They each sat in one of the plush leather chairs surrounding the "coin cabinet" that displayed coins of excellence left by previous VIP occupants. There was no one else in the house to hear their conversation. The kids were in the yard playing with Tiny, unaware of the circumstances of their sudden trip to Fayetteville, while several MPs scanned the surrounding area for any signs of anything out of place. The likelihood of that was essentially zero, but, in the Airborne, missions were not accomplished by making unnecessary assumptions.

It was exactly the response he had expected, but this time he couldn't bend to her wishes. "Anna, I have to do this."

Moments ago he had informed his wife that he would be leaving them here while he went to help Chris get out the danger he was certain would be closing in on him.

"No you don't, Michael! This is way bigger than us, and it's time to go to the authorities. Why would you even consider doing anything else? Once they have what you can give them, the people after us will have to leave us alone, and leave Chris alone, too." It made perfect sense to Anna even as she said it, but she was forgetting one big detail.

"It's not that simple, honey. If I go to the authorities, I will have to explain how I got the discs and that means explaining how Chris got them. Sure, any threat to us will probably stop then, but Chris will be charged with murdering a United States Senator, and I have no doubt he'll be facing the death penalty for it. I have to help him, Anna. After that, I will handle it however you want me to. I promise." By the look on her face, he was pretty sure he hadn't convinced her.

"How, Michael? How are you going to help him?" There were tears starting to collect along her lower eyelids, but there was still plenty of resolve behind her face.

Reece knew that his response, albeit honest, was certainly not going to help his case. "I don't know. I'm working on that, and I think it's best I don't tell either of you," he said as he glanced at both his wife and Tripp. "I'm fully aware that I'm probably aiding a fugitive, and I don't want to include either of you in that if I can help it. I know it doesn't sound convincing, but I have to go, Anna."

"Have you asked Chris? Does he even want you to do that? I can't imagine he would want you to put yourself in that situation. You said it yourself, Michael: he apologized for involving you and only asked you to decide what to do with the discs." Her facial expression pleaded with him as she spoke, but she didn't think she was making any headway. She turned to Tripp. "David, talk to him."

Anna's entreaty to him had snapped Tripp out of somewhat of a trance. He had felt like a spectator in the conversation between the two and was caught off guard by her remark.

"Look, Mike...I think she might have a point. I have no doubt that your intentions are honorable, but this is a whole other level with what you're considering. Not only will you probably be committing a felony, but there are people out there," he said as he pointed out the window "that are *very* dedicated to making sure you fail, by whatever means necessary. I don't think these people are staffers for Sutton; I think these are professionals that wouldn't be conflicted at all about harming you or your family. I think you need to think about yourself at little here. I'm just saying that—"

"No!" Michael interrupted. He seemed genuinely stung that Tripp was taking Anna's side on this. "Don't say that to me!"

David raised his hands to his shoulders. "Look, I just think you need to think this through. That's all I'm saying."

"No I don't, Booger! All the while I'm sitting here in safety is more time that someone has to find Chris, and I don't have any illusions of what they have planned for him. They were willing to threaten me and Anna with kidnapping or harming our kids. Just what do you think they will do to the man that killed Haxton? They see him as a loose end, and loose ends get cut."

Michael stood up and faced both of them while he continued. "There was a time in my life that I was offered a ticket out of something very bad. It was a ticket to better things, and I took it. I walked away from a hell that Chris and Darnell were left to burn in. I went on to find success and wealth and have people lined up to tell me how fucking special and inspirational I am when all I did was abandon two people that were like family to me!"

Anna interrupted him. "Michael, you didn't know that they were being abused. You told me that yourself."

"I didn't know because I didn't want to know! I wanted out so bad that I allowed myself to be blind to what I might be leaving behind. Now look at me! I've got a family, a career, more money than I could ever need, friends, and a lot more. What do they have? Darnell is dead and Chris is on the run from the law, not to mention from people who are going to fucking kill him!" Reece took his own turn at pointing to the window. "He's out there too, you know! He has been abandoned or hurt by pretty much anyone he has trusted, including me, and he needs help. I understand neither of you wants me to go, but I'm going. I'm willing to accept whatever consequences it brings, but I'm not going to turn my back on Manny!"

He hadn't even realized he had said the wrong name, and both Anna and David sat silent for a moment. Neither was accustomed to seeing Michael this way. In fact, David had a hard time remembering a time that he had even seen Reece raise his voice. Nevertheless, both of them now understood what was driving him, and both were certain they wouldn't be able to change his mind.

"Mike, you said Manny...you said Manny instead of Chris."

There was a delicateness in David's voice that belied his anything-but-delicate appearance. It was a side of Michael he hadn't seen before, but he had experienced it in others often. Standing in front of him was a man on a mission, and he wasn't going to be denied. Michael would try to snap him in half if he tried to stop him and, at this moment, Tripp was pretty sure he would succeed.

It took Reece a few seconds to process what Tripp had said to him and realize that both people with him at the moment understood what it meant.

"So what if I did?" he said after a moment's contemplation. "All my life, I have walked away from hellish situations smelling like a rose while others have been left behind. I turned my back on Chris a long time ago for a better deal, and now I have a chance to pay some of that back." He looked at Anna. "I love you, Anna. I love you more than anything in this world. I'm not asking you to understand why I have to do this, but I need you to trust me."

Her tears would no longer be confined and were flowing down her face. She stood and put her arms around her husband and let it all out. It was no longer a question of if she could talk him out of it. He was going. He would leave this place of sanctuary and would be once again among the wolves.

Michael looked at his friend over his wife's shoulder. "I'm sorry about yelling at you both. I need you to watch over my family while I'm gone."

Anna pulled back from embracing her husband and looked at Tripp. "No. David, you have to go with him."

Tripp was looking at Michael and nodding. "You're goddamn right I'm going with him."

Anna looked at her husband. "Honey, we are fine here. I know I can't stop you from going, but you're not going alone."

"No," replied Michael, shaking his head. "Listen, it's not just about you being in danger. You could be possibly committing a crime. I can't put you in that situation. I can't ask you to do that."

"You've got a lot of fucking nerve saying that to me right now," Tripp said, adopting his usual NCO vocabulary. "Don't stand here and lecture me on not abandoning your friends and then expect me to sit here and wring my hands while you go out there against who the fuck knows. It's not a question of you asking me to do it. I'm fucking telling you I'm doing it. I would have never made it after getting shot that night if it wasn't for you, and you goddamned well know it. You saved my life and put yours at risk to do it." He pointed to Michael's left leg. "And you didn't walk away. You were fucking carried away almost dead. No one has a chance of getting to Anna and the kids here. No one gets on this post if we don't want them to. No one but us knows the who and why someone is after you and your family, and it doesn't matter, cause they do know that one of our own is in danger of being harmed. You know and I know that they are not going to let that happen on their watch. If Jesus Christ wanted to pay a visit to Bragg right now, he would have to ask the Provost Marshall's permission. I know you're going, but I'm going with you, and I'll lay down in front of your fucking car if I have to. So go pack your shit and we'll get going. I already have a bag in the car."

Tripp then turned to Anna. "Nothing is going to happen to him. I promise you I will do ANYTHING required to keep him safe, including kicking his one-legged ass if he won't let me go."

Michael knew a lost cause when he saw one. "Yes, sir."

Tripp smiled at the quip and hugged his friend. "Call me Sergeant. I work for a living."

Several minutes later, Michael had hugged his family, promising to be back soon, and met with Tyson as well as the NCOIC of the Ft. Bragg Military Police, who both assured him that no one would be given an opportunity to get close to his family without having to explain themselves first to multiple very serious people. They left Michael's truck at the Sink House and headed west in Tripp's GMC Yukon, with Reece spending almost the entire trip making calls on his phone.

*****

Randall McCray tossed his bag on the bed in his room at the Foothill Lodge. He had requested a room on the front side of the building, which gave him a view of the common entrance that fed to the three hotels just off the interstate in Asheville. This was the location from which the Drone program had gotten several pings from Chris Tyler's cell phone. He indulged in a shower after the long drive from the eastern part of the state, then pulled the desk chair in his room to the window and sat there with binoculars, hoping to get lucky.

McCray's instructions were simple: he was to find Tyler and kill him. The only parts that were left to his judgment were how to do it and how to dispose of the body. In his bag was a 9 mm Beretta fitted with a silencer, zip ties, several industrial-sized plastic garbage bags, an eight-inch hunting knife, and a Taser.

He was not the least bit conflicted about killing a man. He had done it before and he would receive an impressive sum of money if he was successful. His only worry at the moment was finding Tyler. The phone tracking information was helpful but only gave him a general area to focus on, so he scanned the hotel parking lots and entrances for any sign of his target.

*****

Gabriel Drake had departed Grand Bahama Yacht Club after having about a twenty-minute conversation on his phone. After guiding the vessel out of the marina waters, he turned on a heading of 275 degrees for the roughly one-hundred-mile trip to the Old Port Cove Marina in West Palm Beach, Florida. Between phone calls and working his portable computer in the wheelhouse, he had arranged for a two-man crew to take *The Sculpted Lady* from there back to Southport as well as purchased airfare on a flight from Palm Beach International to Charlotte-Douglas International Airport.

His office was not scheduled to reopen for another two weeks, and that would not change despite the early ending to his Caribbean odyssey. The weather was perfect and the ocean surface was smooth. He settled into his plush captain's chair and increased the speed slightly. A man who was hesitant to ask a favor of anyone had contacted him and asked a big one, and it had taken Drake less than five seconds to agree to it.

*****

Chris parked in the parking lot of a local storefront strip mall and walked into Mobile Solutions. He paid cash for three prepaid cell phones with belt clips and tipped the attendant to charge all three with a promise to return in about two hours to retrieve them.

He had chosen this strip mall because its stores could cover his many needs. His next stop was a military surplus store, where he purchased a steel telescopic baton and a pair of binoculars. A camping supply store was only a few stores down, and there he purchased a fanny pack for his baton and a small backpack. He had a little over half an hour before the phones

388

would be ready, so he dropped in to a family-owned Mexican restaurant and ordered a burrito and rice for some needed fuel.

His shopping spree had been spurred by a call from Reece who had caught him up on the events since their last talk, including the episode at the mall. Michael had told him that he had little doubt that Chris was in danger and needed to take precautions in order to be safe—and hard to find. His old friend advised him that anything could be tracked, which led Chris to the first store, and that his pursuers probably meant him harm, which led him to the second. None of that part of the conversation had been surprising, nor had the news that there were now two copies of the discs, one with Michael and the other in a very safe location.

But the latter part of the call had been surprising indeed. After stopping in Charlotte, Reece was heading to Asheville, with the pledge that he was going to do everything in his power to get Chris not only to safety but out of the current predicament his actions on Figure Eight Island had created. Chris's initial irritation that the discs had not been turned over to anyone yet was allayed by the realization that Michael had every intention of exposing Sutton but first wanted to get his old friend to safety. He had listened to the broad strokes of the plan and Michael's request for his permission to go forward with it. At first it had seemed ludicrous, almost like a cheap movie, but as Michael explained how he would go about it, Chris had to agree that it was far better than anything he could manage himself.

The conversation had further convinced him that he had certainly been wrong about the assumptions he had made about Michael's departure from Sycamore. Handing over the discs to the authorities or the media would have certainly put Michael in a position of having to answer some awkward questions as well as having to decide whether to reveal his own tortured past, but shortly after that he could have gone on with his life, which seemed pretty good, and Chris would have considered the two of them all square. What Michael was proposing now not only made him guilty of a crime but also put him, and his family, in considerable danger. This was far beyond what Chris had expected of him, but he was immediately rebutted when he tried to say it was more than Michael should be doing.

As he pushed around the food on his plate, he felt saddened by the fact that their reconnection should be the rebirth of a long overdue brotherhood...but it wouldn't be. Even if he survived the next several days and didn't wind up in prison facing the death penalty, their lives would likely be very separate by necessity. Nothing in the plan changed the fact that he had killed a man in his own home. Regardless of the hideousness of the victim's existence, it was still murder. Dead or alive, there would no longer be a Chris Tyler.

In the end, refusing Michael's offer wasn't an option, and he thanked him for everything. He had told him where to go when they made it to Asheville, which was where he would be going in a little while. As he paid his bill at the restaurant, he realized that he would have been penniless days ago if it hadn't been for Michael. He left the restaurant and picked up the phones from the mobile store. Climbing into the Land Cruiser, he had one more stop to make before checking out of the hotel. He couldn't help smiling a bit as he turned on the fully functional air conditioning in the truck, a decent upgrade from his own pickup that was currently hidden in a storage locker on the coast.

*****

Alex Bradley was right in his prediction that there wouldn't be very much material in the archives on the untimely death of Charles Raymond Potts. There was a transcribed autopsy report as well as several radiograph films. It had not been part of a criminal investigation, but deaths that occurred outside the supervision of a medical facility or professional were required to be evaluated by autopsy.

The first page of the autopsy report listed the usual identifying information about the deceased. It described the presumed cause of death as motor vehicle accident, or "MVA." He could see that the body had been taken directly to the Office of the Medical Examiner and did not first go to a local Emergency Room, which told Bradley that he was pronounced dead at the scene of the accident. There were signatures of the person who received the body as well as the autopsy technician and the pathologist who had performed the actual evaluation and dictated the report. He noted the physician was Dr. Paul Peterson, who had passed away from colon cancer about six years ago and wouldn't be available to discuss the case if Alex needed to do so.

There was a note from the Highway Patrol officer who was in charge of the actual accident scene, describing the condition and position of the car, as well as two photographs of the actual vehicle after the body had been removed. The next heading of the report was titled "Gross Description," which was a summation of the general appearance of the body before any dissection or detailed examination:

"Well nourished adult black male. No obvious skeletal deformities noted. It is noted that the cranial structure appears misshapen consistent with significant head trauma with the appearance of a subdermal hematoma in the occipital region of the skull. There is no bruising noted in the sternal region suggesting that there was not a deployed air bag at the time of the accident. A military-themed tattoo is noted on the deltoid region of the left arm. There is subdermal blood collection in the area above the cervical spine likely secondary to post-mortem migration from head trauma. The lower back, gluteal, and genital area appear free of external injuries."

Nothing so far seemed out of the ordinary. Bradley had long ago lost count of the number of MVA cases in which the deceased had died from head trauma and nothing else. If there was no rollover of the vehicle and the impact was from the front, such as in this case, there was usually significant trauma to either the face or parietal area (commonly called the "forehead"), usually resulting in either significant intracranial bleeding or simple shearing-effect injuries to the brain and brain stem. Paradoxically, the posterior brain tended to show the most damage on examination, from the snapping backward of the brain against the skull after the initial frontal impact. It was called a "contrecoup" brain injury, and its classic characteristics revealed brain hemorrhage or other damage on the opposite side of the actual skull trauma.

It was usual in a frontal impact accident for the chest to show injury from impact with the dash or steering wheel and for the face to show injury from impact with the windshield. Bradley was somewhat surprised by the lack of injury in these areas of Potts's body. But, while it was unusual, it was by no means impossible.

The description in the "Gross Dissection" section mentioned again the presence of hematomas on the back of the head and posterior neck, as well as significant ecchymosis and

391

bruising on the surface of the occipital portion of the brain. Nothing else in the description of this section had been of any significance.

The third section was titled "Microscopic Examination" and entailed a collection of tissue samples from different body organs including the brain, liver, heart, lung, and kidney, which were examined under a microscope after preparation for signs of disease that may not be obvious on examination with the naked eye. It noted some mild atherosclerotic disease consistent with high cholesterol but no signs of blocked coronary arteries that could have suggested that a massive heart attack caused the single-car accident. There were no other signs of abnormalities.

"Ancillary Investigation" was next. It contained one item, which stated that blood samples from the victim showed no signs of alcohol or illicit drugs.

The "Autopsy Summary of Findings" stated:

"Patient is a middle-aged black male overall in good health and well nourished. Investigation is consistent with death from acute significant blunt head trauma from impact resulting in significant intracranial hemorrhage. Frontal impact is supported by the classic contrecoup injury findings on the occipital cortex of the brain. No contributing factors such as alcohol or other agents were identified in the patient's blood. Incidental finding of mild atherosclerotic disease is noted but no evidence of acute myocardial event."

The translation was: this unfortunate man had been in a single-vehicle accident and had sustained head injuries that killed him. He had some high cholesterol but he hadn't had a heart attack while driving. He wasn't high and he wasn't drunk; he probably fell asleep at the wheel.

Bradley was about to close the folder and call his friend to tell him it looked like a tragic, but not unusual, fatal car accident, when he remembered the radiographs. They weren't mentioned in the dictated report but were in the jacket attached to the file. Of all the possible explanations for this, the simplest, not to mention the most likely, was that Peterson had forgotten to do a write-up about them. The question was, however, did he forget to mention it in the report or did he forget to review them? Doctors were human like anyone, and determining the cause of death in the case would have seemed about as straightforward as a three-hundred pound truck driver who eats a steak-and-egg breakfast, clutches his chest, and collapses on the floor. It wasn't that Peterson was a bad doctor; he was quite the contrary, but everyone makes assumptions and mistakes, including doctors.

He pulled the head film out of the jacket and realized something was not right. It was called *scotomata*. Its literal definition is a visual blind spot caused by looking directly at the sun, but an alternative one is a mental blind spot. One's mind can convince itself that it sees what matches preconceived notions or conclusions. A body comes in from a car accident where everything suggests a frontal impact severe head injury. There are obvious signs of head trauma on inspection and no other obvious signs of injury. Maybe he was tired from a bad night's sleep or maybe it was the end of the day. It really didn't matter, but the plain film radiograph Bradley now held in his hand in front of an overhead light above him told a different story.

It could have been easily missed on gross visual inspection, but the x-ray didn't lie. Along the mid-occipital area (also known as the back of the head) was a linear transverse fracture depressing the skull inward that was likely the cause of the massive intracranial bleed that ultimately killed Mr. Potts, with virtually no sign of frontal head trauma. The line of the fracture virtually mimicked the line that the autopsy technician would use to saw the "cap" off the top of the skull to remove the brain for examination. Once the top of the skull was removed, the fracture could be hidden as part of the saw line, and the examining physician would see clotted blood in the skull cavity and a large contusion on the back of the brain that would look very much like a classic contrecoup injury from a frontal impact. There would likely have been enough blood to fill the area between the brain and skull to cause some discoloration of the frontal area. It wasn't a criminal investigation autopsy, and simply forgetting to look at the films from a clear-cut MVA case could have been enough to miss it.

He looked at the photograph of the wrecked vehicle and noted that it had padded headrests. He could see nothing behind him that could have impacted Potts on the back of the head, and Bradley didn't know any scenario where, in the split second before a head-on collision, a man would turn around 180 degrees and look out the back window before he hit. There were probably multiple things that could explain the oddity, most of which would be completely benign, but he did know that it didn't fit the story in the autopsy report.

It wasn't remotely enough to make a hurried call to the District Attorney. All he could conclude was that there were discrepancies between the true cause of death and the official report. There was simply no more information to mine without exhuming the body, and he didn't have anything to justify such a request. But he had done this as a favor for a friend, and he planned to let him know what he'd found.

He picked up the phone and called the number Michael had given him and explained the findings on the radiographs compared to the autopsy report. He was dying to know what had made his friend ask him to look into this particular case, but Reece told him it wasn't a good time to talk and promised to talk to him more another time. Reece thanked him for doing him a huge favor and got off the phone.

Alex was even more confused now, and it seemed that his friend seemed very tired and in a hurry. That being said, he had plenty of current work to do and decided to get back to it until he had a chance to talk with him further. Before getting back to reviewing slides for another case, he checked his email and noted a thank-you note from Special Agent Meredith Scott for supplying the tissue samples requested in a case of a suicide he had performed an autopsy on not long ago.

*****

"They killed him, David," Michael said as he ended the call from Asheville.

"What?" Tripp responded from the driver's seat. They were now on the outer loop of Interstate 485 and minutes away from the Reece home.

"Mr. Charlie...they killed him." By now Michael had told Tripp pretty much everything about his upbringing and what was going on currently, and that included Chris's somewhat cryptic remark about the death of Charlie Potts.

Tripp took his eye away from the windshield briefly to look at his friend. There was a vacancy of emotion, as if he was too tired to even cry. They had both worked some extremely odd and long hours in Afghanistan, but the look of complete exhaustion on Reece's face right now was more than physical fatigue; it was an empty emotional tank. In a short amount of time, he had learned that he wasn't the only one exploited at his childhood home, one of his friends was dead, another was on the run from the law for murder, his family had been threatened, and now he had learned that the man that had been more of a father to him than anyone had probably been murdered by the same people that were after him and Chris.

"I'm sorry, brother. I really am."

There wasn't much more that could be said, but it reinforced the idea that the people pursuing them meant to do serious harm to the man who had saved his life while forsaking his own safety to do so. Tripp's debt to his friend was one that Reece would never ask to be repaid, but Tripp damned well meant to do it anyway.

"We're going to get out of this mess, and there will be a reckoning for them."

Michael's face still showed the vacated look the most recent phone call had triggered. "Everyone who becomes close to me finds harm at some time or another. Maybe I'm cursed. Maybe I'm paying for some horrible sin from a previous life." He rubbed his face as if willing his hands to wipe away the most encompassing exhaustion he had ever experienced.

"That's bullshit, Mike," his friend replied. "I won't argue that the things you have experienced in your life would make you doubt that there is such a thing as karma, but you're not cursed. You're a good man, and I'm pretty sure there is a lady and two kids back at Bragg who would disagree with your theory too. You've had some shitty luck in your life; I won't argue that, but it's going to change after we get through all this. Right now, if you'll forgive me saying, you've got to put all that shit aside. We've got a job to do, and we can argue karma and reincarnation another time."

"Yes, Sergeant." Tripp had achieved some vestige of a smile from his friend. It was brief, but it served its purpose. Michael sighed as he looked out the window to nothing in particular. "I've got to save Chris. I've got to get him out of this mess."

*****

There were perks to being a Colonel in the United States Army. One of those was that picking up a phone and making a request made things happen—and usually pretty quickly. The Asheville component of the 3297th Army Hospital was a reserve unit that mainly served to backfill position needs at Dwight Eisenhower Medical Center in Augusta, Georgia. They had requested one of the medevac helicopters belonging to the Eighty-Second to come to Asheville, where unit members could receive some training on transporting simulated patients.

Before taking off, the crew had received a call that COL Tyson had a meeting in Asheville and would like to catch a ride on the modified Blackhawk if at all possible. This was followed shortly by a call from General Butts asking the same. The requests were enthusiastically approved, and Greg Tyson climbed aboard in his ACU uniform with a medium duffel bag as his only baggage.

He had no idea if he was going to have to do anything while there, but SFC David Tripp had contacted him and filled him in on some rather jaw-dropping details as to what was going on with their friend MAJ Michael Reece. Tripp had informed him of everything, out of respect, since he would be asking the man to possibly break the law to help a friend. Tyson took no time before agreeing. He had simply informed General Butts that he had a personal matter to take care of in Asheville that involved helping out Reece and asked if he would help get him there as quick as possible. Tyson had kept the details from his Commanding Officer to protect him, and if there were consequences to that he would face them and not drag his CO into it as well.

He patted the bag that contained a few days' worth of civilian clothing as he watched the North Carolina countryside pass under him. Tripp had explained that he was asking him to be there "just in case," and it was a request that Reece was completely unaware of, since he would never consider putting his own CO in this type of situation. Tyson knew that he might have to make decisions in the next few days that could cost him his career, but he was willing to do what he had to. The Army is a brotherhood above all else, and soldiers in need will always be able to count on their comrades to come to their aide. He thought about a quote he had in his office from a Filipino named Carlos Romulo, who served with Douglas MacArthur in the Pacific: "Brotherhood is the very price and condition of man's survival."

After the Blackhawk landed at the Asheville airport, Tyson thanked the crew for the ride. He changed into civilian clothes in the airport bathroom and caught a taxi to a hotel, where he checked in and texted Tripp with the information. He would stay here for two days in case they needed help, after which he would head back to Fayetteville and back to his regular duties with no one the wiser.

CHAPTER 30

"Holy shit," Riddle said into his phone. "This is really bad news."

"Just relax," Pierce instructed him. "Yes, our first hit was about 160 miles southeast, but each additional ping is tracing a path right back to you. I think the best thing you can do is to stay put. I'll keep tracing the signal and will let you know if it deviates from a trail back to you or when he's close. Trust me; I do this for a living."

That had been the sum total of the conversation Riddle had with Pierce earlier, and he now looked at the text telling him that Reece (or at least Reece's phone) was just a few miles away. He had no further instructions from Sutton and decided to visually confirm that it was indeed his target before celebrating that he hadn't lost him after all.

The portion of Mountain Island Lake that the Reece property backed up to was a wide, finger-like projection off the main water body with homes on each side. Riddle had been lucky enough to find a home for sale that was unoccupied on the opposite side of the water. It took little effort to break in and confirm that no one had been here in quite a while. He decided to gamble that the depressed housing market in Charlotte meant that no prospective customers would be coming for a tour with their realtor today and opened the garage in order to hide his vehicle from view. There was no furniture in the house, but he located a large empty paint bucket to use as a seat while he trained his binoculars on the Reece driveway across the water.

Less than half an hour later, he observed a large SUV pull up to the house and enter the garage. The tinting on the windows didn't allow him to confirm it was Reece in the truck before it entered and was out of sight. A quick call to Pierce confirmed that the signal from the phone triangulated in the area of the house, so it was safe to assume that Reece's phone had arrived with the vehicle. But he had to make sure it was indeed its owner who was in possession of it. If it had been given to someone else, he would have to make the dreaded call to Sutton to inform him that Reece had eluded him.

Riddle gathered his things and made a quick sweep of the home to ensure he had left no sign of his visit. He would call Pierce after he confirmed Reece was at the house and then simply keep on him until he received more instructions. He pulled out of the garage and manually closed it before leaving the property. He found a public boat-access ramp less than a quarter mile from the Reece home, where he would park and make his way on foot to the house.

*****

Michael and David had done a walking tour of the house to look for any signs of disturbance and hadn't found any. Reece grabbed the first caffeinated thing he found in the fridge and tossed one to Tripp as well. The plan was to be here long enough to get a few items together and then head west to Asheville. The answering machine was blinking the number three.

The first message was from a telemarketing firm, followed by a sleepover invitation for Elizabeth for the upcoming weekend. The third message had a voice that didn't identify himself, but Michael knew who it was immediately.

"Hello, Mr. Reece. We are calling to see if you have a response to the proposal we had discussed earlier. Please call me at your earliest convenience. Thank you and have a good day."

It was telling that this call had been made to his home rather than his mobile phone, which had been the case before. The message was clear: *we know where you live*. He unconsciously looked out the windows for any threats; they purposely left the interior lights of the house off so as to not advertise their presence.

"That's Sutton. He wants to keep the pressure on me."

"I think you're right. I think we should get whatever we need and hit the road. The more we are out in a public area, the better. You go ahead and pack up and I'll keep a look out."

Reece nodded and headed to the bedroom to put some clothes and other items in a bag. He opened his gun locker and clipped his pistol to his belt under an untucked shirt. He thought about calling Chris to update him but decided against it. Chris had given him instructions as to what to do when he got to Asheville and how to contact him, and there wasn't really any new information to share with him. Michael realized he mainly wanted the reassurance that his friend was still OK. Instead, he grabbed a pen and a piece of Anna's stationary from her bedside table and sat on the edge of the bed to write her a note. It was important that she knew how much he loved her and why he was doing this, and he decided to put it to paper for her just in case he didn't come out of this alive. He fought the terrible feelings of guilt for the situation she and the kids were in right now. He had written a "just in case" note like this the day before leaving for Afghanistan and had happily burned it when he made it home alive.

He completed it as quickly as he could, placed it in one of the envelopes she used to send friends and loved ones letters on occasion, and laid it on the pillow on her side of the bed. He kissed his fingertips, touched the envelope, and turned to leave the bedroom—which was when he saw Tripp's massive frame in the doorway. He held a finger to his mouth, telling him to stay quiet, followed by his palm telling him to stay put. The outside light had faded, which made it difficult to see even Tripp's silhouette in the unlit house, but it was clear he had headed to the back door.

Pete Riddle hadn't heard a single footstep before one large hand clamped over his mouth and nose while the other secured his right arm behind him. The leg of a man much bigger than him had curled around the inside of his own and, while he remained upright, he was completely immobilized. He made a token effort to free himself only to be rewarded by upward pressure on his arm to the degree that he felt his shoulder ligaments being stressed to their peak.

"You can do this the easy way or the hard way, motherfucker, but I won't hesitate to snap your fucking neck right now. You need to understand that you are going to do what I want. It's only a question of what I have to do to you first to make you understand."

The breath was hot against his ear, and he knew from the man's size alone that it wasn't Reece. The way the man was speaking to him also made it clear that it wasn't the police, which made him even more terrified.

"Now, flinch again or try to scream and I'll rip this arm right off and shove it up your fucking ass."

Riddle had absolutely zero doubt that the man behind him had both the ability and resolve to do exactly what he had just said. He nodded his head, signaling his surrender, and then found himself being slammed face down to the ground with enough force that he wasn't sure all of his ribs were in the same configuration they had been only moments ago.

"I'm going to take my hand away from your mouth, but if you make any noise, I promise you it will be decision you regret for the rest of your life. Can I trust you to be smart?" said the voice still behind him.

He had no choice. He nodded again and tried to catch his breath once the large and somewhat scarred hand came off his mouth. He dared not breathe too loud for the fear of what might be the consequence of doing so. The release of the hand to his face was quickly followed by a metallic pressure to the back of his head that was unmistakably the working end of some sort of handgun. A knee was pressed painfully between his shoulder blades while the other leg was pinned against the inner side of his right knee. The other hand was now searching Riddle and quickly removed the handgun and knife from his waist, followed by his wallet and cell phone.

Once satisfied that the man was divested of any possessions that could be hazardous, Tripp leaned forward to his ear again. "I'm going to lift you up and you're going to walk where I guide you. Don't make a fucking sound and don't make any sudden moves or I'll turn your heart into ground meat. Can I still count on you to make the right decisions?"

Riddle nodded again and noted with fear that the man lifted him to his feet with almost no effort. As they approached the French doors leading inside, he could see the reflection of his captor in the glass silhouetted against the fading light over the water. He was easily six inches taller than he was, and his shoulders belonged to someone who would chase quarterbacks for a lot of money on Sundays. As the cool air from the inside of the house hit him, he was no longer able to keep from shaking. He was spun around with ease and slammed against the wall while his tormentor pressed the muzzle of his pistol to his forehead.

"I'm not going to ask you twice and I think you know the consequences if you lie to me. Is there anyone else out there who's with you?" Tripp asked.

Riddle shook his head and felt an inner panic as the man moved the pistol from his face and pressed it firmly against his balls.

"Are you sure?"

"Yes…yes I'm sure. There's nobody but me," Riddle replied as he tried to move his backside further into the wall to get some distance between his genitals and the gun. It was definitely not Reece, and Riddle had no illusions that he had any chance of overpowering this hulk and getting away.

Tripp turned to the doorway to the bedroom. "Mike, you can come out now."

Riddle saw Reece come out from the doorway. The border of his jaw was sharply defined as he clinched his teeth looking at their new captive.

"Kinda looks like our guy doesn't it?" Tripp said.

Michael pulled out a copy of the picture Seth had taken on his dog walk and compared the image with the man against his wall. "It's him."

Tripp turned his face back to Riddle and smiled in a way that almost made the man lose control of his bowels. "Man, you're really fucked. This man saved my life, and you threatened his wife and kids." Looking back at Reece, he said, "I need something to tie him up."

*****

Their meeting began as they always had: with prayer. Both men arose from their knees and sat on a pew at Victory Assembly Church of Christ. The Reverend Billy Cash looked at his friend, noticed the bloodshot eyes and look of exhaustion, and had a direct question for him.

"Chris, do you have something you want to tell me, brother?"

Tyler didn't get the inferred meaning of the question. "There are so many things I want to tell you, brother Billy, but I can't right now."

Billy leaned toward his friend and placed a hand on his shoulder. "Brother, there is nothing that you can't tell me. What made you do it?"

Chris was shocked by the question. How does he know? And if he knows, who else knows? He had to think about his answer after recovering from the jolt of the query.

"I didn't mean to...it wasn't something I planned to do. I didn't even realize it until after it happened."

Billy shook his head slightly and adopted his mentor tone. "Brother Chris, temptation can happen at any moment, but one must take responsibility for his actions. The devil's hand of temptation is always present, but we as God's children must keep the strength to resist." As he often did with his flock, he followed up his admonishment with encouragement. "It's all right. Many have fallen off the wagon...and many get right back on. We'll get through this."

It all came together with the last two sentences. Chris actually began to laugh at the misunderstanding. It was the first moment of humor he could remember in a long time.

"Billy, I haven't fallen off the wagon. I'm as clean as the last time we saw each other. Those days are behind me, brother."

Cash adopted the look of a somewhat suspicious parent. "Chris, it's all right if you did. You are here and I'm your sponsor and we can work through it. I promise I'm not mad at you, my brother."

As humorous as the misunderstanding was, he had things that he had to do, and he didn't want to stay in one place for very long right now. He pulled the Holy Bible out of Billy's lap and put his hand on it.

"I swear on my faith as a child of God that I haven't used drugs of any kind or alcohol of any kind since we last saw each other." He handed the book back to his friend.

Billy was immediately satisfied. Chris had made his share of mistakes, but since he had embraced the love of God and the teachings of Jesus Christ he had exhibited faith that was stronger than almost anyone he had in his congregation. There was nothing that would allow him to place his hand on the Lord's book and lie to his friend, sponsor, and pastor.

"All right, brother Chris, I believe you. What, pray tell, were you talking about then?"

"That's something I can't share with you right now," Chris replied. "I do have to ask you a question, though. Do you trust me, Billy? I mean really trust me?"

"Of course I do, Chris. You should know that by now," was Billy's somewhat confused response.

"I don't mean to doubt anything about you. I need you to do something for me." He handed two cell phones to the reverend. "There's a man named Michael that's going to come here. When he does, I need you to give these to him. It will let him keep in touch with me for the next several days. He's going to help me, and I trust him as much as I trust you. My faith in him is the same as my faith in God." This elicited raised eyebrows from his friend. "He should be here within the next twenty-four hours, but I'm not sure what time. You can trust him."

"Of course, Chris; I'll give them to him. Are you in trouble?"

Chris paused before speaking. He rejected his initial impulse to reassure his friend, which would require a lie.

"Yes, I am. There are some people out there who are trying to hurt me. They are the same people that drove my brother to do what he did. They're also trying to harm my friend I just told you about." Chris's eyes conveyed an apologetic look. "I can't say more than that right now, and you won't be able to get in touch with me for a while. If you trust me, I need you to not ask anything more else."

Billy looked at his friend and decided that he had come a long way from the wayward knucklehead that had let drugs lead his life that he used to know. "You can count on me, brother. You just make sure that you do get in touch with me when the time comes."

The two men embraced, and Chris handed him the two phones. Billy placed one in each of his front pockets. They both decided to pray once more, and then Chris left out of the back entrance.

*****

The blinds in the windows surrounding the living room had been closed and a few lights had been turned on. Riddle sat in a dining room chair but was by no means comfortable. His wrists and ankles were bound together with zip ties along with duct tape just above the joint line. He was surprised that he was asked if he had to go to the bathroom before he was immobilized. In addition, he was not gagged. But it was clearly understood that if he made any noise beyond answering their questions, he would soon be requiring significant dental work.

"Are you going to kill me?" Riddle asked his captors.

Michael was sitting across from him. "No. I'm not like you. But I do need some information. It is important for you to understand, however, that if I feel you have any future plans to harm my family, I will have no reservations about ending your life."

"I understand," was his reply.

He was no longer shaking, as he had come to realize that he probably wasn't going to die here. He noted that when he had been bound, Reece had made sure to put a layer of Ace wrap bandage under the zip ties for comfort and made sure he had water and the ability to go to the bathroom if he needed. He had heard Reece call the other man David, but he was no less terrified of the guy as he had been when his pistol had been pressed against his balls.

Michael had gone through his wallet then placed everything back inside, including the money. David had taken the knife and gun and disassembled them. He took the pieces to the garage and worked them over with a steel mallet, rendering both forever useless.

"Why are you following me?" Michael asked.

405

"I was hired to," he said. There was no reason to lie about it anymore. The movie scenes of people willing to be tortured and maltreated to protect secrets did not apply to Riddle. He wasn't about to have anything bad done to him for an asshole like Sutton.

"Was it Sutton who hired you to follow me, and what did he want you to do to me?"

"I was told to just follow you and await further instructions." Riddle saw David lean forward with a look that conveyed he wasn't convinced that was true. "I swear. We were following your friend, and when he gave you something, I was told to watch you too. It was Sutton that hired us."

"You said us," Tripp interrupted. "I thought you said there was no one else with you."

"There isn't...I swear. The other guy is following your friend," he said as he looked back at Reece. He noticed that Michael's body language changed with that remark.

"Does the other person have the same instructions as you? I mean is he only supposed to observe?" Michael asked.

"I don't know." Riddle didn't think this was technically a lie, since he didn't know if McCray instructions had changed or not. "We haven't communicated with each other since I was told to follow you."

"Do you have any instructions to do anything to my family?" Michael had a very different demeanor as he asked that particular question.

"Look, I wasn't going to do anything. I just wanted to scare them a little bit and see if you would back off. It wasn't a big deal."

The open-handed slap that came from David made Riddle see stars and taste blood. When his visual focus came back, the giant had moved his chair very close to him.

"I won't go easy on you next time, motherfucker. Just answer the questions and let us decide what is a big deal and what isn't. Do you understand?" Tripp was given a vigorous nod.

"No. There are no instructions to do that," Riddle said to Michael.

It was David's turn. "Are you supposed to check in at certain intervals or communicate in any way with anyone, so if you don't they will assume you're exposed?"

"No. In fact, I was starting to think about telling Sutton to go fuck himself. I have other things to do besides being his errand boy. I'm just supposed to keep up with you until he tells me what to do next. I hate the fucking guy too. He's got me by the balls with some information. I guess you could say that we both could fuck the other guy over enough that we have to do each other favors sometimes."

Michael sat in silence for two full minutes and gestured to Tripp to wait as well. Afterward, he leaned forward to Riddle.

"Would it be fair to say that you don't feel compelled to protect Sutton if you had the opportunity to walk away from him?"

"Well...yeah...absolutely. I don't owe him shit."

Michael nodded, and Tripp could see wheels turning in his mind. "My friend and I are going to talk over there in the next room. It's important for you to understand that we can still see you. Do you need any water?"

Riddle shook his head and watched the two men walk out of earshot but not out of sight.

"Why don't we just drop his ass off at the police station with a note?" Tripp asked Michael.

"We can't...at least not until I make sure Chris is safe. I really don't know what to do with him right now. I can't let him go, but I've got to get to Chris."

"We'll take him with us," Tripp told him.

He explained (and apologized for freelancing a bit) that Greg Tyson was in Asheville at a hotel waiting to help them in any way they needed. Tripp quickly told Reece that he had explained fully what was going on, and Tyson had not been put in a situation that could bring him personal or professional harm without really knowing why.

"Listen, if my idea of getting Tyson involved backfires, you can put your one good leg right up my ass and I won't complain. But think about it. We don't really have a choice."

Reece couldn't argue with that point and surrendered to the logic of it.

Tripp had one more idea, though. "I'll get him ready to go, but there's a phone call you need to make. But don't let him know we have this guy." He explained why, and they agreed that it was their best option going forward. He walked back to the dining table while Michael went to make the call in private.

Sitting down directly in front of Riddle, he checked to make sure that all the zip ties were still secure. "OK, I think you're too fucking stupid to realize it, but you might have a way out of this. You're going to go on a car ride with us, and you're not going to cause any trouble. We have a friend that's going to keep an eye on you while we do a few things, and then, just maybe, you might be able to walk away from this." He slid his chair to where his face was mere inches from Riddle's. "But you understand this and you understand real fucking good. If you do anything that makes it more difficult for my friend, I'm going to kill you and I'm going to kill you really fucking slow. Do you doubt that I'm willing to do it?"

"I don't doubt that at all," Riddle replied. He decided that he better take them up on the offer to go to the bathroom after all.

*****

The cabin fever was about to drive the extroverted Hal Sutton to madness. He had ventured out to dine at the resort's Sunset Terrace and was about to cut into his beer-braised lamb shank when his phone rang. He fished it out his pocket; the number was familiar to him.

"I was beginning to wonder if something bad had befallen you," he said as a greeting to his caller.

"I'm sure that would be devastating news to you," Reece replied.

Sutton had asked for a table that afforded privacy, stating he was dining alone but was expecting an important call. "It's a dangerous world we live in, Dr. Reece."

"It certainly is...especially shopping malls." There was no effort to hide the acid in the remark.

Sutton gritted his teeth as he silently cursed the drug-dealing pimp who had chosen a most inopportune time to freelance his efforts. "Look, I want to assure you that I had absolutely nothing to do with that foolishness, and I immediately handled that most unfortunate event." He sounded like a restaurant manager speaking to an unhappy customer. *My goodness, I'm so sorry your steak was undercooked. I will have a new one prepared immediately for you on the house.*

"You'll excuse my lack of faith in your assurances, Mr. Sutton." Calling attention to the fact that he knew it was an error by Riddle could tip Sutton off that he knew more than he should.

"I understand your skepticism, Dr. Reece. I want you to know that my offer still stands, but you must understand that it will not be available in perpetuity. Circumstances demand that I know your decision in a timely manner." Anyone watching Sutton's face would have thought he was chatting with an old friend or business associate. The man's poker face was legendary.

"Really? Why would that be, Governor?" Reece was mentally doing some very bad things to his conversation partner at the moment.

"Let's not get into unpleasant details, Dr. Reece. I think the offer is an excellent opportunity for you and Mr. Tyler. Any potential ugliness on either side can be avoided, and both of you can walk away very wealthy men. I know you have achieved an impressive degree of financial success yourself, Dr. Reece, and no one deserves it more, in my mind. But think about Mr. Tyler, if I might be so bold to suggest. I would hardly think he has much prospect for a bright financial future, not to mention such funds could help him disappear and avoid some very unpleasant legal entanglements. I even might have some associates that could help him in that matter," Sutton offered.

"Help with what...the legal entanglements or the disappearing part?"

"Why, either, Dr. Reece...and not the type of disappearing you might be thinking. I am just as interested as you are in this ending with satisfaction for everyone, I can assure you." Sutton was worried that the conversation wasn't going well. "The amount could even be negotiable as well."

Michael had listened to all he could stand from the man. He initially had no intention to call him with an answer at all, but Tripp had convinced him of the utility of casting this bait in the water.

"Look Sutton, I don't want to spend any more time listening to you than I have to. I called to let you know I have spoken with Chris and I have an answer for the both of us."

Sutton unconsciously leaned forward in his padded dining chair over the aroma of mint jam and roasted lamb. "Well that is fantastic, Dr. Reece."

"I'm afraid it won't be fantastic for you, Governor. Our answer is go fuck yourself." Michael hit the kill switch on his phone.

Sutton sat in silence, still holding the dead call to his ear. Slowly he lowered the device and got up from the table. Suddenly he no longer had much of an appetite. He apologized to the maître d' and claimed to have an urgent matter to attend to. He headed up to his suite with plans not to leave the property until things were taken care of.

Michael walked back into the dining area. "It's done," he said to Tripp.

He nodded. "All right, let's get him in the truck and get going. I've explained the importance of his cooperation on our trip as well as the consequences of any nonsense. He's going to be a very good boy."

Riddle nodded in the direction of Reece. "That's right. I won't be any problem."

Reece and Tripp loaded Riddle into the back seat and buckled his seat belt. Tripp then used additional duct tape to secure his hands to the handle above the window so they would be visible; all while the garage door remained closed. He turned to Michael with a sly grin. "Always knew tinting the back windows would pay off sometime."

Michael secured the house and turned on the alarm, after getting the original discs out of the family safe but leaving the copies stuffed among the Christmas tree lights in the attic. The pulled out of the driveway in the darkness with Riddle's cell phone on the dash. They had gone less than two miles before it vibrated announcing a new text message.

Kill him

*****

"Maybe it was there before the murder," Special Agent Frierson said to the people gathered at the conference table in the Asheville FBI Headquarters on Patton Avenue.

Special Agent Meredith Scott shook her head at the table surface. "I don't think so. We're missing something."

The ten-person team had sat around the table for over an hour after receiving the confirmation that the DNA on the door handle at the residence of the late Senator Haxton matched the samples supplied by the Buncombe County Medical Examiner's Office, confirming the initial hit in the CODIS system identifying one deceased Darnell Tyler as the owner of that particular DNA.

"Well, unless Mr. Tyler was resurrected several days after his death and made a trip down to Figure Eight Island to commit a homicide, I don't really know what to say," Frierson replied. He wasn't being disrespectful to his boss. On the contrary, Scott valued bluntness in her team members and never got caught up in the hierarchy. It probably explained her astounding success rate in case investigations as well as the fierce loyalty of her team members.

Meredith chuckled. "Maybe he's the Messiah." The remark garnered tired laughter around the table and broke the tension. "All right, everyone take a break. We've been beating the shit out of this dead horse for over an hour. Go get something to eat and we'll gather back here in an hour to start tackling new angles."

The team members gathered their papers and filed out of the room. Frierson asked if she wanted anything to eat, and she gratefully declined. She was going to call the Deputy

411

Director and update him on new leads, which could be summed up in two words: "jack" and "shit."

Something made her stop as she neared the door leading out of the conference room. She backed up one step and looked in the mirror that was on the wall near the door. It was aligned with one across the room and created the effect often seen at children's museums where it appears that a copy of your image repeats itself in succession. She kept staring at the images, not quite getting why it had grabbed her attention, but something was gnawing at her.

Frierson noticed that she had stopped in front of the mirror. "You worried you look as shitty as I do right now?"

"Son of a bitch," Scott said into the mirror.

"What? I was just messing with you," her assistant said.

She turned to him. "Come with me," she said as she started walking toward her temporary office with a rapid pace. It was a long shot, but it was more promising than any other idea she had right now. She would delay her call to the Deputy Director for a little while longer.

*****

"Goddammit," McCray muttered to no one in particular as he shifted in the chair at his hotel room window. The coffee pot had greatly aided him in staying awake for the many hours he spent waiting for Chris Tyler to pass in front of his binoculars. The same appliance had also made him need to piss so bad he was tapping both feet. But he wouldn't dare get up to make the ten-foot walk to his bathroom. After hours of waiting, he had caught a man that looked a lot like Tyler get out of a Toyota SUV and walk into the entrance of the hotel across the street from his own. He was convinced that the man would exit and leave at exactly the time McCray decided to take a leak. He finally improvised by pissing in an empty water bottle while still standing at the window and laughed at the image he would be advertising if there had been lights on inside his room.

At the same time, Chris was treating himself to a shower before packing up his things to move to a different location. He had no idea that checking into the hotel with his dead

412

brother's driver's license and paying with cash was probably saving his life, as the front desk worker downstairs had just informed a caller asking for Chris Tyler that they currently didn't have a guest under that name.

Randall was tired of waiting. He grabbed his backpack and ventured out of his hotel for a walk, taking an indirect route toward the Toyota in the parking lot and all the while watching the hotel entrance to make sure that the man he had seen from the window wasn't heading his way. He walked between the SUV and the car beside it and didn't see anything of substance inside that would give away the identity of its driver. It was at this point that he remembered that someone involved was a private investigator.

Satisfied he wasn't being watched, he walked by the rear of the truck again, snapped a picture of the license plate, and sent it to Riddle, asking him to find out who the car was registered to. He made a quick walk through the hotel lobby, didn't see his target, and decided to drive his own car to a parking space nearby that was shaded and could hide the fact that someone was sitting in the driver's seat. He planned to stay there until he either saw the man and identified him as Tyler or until Riddle got back to him about the license plate number.

*****

The words on the previous text on the confiscated phone had been chilling, but at least they knew what they were facing. The ride had been pretty quiet after that, not only because of the ominous instructions given by Sutton but also because they didn't want to discuss any plans in front of their passenger in the back seat.

The silence had allowed Michael to remember how exhausted he was, and he found himself fighting the urge to drop his head on his chest and enjoy a few blissful moments of sleep. The vibration of the phone on the dash actually made him jump. After reading the message and seeing the attached picture, the surge of adrenaline took away any desire for sleep.

"Pull over," Michael said to Tripp.

"What?" Tripp asked to make sure he heard him right.

413

"Pull over now!"

Tripp was surprised by the unusual bark from his friend and pulled off the interstate quickly. He was even more surprised to see Reece pull his pistol from his belt and point it at the suddenly panicked face of Riddle.

"Who is Randall McCray? You have five seconds to answer me before I blow your fucking brains out right here."

*****

Chris was part confused and part irritated when he saw the number on the caller ID display of his phone. "I told you not to use this number, Mike—"

"You've got to get out of there Chris. You got to get out of there now. Someone is outside your hotel and thinks you're there. I don't have time to explain how I know, but a guy named Randall McCray is following you and I don't think he plans to do nice things to you. He's about your age and he supposedly looks a lot like you. He's being paid by Sutton, so you can guess what his instructions probably are." Michael was pacing outside Tripp's truck, which was still pulled over on the side of the road. "Listen, we are about thirty minutes from the church. I will call you on the new phone as soon as I get there, but call me on this one if you get in a pinch before then, all right?"

Reece told him the type of car McCray was probably in, based on what a scared shitless Riddle had told him with a gun in his face. He climbed back in the passenger seat and looked at Tripp, who was as shocked as Riddle was scared. "Sorry, David. We need to get there as quick as we can."

The V8 engine of Tripp's truck roared as he spun his wheels getting back on the interstate. They made it to the Victory Assembly Church of Christ in twenty minutes.

*****

It didn't take very long to see him. Chris stood at the narrow vertical window of the third-floor stairwell located on the eastern side of the hotel. The car description was invaluable

414

in narrowing down his search. He had seen a matching vehicle parked in the shade at the side of the building and could make out that someone was inside.

It presented quite a dilemma. He could make a break for the truck and get out of there with a very low likelihood of actually shaking him. Confronting him would either get him shot or cause enough of a scene where the police would be called—definitely the last thing he needed at the moment. If this McCray guy could stay with him, it would be a matter of time before there wouldn't be anyone around, and then it would be all over.

He made a mental inventory and was happy that everything he needed was in the duffel and the backpack that he had with him currently. There was nothing that could link him to using Reece's truck either; that was important to him too. He walked to the other side of the building to check that stairwell and then dialed his phone.

*****

"Reverend Cash, my name is Michael Reece, I believe our friend left something for me," Michael said to the man that came to the back door of the church.

"I do. Would you gentlemen like to come inside?" Billy responded.

Michael looked back to the truck. "I'm afraid we can't, sir. We have one other person with us in the car and we have to stay on the move for right now."

Cash handed Reece the two phones with the chargers. "My friend said that he trusted you as much as he trusted his Savior. Is he right to think that?"

"There is nothing that I won't give to keep him safe, including my own life. There was a time that I failed at protecting him, and that will never happen again. I'm afraid I can't tell you more right now, but you have my word that is given in this house of God."

The two men shook hands, and Billy gave him a church bulletin from the week before. "I wrote a phone number on the back that you can reach me at any time of the day. I am a shepherd of my flock, but I am not afraid to fight the wolves."

As he watched the tail lights fade into the distance, he said one more silent prayer for Chris and his friends.

*****

Chris put the phone to his ear. "Hello?"

"This is Darryl from Asheville Taxi. Dispatch said to call this number when I was about ten minutes away," was the response on the other end of the line.

"That's right. Thanks for calling. Listen, it's a little crazy in the parking lot of the hotel. Can you meet me on the left side of the building? It's the opposite side from the pool. There is a stairwell exit on that side and I'll meet you there. I'll make it worth your inconvenience." Chris was in the ice/vending machine room on the third floor, chosen because there were no security cameras that he could find there.

"Sure, that's no problem. My cab is yellow with a green hood." The taxi driver didn't give a shit where he picked up his fare, and driving an extra fifty feet sounded like it would get him a bigger tip. "I'll see you in ten minutes."

"Thank you. See you then," Chris replied and ended the call. He made a quick look down the hallway and saw no one there. Dipping back in the room, he took a deep breath and pulled the fire alarm.

*****

"Mr. Riddle, this is Mr. X," Tripp said, introducing the man to Tyson who had let them in a side entrance that wasn't near any streetlights.

Tripp had walked down the hall to the elevator and then to the room with his arm around Riddle, acting like two men who had enjoyed a little too much to drink and were holding each other up. He had taken off the zip ties from around his ankles to allow him to walk but had affixed one that connected the two men by their belt loops just in case Riddle had any thoughts of making a run for it.

416

"He will be your host for a while. The same rules and consequences that you and I had agreed on are still in effect with Mr. X. Do you have any questions?"

"Is he going to kill me?" Riddle asked with more than a little fear in his voice. "Mr. X" was a pretty big guy himself and shared the same intense look as the man who had thrown him around like a rag doll outside of Reece's home.

Tyson helped re-attach the zip lines to Riddle's ankles. "I won't lay a finger on you unless you give me a reason to, Mr. Riddle. I am a very reasonable man as long as you don't make me become unreasonable."

"I won't give you any trouble, Mr. X," Riddle replied.

Tripp smiled and patted Tyson on the back. "Excellent. In that case, you two guys will get along just fine." He turned to his commanding officer. "I'll text you updates when we can, but let's not talk on the phone in front of our guest. Oh, we got this for you and Riddle." He handed him a bag that contained sandwich items, chips, apples, and bottled water. "We will be as quick as we can."

Michael shook Tyson's hand at the hotel room door and spoke to him quietly so as to keep Riddle from hearing. "Thank you for helping, sir. I'm sorry I've put you in a situation like this."

"You didn't put me here, Mike. I chose to be here." He looked at both the men. "Airborne."

"All the way," Tyson's two subordinates said in unison.

"We'll be here when you get done, and call if you need anything." Tripp and Reece headed down the hall to the elevator, and Tyson closed the door and turned to his new roommate. "We can watch SportsCenter or pay-per-view. Any requests?"

Riddle was speechless. He had no doubt that any of these men would seriously jack him up if he went out of line, but none of them were interested in harming him if they didn't have to. There was a professionalism to them that he didn't see in men who worked in his line of business. "Umm, either is fine."

"Why don't we catch some SportsCenter then? Let me know if you need to go to the bathroom and need anything to eat or drink. I'm afraid I'll have to watch you in the can, though."

*****

McCray heard the blaring of the alarm coming from the hotel, followed shortly by customers and employees streaming out into the parking lot like ants from a disturbed hill. He thought it would be wise to stay in his car in case he needed to pull out to give chase, but he scanned the growing number of people outside. He thought to himself that this could be a stroke of good luck since this might flush out the man he thought could be a match and he could be sure one way or another.

That unreliable piece of shit Riddle hadn't gotten back to him on the license plate number, so this was pretty much his only option. His parking spot was on a slope slightly higher than the rest of the lot, so he had a good viewpoint for scanning the faces in the crowd. If he saw his guy, he would follow him and wait for the right opportunity to finish him off. If the man went back inside, he would simply wait for him to leave or show himself in his room window. *Why didn't I think about pulling the fucking alarm an hour ago?*

His inner celebration of good fortune was brought to an end as two large fire trucks drove onto the property, the second one stopping right in front of his car and not only blocking his view but pinning him in his space until they decided to leave. He had to get out of the car now. Walking around trying to appear as just another guest who was pissed about being outside for a likely false alarm, his eyes went from face to face without noticing the yellow and green cab that exited from the rear of the building and turned onto the main road below.

*****

"No, they wouldn't," Dr. Stan Rosen's voice announced over the speakerphone in SAC Meredith Scott's temporary office.

418

It was deflating the "eureka" moment she had experienced about fifteen minutes ago in the conference room. She didn't realize she had made a wrong assumption when she framed the question. She had thought that an identical twin would be exactly that and had asked the faculty geneticist at Wake Forest University that one of the team members had been able to get on the phone if those twins would have the same fingerprints.

"Oh, well, sorry to bother you, Dr. Rosen. I'm a lay person in genetic studies, and I was hoping that identical twins would have the same DNA."

"Well, on that issue you are completely correct Agent Scott," Rosen replied. "They would have the same DNA."

Scott nodded vigorously to Frierson who was listening to the conversation as well. "I'm a bit confused. I just assumed that if someone had the exact DNA, they would have the same characteristics like fingerprints."

"Agent Scott, you are confusing genotype with phenotype," Rosen said as if leading a discussion in his undergraduate class. "You see, a person's DNA makeup is called their genotype, but a person's appearance and physical characteristics are determined by how that DNA is expressed, which can be altered by conditions in the womb and other factors. That is called a person's phenotype. Now, granted, the alterations in phenotype in identical twins are subtle, which is why they look almost exactly alike, but things such as fingerprints would be different because of gene expression. It's a common mistake, Agent Scott, but that is why people can often tell one identical twin from the other by a certain birthmark or slightly different shapes of their eyebrows. Identical twins are one fertilized egg that splits after fertilization, so the DNA is identical. Fraternal twins, on the other hand, are two separate eggs that are both fertilized at conception and therefore have differing genotypes."

"So, Dr. Rosen, just to make sure I'm hearing you correct, identical twins have the same DNA and would have the same results on a DNA probe test done on a tissue sample, correct?" Scott was now leaning forward in her chair toward the speaker phone.

"That is correct, Agent Scott," the professor replied.

She quietly held her hand up to Frierson and crossed her fingers. "Dr. Rosen, I really appreciate you taking the time to speak with me today. You have been most helpful."

The two exchanged goodbyes and Scott high-fived her second-in-command.

"You realize that this is still a very unlikely explanation, Meredith," Frierson said to her. "It is much more likely that that blood does belong to Darnell and it was put there for whatever reason before the crime."

"Maybe, but I don't think so, Mitch. Remember, it was on a door handle. It would be hard for something like blood to be on a location like that for very long without being disturbed or noticed and cleaned. Think positive, because this is about the only lead we have right now."

"Look, I hope you're right, but I don't like our odds. That's all I'm saying." Mitch leaned back in his seat. "My fingers and toes are crossed."

As if on cue, Scott's cell phone began chiming, and the caller ID showed it was the junior agent on the team she had dispatched to the Buncombe County Department of Vital Records. She was very pleased with what he found.

CHAPTER 31

Landon Pierce stepped out of a chartered Gulfstream G150 at the Asheville Regional Airport after negotiating an additional hundred-thousand-dollar fee plus expenses for the more on-site role that was recently requested. Sutton was in full panic mode now. He had been unable to get in contact with Riddle for hours despite multiple heated voicemails and felt that the FBI would start making connections at any minute. His demeanor wasn't improved at all when Pierce informed him of the pirated text message McCray had sent to Riddle's number, which had revealed that the vehicle in question was registered to Michael Reece and, despite it still sitting in the same parking space, Tyler had disappeared.

There was no doubt anymore that Reece was actively helping Tyler, which meant that they both needed to vanish—the sooner the better. Riddle was missing in action, and McCray struck Sutton as unlikely to have been valedictorian of his class. He had pleaded to Pierce to drop everything else and get more involved with locating both of them, money wasn't an object. Pierce had flown in a private jet out of Reagan National Airport shortly after their conversation and had spent the short flight gathering intelligence from his contacts.

Reece had not used his phone in a while but, unfortunately for Reece, it was still connected to its battery, and therefore the signal would still ping off towers. Tracing the phone locations made it quite clear that he had gone to the Asheville area fairly recently. A short negotiation with the pilot altered their flight plan from Charlotte to Asheville. Pierce had made it very clear to Sutton, however, that he was only there to locate two people and would not participate in any activities beyond that. Sutton had no choice but to agree.

This case did not pose much of a challenge except for the timeline. Both his targets were likely in the same city. He had DMV pictures of both of them, and the fact that one had a prosthetic leg would make identification from a distance much easier. One of his freelance computer hackers had described getting Reece's credit card number as "child's play," and he had another "consultant" that worked for VISA monitoring any activity on the card. The only problem was that Sutton wanted them located immediately, and a bonus of six figures was promised if it occurred in less than twenty-four hours.

Pierce didn't need the money, but he liked the fact that he was known as someone who delivered. There were plenty of other rich douchebags out there that needed secrets hidden or exposed, and his reputation for results and discreetness was second to none. Every professional had a monetary number that they set as a goal for when they would walk away, and Pierce was getting pretty close to his. He wanted to be able to retire from this when he was still young enough to enjoy the fruits of his labor. If he pulled this off, he figured he was less than five big jobs away from reaching his "walk away" number.

After securing a rental car, he drove to McCray's hotel and listened to him describe the events of the past several hours. He was struck by how much this man favored the photograph of Tyler he had in his briefcase. Pierce had little doubt that the fire alarm had been triggered by Tyler as a way to escape, and there was little chance that he would return to the truck that was parked a short distance away. A brief inspection of the vehicle revealed little useful information, and Pierce instructed McCray to stay put, watch the truck, and await further instructions. It was unlikely to bear any fruit, but it gave McCray something to do while Pierce focused on gathering more information.

*****

Reece saw the taxi pull into the parking lot of the local chain restaurant they had agreed upon. Tripp grabbed his arm as he made to get out of the vehicle.

"I want to see if anyone is following him," Tripp said as Michael settled back into his seat.

Michael called Chris's new number using his own new phone and told him to go inside the restaurant and get a table for three. If no one followed him in, they would meet him shortly. Moments later, they watched Chris exit the taxi and go inside the restaurant. After fifteen minutes, neither of them saw any sign of a tail (but both joked about their complete lack of urban counterintelligence training).

After entering the restaurant, Michael saw Chris waving from a corner table and walked over and embraced his old friend. "Chris, this is David, and you can trust him with anything. He knows everything about both of our situations and is here to help."

Chris shook Tripp's hand and looked at his massive frame. "Jesus…I'm guessing you don't get challenged to many bar fights, do you?"

Chris had been smart to ask for a corner table that was not in earshot of other patrons. They all agreed that this was as good a place as any to talk and get something to eat.

"How're you holding up?" Reece asked Chris.

"All right, I guess. Thanks for the heads-up at the hotel. I made the guy in the parking lot pretty easy, and I would have pretty much been fucked if you hadn't called."

His remarks seemed to hammer home the fact that there were people after them and they weren't far away.

"How did you get away?"

"I pulled the fire alarm in the hotel. I was going to try to slip away in the crowd of people who had evacuated, but I got lucky. The fire trucks pulled in and stopped right in front of the guy's car. I had called a cab to pick me up in the back and I just left." Chris shrugged his shoulders. "I guess I was due for a little good luck. The truck is still there. Sorry about that, Mike."

"Don't worry about that, brother. I think we should leave it there for now. Whoever is following you sent a picture of the license plate, so they know it's yours." Reece paused the conversation as the waitress brought drinks and the men placed orders. "Let's talk about where we go from here."

Chris took a long pull of his caffeinated drink and turned to Michael. "Listen, man, I know I said I would trust you to decide what to do with the package, but I'm a little confused that you haven't done anything yet. Are you planning on burying them?"

Michael shook his head emphatically as he brought his glass away from his face. "No, Chris...I would never do that. I swear to you: no matter what happens to us, people are going to know what they did. But that's a secondary concern right now."

"What the fuck could that be secondary to, Mike?" Chris asked.

"Getting you the hell out of trouble, that's what. If those discs get out now, I have to explain where I got them. Now, even if I don't tell them, it still gives the FBI two guys who had one hell of a motive to kill someone. It's pretty obvious that the tape was made in Haxton's bedroom, you know. It makes it a hell of lot harder to get you out of here if every law enforcement officer in the country is looking for you."

"Look, Mike, I'm not asking you to do that. That part's on me, and if I get caught, I am more than willing to answer for what I did. You don't have to do that," Chris told his friend.

"The hell I don't," Michael said as he shook his head. "I walked out on you once when you were in a bind, and I won't do it again."

"I know why you did it now, Mike, and I understand. I'm just saying...we're all square." Chris looked at Tripp. "Help me out here, David."

"Don't look at me, man. I tried the same logic and almost got my ass kicked. He's committed to doing this, which means I'm committed to helping him. We get you in the clear, then we worry about the discs."

Both men stopped as they both saw a change in Michael's expression. Reece pulled Tripp's keys off the table top and slid them to Chris while looking toward the bar behind them.

"Chris, take the keys and go to the car. Don't say a word and get up and go to the car. We'll be there in a minute," he said under his breath.

Tyler looked at the keys and then to Michael. "Mike...what are you..."

Reece looked at him and spoke quietly with his teeth clinched. "Chris, take the fucking keys and go to the fucking truck right now."

Chris took the cue and grabbed the keys and headed to the exit.

Tripp looked at his friend waving to their waitress and was completely baffled. "What gives, Mike?"

"Look at the television," Reece replied.

While Michael apologized to the waitress, claiming they had to go and paying for their order along with a generous tip, Tripp looked at the monitor hanging above the bar. There was a middle-aged woman speaking at what looked like an impromptu press conference. Tripp didn't get what had spooked his friend until the image became a split screen, now showing a face that he had just gotten familiar with.

*****

"We want to emphasize that Mr. Tyler is only a person of interest and is not considered a suspect. Anyone with information that they believe could help our investigation can call the number that should be listed on the bottom of your screens. We ask Mr. Tyler to contact us at the same number or present himself to the nearest police station so we can discuss matters related to this case. Anyone who sees Mr. Tyler should not try to engage him directly and should simply call the number listed below." Agent Scott stood in front of a collection of local and national news affiliate microphones. "I can answer a limited number of questions, and then I must ask that you let us get back to work."

"Could we have your name?" was the first question that came through over the din of reporters all speaking at the same time.

"My name is Special Agent Meredith Scott. I am the Agent In Charge in the Charlotte Field Office of the Federal Bureau of Investigation. As you know, the FBI received a request from local law enforcement to take the lead role in this investigation, which we were happy to do. We have enjoyed invaluable assistance from New Hanover County Sheriff's Department as well as the North Carolina State Bureau of Investigation."

"Agent Scott, what made you seek out this person of interest?" asked the local NBC affiliate reporter.

"Unfortunately, I cannot comment on details of this ongoing investigation. We believe that Mr. Tyler may have information about this case that we have not discovered at this time," Scott had been through enough of these that she could almost predict what the first several questions would be.

"Is he considered a suspect in the murder?" this question came from the on-site CNN contributor.

"I think I have already answered that question in my opening remarks. Mr. Tyler is considered a person of interest." She knew what the next question would be.

"Follow up, Agent Scott, if I may. You said that, if sighted, he should not be approached directly. Is that because he should be considered dangerous?"

Scott knew she had to wrap this up. "I did not say that. It is a matter of policy that we ask citizens not to get directly involved in investigations, which is why we ask to let trained law enforcement professionals handle any contact and discussions with persons of interest. I'm afraid that is all the time I have for now."

She walked away from the collected microphones and cacophony of shouted questions. She already had agents dispatched to his last known address on the coast and had furnished the press with his DMV photo so that it could be displayed to the public. In cases such as this, breaks in the case were much more commonly made from a tip on the hotline than actual agents making contact. There was work to be done, but she mentally crossed her fingers as she walked back to the Asheville Field Office entrance behind her.

*****

Tyson had changed Riddle's phone to vibrate several hours ago but, using his own phone, had sent a copy of every text Riddle's phone received to the number Reece had given him. The most recent message was more chilling than the others to this point:

Tyler discovered by FBI. Running out of time. Eliminate both immediately.

After sending a copy, he decided to pick up the phone to make sure they were all right.

"Hello," came the familiar voice of Sgt. Tripp.

"Booger, it's Tyson. You guys all right there? Did you get the new text?"

"Yeah, we're good. Can't really talk now, though. Any problems with our guest?" Tripp replied.

"No problems at all. Anything I can do right now?"

"No, sir. Just stay with Riddle there and we'll call you when we can. I gotta run, sir."

"Roger that. I'll be standing by."

For the first time since he had taken custody of Pete Riddle, he looked at him with a decidedly unfriendly expression. "You better fucking pray nothing happens to those men."

Riddle was about as far from a man of God as one could be, but the expression on Tyson's face made him consider engaging in some serious prayer for the safekeeping of the two men who had brought him to Asheville.

*****

The new phones that had been purchased by Chris did not have internet capability, so Reece was sitting in a small internet café several miles from their recent restaurant exodus. He had reserved a rental car from a nearby Avis and finished his second transaction renting a cabin on the outskirts of town. The stay there wouldn't be very long, but it would give them a chance to get out of the public eye and figure out more details of how to get Chris out of trouble.

"We're set with the car, and I have a cabin reserved outside of town," Reece said as he climbed inside.

Not long after, Tripp was following Michael, who was now in a rented Jeep Patriot equipped with a GPS system. Both had decided to keep Chris in Tripp's truck behind the tinted rear windows. They had gotten the keys for the cabin from the main office located near downtown and watched the population density fall as they drove out of town.

The seclusion of the cabin was exactly what they had been looking for, and there was a collective exhale as the three men walked into the three-bedroom log cabin near Arden. The gravel driveway meandered through hardwoods and evergreens with the property backing up to one of the southern fingers of Lake Julian. Other than the raccoon-proofed trash bins, there were no other manmade structures visible from the large back deck. Michael stocked the meager groceries they had picked up on the way in the kitchen cabinet and refrigerator, and they all collapsed into the soft leather furniture in the living room.

Michael had hoped that they could get Chris away before he had been identified as a suspect in the murder, but it couldn't be helped now. Always one to be hesitant about asking others for favors, he had come to the realization that it wasn't possible for something like this.

He had spent a lot of time on the phone the past several hours and had yet to find one person, even some who were fully aware of what was going on, that declined to help in any way they could. It had started with David who had steadfastly refused to stay in Fayetteville and had probably kept Michael from being executed in his own home not long ago. The list had grown by many more since that time, and, although disheartened that the others were subjecting themselves to possible legal trouble in the future, he knew he couldn't do it alone.

They spent several hours going over the details of what would be Chris Tyler's exodus from everything he had known to this point. Although there wasn't really any other option, it was important to Michael that Chris agree to it. If everything went according to plan, Michael would return to his previous life, with a few changes, but Chris would no longer even have his identity anymore.

It wasn't perfect by any stretch, and they would need more than a little good luck for the plan to be successful, but they all agreed that it was far better than any other option they could think of in the rustic mountain living room. They all knew that getting him out of the country wouldn't be the end of it either, since the manhunt for someone who could have possibly been the next President of the United States would be a worldwide effort, but they could make the search as difficult as they could. Chris agreed with gratitude, and Michael started making calls on his new cell phone in the other room. Chris and David turned on the television to get updates on the manhunt.

David found Fox News on the satellite channel menu and entered the number. They were greeted by a correspondent reporting from a location that was quite familiar to Chris.

"That's the road that went to my house," he said to Tripp. "I had been there for a couple of years. There ain't nothing that will help them find me there."

The only new item they heard was that it was DNA evidence from the crime scene that made Tyler a person of interest. Chris looked at his hand when he heard that news tidbit.

"How did you wind up on the coast?" Tripp asked his new friend.

"Not really sure, to tell you the truth. I had to get away from the life I had in Asheville. I had gotten clean but had to put some distance between my new life and my past. I tried to get Darnell to go with me, but drugs still had him. I had never been near the ocean except for when I was taken there by them." Chris used the word "them" in a way that made it very clear to Tripp who he was referring to. "I just drove there and let God guide me."

"What did you do when you got there?"

"Well, there was plenty of work in construction there at the time. The housing crash hadn't come yet, and I got work with a good guy who built beach houses by the name of Jimmy Hardy. The pay was pretty good, and I always liked working outside. A little sweat is good for you, I think." Tripp nodded agreement with a smile. "I worked hard and tried to learn everything I could. Mr. Hardy always took the time to teach me new skills. He was a good man. When the housing crash came and he told me he had to let me go, he cried like a baby. He always looked after people he was close to and never judged them."

Tripp nodded toward the next room. "Sounds like someone else we know."

"You got that right," Chris chuckled. "I spent about a year and a half doing odd jobs, mainly on shrimp boats. I learned how to do pretty much anything on the boat including working the nets and driving the boat. I even got handy enough fixing engine problems that one of the captains would let me take the boat out with a net crew without him sometimes. He said it was because he wanted to train me to be a captain, but I think it was because he had a new young girlfriend that he didn't like to leave on land. Anyway, I didn't have the money to get a captain's license, and my main captain had a heart attack, so the work became spotty. That's when Mr. Hardy called the manager at the Lowe's in Shallotte and got me a job there. I worked there until everything went bad."

"What made you decide to go to Haxton's?" Tripp asked. "Oh, and by the way, if you don't want to talk about any of this, it won't hurt my feelings."

"No, I don't mind. You've stuck your neck out for me and you hadn't even met me. You deserve to know whatever you want. Well, you know that Darnell killed himself. He left me a note and I think the memories of what we went through finally became too much. He had always been very bitter about them not being held responsible for what they did. I had been the one to discourage coming forward. I told him that Haxton and Sutton were powerful men and they could destroy us, not to mention the fact that they would probably stop supporting the Sycamore House. That didn't bother him because he had always suspected that they knew, but I don't think they had any idea. Anyway, I think his death made me feel like a coward."

"Did you mean to kill him when you went?"

"No, I swear I didn't. I won't lie, David; I'm not sad he's dead, but that's not what I intended to do. I just wanted to get those videos. I was pretty sure they were still there. I had seen Sutton put them in that safe before, and I wanted to show the world what kind of animals they were. I stole a boat from a marina and took it to the dock of his property. I prayed he would be alone, and he was. He was in his backyard playing on a putting green when I showed up. He didn't recognize me at first and came up to the dock to tell me it was private property. I think he realized it was me right about the time I pointed a pistol to his face. It was the same one Darnell had used to shoot himself. I took him inside and told him to get the videos out of the safe. He acted like he didn't know what I was talking about, and that's when I knocked the shit outta him with the pistol upside his head. I'm pretty sure that I pinched my hand when I did it, and that's probably where they got my blood at the house."

Tyler showed the almost completely healed cut on his hand. "Man, shitty luck dude," Tripp said.

"Yeah, I agree. Anyway, that persuaded him to go upstairs and get the videos. I took him back downstairs and tied him up in his office. He was trying to get me to not take the discs. He offered me all kinds of money, and I told him I wasn't interested. That's when he started threatening me. He told me no one would believe me and that he could ruin me. He said in the end he would make it look like me and Darnell were 'two little faggots looking for a payout.'" Chris used his hands to make quotation marks to show the last few words were a direct quote from Haxton. "That's when I snapped. I didn't even know I had done it until the noise made me jump. I shot him right between the eyes. I planned to take the discs and give them to the police and tell them that he was tied up at his house where they could go get him. I guess I blew it, but he just made me snap. I'm not a bad guy, man. I even returned the boat and left some money to cover the inconvenience...I never meant to kill him."

Tripp gave a knowing look to Chris. "Look man, sometimes being in a bad environment can make you capable of doing things you never thought you could...good and bad. See that guy over there?" he said, motioning to Reece. "He's pretty mild-mannered, don't you think?" Chris nodded and David continued. "I watched him take on probably a half a dozen Taliban fighters on his own to protect me and another guy. He might tell you he was scared shitless now, but at the time he was an ice-cold motherfucker. He wasn't going to let anyone get to me or another soldier who was wounded. It cost him his leg and almost his life. Sometimes you only find out what you're capable of when you're put in a bad situation. I think you were protecting yourself and your brother's memory, not to mention probably some kids in the future, when you did what you did. You're OK in my book." Tripp smiled. "By the way, sorry about my cussing. I know you're a man of faith."

"No problem, man," Chris reassured him. "I've been known to throw a few bad words around myself. Look at me now, quite a ways from framing beach houses and running shrimp boats."

Something in his last sentences had changed the look on David's face, and he sat looking at the floor in deep thought for about twenty seconds then looked back at Chris. "Hang on one minute, Chris."

431

Tripp got up and waited for Michael to finish his current phone conversation before speaking. "I think we can do more than just get him out of the country…"

He spent the next several minutes explaining his plan, which would require letting one more person into the circle of knowing what had happened. It took a bit to overcome Michael's objections to asking one more favor of someone, but in the end he was convinced it was worth a try.

CHAPTER 32

None of them were trained investigators or career criminals, so the expectation that there wouldn't be some sort of mental slip-up was unreasonable. Although Michael had been smart enough to use cash for his transactions since leaving Fort Bragg, he was required to give a credit card number for incidental charges when he had reserved a three-night use of the cabin. The clerk had assured him that it would only be charged in the event of damage that went beyond the security deposit he had given and the full insurance option he had purchased. But there was no way to get the cabin they needed without submitting the card, and to insist on cash only could have raised unnecessary suspicions.

What wasn't understood was that it was company policy for the Great Smokey Vista Cabin Rentals to ensure there would be sufficient funds in a credit line to cover a theoretical damage expense of five hundred dollars. The actual account was not charged, but the inquiry was logged in the massive VISA server network as a transaction nonetheless. At the end of a guest's stay, when the company was satisfied that there was no damage that would require compensation, the transaction would be wiped away from the record.

The twenty-seven-year-old IT Department employee who was getting a hundred bucks for each search of Michael Reece's VISA account every hour until instructed to stop didn't know why the information was needed nor what it would be used for, and, truth be told, he didn't really give a shit. The money was good. His department was in the fraud protection division, and his repeated queries would not attract any attention given that it was done thousands of times a day on countless accounts and almost always for the altruistic reason of protecting their customers. The only difference in this instance was that any "hit" on the account was encrypted and sent to a dummy company account, which wasn't listed in the security department and which would be hard to find without a line by line code search, and then immediately sent to a generic Hotmail account.

Any time the Hotmail account received an incoming item, it sent an alert to Landon Pierce's mobile phone. His suite at the Grand Bohemian Hotel (Pierce was partial to the Grove Park, but, for obvious reasons, it wasn't a good idea) had four running laptops as well as six prepaid mobile phones scattered around the plush accommodations. He made a copy of the transaction "hit" and forwarded it to one of the five prepaid phones he had given to McCray, who was under strict instructions to destroy a phone after receiving any information; further contact would occur on another one until he was down to his last phone, at which point he would be provided with more. Along with the transaction copy, McCray received an address of the office where the transaction occurred and notification by text that both targets were likely there.

Across town, McCray left his observation perch at his window and took the elevator down to his new rental car that, if investigated, would have been rented by a corporate account of a company that didn't exist beyond a post office box and a MasterCard account. He plugged in the address to his GPS system and headed to Dogwood Road to the rental headquarters of Great Smokey Vista Cabin Rentals. Despite the condescending way the suggestion had been made, McCray now had on khaki pants and an untucked short-sleeved golf shirt instead of his outfit from earlier in the day, which Pierce had said made him look like he should be selling weed behind college fraternity houses. Despite his more tame appearance, he still had his gear in a pack in the passenger seat and a 9 mm pistol tucked in the back of his pants.

The drive was only ten minutes, and he put on his best well-meaning innocent look as he approached the counter that was bedecked with countless pamphlets touting area attractions such as whitewater rafting and fly fishing. It was a small stand-alone building with a fake log cabin façade that Randall noted only had one employee behind the counter.

"How may I help you today, sir?" said the friendly middle-aged gentleman from behind the counter.

"I'm sorry to bother you with this. I was supposed to meet my friends before checking in, but I'm running late. I know my guys rented the cabin here, but I don't know which one," McCray said, looking apologetic for intruding on this man's time.

"I see...Well, sir, I'm afraid—"

"Again, I'm sorry to bug you with this, but you know cell phone reception can be tricky in the mountains and I can't reach them. If you could just tell me which cabin it is, I can meet them there. The cabin would either be in the name of Reece or Tyler I think. They were probably just here a few hours ago. We all take a two-week trip together every year."

Something wasn't quite right. The man knew exactly who this fellow was referring to, but he remembered the cabin was only rented to three nights. "Yeah, cell reception can be hit-or-miss sometimes, but I'm afraid I can't be any help to you. I can't release the names and locations of any clients. I'm sorry, but it's company policy."

McCray slid a one-hundred-dollar bill across the counter toward the man. "Are you sure you can't help me out just this once? It will stay between us...I promise."

He was certain something was amiss now. "I'm sorry, sir, I can't help you. It's company policy. I suggest you keep trying their phones from a few different locations until it goes through. I'm afraid unless you want to rent a cabin, there is nothing else I can help you with."

*****

Seth Katz punched in the code to open the garage door and then used his key copy to open the door into the Reece home. His longtime friend and neighbor had asked a favor, and the tone of his words had made him think it was important. It really didn't matter, there wasn't much Michael could ask him that he wouldn't do without hesitation.

He put the past few days' mail that he had collected from the Reece mailbox on the kitchen counter and did a quick look around the house to make sure everything looked in order. Next he climbed the stairs up to the second floor and found the dangling cord in the hallway overlooking the downstairs family room. Katz pulled the cord, lowering the door, and climbed into the heat of the attic. Based on Michael's directions, he looked to the left and saw three plastic tubs labeled "X-mas Decorations" and took the top two off the stack and opened the lid to the bottom container. Just like he was told, under a few decorations was an unlabeled padded shipping envelope. After putting the containers back the way they had been, he climbed back into the air-conditioned coolness of the house.

Once the house was locked behind him and he was back in his own home, he placed the package in his own family safe. Satisfied everything was done, he dialed the number his friend had given him.

"Seth?" came through the speaker held to Katz's ear.

"Hey buddy. It's all done. The package is locked in my safe," he told his friend.

"I really appreciate it, Seth. I might need you to take it to someone later, but I'm not sure yet. I'm sorry to be all cloak and dagger about this," Reece said.

"Don't worry about it. I trust you implicitly, and I'm there for you, buddy. You all right?" He couldn't help but notice that his friend's demeanor seemed a little rushed and nervous.

There was a pause. "I'm OK, Seth. Listen, if anything happens to me, Anna will know what to do with the package. I know that's a big bomb to drop in your lap without explaining, but I really can't right now. You're a good friend, Seth, and I'm sorry for not being able to say more but I've gotta go."

"OK, Mike...but call me when you can, and take care of yourself. Just let me know anything I can do and I'm on it. No questions asked."

After the call ended, Seth leaned against the same counter his neighbor had just a few days before and felt genuine worry that something was very wrong and that his friend could be in trouble. All he could do was wait for a call and do whatever he needed. For the entire time he had known him, Michael had never given him a reason to distrust him or even be mad at him. If he wasn't telling him everything right now, Seth decided there was a good reason for it, and that was that.

*****

Michael's marathon of phone activity had ended after about ninety minutes, and he returned to the living room. Shortly after, Tripp entered from the outside deck and nodded to Reece, silently saying, "We're good."

"OK," Reece said as he sat down with his two friends. "I think we're all set."

He explained the plans for the next several days to each of them. They decided it would be best to travel at night, including waiting for the rental car agency to close and use the key drop box to get rid of the second car. They could leave the cabin keys in the house when they left, as instructed, where housekeeping would collect them when they did their post-checkout clean-up. This would minimize the amount of contact they would have to make with other people who might remember them later. It was decided that they would leave around two a.m. and head east and that they should try to get some sleep until then. None argued, since the solitude and security of the cabin had allowed them to realize how tired they all were.

*****

Sorry for the hassle but our office had to close early today.

Please come back in the morning.

Management

This would be the note any potential cabin tenants would find on the door of the office of Great Smokey Vista Cabin Rentals. It was only an hour before closing anyway, and McCray hoped it would buy some time for him before anyone noticed the body of the middle-aged father of three who now was face down on the floor behind the counter, a growing pool of blood emerging from the gaping hole in the side of his head.

The man had been forthcoming about the cabin location almost immediately after the gun had been taken out, but he had seen McCray's face. That could have been a big problem if things went as he expected when he got to the location that he had extracted at gunpoint just minutes ago. Left with no choice, he had wrapped the pistol in a sweatshirt that was for sale on the wall and, with one muffled boom, ended the man's life. He had swept the office as best he could to make sure he hadn't left any signs of his visit and had left for the outskirts of town. He had a different plan to cover his tracks at the cabin.

*****

Reports from the coast had made Scott even more certain that she had her man. Chris Tyler wasn't at his home and it looked like he hadn't left much, telling her that he didn't plan to return. A visit to his most recent employer had uncovered the fact that he had quit his job abruptly and told his boss he wouldn't be coming back. She learned that he had grown up in Asheville and had lived at an orphanage whose main benefactor was none other than the murder victim.

Unfortunately, he had vanished from the earth, from what she could find. No one had been found yet that knew him any more than working with him, and all described him as a nice guy who usually kept to himself. Fugitives will often turn to their roots when on the run, which was why she had decided to remain in Asheville at least until any other location produced any lead of substance. The manager of the orphanage was devastated with the events of the past several days and informed Frierson that she didn't know where he was. Mitch had told her that she seemed to be telling the truth, and she had promised to contact them if she heard from him.

Subpoenas would be available by the morning to try to ascertain if he had any credit cards that could be tracked. He had no phone number in his employee file at the home improvement store, and there was no landline phone service to his home near Wilmington. This made her certain that he had a cell phone, and that was the reason for another subpoena being requested. Tomorrow would be the full-on launch of one of the biggest manhunts in recent history, so she decided, for the moment, to close her eyes in her high-backed desk chair and steal a brief moment's rest.

*****

After several hours, Tripp gave up and got out of his bed. Sleep was a gift that he wouldn't receive that night. Although he had absolutely no second thoughts about helping his friend, there were nerves about the upcoming day. If they were caught with Chris from this

438

point on, there was no way to deny the fact that they were aiding and harboring a fugitive from the law. His career would be over, and he could very likely wind up in prison. It was a price he was willing to pay, but he would rather get away with it if he had the choice.

He was greeted by the smell of brewing coffee from the kitchen and found Michael sitting in the living room watching CNN with the volume on low. Reece's bag was already packed and on the table near the door.

"I guess I'm not the only one who couldn't sleep," Tripp said as he filled a mug with the fresh coffee.

"I just couldn't force myself to relax. There are still a lot of things that can go wrong," Reece replied. "Listen, David, I will completely understand if—"

"Stow that shit, sir," he interrupted. "I'm still on board with the plan, and I'm not bailing until the job's done."

Michael nodded in surrender. "OK. I just had to put it out there." He looked over at the closed bedroom door that Chris was behind. "At least one of us was able to sleep."

"I can't imagine how tired he had to be. Chronic stress like he's had can be more exhausting than running a marathon. I guess this is about the first time he has felt some degree of security, and he probably just hit the wall."

Tripp thought about times he had returned to the relative safety of an operating base after being outside the wire for several days with his adrenaline stores completely depleted. He could remember going from complete mental alertness to overwhelming fatigue just by crossing the Entry Control Point (ECP) of the FOB. At those times he felt like he could have stretched out on a table in a full chow hall and slept without difficulty. It was probably similar to how Chris felt when he put his head on his pillow a few hours ago.

"Anything new on the news?"

439

"Not really. They are just cycling the same stuff over and over again," Michael said. He had been channel hopping between CNN, Fox News, MSNBC, and Headline News, looking for any updates on what the press or the authorities knew.

Tripp patted the side pocket of his tan cargo pants. "I'm going to get a little fresh air before we get going."

"It won't be very fresh with all that bullshit you're talking," Reece said with a grin. He had learned long ago what getting fresh air was code for. "I think I read somewhere that they are not healthy."

Tripp was in superb physical condition and maxed out his physical fitness test every time he took one in the Army, but a Marlboro Light about twice a day was a vice he hadn't been able to shake. "Yes, sir Doctor sir…How about if we get through this, I'll quit forever."

"You've got a deal," Reece said to his friend's back as he walked out the door toward the wooden dock that was about fifty yards below the back of the house.

The moon was at about a quarter phase and gave him barely enough light to get down to the lakeside without a flashlight. He sat facing the water that reflected the small glimmer of the crescent moon high in the sky. There were several days to go, but the next forty-eight hours would likely decide whether they came through this or not. He savored every puff of the cigarette and decided to have a second, since he fervently hoped to be quitting in a few days.

Since there was about thirty minutes before he would have to roust Chris from his slumber, Michael decided to pull out the groceries they had purchased and put together breakfast for the three of them. He had never been accused of being an accomplished cook, and his selections at the grocery store had reflected that. Nevertheless, there was fruit to be sliced, along with frozen waffles, maple syrup, and microwave bacon, which he started to prepare as he heard the side door open. Reece's plan to give Tripp a little more grief about having a smoke evaporated as he turned around to see a pistol pointed at his face.

The man wore khaki pants and a short-sleeved shirt and held what looked like a 9 mm handgun that was aimed at his head. African-American and a bit taller than Reece, he stood about ten feet away. "Keep your fucking hands where I can see them," he said to Michael in quiet, measured words. He didn't seem nervous at all, which seemed all the more ominous. "Sit down on the couch over there and don't say a word unless I ask you something."

Michael lifted his hands to shoulder height, showing the man his palms. "No problem," he replied as he followed the instructions. There was a sense of defeat starting to consume him. After all they had done and how close they had come, it was going to end right here. He hoped against hope that maybe Chris and David would get away.

"Where is your friend?" McCray asked as he scanned the room and hallway.

"I'm here by myself," Reece replied and was rewarded with the sound of the pistol being cocked.

"Look here, Dr. Reece; I know who you are. Where is Chris Tyler?" his words were still calm but more direct. "I will not ask you a third time."

Tripp could see the back of the man standing in the living room through the window as he approached the cabin door and assumed that Chris had gotten up while he had gone down the waterfront for a smoke. He opened the door.

"It's cooled off quite a..." He stopped cold when he realized that the man wasn't Chris and he now alternated pointing a gun at him and Reece.

"Who the fuck are you?" he asked Tripp, who stood mouth agape in the doorway.

"My name's David," he said as he raised his hands up in a similar manner to Reece. "I'm just a friend. Sorry about barging in; I didn't know we had company."

Tripp was calm, but inside he was angry at himself for making the assumption he had when looking through the window from the outside. Not to mention that he left his own gun in his room, which was down the hallway behind their new guest.

"There's no need for the gun, sir. We don't mean you any harm."

"Shut the fuck up and sit down beside your friend. You picked a bad night to be here, dude." He looked back at Reece. "Where's Tyler?"

"He's not here. We came here together, but he didn't want to stay in the same place very long so he took off a few hours ago," Reece replied, hoping to sell the lie. He was pretty sure he was as good as dead but hoped he could find a way to be the only one.

"We'll see about that. Both of you get on your knees and face the other way," McCray instructed.

Tripp made a quick evaluation of their current situation. The man was standing too far from him to make a move to overpower him before he could drop him with a shot. There was no twitchiness to the man, which made David think that he had done this before and wouldn't chicken out. He didn't have any options that he could see.

"I'm sorry, David," Reece said as he got on his knees as instructed.

"Nothing to be sorry about, brother," he replied as he did the same.

The gunshot was deafening inside the cabin. Both men looked at the other to see who was shot. They jumped a second time as they heard the body of Randall McCray fall on the coffee table and roll to the floor. His eyes were vacant and the left side of his head was no longer there. His right leg gave a sickening death quiver as his last exhale gurgled and hissed.

Chris stood at the corner to the hallway, still pointing the gun to a person that was no longer standing there. After lowering the pistol, he looked at his two friends. "You two all right?" he asked.

"I think so," Michael replied.

"Yes," echoed Tripp.

Chris rubbed his right jaw, looking around the cabin as if doing a mental inventory of what was there. "Both of you get all your belongings and load them into Tripp's truck," he said, then pointed to Tripp's belt which had his Leatherman multitool attached. "Does that thing have pliers?"

442

"What?" Tripp asked completely confused.

"That tool on your belt...Does it have pliers?" Chris asked again.

"Um...yeah. It has pliers."

"OK, give it to me and do what I told you." After those instructions, Chris walked out of the cabin door and went to the garage area below.

Reece and Tripp gathered their limited possessions that they had brought into the cabin and loaded them into the truck. They walked down to the garage area and found Chris behind a Briggs and Stratton generator that was a common finding in the isolated cabins in the area. He emerged with a ten-gallon gas container. "It's about two-thirds full, but it will do. Come with me," he said, looking at the two men.

The Leatherman had been opened and the pliers had been unfolded. The tool now lay on the coffee table beside the body, along with the thick leather wallet that belonged to Chris. They watched him go into his room and emerge about a minute later with his own bag.

"Mike, I want you to put this in the rental car and leave the keys to it. Then I want the two of you to get the hell out of here. I will be down at the end of the gravel road in about ten minutes, but I want both of you to know that I don't expect either of you to be there. David, I appreciate your help these past few days." He then turned to Reece. "Mike, I want you to know that whatever debt you thought you owed me is paid. We're square, and I don't want you to feel like there is anything else you have to do for me. I trust you to do whatever you think is right with the discs, but you don't have to do anything more than that. I promise you if I get caught, I will never mention that you did anything for me."

"No," Reece said. "I'm not bailing on you now."

"You're not bailing on me, Mike. I'm telling you to get the hell outta here. This is spinning out of control, and you both have too much to lose. Whether you think I had the right to do what I did or not don't change the fact that I made the choice. Don't get me wrong, boys; I'm going to try to get away. But if I get caught, I will face the consequences of what I did. I will

443

pray for God's forgiveness and await his judgment when it's all said and done. But until those videos get out, this won't stop, and that's why I need you to get somewhere safe."

He walked across the room and embraced Reece who seemed to be unable to process what he was saying.

"I love you, man. I love you as much as I loved Darnell, and at least one of us has to come out of this alive. People have to know what kind of animals they were, and I need you to do that for me, because they'll believe you a lot easier than me. That's why I need you to get the fuck outta here now."

Chris looked at David. "Do you trust me?"

"Yes I do."

"Do you want what's best for him?" he asked while nodding toward Reece.

"Absolutely," Tripp replied.

"Then get him the fuck outta here."

David turned to Reece and approached. "He's right, Mike. You have to trust him now that he knows what's best."

Michael shoved Tripp back. There were tears in his eyes. Chris quickly stood between the two.

"No, Mike. Look at me. I'm asking you to do this for me. Just get down the road and you'll see that it's for the best," Chris said. "Do this for me. If you value you what we had as brothers though all of this, I'm asking you to trust me and do this."

The childhood friends hugged once more. Reece's shoulder bounced up and down slightly as he fought back his emotions. They let go and Michael wiped his nose and looked at Chris. "What are you going to do?"

Tyler nodded his head toward the body in the living room. "I told you we looked alike. Now get the fuck outta here."

David and Chris shook hands briefly then embraced, sensing that the first gesture was inadequate to reflect what they had been through together in such a short time. The two came from different backgrounds and perspectives but they shared a devotion and respect for the man that stood beside them at the moment. Tripp put his hand on Reece's shoulder and walked him to the truck. Once there, Michael turned around one more time to look at his friend in the doorway.

"I know," Chris said. "I love you too. Now get the hell outta here."

After watching the tail lights of Tripp's truck head down the gravel drive toward Beale Road, Chris turned around and went back in the cabin. After ten minutes, he exited the same door of the cabin, using a wet dish towel to wipe off his hands. He circled the cabin to the front door and, using his own pocket knife to reopen the healing cut from Figure Eight Island, let several drops of blood drip along the sidewalk that led from the porch to the driveway. Before getting close to the car, he used a strip of one of his t-shirts to wrap his hand so that no blood would spill in the interior.

He held the steering wheel with his uninjured hand to take further care not to contaminate the car as he drove down the same gravel road. It was still hours from sunrise, so the ride was dark under the canopy of long-leaf pine and maple trees. He was almost on top of them before he came to stop. Looking through his windshield he could see his friends leaning against Tripp's truck waiting for him.

"What the hell are you two doing?" he asked as he climbed out of his car.

"Exactly what you told us to do," Michael replied. "You told us to leave the cabin and drive down this road and that's what we did." He pointed to the Chrysler sedan parked on the side of the road. "I imagine this belonged to our friend."

Chris pulled out an Avis keychain. "This was in his pocket." As expected, the remote key fob unlocked the vehicle. "I'll deal with it. You guys need to get going."

"The hell you say," Michael replied. "Listen, we've got one rental car to turn in and another to get rid of. After that, I don't see why our original plan can't move forward. We've got three cars here, so we need three people."

"Wait...listen...we," Chris stammered.

"Nope; it's my turn to give orders for a little while. Why don't you drive the...holy shit," Michael said as he looked in the direction of their cabin. It was barely visible through the trees, but there were clearly flames flickering from the windows of the first floor.

"Oh, yeah...we should probably get going," Chris said to the two others staring open-mouthed at the cabin up the hill.

The three-car convoy became two after they dropped off Reece's rental car at the closed agency putting the keys in the night drop box. Several minutes later, the late Randall McCray's rental car was parked in a parking deck of a local hospital which, they hoped, would allow it to sit for a long time without any notice. After Reece made a few phone calls, the three then headed east to Charlotte, making one stop on the side of the road where Chris threw a bloody Leatherman, a blood-stained t-shirt, and a small white object that neither David nor Michael could make out from inside the truck into the Catawba River.

The sun was just starting to climb over the eastern horizon when they pulled into the empty parking lot of The Drake Center for Cosmetic Surgery and Michael texted Anna to let her know they were all right. The notice on the front entrance explained that the office was not scheduled to reopen for another ten days due to Dr. Drake being out of town, and it listed the numbers of two plastic surgeons who had agreed to cover any urgent patient needs before then. That being said, there were two other cars in the back parking area that could not be seen from the road, and there were a few lights on inside.

*****

The team had gathered back in the conference room to go over assignments for the day. The Wilmington Office would be interviewing additional employees at the Lowe's Home Improvement where Chris Tyler used to work, as well as another previous employer who used to be a shrimp boat operator. The Asheville team would be visiting The Sycamore House as well as Tyler's former probation officer from many years ago. There were not high hopes of any of these contacts bearing much fruit, but you looked at every possibility, since one couldn't predict where a break would come from.

The hotline, on the other hand, had been a bevy of activity since the press conference. Agent Scott knew that the overwhelming majority would be dead ends or mistaken information, and she had two members of her own team to help organize the tips in terms of what was most likely to be legitimate. As expected, sightings of the "person of interest" had been reported not only throughout the state of North Carolina but in several other states as well, not to mention one repeat caller who was certain he was living in Spain.

There would be a press conference at four p.m. today to update the press on new developments (if any), preceded by a phone conference with the Director and other senior Washington staff. The problem with being the Agent in Charge of the case was that everyone thought that what they had to tell her was the most important, and it was near impossible to have five minutes of uninterrupted thought without someone needing her attention.

She did notice Frierson being pulled out of the conference room while she was being briefed by each section leader of the team. There were sections for the hotline, a Wilmington section, an Asheville section, a section that served as a liaison between the FBI team and local law enforcement, a media team, and a forensics team. About halfway through the team leader updates, the door cracked open.

"Agent Scott, we need you out here for a moment," said one of her best field agents.

She felt a surge of irritation as she expected yet another interruption of thought by something that could have easily waited until the end of the briefing. As she exited the door, the agent who had beckoned her simply pointed down the hallway to the left, where she saw Mitch talking on the phone loudly and urgently motioning her over. Mitch was not one to get excited over trivial things, and her pace quickened as she walked the twenty carpeted feet to him.

"Chief, hang on one moment. I'm going to hand you over to Special Agent Scott, who is our team leader," Mitch said before thrusting the cordless phone over to her. "I think we got him," he whispered as she brought the phone to her ear.

"This is Special Agent Scott," Meredith said in greeting.

"Agent Scott, this is Chief Keith Foster of the Arden Fire Department. I think I have something that you should see immediately."

Scott listened to the conversation and her eyes popped open about one minute into it, as Frierson vigorously nodded in silence. Less than five minutes later, the two agents were in a caravan of four sedans and two forensics vans blatantly breaking the speed limit with dash lights on heading south toward Arden.

*****

The mid-afternoon sun brought heat and humidity to Charlotte, as was customary this time of year. Eric Daniels shook hands with Michael and Gabriel before heading out the back door of The Drake Center. The two watched his car pull out in the direction of his home before facing each other.

"Are you sure you want to do this?" Michael asked his friend.

"Absolutely," was Gabriel's reply.

Reece looked over his shoulder and then back to Drake. "I'm not sure, Gabe. I mean, maybe I should stay with you guys for a little while longer."

"Mike, it's time to trust us. We'll be OK. Everything is arranged, and everyone involved is on board. Just pray for good weather." Drake patted him on the shoulder and was shocked to see how tired his friend looked. "Just don't fall asleep at the wheel, OK? I mean, I don't give a shit about you, but I don't want my car all messed up."

The joke was not as funny as Michael made it seem. He laughed the punchy giggle that one gets when one is beyond tired. But then again, it wasn't just fatigue that made him laugh; it was the realization that he had good people around him who wanted to help no matter what.

448

He walked to the adjoining room and said goodbye to his two companions of the past several days and got the same assurances from Tripp as he had from Drake.

Shortly after, the back entrance to the office/surgery center was locked, and David, Gabriel, and Tyler headed east in Tripp's SUV while Michael headed west in Drake's Jaguar. He connected his cell phone to the Bluetooth in the luxury sedan and called his wife. He talked with her for over an hour, partly to help stay awake but mostly just to hear her voice. "Not much longer," he promised her.

Several minutes later, Seth Katz hung up his phone and walked to the family safe. Once he had extracted his neighbor's package along with a few phone numbers he had scribbled down during his phone conversation, he kissed his wife goodbye and climbed into his car, heading west as well.

CHAPTER 33

Agent Scott was happy to see that the virtual fleet of local law enforcement vehicles had been stopped at the main road and not allowed up the gravel entrance. The Deputy Sheriff who had been placed in charge of access had been told to expect the FBI team and waved them through the cordoned-off entrance. As they ascended the gravel road, the air conditioning vents of the car announced the smell of burned wood, plastic, and roof tar. Only one pump truck remained from the Fire Department in case flare-ups occurred. One Sheriff's department cruiser and the van from the Medical Examiner's office were flanking the fire engine, but overall she was pleased to see that a fair amount of effort had been made to preserve the integrity of the scene.

The Sheriff and the Fire Captain walked up to the lead vehicle to greet the incoming investigators. The acrid smell was elevated tenfold when she opened the door.

"Special Agent Meredith Scott. Thank you for calling us," she said as she shook the offered hands of the two local officials.

"Not a problem, Agent Scott. I'm Sheriff Dan Westman of Buncombe County. Chief Norris called us when they found a body in the remains of the house. I will let him explain it up to that point," the lawman said.

"I'm Chief Leslie Norris of the Arden Fire Department, ma'am. We received a call before dawn about a house fire. One of the local residents across the lake noticed the flames and called 911. The house was pretty much engulfed when we arrived, and I would estimate it had been burning for about an hour. There are signs of an accelerant being used, and we found a body in the main room of the first floor."

Westman picked up the conversation at that point. "The body was fairly charred, but the coroner could say it was an African-American male approximately six feet two inches in height, and it certainly looks like the fire didn't kill him. Preliminary examination revealed a gunshot wound to the head. That's when we found this." He handed her a plastic evidence bag that initially looked like a large piece of square charcoal. "It's pretty amazing how the inside of these can be preserved in a fire."

Scott donned a pair of latex gloves and pulled out the item. It wasn't charcoal but a leather wallet that was certainly charred extensively on the outside. Black carbon dust fell from it as she carefully opened the middle fold. It showed some distorted remnants of likely credit cards, but she was amazed at how little char there was on the inside.

Westman handed her another plastic evidence bag. "This was what made us get on the phone."

It was clearly a driver's license that had some melting around the edges, but the middle portion was quite legible. The picture was instantly familiar, since it was the same DMV photograph of Chris Tyler she had provided to the media before her press conference not too long ago.

"There are no other bodies and no weapons that we have found, so I pulled my boys back until you arrived to do a proper forensics examination," Westman offered.

"We really appreciate everything you did here, Sheriff," Scott said as she shook his hand once more. Local law enforcement was often scoffed at by the FBI, but in Meredith's experience, more often than not they had their shit together. Besides, usually the first ones to poke fun at the locals were the same assholes that didn't think a woman should hold her position. She had joked to Mitch before that the likelihood of agents to come down on other professionals was inversely proportional to their penis size.

Without any direction, the forensics agents were systematically and carefully doing an outside-to-inside inspection of the property, and it didn't take long before one called out, "I've got some blood spatter here." The team had found what looked like a spatter trail along the sidewalk toward the front entrance, but the charring near the front porch prevented them from making that a firm conclusion. Samples were taken, and one was immediately dispatched from the scene for comparison studies.

Examination of the body yielded a patch of hair that had been in contact with the stone hearth that had not burned away completely, confirming the tight curled pattern of an African-American. The remainder of the body was pretty badly burned, making identification of gender fairly difficult, but there was enough there to conclude the victim was male. The skull showed a fairly textbook example of an entry wound on one side and a more gaping, explosive exit wound on the other, leading the team to suspect it was done at close range.

Samples of the flooring, walls, and other areas of the house were taken to confirm the use of some type of accelerant. The Sheriff had already determined that it was a rental property and had dispatched a deputy to the rental office, which would open shortly, to see what they could find out about the customers.

Once the on-site evaluation was complete, they released the body to the Buncombe County Medical Examiner, while Agent Scott walked to a more private area to make a call to the Director. This couldn't wait until their scheduled conference call.

"Director Purser, we have a body at a burned home in Mr. Tyler's home county. The victim appears to have died from a gunshot to the head prior to the fire. The physical dimensions, gender, and race all correlate with our suspect as well as his driver's license being on the victim's person inside a wallet that allowed fairly easy identification. We have found blood spatter outside the home that will be rush-compared to his known profile, but I would say we have a high likelihood of this being our suspect." She answered a few more questions and promised to update him when the DNA comparison was complete.

It was about that time that Westman received a call from his deputy informing him of another body being discovered at the cabin rental office, which he passed on to Scott. After thanking him for the update, she pulled Frierson aside.

"Who the hell was after this guy besides us?"

*****

Reece sat on one of the matching queen beds in the hotel room across from Pete Riddle. Tyson had taken a much-appreciated break to leave the hotel room and go for a run, armed with the knowledge that the following day he would be going back to Ft. Bragg. That being said, his guest had been more than cooperative and hadn't given him much trouble beyond the occasional complaining of being handcuffed almost all the time for the past couple of days. "Mr. X" had reminded him that he had received three meals a day, bathroom breaks whenever he wanted, unlimited television and newspaper access, and no physical abuse whatsoever. Riddle had been told that, if it was too much to take, he could walk out the hotel at any time he wished, minus his cell phone and wallet, at which time Tyson would call the police and he could try his luck as a fugitive.

Likewise, Reece now sat across from the man and assured him that, one way or the other, he would be leaving the hotel the following day. One option was the same as Tyson's, which was as a fugitive from the law who had left behind some rather incriminating evidence in the hands of men who didn't care for him one bit. His mouth feel open as the second option was explained to him, but he had to agree it would probably work and it was, by far, his best option. He agreed without much deliberation.

"This comes with a couple of conditions," Reece told him. "First, you cannot withhold any information that is asked of you if they accept your proposal. Second, you have to answer a few questions from me right now honestly. If you don't agree to either of these conditions, the deal is off, and I'll turn you lose today right before calling the authorities."

"I agree," replied Riddle. Although he had been treated much better than he had expected, he still had more than a small suspicion that he would be killed at the end of this adventure by his captors. What he was being offered (if it worked) would allow him to swim through decades of shit and walk away clean as a whistle.

"OK. I will take you tomorrow." Reece shifted uncomfortably before going on. "How long have you been doing things for Sutton?"

"I don't know...a long time. We have had an odd relationship since I was very young. We both have information that could bring down the other, and he started paying me to handle things for him a long time ago. It was mainly stuff like blackmail or intimidation, but sometimes it was a little uglier than that."

"Did anyone else do things like this for him?"

Riddle thought for a minute. "Not that I know about. I would imagine that he would want to keep the number of people who did this kind of thing for him pretty low. I can't be sure, but I would doubt it."

The thermostat in the room was set at a comfortable temperature, but Michael could feel the tingling of perspiration on his forehead. It wasn't an answer that he was sure he wanted to know, but he would regret not asking the question for the rest of his life. "Did you ever kill anyone for him?"

"No, never directly for him," Riddle said.

Reece wasn't allowed much time for relief before the unsolicited addition from Riddle.

"But he did ask me to do it once for someone else."

*****

The same yellow caution tape was wrapped around the office of Great Smokey Vista Cabin Rental as the gravel road leading to its now-destroyed rental property. As expected, although not welcomed, there were countless fingerprints inside the office, and the hope that there would be any lead from them was slim. The victim's next of kin had been notified, and the body had been removed from the scene. Because of the time proximity and other logistical connections of the two crimes of the day, Asheville Police Department Homicide Division had granted the FBI access to their investigation.

Agent Frierson leaned against the hood of his official car as he drank what seemed like his hundredth cup of coffee of the past few days. The ballistics expert on the forensics team had informed him that the dimensions of the exit wound of the victim suggested a fairly close-range shot, but it lacked the pressure indentations at the entry site that mark a self-inflicted bullet. That, along with the fact that there wasn't a weapon at the cabin, made him quite certain that the burned corpse they had found earlier was not a suicide case.

His working theory was that whomever had killed the man in the rental office had likely killed Mr. Tyler (if that was who it indeed was) as well. It was noted that the key to the cabin had been issued from the office several hours before the employee was murdered and that, based on the transaction log in the office, there had been other customers who had come in after that. He thought that the person who had killed the rental agent was looking for Tyler, and he either killed him to get the information or killed him because he had seen his face. He hoped he would get answers to his questions in due time, but the likelihood that these two murders were not connected in some fashion seemed very low indeed.

Mitch saw one of his junior agents walking toward him while putting his mobile phone back into his belt clip. "You got anything?"

"Maybe. Well, no surprise that the registration for the cabin was not in Tyler's name. It was in the name of a Michael Reece, and the credit card number left for incidental charges matches a Michael Reece from Charlotte," his subordinate answered.

"You thinking a stolen credit card?" Mitch asked.

"No…Actually I did a little digging, and there is a Doctor Michael Reece that lives in Charlotte. Does that name ring a bell?"

Frierson thought for a moment. "I can't say that it does, but I haven't slept in about a year. Why don't we save the dramatic build-up and just get to the point?" He had always been a no-nonsense kind of guy, and this trait was now amplified by his exhaustion.

"Sure, sorry about that. Dr. Michael Reece is the guy who was awarded the Congressional Medal of Honor not long ago. He was on the news a lot during that time. But that's not what set off my alarm. He grew up at Sycamore House…the same place as Tyler. Not only that, he knew Haxton and had run into him in Washington the day he was given the medal. Evidently, Haxton was some sort of mentor to him when he grew up."

"Wow," Frierson replied. "I think we need to have a talk with Dr. Reece. Good work, and sorry about being a little snippy."

The junior agent gave him a dismissive wave. "No problem, Mitch. We are all entitled to be a little punchy after this case."

Mitch called his supervisor, who informed him that she was arriving at the Asheville Field Office. He pulled out of the parking lot headed to the same location to update Scott on the new development.

*****

Katz sat speechless in front of Michael at a corner table in the bar of the Hilton Biltmore Park, where he had checked in earlier. When they had first sat down, his neighbor had slid a one-dollar bill across the table to him and asked if it could be considered a retainer for his legal services. Katz had initially laughed at the suggestion, thinking his neighbor was messing around with him, until he saw the look on Michael's face. After telling him that it could be considered just that, Reece then asked if that meant their next conversation would fall under attorney-client privilege, and again the response was in the affirmative.

Over the next half hour, Michael had explained (just about) everything of the events of the past several days, including the history between himself and the late Senator James Haxton. At many points during the explanation, of course, Reece apologized for getting his friend involved. After taking a while to digest what his friend had just told him, he had some questions.

"Mike, are you and the family safe now?" It wasn't just the first question of a list; it was Seth's biggest concern. Yes, Michael was now his client, but he had been his friend for far longer.

"Anna and the kids are on an Army base not too far away and are well protected," Michael responded.

"So you gave Tyler some money and the use of your vehicle and rented a cabin for him later, correct?"

"Yes, but there is more to it than that, Seth. You see, I initially—" Reece stopped as his friend held up the palm of his hand.

456

"Michael, I am speaking to you right now as your attorney. Let me ask you a question. Do you know what time it is?" Seth asked.

"It's five forty," he responded somewhat confused.

"No. That is not the right answer. The correct answer is yes. I only asked you if you knew what time it was. If I wanted you to tell me the actual time, I would have asked that." Seth could see his friend wasn't getting it. "Look, what I'm trying to tell you is that for some of this conversation, and for *all* of the conversation tomorrow, I want you to *only* answer the question. If I or anyone else wants more information, we will ask for it. I think you don't have much to worry about from a legal standpoint, but if someone has a hard-on for you there, they could make some trouble for you. That's why you should keep your answers short and limited only to the question. I want you to practice with me now, OK?"

"OK," Michael answered. He was imminently grateful that his best buddy was a criminal defense attorney and not a tax lawyer at the moment.

"Where were you at the time that Haxton was killed?"

"I was in Dominica on a diving trip with several of my friends," he saw the reproaching look from Seth. "I mean, I was in Dominica."

"Very good. Are you aware of the location of Chris now?"

Michael had not told Seth anything that happened after reserving the cabin for Chris. "No." It was not the entire truth, but it wasn't a lie either.

Seth looked over his shoulder before leaning forward. "Now Mike, you don't have to answer the next question to me or anyone else, but I want to be upfront with you. If you don't answer this question, I will decline to be your legal representative any longer. Rest assured, our conversation to this point is still protected, but here goes. Did you have anything to do with the murder of Senator Haxton?"

"No." Reece saw his friend about to apologize but kept going. "Seth, I know why you're asking, and I understand. I swear on my family that I didn't have anything to do with it. If you were to ask me if I mourn him, I would tell you I don't. That being said, I played no part in his death, and yes, I know that's more than you asked me."

Katz chuckled. "I knew the answer, Mike, but I had to ask."

They spent an additional two hours discussing the plans for the following day, including the destination of the second copy of the videos. During that time, Michael received a cryptic text that simply read "Arrived. No Problems. GD." After shaking hands, they headed up the elevator to their respective rooms, both of which were reserved in Seth's name.

Michael's exhaustion was reaching levels of delirium, but he had a few more calls to make and then he would surrender to the sleep that had pursued for longer than he could remember. He called Anna to let her know things went well, then he got to work on the other phases of the plan.

*****

Mitch walked into the conference room with two cups from Starbucks. "Let's try tea for a change," he said to Meredith who was already there.

"DNA matches the Tylers," she said as she held up several fax pages in her right hand and gratefully accepting the tea with the left. "Thanks, Mitch. Director Purser is going to call for another update in about two hours."

"You need to hear about this first," Frierson said as he passed the Nutrasweet packets across the table. He explained his theory about how, based on the timing of the encounters and the evidence, the killer of the rental agency employee was probably the same person who had killed Tyler. He then went on to explain how the information had been found regarding Michael Reece, including a nod of credit to the junior agent who had joined them in the conference room. "Reece could be involved in the murder of Haxton, or maybe he was simply helping an old friend. Either way, I think we need to have a little chat with him in the near future."

"I agree. Good work, both of you," she said as she punched the intercom line on the phone and hit the connection button for the receptionist. "Maggie, I need to get contact information for a Dr. Michael Reece in Charlotte as soon as possible please."

"Agent Scott, did you say Michael Reece?" the receptionist replied.

"Yes, ma'am. Dr. Michael Reece."

"Why, that is really strange," Maggie said over the speaker. "A Michael Reece just called about ten minutes ago and left a message for you to contact him. I have the number and will bring it to you if you would like."

"Um...OK, Maggie, that would be great." Meredith looked at Mitch with a bewildered expression and then peered into the paper cup he had given her. "What in the hell did you put in this, Mitch?"

*****

"The body exhibits extensive charring throughout. Gross observation supports that subject is male and, based on bone measurements, would be somewhere between seventy-two and seventy-six inches in height. Post-mortem contractures from exposure to intense heat precluded a more accurate height measurement," Dr. Alexander Bradley said into the small microphone beside the corner of his mouth that led to its attachment over the top of his ear. "Examination of the skull is consistent with a ballistic injury that has an entry point in the right temporal area of the skull, with a likely exit wound on the contra lateral side measuring approximately three point five centimeters.

"There are no other obvious signs of ballistic injury on any other part of the body. However, the extensive burn damage precludes making this a conclusion with absolute certainty. It is of note that there is a small two-centimeter area just right of the sagittal midline that appears to have some remaining hair. It is consistent with the appearance of hair that would belong to a patient of African-American descent, but this would not be considered conclusive. Thermal damage extends to the internal organs and cavities of the subject, and no usable blood or spinal fluid samples were able to be collected."

Bradley removed the protective gown and latex gloves and left the autopsy room, waiting until he closed the door behind him before removing the surgical mask, the inside of which he had wiped with Vick's Vapor Rub to help block the scent of charred human flesh that, despite his medical training, he had never been able to get used to. He walked to his office and picked up an old film from the Radiology Department of the hospital that was only three blocks away.

After being arrested for involvement in a bar fight many years ago in Asheville, Chris Tyler had been brought to the emergency room by the police before booking him for simple assault to have his own facial injuries evaluated. Part of the testing done by the attending physician had been a flat film head series, which were simple x-rays of the skull in both a frontal and side view. There had been no fractures or other signs of head trauma, but that wasn't what Bradley was interested in at the moment. He placed the film in the viewing box above his desk alongside a similar film taken of the body down the hall.

He pressed the button on his dictation microphone again to enable the voice-activated digital recorder. "Identification was found on the body of the subject on scene that revealed a name and birth date of a Christopher Tyler. Comparison between radiographs of the subject and radiographs of a patient of the same name and birth date done twelve years ago revealed both were absent of any fillings or dental work of any kind. The film of twelve years ago reflects the physician documentation that the patient had lost tooth number 12 in the left maxillary region in an altercation. This same tooth is noted to be missing in the radiograph of the subject today."

Bradley leaned back in his desk chair and rubbed his eyes after staring at the lighted radiograph viewing box. "In conclusion, examination supports the identification of a male subject between seventy-two and seventy-six inches in height, likely of African-American descent. Cause of death likely a ballistic injury to the head, with the body being subsequently involved in a fire, resulting in significant thermal injury and distortion to the body. Review of dental x-rays and the presence of identification on the body support the identity of Christopher Tyler; date of birth and other specifics to be listed in Appendix One of this report. Due to the significant amount of full-thickness thermal destruction of the body, collection of tissue suitable for DNA analysis would be unlikely to be satisfactory. Using CTAB lysis buffer along with isoamyl alcohol-chloroform extraction of bone tissue could be considered for this purpose, but the reliability would still be suspect. End of dictation; signed Alexander Bradley, MD, Chief Medical Examiner."

Bradley's department had installed Dragon voice-recognition software two years ago, so his report was transcribed in real time as he spoke. He read the remarks one more time to ensure their accuracy and electronically signed the document. After printing a copy, he walked over to the department's fax machine and sent a copy to the attention of Special Agent Meredith Scott, Federal Bureau of Investigation, Asheville Field Office.

*****

The seats were plush leather with thick carpet under her feet. Rachelle MacLean had never been on the corporate jet of the National Broadcasting Company and marveled at how the experience made first-class tickets on any domestic airline seem like you were on a Greyhound bus. *So this is how the other half lives.* She put down her water with lime that was in a real crystal glass and started jotting down notes again on her legal pad.

Two hours ago, she had received a phone call that she had thought initially was a prank. Describing the information as "explosive" would have been the understatement of the century, and within ten minutes of informing her director she sat in the office of the Chief of the News Division. There were no flights that could get her to Asheville before the agreed-upon meeting time the following morning, so the corporate jet was fueled up to be at her disposal for the relatively short flight to the North Carolina foothills.

In her briefcase she had a notarized one-page document signed by her and the News Division Chief agreeing to the terms of the offer. She was not a big fan of agreeing to any conditions in exchange for information, with the exception of guaranteeing protection of identity, but this was simply too big to let go, and it was a quick decision of both the signers that it was more than worth it. She would have about six hours before the meeting, and she planned to use every minute researching the background of this story—without contacting anyone directly, which was part of the agreement.

She was accompanied by her cameraman, who was currently catching a nap in a plush leather seat behind her, and a bodyguard contracted by the network that came along at the

461

suggestion of the man who had called her several hours ago. She reviewed her notes that she had written so far, including the first entry, a quote by Noel Coward: "It is discouraging how many people are shocked by honesty and how few by deceit."

CHAPTER 34

There were too many people involved in the 911 response to the Buncombe County woods fire for it not to happen. The igniting incident for this firestorm was a Sheriff's Deputy who had come home after his shift to his wife, and who had greeted her with something like "You won't believe what we found tonight." That conversation was followed by one between the wife and a friend who happened to have a favorite nephew who was a production assistant for the CBS affiliate in the area. From there, the spread of information became exponential.

The country road that led to the gravel turn-in to the charred remains of the rental cabin was now overrun with satellite-communication-equipped news vans with reporters jockeying for a position where they could make their live segment updates. The few areas from which a portion of the cabin could be seen in the background were the most prime and were staked out first.

Every correspondent would try to give their own spin of the fairly limited information that was available. All could confirm that a body was discovered after the fire was doused, and the FBI had been seen with local law enforcement on the scene. Confidential sources were also quoted as saying the there was a high suspicion that the identity of the victim was Chris Tyler, who had been labeled a person of interest in the investigation into the murder of Senator James Haxton. Some reporters were citing confidential sources "close to the investigation" who had stated that Mr. Tyler was more than a person of interest and was considered the lead suspect in the murder.

"Local officials with the FBI investigative team as well as the Buncombe County Sheriff's Department have declined to comment, saying it is an ongoing investigation," Parrish Winston of MSNBC said to the camera mounted on a tripod in front of her. The split screen broadcast to the nation had pictures of Tyler and Haxton on one half while she occupied the other. She had been surprised at getting the assignment for this, given Rachelle's breaking news on Haxton not long ago, but she wasn't going to question being the lead correspondent on a national story.

She had been in Raleigh on assignment with the coverage of potential appointees to fill Haxton's now vacant Senate seat, was scheduled to interview the current Governor's Chief of Staff in two days, and was hoping to keep that as well and become the network's go-to reporter on all things Haxton. She wasn't aware that her colleague had landed at the airport only a few miles away just hours ago.

The red light went off on the camera, reflecting that she was no longer on the live feed, while she saw the encouraging thumbs-up from the man behind the lens. She looked over her shoulder at the partial view of the destroyed cabin and wished it was still smoking a little for dramatic effect, but you couldn't have everything can you? There were similar setups from other networks for at least one hundred feet on each side of her, all saying essentially the same thing every thirty minutes of the refreshing news cycle.

*****

Sutton swirled the drink in his left hand as he watched the cable news coverage of the fiery demise of one Chris Tyler. *One down, but one to go.* The fact neither he nor Pierce had heard from McCray wasn't concerning. He had done his job and he had to disappear for a while. He would surface in due time to collect his handsome payment for services rendered. Sutton's only wish was that he could have Randall start hunting Reece now for additional reward, since that fucking retard Riddle had vanished of late. The job was either too difficult for Riddle or he had cold feet.

"Where's Reece?" he asked into his phone.

"I don't know currently," Pierce replied. "He will pop up in one of my nets pretty soon, but I don't have an answer for you right now."

"I assumed that my generosity would emphasize the urgency in this matter." The Governor began pacing in his suite, which was often his custom when having direct conversations. "What kind of figure would be required for you to take a more hands-on role in this issue?"

"I'm not certain what you mean by that," responded Pierce. He was a man of few words, but the message was clear.

"You know goddamn well what it means. I'm under a rapidly diminishing timeline on this and I might need more people involved in order to resolve the matter definitively in a rapid fashion," Sutton said. "Does that make it a little clearer?"

"A little," Pierce said with no emotion. "The answer is none. There is no figure that would allow me to perform such a service for you. It is not part of my expertise or part of the menu of services that I offer."

"Every man has his price." Sutton had stopped pacing. *Come on, you fucking robot. Help me get out of this mess.*

"I have no further information since I answered you the first time," was Pierce's clipped and cold reply.

And that, as they say, was that. Sutton knew from his experience with Pierce that there was no reason to pursue it further. The answer was no and it wasn't negotiable. He gritted his teeth and kicked a sofa pillow across the plush carpeted floor. "Then find Reece...and Riddle and McCray too while you're at it. Prove that you're worth the ridiculous amount I'm paying you."

With that, he ended the call and tossed his phone on the sofa in frustration. He couldn't celebrate Tyler being dead until the other part of the equation was eliminated as well. As opulent and comfortable as this place was, he was ready to get the hell out of there and return to his life of influence and privilege, but he would remain holed up here until Reece was silenced. He looked out the window at a view that could be inadequately described as breathtaking and told himself there were worse places that one could have to hide.

*****

They met at a parking lot two blocks away from the FBI field office as the first morning commuters were starting to occupy the streets of Asheville. As instructed, the cameraman did not come with Rachelle to this meeting, but her bodyguard stood far enough away not to encroach on the conversation but close enough to act if needed. She shook the offered hand of the man that she recognized from the Capitol hallway several days ago, but she was not familiar with his companion.

"Ms. Maclean," Reece said, "this is my friend and attorney Seth Katz."

Katz shook the reporter's hand. "It's a pleasure to meet you, Ms. MacLean. Do you have the document that we discussed?"

Rachelle reached into her briefcase that was slung over her right shoulder and produced a manila envelope. "I do indeed, Mr. Katz." She handed him the document and watched as he reviewed the statements and signatures and gave a nod to Reece.

Michael handed her a padded envelope. "This contains the video footage we discussed. You cannot report on any part of this matter until I text you the go-ahead. It should not be more than a couple of days. I will be giving the other copy to the FBI in about an hour. If any reporting is done by you or anyone with your network before I consent, I will come forward with this document showing that you violated the terms of our agreement and you screwed over a source." He held up his hand in apology. "Please understand, Ms. MacLean, I don't think you would do that. I picked you because you have been part of the story about Haxton and I, and you seem to be respected in your field. I am merely protecting myself and others."

"You don't have to worry about hurting my feelings, Dr. Reece. I completely understand your caution," she replied. "I do have one concern. It is possible that his could be leaked once the FBI has the evidence, and then I don't have any exclusive material."

"That is a chance you will have to take, Ms. MacLean. You will still have an actual copy of the video, and I will give you access to interview me before anyone else, besides the authorities. If that's not enough, I understand, and I will try to contact someone else."

"Why are you giving me a copy instead of just turning a single one over to the authorities, if you don't mind me asking?" Rachelle asked.

"Because this is pretty damning evidence against very powerful people in government and I don't want it buried. Also, if anything happens to me, I wanted more than one person to be in possession of this information. That may sound paranoid, Ms. MacLean, but you may feel differently after reading the affidavit in that envelope."

MacLean silently appraised the man that stood in front of her. It was pretty clear that he was a novice at intrigue and dealing with the press, but he wasn't stupid. He also seemed pretty damn honest, and she trusted he wouldn't screw her over. She had interviewed people who knew him when she was working the Sycamore connection, and everyone respected him and saw him as a stand-up guy. "That won't be necessary, Dr. Reece. I agree to your terms. I'm sorry, should I call you Dr. Reece or Major Reece?"

He gave a shy smile. "I would prefer you call me Michael. Thank you for your time, Ms. MacLean. I'll be in touch."

She shook the men's hands and watched them pull away only to turn into the FBI office just a few blocks down the road. While her bodyguard drove back to the hotel, she opened the envelope, placed the two DVDs in the seat beside her, and began reading the five-page affidavit written and signed by Reece. Her eyes opened wider with each page. *Holy shit.*

Reece now sat in the same conference room that Scott had been using for her team meetings throughout the investigation. Scott introduced herself and Frierson, as well as a representative from both the North Carolina and the United States Attorney General's Office. They all sat down and both Reece and Katz declined the offer of coffee, while down the hall in a small holding room Pete Riddle sat at a table with a cup as well as instructions from Katz to not speak a word to anyone unless he was present with him.

Agent Scott decided to break the silence. "Dr. Reece, let me first say thank you for contacting me and agreeing to come here and speak with us. I must say that some of the accusations you make are quite shocking."

Katz leaned forward. "Before we go any further, I'm afraid we have to agree on the terms of Dr. Reece's cooperation in this matter. My client is requesting immunity for any actions that could be construed as illegal in regards to how he came into possession of the material he plans to turn over to you, as well as any charge of obstruction of your investigation into the murder of Senator Haxton."

Gavin Knight, the representative from the US Attorney General's Office, raised his hand and everyone turned their attention to him. "Mr. Katz, I think we are ignoring an elephant in the room. Dr. Reece has claimed that he was the victim of childhood abuse at the hands of Senator Haxton. That could certainly be considered a motive for murder."

Katz was unfazed by someone suggesting that Michael could be a murderer. "My client wasn't in the country at the time of the crime. This is an alibi that can be corroborated by several people that include respected doctors and decorated soldiers."

"That may be the case," Knight replied, "but the man who pulled the trigger is not the only one who can be charged with murder."

"Dr. Reese had no part in the murder of Senator Haxton and is willing to waive prosecutorial immunity in the matter of that crime." It was a big gauntlet to drop on the table, and the exchanged looks between the people across the table was not unnoticed. "We are only asking immunity for actions after the crime took place, including obstruction of justice—for which, I might add, there is no evidence that he engaged in."

"Your offer is noted, Mr. Katz. I also have significant concern about aiding a fugitive from the law. Would that be part of the immunity request as well?" Knight asked.

"The answer to your question would be yes, but let me ask you a question. Do you have any evidence whatsoever that my client performed favors, material or otherwise, *after* it was made public by authorities that Mr. Tyler was a person of interest? Do you have any evidence whatsoever that my client was aware of Mr. Tyler even being a suspect, since the FBI was very careful in the press conference to refute that very suggestion? Finally, do you have any prospect of getting such evidence, since the main suspect in the crime is deceased? Furthermore, there is certainly no indication that any of my client's actions delayed your ability to discover that Mr. Tyler was a suspect, nor can it be claimed that it delayed your finding of the suspect either." Katz leaned back in his chair while Reece marveled at him in a role he had never seen him play before. "Folks, we are asking immunity from offences that you can't possibly prove even occurred. In exchange for this, you will be presented on a silver platter ironclad evidence for multiple crimes, including repeated sexual assault against a minor, pandering, kidnapping, and murder." Katz pushed the agreement across the table.

There was a silent consent among the gathered professionals. "We agree to your terms, Dr. Reece," said Knight.

"Thank you," Reece replied.

"Before we go any further," Katz interjected, "we need come to an agreement on the broader terms for my other client down the hall. He has agreed to cooperate fully with any and all requests in exchange for full prosecutorial immunity. He had firsthand knowledge of not only crimes committed related to the Haxton case but also ones that have occurred years ago, including child sex offenses, prostitution, conspiracy to commit murder, as well as an unsolved murder that took place in this county several years ago related to covering up illicit and illegal sexual activities by both Governor Hal Sutton and Senator James Haxton. Your agreement will not only include the cooperation of Mr. Riddle but possession of his cell phone, which has traceable instructions from Governor Sutton himself to kill Dr. Reece. We can give you the room if you would like to discuss the matter in private."

"We would be grateful for that, gentlemen," replied Agent Scott. "There is a break room down the hall to the right. Please help yourself to anything you might need there."

The door had not come to a complete close before every person left in the room had picked up a phone. Michael turned to Seth.

"That was pretty amazing to watch. I'm used to the Seth Katz that helps me clean my gutters and shares carpool duties. You're kind of a badass. Do you think they'll agree?"

"They'll take it. I guarantee you that. They have the chance to prosecute an ex-Governor for molestation and murder, and the only thing they have to give is granting immunity to a guy that they would have probably never arrested anyway," Seth told his friend. "Remember, I worked in the Mecklenburg County District Attorney's office for a few years after law school. Not only would I have taken this deal, I would have jumped across the table and tongue-kissed you. It's a done deal; they just have to call their superiors so they're covered."

They sat at the break room table. Seth sipped a Styrofoam cup of coffee while Reece grabbed a cup of water from the cooler. Neither had time to finish half of their beverage before Agent Scott came in.

"Gentlemen, you can return to the room, if you don't mind."

She escorted them back to the conference table where she handed Katz a signed document. "Director, the men are back in the room," she said toward the speaker phone sitting in the middle of the table.

"Dr. Reece, this is Director Sam Purser of the FBI. On behalf of myself, the United States Attorney General, and the Attorney General of the State of North Carolina, I want to inform you that we all accept the terms of your offer and the offer of Pete Riddle. You will find signatures from the representatives of each office on the document just given to your attorney, but I wanted to inform you personally that we will honor every aspect of your agreement. It is with regret and some degree of shame that such a high representative of our government has treated you in a way that no child deserves."

It was one of the first moments of humanity that Reece had experienced in a while, and it brought the original reason for this whole saga back to the forefront. He looked down to the table. "Thank you, sir."

Frierson left to speak with Riddle who, armed with complete immunity, waived his right to have an attorney present during the questioning. Both the state and national representatives for the Attorney General left the room, the former to sit in on Frierson's questioning of Riddle and the latter to call his boss. This left Meredith Scott alone with Reece and Katz.

"We can start the questions tomorrow if you would like, Dr. Reece. I'm sure these past few days have been exhausting," Scott said.

"I would prefer if you would call me Michael, if that's OK, and I would like to start now if at all possible. I have a family that is basically being guarded on an Army post, and I'm ready for them to be able to return to our home. And I won't be comfortable about that until Hal Sutton is not able to go after them. I want him in custody as soon as possible."

"Well, in that case, I ask that you call me Meredith. I'm happy to start the questions now, but please let me know any time you need a break. Unfortunately, I cannot give you a firm time of when we would look to apprehend Sutton. Some of that will be based on the information you give me. I understand your concerns about your family, but these things can take time," Scott replied.

"I know I can't make you go any faster than you decide to, but I want you to know that I have given a copy of everything I have given to you to a reporter. In the interests of not hampering your efforts, I made them agree to sit on it until I gave them the green light to go forward with the story. That being said, if I feel that any agency involved with this investigation is dragging their feet, I will tell them to go forward. It is certainly not my intent to tell you how to do your job or bully you into doing something, but Sutton is well connected in government circles and I decided to take a little insurance policy on this matter. Please understand, I don't mean to imply that you would do this yourself, but this will go above both our heads pretty quickly." Reece's face had a guilty look for being so direct about this to someone who had done nothing but help him. "I hope you don't take any personal offense to that, Meredith."

"How about this: if our conversation agrees with the evidence you have given us and we can fill in a few blanks, I think we can probably scoop him up within twenty-four hours. There is no offense taken at all." The man across from her wasn't a lawyer or a cop, but he was smart and he wasn't bullshitting around. Meredith liked him immediately.

Before beginning, Michael requested that he be able to step outside for one moment, where he was met by a tall African-American gentleman in impeccable physical shape. He reached out and shook the hand of Colonel Greg Tyson.

"We're all set, sir," Reece said. "They agreed to our terms."

"That's fantastic, Mike. I'm going to head back to Fayetteville. Our boys said to tell you your family's fine. They took your kids for a ride in a tank this morning, and your wife's parents have come down as well. No one we don't want to will get within a hundred feet of them until you tell us to relax," Tyson told him.

"Colonel, I know what kind of risks you took to do this for me and my family, and I don't have the words to say how much it's meant to me. It's been overwhelming..." The cracks were starting to come in his voice.

"Let me ask you a question, Reece. Would you have done the same for me?" Tyson asked.

"Yes...of course I would...without a doubt."

Tyson put his hand on Reece's shoulder. "I know." He walked back to his car and turned toward the most decorated soldier he had ever commanded. "Airborne leads the way, Reece."

"All the way, sir," Michael replied while waving to yet another friend who possessed integrity and honor in amounts that could never be adequately measured.

Reece returned to the conference room, where they spent over six hours, with occasional breaks and take-out food. They discussed not only the evidence that he had provided but also often painful details about his own abuse and the death of Charlie Potts. Seth remained by his side the entire time and was visibly shaken at the history of one Michael Reece. He had always been an admirer of his neighbor, but the degree of his perseverance in life was nothing short of astounding.

At the end of the marathon session, Scott thanked both the men for their time and patience. "I want you to know that we've located Sutton. He is actually in a hotel in the city and we have him under surveillance. We certainly have enough to get a warrant for his arrest for the Potts murder as well as conspiracy to commit murder in regards to you. We should have no problem getting that from a judge tomorrow morning. I would like for us to meet again in the morning after I have gone through the notes of everything today, if that would be OK."

Everyone agreed, and Michael went for a bathroom stop before they left for the evening. Scott had arranged for two agents to keep watch at their hotel until the morning, just in case.

"Did you know about all of this stuff when he was a kid?" she asked Katz.

He shook his head. "No, I didn't know anything about it. He has so many reasons to hate the world, but he doesn't."

She looked down the hall toward the restroom where Michael had gone. "He's the real thing, isn't he?"

"As real as they come, Agent Scott. I hope this ends well and the system doesn't chew him up. A lot of people want him back when this is over," Katz replied.

"He will come out of this OK, Seth...I promise you that."

*****

Jack Pulaski walked into the office of First Caribbean Trust Bank with his proper identification documents. The marble floors were polished so perfectly that they reflected the rotating mahogany blades of the ceiling fans above. After introducing himself, he was taken to the branch supervisor's office, whose occupant welcomed him warmly and offered refreshments, which Pully politely declined.

The supervisor was friendly and professional, with tailored business slacks offset by a lightweight cotton short-sleeved shirt, in deference to the climate. He would execute a healthy transaction today that would require about two minutes of work and would gain the branch a 4 percent commission on the amount transferred, which wasn't a miserly sum. He inspected his visitor's identification papers and was satisfied that everything was in order.

"Would you like a cashier's check for the amount of the transaction, Mr. Pulaski, or might I suggest initiating an open withdrawal account with our institution, and you can have access to it at any time you wish?" The latter option would be a double-dip into the amount, which would make his own supervisors very pleased indeed.

"No thank you, sir. I would like the full amount in cash," Pully replied.

"That is not a problem, sir, if you so wish, but the full amount is fifty thousand American dollars," the man replied. It was unusual but not unheard of for such a request to be made. All

473

kinds of issues on the island nation could be lubricated with the right amount of cash to the right person. "I just wanted to make sure you were aware of the full amount."

"That's very kind of you to ask, but cash will be preferred."

The lean banker almost asked his customer if he would like security to accompany him anywhere while carrying such a large amount of cash but decided against it upon seeing how the seams in the customer's shirt sleeves were barely able to contain the muscles within.

"Very well. I just need you to punch in your access code on the keypad to execute the transaction, and I can prepare your funds for you."

Jack punched in the six-digit code that had been given to him, and the computer announced its satisfaction. He assured the banker he didn't need anything to drink while his money was being put together and leaned back in the chair for what turned out to be a short wait.

"Here you are, Mr. Pulaski," said the supervisor. "The transaction was for fifty thousand dollars, minus a two-thousand-dollar transaction fee, for a total of forty-eight thousand dollars. You are welcome to count the cash to verify that it is correct, if you would like."

"That won't be necessary. Forgive me, but it's Mr…"

"Washington, sir…Niles Washington," he replied. "It was a pleasure to serve you today.

Pully folded a one-thousand dollar bill into his right hand and transferred it to Washington as he shook his hand. "The pleasure was mine, Mr. Washington. I may have further business to do here, and I would be honored to consider you my personal banker."

Washington transferred the bill to his pocket with one smooth motion. "I will be happy to help you with any needs you require with our bank, Mr. Pulaski."

"Good day, Mr. Washington," Pully said in goodbye and headed to his truck outside.

Pully would be having one of his regular dinner parties he put on for various government officials, most of whom worked in the tourism division. One of the regular attendees and a personal friend of Jack's had been asked to bring along another official from the Ministry of National Security, Immigration, and Labour for an evening of good food, good drinks, and good conversation.

*****

"I drive all the way here and serve as your lawyer for one dollar and this is how you repay me?" Katz was desperately trying to catch his breath and not vomit. "It doesn't help that you had to slow down for me with one leg!"

"You'll feel more energetic for the rest of the day," Reece replied. "It will also make us feel better about the terribly unhealthy breakfast I plan to have in a little while."

Despite the objections of his lawyer and the two FBI agents at the hotel, Michael had gone for a run at sunrise. It was mainly to clear his head but also just to get outside. Seth wasn't a sloth by any means, but he wasn't a runner, and the three-mile route along the hilly topography of Asheville had nearly killed him. The only condition was that Michael had to loan a younger and fitter FBI man some of his workout clothes so the agent could keep pace about ten yards behind them throughout the run, all the while with a shoulder holster and an FBI-issue handgun under his windbreaker.

After showers and fresh clothes, the party left for the Asheville FBI Field Office, with a stopover at a country breakfast buffet. Reece threatened to spray paint "Undercover FBI Car" on the agents' vehicle if they didn't let him pay for their breakfast. The only rule was that the case or politics couldn't be part of the conversation at the four-person breakfast table. It wound up being the two neighbors telling embarrassing stories about each other to the delight of the two agents with them. It was the first moment of levity Reece had enjoyed in several days and, although he wasn't aware, it was purposely engineered by his friend this morning to help him forget about all the bad things going on at the moment.

Although all four felt more like a nap than police business after thirty minutes of cholesterol-induced bliss, they made the short trip to the field office where Meredith Scott was waiting for them. The exchange for the morning was only about two hours, mainly devoted to clarifying remarks about points made the day before. Once satisfied all the information had been covered, Scott would have the morning's interview transcribed to go along with yesterday's, to be signed as accurate by both Dr. Reece and Special Agent Scott.

"Would you gentlemen like to take a walk for an off-the-record conversation while we wait on the document?" Scott asked Michael and Seth.

Both accepted, and they decided to take a three-block leg-stretcher to the local Starbucks to get some fresh air.

"Can I ask you a few questions not really for the case but for my personal curiosity?" she asked. "None of it is on the record, and I won't be offended if you decline."

"Sure," Reece replied.

"Pete Riddle has about the most sweetheart deal I have ever seen someone get. Why did you do it? I mean, why not just turn him in? It seems pretty clear that he was your guest-without-consent, although I won't ask you that officially." The answers would have no bearing on the investigation, but she just wanted to feel him out.

"I worried that he would just lawyer up and not tell you guys anything, and that would be one less person giving evidence against them." After pausing, Reece continued, "I mean, I won't lie. I also thought it would make him feel grateful to me, and that might be helpful since he was trying to kill me before and all."

"It seems pretty clear that you were pretty close to Mr. Potts." Scott tried to tread delicately on this subject, because it was apparent during questioning that the man's death had been devastating to Reece.

"He was the closest thing to a father I ever had."

"The reason I ask is...it seems pretty clear that Riddle killed him at the direction of Haxton and/or Sutton. And then you have him with you the past couple of days. It seems like...I'm not sure how to ask this..."

"You want to know why I didn't kill him," Reece said, pointing to the elephant in the room.

"Well, yes, I guess that's exactly what I want to know."

"Because it's wrong. Look, Chris was a good person, but I don't condone what he did to Haxton. He made a snap decision that was a bad one in my opinion. Killing Riddle would have been a short-term satisfaction followed by a life of regret. Don't get me wrong, Agent Scott; I have a lot of hate for Mr. Riddle." He stopped walking and faced her. "I have seen good people killed out of hate right in front of my eyes. I'm not a perfect man, but I have to believe that there is a difference between me and the Pete Riddles of the world. I feel like I owe the guys that have lost their lives trying defeat hate and evil to make the decisions that a good man would make. I would dishonor their legacy by doing anything different."

Scott smiled as she realized that Katz's remarks the day before about Reece being the real thing were right on point. "I have one more thing I would like you to do for us on the matter of Hal Sutton, if you don't mind, and I think we're set. This would be completely optional, and I will understand if you refuse." They walked into the coffee shop and she explained her idea.

"Absolutely not," Katz said before his friend could even speak. "You have everything you need, and this could involve unnecessary risks."

"He is the only person in the room, Mr. Katz. I assure you the threat would be minimal," replied Scott.

"Minimal and none are not the same thing, Agent Scott." Katz was part uneasy at the suggestion and part irritated that it was being asked. "This is not the time to try to make this like some detective drama on television. I don't think this is—"

"Would it help the case?" Michael interrupted.

"Yes," Scott replied.

"I'll do it."

CHAPTER 35

Frying Pan Shoals are a collection of shifting areas of shallow water along the confluence of the Cape Fear River and the Atlantic Ocean. Well over one hundred wrecks sit along the bottom in the area as a testament to the dangers to shipping. It now functions as a popular diving and fishing location where charters can catch redfish, grouper, and bluefin tuna among others. Built in 1966, the Frying Pan Shoals Light Tower stood at the southern edge of the shoals approximately forty miles of the coast. Along with a patrolling vessel aptly named *The Frying Pan*, the two structures served as a point of reference for ships in the area to caution them about dangerous depth changes.

In 2003, the tower and ship were replaced by a permanent buoy, and the tower, formerly operated by the United States Coast Guard, stood vacant for several years. In 2010, an entrepreneur purchased the tower from the US government after putting forth the winning bid. With an eighty-foot tower and two levels of the superstructure, efforts were begun to convert the abandoned ocean mark into an alternative to a traditional bed and breakfast, one that would cater to not only fishermen and divers who wanted to be on-site but also people simply looking to get away or put on unique events.

In between ongoing renovations, the tower became available for rental use in 2011, with sporadic bookings. The replacement of the water-access staircase, which had been destroyed in 2008 by Hurricane Irene, was certainly picking up business, since access was no longer restricted to hoisting or helicopter. Groceries had to be brought with the guests, since a nearby store or nearby anything didn't exist. Most guests were looking for a unique experience away from the hustle and bustle with a rental that offered stunning ocean views from every side of the property.

Janice and Betty Davis had started a business cleaning rental houses in the Southport area in between guest departures and arrivals. It had grown over the years to the point that they had six employees and were a favorite of the local rental agencies due to their promptness and quality of work. The local sisters were an example of small business success gained from risk, perseverance, and good old-fashioned hard work.

One of their newest clients was the operating trust of the Frying Pan Tower, and, although fairly infrequently, it offered a generous fee indeed for a post-rental clean-up. The sisters would take a chartered boat to the tower, and a cleaning usually took about three hours. The work was fairly easy since the location and price was discouraging to the average Spring Break party crowd and catered to a more mature (and clean) clientele.

They had been informed by the owner that there would be larger buoy cushions at the boat docking area that had been brought by the tenant, who had agreed to leave them there for use by anyone who had a larger boat than the average size used to ferry clients back and forth to the coast. The buoys were still there, but it was clear that the tenants had already left from their short stay. It had been fairly short notice, but the client had made it worth the operator's effort to make the property available.

The sisters realized quickly that today would be one of the easiest fees they had earned out here on the former Coast Guard Station. Most of the beds had not been used, and it was obvious that the occupants were tidy people. The trash had been collected in two large bags and left at the entrance to the property. A note had been left about some unused food in the refrigerator and cupboards that the cleaning crew was welcome to take with them. They had been notified that there would be a red plastic "sharps" container, as one of the occupants was diabetic and required insulin shots. They only had to bring the sealed container back with them, and the owner would take care of disposing of it properly. They could not see the bandages and other non-sharp medical waste that was tucked away in the middle of the paper towels and disposable plates.

Derrick, the charter boat operator, was surprised when the ladies told him they were ready to go after only ninety minutes. Usually, while they cleaned he stayed on the property and climbed the stairs to the top of the tower structure to enjoy the view and occasionally steal a cat nap. He gathered his magazines and took one last look at the beautiful view, the blue ocean water, and the fishing boats. Just near the horizon, he could see an impressive luxury yacht heading south.

*****

"Hello?" Sutton said as he picked up the hotel phone in his suite.

"Governor, this is David Heinberg. Sorry to disturb you, but you have a guest at the front who is asking to see you. I haven't confirmed that you are here but did not want to send him away if it was someone you wanted to meet. I have stepped back to my private office so I could call you in privacy…Again, sorry to disturb you."

This was a little unusual. Just about everyone who knew he was here would have contacted him directly on his mobile phone. If it was a member of his staff at the lobbying firm, he would have thought they would have called ahead first. "Did this person give a name?"

"He did, sir. He said his name was Dr. Michael Reece." The name hung there for a few moments while Sutton decided if he was hallucinating or not. "If you would like, I can tell him you are not here and send him on his way."

"Is he alone?" *If that motherfucker Riddle brought him here, I will cut his balls off.*

"He is, Governor."

"Can I call you back in about two minutes, David?" Sutton was back to his usual pacing while he talked. "In the meantime, don't tell him that I'm here yet, please."

"Of course, Governor. I will inform the operator to patch you through to my private line as soon as you call."

Heinberg returned the phone to the receiver. He had not lied when he said that Dr. Reece was alone in the hotel lobby. But Heinberg was not the only person in his office during the phone conversation.

The cordless phone was back in the carriage, and Sutton's pacing had resumed. *What in God's name could Reece want with me, and where the hell was Riddle?* He had presented himself at the front desk and given his actual name, so Sutton thought the likelihood that he was here to do him physical harm was very low. He would have to know that he would be on camera in the lobby, and by giving his name he couldn't hope to get away with coming in and offing a guest. Sutton decided that the most likely explanation was that he had decided to agree to the terms after seeing the fate of his friend in the mountain cabin. It wasn't a sure shot, but it was worth the risk to possibly settle this matter and pay the guy off and be able to return to the world without fear of his past catching him. He dialed the front desk, who patched him through to the boss.

"Send him up please. Thank you, Mr. Heinberg."

It wasn't long before his suite door chime rang. Sutton opened the door with his trademark politician smile. "Well, Dr. Reece...I must say this is a surprise."

"May I come in, Governor?" The tone was by no means friendly but seemed to lack the brusqueness of their previous conversation. Sutton took this as a good sign.

"By all means, Dr. Reece...Please come in," he couldn't help but sneak a glance outside the door as his guest entered the suite. There wasn't a soul around. "Have a seat if you would like. Can I offer you something to drink?"

"No thank you," Reece replied as he sat down in one of the leather chairs.

Sutton took the matching model directly across from him. "What can I help you with today?"

"I wanted to know if we could revisit the offer you made several days ago."

Bingo. "Why, certainly we can. May I ask if you're considering changing your mind?" Sutton's ability to conceal his utter excitement had been perfected over decades of bullshitting all kinds of people in his career. "Is it a matter of the amount? We can certainly revisit that if it would help you come to a decision."

"No, it's not that. Although I would ask that the amount that had been designated for Chris be given to any family of his we could find. I think that would only be fair."

Michael didn't have to put on an act to look uncomfortable with the conversation. It wasn't that he was afraid or nervous, as appeared to Sutton. It was because it was taking every fiber of his being not to come across the coffee table and snap the neck of the pot-bellied charlatan that sat in front of him with that famous shit-eating grin.

"I need to know exactly what is expected of me if I accept this offer."

"Well, first of all Dr. Reece, it will not be a problem to get those funds to Mr. Tyler's family in some way or another." He shook his head as if he was visiting a tornado-stricken small town as the concerned Governor. "Terrible tragedy that he couldn't make a more wise decision. Second, the payment would be conditional on you not speaking to anyone about the circumstances that led to the Senator's death. That would include any discussion on the nature of the relationship between you and the Senator as well as the relationship between myself and the Tyler twins, including any unpleasantness that has occurred since the Senator's death. It would also be contingent upon you not disclosing the contents of the safe, which I would have to insist that you return to me."

"What about my safety and the safety of my family?" Reece interrupted. "My condition would be that the deal would be null and void if I thought there was any threat to our safety. You will have to forgive me, but you threatened to kidnap my son and you have been trying to have me killed."

"Why would I have any reason to wish you or your family harm if we can come to an agreement here today?" Sutton actually looked like the suggestion had hurt his feelings.

"I know you have someone following me and I know what you want him to do if he finds me, so don't play around with me. I will insist that you call him while I am here and call him off. I have the discs on site and will give them to you before I expect you to call him, as a gesture of goodwill."

"I think that is a reasonable expectation for you to have. I agree to your stipulation," Sutton replied, acting as if Reece had won a monumental concession.

"What about Charlie Potts?" Reece asked.

Sutton seemed confused about the question, but a moment later his appearance revealed he had recognized the name. "What about Charlie Potts?"

"Am I free to discuss his death and pursue any details about it?"

"What in the world would that have to do with me, Dr. Reece?"

Michael leaned forward in his chair. "Go ahead and bullshit with me, Sutton, and watch me walk out the door. Walk out the door after me and my one leg will kick your fat fucking ass until you bleed all over this luxury carpet." Reece started to stand and was more than willing to deliver on his promise.

Sutton held his palms up and gave a friendly chuckle. "Why, Dr. Reece, there is no reason for this to be adversarial. I only mean to say that any unfortunate events that may have occurred to Mr. Potts were between him and Senator Haxton."

"That may be so, but you made the arrangements for him to die." Reece held his hand up to keep Sutton from interrupting. "Don't ask me how I know that, just assume that I do."

"Well, you have a point there, Dr. Reece. Boy, ol' James certainly shit his drawers on that night. We certainly had to improvise. What a stupid thing that Charlie Potts did."

Michael had sat back in his chair and was gripping the armrests to keep control over his reactions. It was hard to hear what he was saying, and it was about to get harder. "What do you mean?"

"I mean, Jesus...what did he expect was going to happen?" Sutton continued. "Calling up Haxton and threatening him? Who the hell did he think he was barking at? If it wasn't for James, he would still be flipping burgers and bussing tables at the country club. Did you really think a man with the prospects and influence of Haxton was going to let some stupid nigger ruin his life because he had discovered some dirty laundry on him? Come on, Dr. Reece, you can't be that naïve."

Reece felt the acidic heat of vomit working its way up his esophagus, and he swallowed hard and willed himself to remain in control for a little longer. "Haxton couldn't have done something like that without you and your contacts, but if you say I'm free to pursue that then I'm OK with that. I'm trying to do you a favor for reasons I can't fathom right now."

"Fair enough, and I appreciate the completeness of your thought, Dr. Reece. Haxton called me freaking out like a goddamn child blabbering on about it could ruin us both. I knew that if he went down, I would go down with him. I put one of my, let's just say "off the record" associates in touch with him so we could bring that unfortunate event to a quick end. So I guess the answer would be yes, pursuing Mr. Potts's death would have to be prohibited in our agreement."

"If that's the case, I want a million more than the original amount," Reece said with a steadiness that hid the rage he felt under the surface.

Sutton belly-laughed like he had heard a new punch line from a good buddy. "Well, all right, Dr. Reece. I guess everyone has their price. Agreed…an extra million."

"Very well," Reece responded. "I left the discs in a shipping envelope at the front desk with a Mr. Heinberg. I can go get them or you can have someone bring them up to you. It's up to you."

Sutton picked up the hotel phone and hit the button for the front desk. "Yes, this is the Timberlake Suite. Please inform Mr. Heinberg that he can bring Dr. Reece's package up to the suite directly. Thank you." He turned back to Reece. "As a gesture of goodwill, I will trust that the discs contain what we think they do, and I will call off your pursuers without verifying. Please understand that if I discover they are not the ones we are both referring to, I will have to call him right back and tell him that you are not a friend to me. Is that a fair assumption?"

"It is a fair assumption. Inside the envelope you will find two account numbers for an overseas bank: one for myself and one for Chris."

The door chime rang, and Sutton retrieved the envelope from Heinberg and dispatched him with a thank you that would make anyone think he was considering the man for sainthood. Sutton opened the envelope and verified the presence of two DVDs as well as a slip of paper with a bank name and two account numbers.

"It's time to make the call, Governor, and I want it on speaker so I can hear it," Reece said, standing from his chair.

"Very well, Dr. Reece," Sutton said as he dialed a number on his mobile phone.

"Riddle," was the greeting the two men heard on the speaker.

"Mr. Riddle, this is Sutton. I want you to end your pursuit of Dr. Reece. That matter is concluded."

"Do you want me to just stop trying to find him and you will let me know where he is? Do you still want me to kill him?" Riddle replied.

"No, Mr. Riddle...I want to stop both assignments," Sutton said as he shook his head in irritation to show Reece that he was dealing with someone obviously not as brilliant as he.

"What about McCray? Do you still want him to kill Tyler?"

"It appears that Mr. Tyler is already dead, and you can tell Mr. McCray that his job is also considered complete. Now if you don't mind, Mr. Riddle, I have other things to attend to," Sutton said as he ended the call. He looked at Reece. "Can I conclude that we are in agreement and we understand each other's terms?"

"We can, Governor." Reece pulled an envelope from his back pocket. "Do you like Shakespeare?"

"I'm sorry?" Sutton responded somewhat confused.

"It's a simple question. Do you like Shakespeare?"

"I certainly do, Dr. Reece. I'm kind of partial to *Macbeth*, if I were to be asked," Sutton said with a snicker.

"This is for you then." Reece handed him the envelope. "Good day to you, Governor." He turned his back to Sutton and left the suite without another word.

Without knowing that Reece had went down the fire escape steps two at a time so he wouldn't lose his composure in sight, Sutton peeled open the envelope marked only with his name. Inside was a page torn out from the play *Richard III*—Act I, Scene III. There was one quote highlighted:

And thus I clothe my naked villainy

With odd old ends, stol'n out of holy writ;

And seem a saint, when most I play the devil.

The door chime rang once again as he stood staring at the paper. Opening the door, he saw a woman flanked on each side by some very serious-looking men.

"Governor Sutton, my name is Special Agent Meredith Scott of the Federal Bureau of Investigation…"

He had offered no resistance, more out of shock than resignation. As the elevator doors opened to the lobby, there were several more agents in attendance. The realization came crashing down on him as he saw a stone-faced David Heinberg with a look of utter contempt, and beside him a federal agent and then none other than Pete Riddle. The agent lifted a cell phone and shook it at the Governor as he walked by. It was at that moment that Sutton lost all muscle control in his legs and was dragged to the awaiting vehicle sobbing like a child. There was only one press presence that caught a shot of the Governor being taken away in handcuffs, and it was Rachelle MacLean and her cameraman, who just happened to be on the property as the Governor came out.

*****

Director Purser stood before the massive assembly of media members as he read his statement:

"Based upon identification evidence that includes DNA at the scene, physical characteristics, and accompanying property of the victim, we have concluded that the deceased was indeed Christopher Aaron Tyler. We are also in possession of conclusive evidence that identifies the same Mr. Tyler as the man who murdered Senator James A. Haxton of North Carolina.

"Also, in connection with the ongoing investigation, former Governor Harold Sutton has been arrested and charged with two counts of murder in the first degree, two counts of conspiracy to commit murder, and multiple counts of kidnapping and felonious sexual assault of a minor. He is currently in custody in a maximum-security prison pending a bail hearing on suicide watch. The Attorney General has already stated on record that the prosecutor will oppose any consideration of bail in this matter, due to the heinous nature of the crimes as well as the substantial flight risk that we believe the defendant poses.

"We have also requested the assistance of the United States Marshals Service in our efforts to apprehend Mr. Randall McCray, whose information we will distribute to you shortly.

"Finally, we are in possession of definitive evidence that the late Senator James Haxton was also engaged multiple counts of felony sexual crimes against a minor. We have initiated an investigation as to whether there were any other parties involved in the criminal activities of Mr. Sutton and Mr. Haxton but have no further information on that matter at this time.

"This concludes my statement, and I will not be able to take any questions. We hope to update you further at a press conference at ten a.m. tomorrow, and we will be taking questions at that time. Thank you."

Purser exited the stage to a deafening roar of questions from the assembled members of the press.

*****

The rotor wash from the UH-60 Blackhawk helicopter stirred the dust from the parade grounds, creating a glittering bowl-like appearance from lights that illuminated the area under the cloudless Carolina night sky. Colonel Tyson had commandeered yet another chopper for yet another flight to Asheville, with the approval of General Butts. Tyson had picked up Reece at the FBI office and waited while he said goodbye and embraced his neighbor and friend, who climbed in his car to head home to Charlotte. They had made one unscheduled stop at the Victory Assembly Church of Christ, where Reece had asked Tyson to remain in the car while he had a short conversation with a man who met him at the door. Tyson had no idea what the conversation was about, but it ended with the man hugging Reece with obvious tears in his eyes. The flight had been uneventful, and Tyson had noted that Reece was sound asleep within two minutes of taking off.

There were over two hundred Airborne soldiers in their ACU uniforms along with the Division's flags and battle streamers. Every soldier snapped to attention and rendered a perfect salute in unison as Reece climbed from the side door of the chopper. Even though he was in civilian clothes, Michael snapped a salute as he saw General Butts there to greet him. The men shook hands and Butts kept his welcome brief, as he couldn't help but notice Reece's eyes darting to his left where his family was waiting.

"Major Reece," Butts said. "Get outta here and go hug your family."

"Yes, sir. And thank you, sir." He looked at Tyson. "Thank you to all of you."

"Not a problem, Mike. Just tell Tripp he probably needs to get back to work when he finds it convenient," Butts replied while Tyson didn't even try to hide a snicker.

"I will do that, sir. Airborne leads the way, sir."

"All the way," Tyson and Butts responded in unison.

Charlie could not be contained any longer, and he came running with Elizabeth and Anna not far behind. Reece fell to his knees and enveloped his family in a warm and long overdue embrace. There was no reason to have to hold it in anymore, and the tears streamed down his face. He thought of what he had right in his arms and the safety they could enjoy once again; he thought about his son's namesake and how he could rest in peace now that justice would be served. Anna couldn't help but notice that General Butts and Colonel Tyson seemed to be having some problem with dust in their eyes also.

She looked at her husband and kissed him. "What do you want to do now?"

"Let's go home."

EPILOGUE

SIX MONTHS LATER

Michael stepped off the small plane that had taken himself and Tripp from San Juan, Puerto Rico, to Melville Hall Airport on the northeastern end of Dominica. This would be the last week of what had been an extended sabbatical from his work in Charlotte. It had been a whirlwind six months since climbing in the family car in Ft. Bragg and driving home.

He had granted a single prime-time interview, in which he stood with other victims of childhood abuse and explained the horrors of his childhood at the hands of Senator James Haxton. He would speak on the subject no more except for efforts to help child victims, with absolutely no media around. Although the value had been kept from the public as part of the agreement, a settlement had been made with the Haxton estate in the amount of thirty-five million dollars. Not a cent would find its way to any account belonging to the Reece family.

Not long after the settlement was reached, an endowment was created in the amount of ten million dollars to keep the Sycamore House fully funded in perpetuity. It was made on the condition that Theresa Williams rescind the resignation that she had submitted after the story of the abuse broke. The same day, the Western Carolina Foundation for Christian Outreach and Substance Abuse Treatment received a five-million-dollar donation anonymously in the memory of Chris and Darnell Tyler. Red Creek AME Zion Church received a similar check in the memory of Charlie Potts. Another five million had been transferred to an account at the First Caribbean Trust Bank, with Jack Pulaski listed as the sole withdrawing authority.

After being asked again by political operatives, Michael had once again made the request not to be considered to fill the vacant Senate seat of the late James Haxton, Senior Senator from North Carolina, Pedophile and Murderer. Two weeks later, the current Governor appointed his nephew to fill the seat, and he hired local legend Chip Johnson to be his Director of Communications.

The continued investigation into the Sutton matter had resulted in the arrest of several prominent members of the North Carolina community on prostitution charges, as well as the arrest of Landon Pierce on charges of tax evasion, wire fraud, and accessory to murder. Randall MacCray still had not been found.

The remainder of Michael's time had been spent with his family, as well as performing duties and functions associated with being a Medal of Honor recipient, which included speaking to soldiers and disabled veterans, testifying to Congress on the need for increased funding for mental health services for veterans, traveling to countless welcome-home ceremonies for returning troops, and, his son's favorite, performing the coin toss for the Carolina Panther's opening playoff game, where Charlie got to run out on the field with the team beside their star quarterback who was on three posters in the little man's bedroom.

He had wandered to the hospital on occasion to take care of a patient whom he had a close relationship with; this was under the guise of keeping his skills sharp, when everyone knew he sometimes just simply missed his work and his patients. The remainder of the time had been devoted to cherished activities such as driving carpool, date nights with Anna, going on runs with Tiny, and, yes, picking up dog crap in his yard.

His final week had begun with a stop in San Juan where, due to his ten-million-dollar donation matched by the Wounded Warrior Foundation, he and David had cut the ribbon on the Manuel Torres Institute for Veterans Health. It would be the newest addition to the VA Medical Center and would not only provide direct patient care but would perform research on health issues such as traumatic brain injury, prosthesis science, and post-traumatic stress disorder.

After posing for the cameras in their Army Dress Uniforms alongside Giselle Torres, the two men had boarded a plane to Dominica. Lt. Col. Dwayne Collins informed the media that the now Lt. Col. Michael Reece was heading for a vacation for the last week of his sabbatical from work and asked everyone to respect the privacy of a man who had been more than accommodating with the spotlight for over half a year.

They were met by Pulaski at the airport and took the short drive to the dive center. Pully's business had continued to grow, and he now operated six boats. It was the end of the day, and the last customers were driving away in their rental cars or boarding shuttles to take them back to their cruise ships. Pully had sent the entire staff home early and had the grill heating for dinner; the only remaining employee was his chief boat operator.

Tripp and Pully remained by the truck as they watched their friend fall into the embrace of Pully's boat operator. Standing several inches taller than Reece with short dreadlocks that were beginning to show a lighter tint from exposure to the daily Caribbean sun, the boat operator's tears were glistening from the pit fire that had been made in the white sand. The facial features were altered and no visible surgical scars could be seen, but the in the eyes was a familiarity that could not be taken away by a surgeon's knife. Chris had a new look, but he was still Chris...and was now safe.

The four men spent hours on the beach eating, sharing stories, and laughing by the light of the fire and smell of fresh grilled fish. At one point, the eyes of Reece and Tyler met and a silent understanding was shared between them. Reece thought of the story of Pandora's Box from Greek mythology. It is often told with emphasis on the box containing all the evils of the world which Pandora released. But there was more to the tale. At the bottom of the breeched vessel was a new discovery; hope. Elpis, or The Spirit of Hope, was found after the horrifying onslaught of misery that came after Pandora's fateful decision.

The two men shared a bond of suffering that would be unimaginable to most, but each had found their own exodus. And at the end of the journey, they had found brotherhood and justice. They both smiled and shared nods with each other. The waves of the ocean could be heard along with the cracks of burning driftwood and the salty breezes bathed them in a feeling of contentment.

As the light diminished from the waning fire and the stars were visible in the clear tropical sky, the men took the short drive to the home of Pully's chief boat operator where they would be guests. It sat on a large lot that gave a staggering panoramic view of the ocean behind its gates...and seemed far more opulent than one would expect from the meager salary of a boat driver for a scuba diving operation.

The following morning, long after sunrise, Michael awoke to the sounds of the steady breaks of the ocean waves in the distance beyond the gossamer rolling motions of the white curtains that swayed at his open window. His night had passed without a single dream.

Acknowledgements

What had begun as a "Bucket List" item to perform became a process of many friends and colleagues encouraging me to publish this story and share it with others. What you have just read would never have been completed without the support and inspiration of many others, which I will probably do a poor and incomplete effort of recognizing here.

I am blessed with a patient and supportive wife and children who tolerated countless hours of watching me peck away at my laptop during time that could have been shared with them. Also, the sacrifices made by the families of soldiers who are called to duty should be recognized as much as the ones made by the soldier. They remain my inspiration to be a better man every day of my life and any accomplishments I have are because of them. I am grateful to the rest of my family as well, especially my mother, who is the epitome of perseverance and toughness.

I want to thank the United States Army for allowing me to be a part of an institution that will give me pride long after I am no longer a soldier. In particular, I want to thank Lloyd Jackson, Michael Lynch, Randall Moore, Chuck Dietrich, Doug Yoder, John Sorensen, Joe Alderete, Mary Link, Dave Buczinski, Scott Turco, Sharon Henry, Curt Alitz, Doug Elmore, Gino Trevasani, Steven Sutterfield, Adam Parnell, Robert Peyton, and the countless other soldiers that have shared the experience of combat deployment with me and have taught me by their words and their deeds what it means to be a hero.

I thank Jerel Law, a real author, who pushed me to move forward with this story and gave invaluable advice on more occasions than I can count. Much credit should be given to Julia Fatou for her hard work and patience as my editor as well as the entire team at CreateSpace.

Joe Gaydeski and the rest of the team at Open Water Adventures were always generous with their time with countless random questions about diving and I thank his wife, Heather, of Heather Gaydeski Photography for her help in the cover design of this book and allowing me the use of her studio at any hour of the day to write in seclusion. All undertakings require a core group of friends who give unconditional support and encouragement, and that was certainly the case with this book with special thanks to Mac Goodrum, Iris Goodrum, Charlie Szymborski, Hayworth Szymborski, Michael Ryan, and Steffany Ryan. Also, to Greg Hemsley for the random questions about legal procedures and jurisdictions.

Finally, I thank the soldiers that have given the ultimate sacrifice, often in faraway lands, allowing me to live in the greatest country on this planet with freedom of expression. Their heroism along with the sacrifices of their families and loved ones can never be acknowledged enough.

Made in the USA
Lexington, KY
26 September 2013